TREASURE OF THE ABYSS

THE KRAKEN #1

TIFFANY ROBERTS

Copyright © 2017 by Tiffany Freund and Robert Freund Jr.

All Rights Reserved. No part of this publication may be used or reproduced, distributed, or transmitted in any form by any means, including scanning, photocopying, uploading, and distribution of this book via any other electronic means without the permission of the author and is illegal, except in the case of brief quotations embodied in critical reviews and certain other noncommercial uses permitted by copyright law. For permission requests, contact the publishers at the address below.

Tiffany Roberts

authortiffanyroberts@gmail.com

This book was not created with AI, and we do not give permission for our work to be trained for AI.

This book is a work of fiction. Names, characters, places, and incidents are products of the author's imagination or are used fictitiously and are not to be construed as real. Any resemblance to actual events, locales, organizations, or people, living or dead, is entirely coincidental.

Cover Illustration & Chapter art by Fadhila Inès (IF_Art)

Character Portrait by Marespinosa

❀ Formatted with Vellum

TREASURE OF THE ABYSS

HIS TREASURE AND HIS OBSESSION...

Despite her longing for the sea, Macy has clung to the safety of land for half her life, devoting herself to her daily routine — until she agrees to go sailing with a childhood friend. Her fears come to fruition when a sudden storm capsizes their boat, rekindling her old terror. She awakens to a rescuer who is anything but human — and he refuses to let her go. Treated like a curiosity and a possession, she's desperate to go home. Yet Macy is undeniably drawn to this strange creature. Can she give up her old life, her family and friends, to embrace this adventure...and Jax?

HER SAVIOR AND HER CAPTOR...

Jax the Wanderer is a hunter, an explorer, and an oddity among his kind. While other kraken are content near their dens, Jax is driven by a deep need to journey far and wide, discovering the unknown corners of the sea. Macy challenges everything he's known; she is the most alluring creature he's ever seen on his travels. He must possess her, though he knows it can only end in disaster. How much is he willing to forsake for the female he desires?

Dedicated to my true love. Without you, this book wouldn't be.

And to you tentacles lovers!

CHAPTER ONE

361 Years After Landing

MACY WIPED the sweat from her forehead with the back of her hand and angled the brim of her hat to block the glare of the bright afternoon sun. Every day was warm on Halora, but today was unusually hot, and there wasn't a spot on her that didn't feel damp with perspiration.

Her knees sank into the soft dirt as she crawled forward. Tall stalks of corn towered over her to either side, planted in neat rows, and the scent of earth and growing plants permeated the air. She stopped when she reached a mass of red vines.

She dug her fingers into the ground to grasp as much of the crimson creeper's root as possible. When she pulled up, the plant resisted briefly before coming loose with a spray of dirt. The thin, red vines were harmless for a few days, but they quickly killed most Earth-crops when left untended. Macy shoved it into the bulging sack of weeds hanging over her shoulder.

"Ugh!" exclaimed Aymee from the next row of corn. "I

should've stayed at the Doc's today. If I keep volunteering to help you here on the slow days, I'll be walking like an old crone before the year's out."

Macy chuckled and shook her head as she pulled up another root. "Guess we'll be old crones together."

"You better believe it."

There was a rustle of leaves; Macy glanced up as the stalks parted and Aymee poked her grinning face through. Her dark, curly hair was pulled back and stuffed beneath a wide-brimmed straw hat, just like Macy's, and her brown eyes danced with humor. "Wasn't that the plan? To cause mischief together until we're so old that nobody will believe we'd cause trouble anymore?"

"*You* are the mischief maker, Aymee." Macy tore up another cluster of roots and stuffed it into the sack.

"Yeah, and you're *always* the voice of reason." Aymee rolled her eyes. "Admit it, Mace. Without me, your life would be dull."

Macy sat on her heels, stretched her sore back, and rested her hands on her thighs.

Life in The Watch was monotonous. Each day bled into the next with little deviation; everyone had a job to perform, and the entire community's prosperity was dependent on those duties being performed. Sure, people usually gathered for food, drink, and song after dark, but even that had become predictable and routine.

Aymee brought a hint of unpredictability. She added color to life, and that made it all a little more bearable.

Guilt filled Macy.

She should feel the same about Camrin. Where Aymee exuded vitality, Camrin was a steady presence she could always count on.

Camrin's father, like Macy's, was a fisherman. It had always been expected that Macy and Camrin would form a relationship and eventually join — they'd been friends since they were toddlers, and their parents had always been close. Much to the delight of their families, Camrin had begun courting Macy when she'd come of age at eighteen.

Macy was approaching twenty-five; most people had already joined their partner and started a family by her age. Camrin had always been sweet, had never pushed her, but she sensed he wasn't going to wait much longer.

Her guilt morphed into anxiousness. It curled in her gut, tying her stomach into knots. As much as she cared for Camrin, she couldn't see life with him as anything beyond the same routines. The same thing she'd been doing all along.

"Macy? You okay?"

"What?" Macy asked, blinking. She met her friend's gaze.

Aymee carefully squeezed between the stalks, crawling into Macy's row. "You had this look on your face. Like you were going to be ill."

Macy lifted her hands to rub her eyes, stopping abruptly when she noticed the dirt clinging to her gloves. She dropped her hands back to her lap. "Camrin wants to take me on his boat tonight."

"What? You hate the water! Camrin knows that!"

Macy turned her palms up and stared at them as she brushed away the clumps of dirt. "He said he wants to show me something. A place he found while he was sailing. And I...I need to do better, Aymee. *Be* better. For him. He deserves it."

"Oh, Mace!" Aymee knelt before Macy and took her hands. "You don't need to be *better* for anyone! Why are you settling?"

"Settling?" Macy flicked her eyes up to meet Aymee's. "I'm not settling."

"You *are*. Camrin's a wonderful guy. Hardworking, patient, kind. He'll make a great life partner—"

"I know—"

"—but not for you. I know you, Macy. I know what they

expect of you. But this is your life. Just because your parents want it doesn't mean you have to."

Macy pulled her hands away. "I can't disappoint them. Not again." She'd already caused her parents enough heartache and grief.

"Do you love him?" There was no judgment in Aymee's question; she was as close to being a sister to Macy as anyone could be and knew the guilt Macy carried in her heart every day.

"Of course," Macy said, more defensively than she meant to. Loving him wasn't the same as being *in love* with him, but it had to be enough. "I think...he's going to ask me tonight."

"Tonight?" Aymee's eyes were wide, her jaw agape. "He's going to ask you *tonight*?"

Macy nodded.

"Mace...you know I have your back, right? No matter what you choose, I'll always support you. I just want you to be happy. You sure about this?"

Swallowing, Macy nodded again. "You said it yourself, Aymee. He'll make a wonderful partner. It's about time I make some effort to be the woman he deserves."

He deserves so much better.

Despite her guilt, despite her misgivings, she would try. She'd spend the rest of her life trying to make him happy. Her doubts would fade after they were joined, and she would view him differently. She'd see the man, rather than the boy she'd grown up with. Her love for him would change and grow.

Wouldn't it?

"I better go," Macy said, brushing dirt from her knees as she stood. "I need to wash up and pack before I go meet him."

"Pack?" Aymee rose with a frown. "You're going to be out there all night?"

Macy took in a deep breath. "I trust Camrin. Wherever he's taking me, it'll be safe."

The fear slinking through her chest didn't diminish.

"You're right. I just…" Aymee sighed and smiled. "Be careful, okay? I expect to see you when you get back, so we can keep working toward being old crones together."

Tears blurred Macy's eyes, but she laughed, and stepped forward to embrace her friend. Aymee squeezed her tight.

"I love you," Macy said.

"Love you too, Mace. Even if you stink."

Macy drew back. "What? Do I?"

"Can't meet Camrin reeking of sweat and dirt, can you? Go on." Aymee waved her hands, shooing Macy away. "I'll see you when you get back, and I expect to hear *everything*."

Laughing, Macy said goodbye and maneuvered through the rows of corn. When she finally emerged, she stretched her aching legs and back and walked to the burner. She upended the sack, dumping the weeds into the flames, and turned to stow the pouch and gloves in the battered metal locker nearby.

"Leaving early? That isn't like you, Miss Macy."

She turned and smiled. "Hello, Uncle Malcolm."

He limped toward her, his gait slow but steady, his expression full of its usual warmth. Malcolm wasn't related to her — he only had his wife, Tammy, as far as Macy knew — but his amiability and kindness toward everyone had earned him the title of *Uncle* to most of the town.

Uncle Malcolm worked in the greenhouses and fields, just like Macy, but he'd been a mechanic when he was younger. He'd worked on the complex machines that had been brought to Halora during the colonization, had kept them running for the good of The Watch. But time hadn't been kind to the old equipment; every year, more of it broke down, never to run again. After Malcolm was injured by one, he taught another man his trade and went on to different duties.

"Where you off to, girl?" he asked.

"Home. I need to get cleaned up before I meet Camrin."

"Truly?" He grinned, the lines around his eyes crinkling.

"Don't let me hold you up, then. Tell that boy to make his move already, or a more experienced suitor might move in."

Macy chuckled and gently patted his whiskered cheek. "Aunt Tammy would have something to say about that."

Malcolm snorted. "You're right. Wouldn't want a limp in the other leg, too, would I? Already takes me half the day to walk across town."

"Do you want me to walk with you?" She asked before thinking.

"And keep your man waiting? Get on with you, girl."

Though it felt dishonest, she smiled at him before continuing toward town; the sinking feeling in her gut had returned. She knew she'd only offered to walk with Malcolm to delay the looming excursion. Glancing at the sun, she increased her pace. If she wanted to wash and change without being late, she'd have to hurry.

This was important to Camrin. Macy didn't want to disappoint him.

It was only fifteen meters from the edge of the cornfield to The Watch's outermost buildings — several tall, metal silos constructed for storing crops in the early days. Macy walked between two of them and onto the dirt road leading into town. She passed between pastures and smaller fields without noticing; she'd made this walk almost every day for years and knew the sights by heart.

The lighthouse was the first building in the town proper to come into view. It towered over everything else from its perch on the cape. The structures immediately around it were all from the colonization — metal and concrete, built for functionality and durability. They were weatherworn and sun-faded but had withstood the test of time thanks to their tough materials and diligent maintenance. Most of them stood near the edge of the cliffs, overlooking the sea.

In Macy's eye, it was the newer buildings that gave The

Watch its true character. They were all more haphazard affairs, constructed of native wood and repurposed scrap — taken from broken-down machinery and structures that had lost their purpose — and so lacked the precision of the original structures. But they were hand-built, crafted with pride, care, and no small amount of trial-and-error.

That meant something.

The dirt path gave way first to cobblestones and then to the original concrete roads as Macy entered town. She greeted the townsfolk she passed with smiles, waves, and pleasantries, betraying nothing of the turmoil inside. It was no one's burden but her own.

Her home was an old residence near the ramp to the dock. It was empty when she arrived, and she was relieved. Her mother could be difficult to deal with even on good days; Macy didn't think she could handle her now.

She slipped into her room and packed a change of clothing and a few necessities, hesitating when she saw what she'd decided to wear for tonight. It was a white, knee-length dress her mother had made in anticipation of this occasion. Of Macy's joining. The dress was finer than anything else she owned. She held it up by the shoulders, running her fingertips over the soft, silky material, and cringed as it caught on her callouses.

Laying the dress on her bed, she went to the bathroom, undressed, and ran a cold, wet, soapy cloth over her body, scrubbing away dirt and sweat. After rinsing off, she brushed her hair and returned to her room.

Macy allowed herself no hesitation this time; she picked up the dress and pulled it over her head. The fabric flowed over her body as easily as water. She hurriedly buttoned the front and turned to the mirror.

The dress was held up by two thin straps, and the hem hung

just above her knees. It was lovely, nothing like the rugged work clothes she normally wore.

She longed to tear it off.

A stranger stared at her from the mirror. There was no sparkle of happiness in the woman's eyes, no joy in her expression; nothing that said she was going to join with the man she loved. There was only fear. Regret. Shame.

Life with Camrin wouldn't be bad. He'd work hard to keep Macy content, and they had been close friends since childhood. But it would always be missing something. It would always be somehow empty at heart because she would forever hold back a part of herself.

She'd try; it was all she could do.

Macy stood straighter and forced a smile. It didn't reach her eyes, but it was enough. Enough to hide the conflict raging within…because, as though her reservations about joining with Camrin weren't enough to deal with, he was taking her out on the *ocean*.

She moved to the wooden box atop the nightstand and held her hands over the lid. Swallowing, she opened the box. Inside lay a necklace — strands of thin rope, braided around a light green rock. Such stones could be found anywhere along the beach. They held no value, save to imaginative children who saw nothing but wonder when it came to the sea. And to Macy; it was priceless to her.

The necklace was all she had left of Sarina.

Macy lifted it from the box and gently closed it in her fist, which she pressed to her chest. She squeezed her eyes shut at the sting of tears. Her throat tightened with overwhelming guilt. Sarina would never join with anyone, would never make her own home, would never grow up.

Releasing a long, shuddering breath, she replaced the necklace.

"I can do this."

She closed the lid, fingertips lingering on the smooth wood, and nodded.

"Camrin's been on boats since before he could walk. He knows what he's doing."

After slipping on her shoes, she collected her pack, took another steadying breath, and departed for the dock.

The concrete road descended gradually, angling down from the cliffs to the ocean below. Macy's heart beat faster with each step. The wide loading platform at the base of the path was a meter above the water — mid tide. There were a few workers there, strapping together barrels of fish to haul up to the warehouse with the crane.

She greeted them as she walked by, and worried they'd see through her forced pleasantries.

The dock stretched before her, floating atop the sea; the first few sections were angled downward to meet the water's current level. They felt solid enough beneath her feet as she stepped on, but the dock's swaying was undeniable as she proceeded. The sound of the ocean filled her ears, raising goosebumps on her arms.

It'd been so long since she last stepped foot here.

Camrin was near the end. When he looked up and noticed her approaching, he waved, a huge grin on his face.

He dropped the rope he'd been fiddling with and strode toward Macy, quickening to a run as he drew closer, until finally he took her by the waist and drew her close. Her stomach lurched, and her heart leapt into her throat.

"I missed you," he said, either not noticing or unaware of the desperate way she clutched his shoulders, and lowered his mouth to claim hers.

He'd kissed her before, but never like this. This was more than a brief brush of lips, more than a stolen peck. This was intimate, eager...sealing.

Macy stood still, willing it to end. Longing for solid ground beneath her feet.

"That's enough, you two," said a familiar voice behind her.

Camrin paused and lifted his head, grin returning. His blue eyes were bright as they shifted to look past her.

"I expect you to take care of her," Breckett said, placing a big hand on Macy's shoulder to give it a gentle squeeze. "You look beautiful, Macy."

"Thanks, dad." She turned, slipping out of Camrin's hold, and hugged her father. She shut her eyes as his big arms encircled her. One of his hands cupped the back of her head, smoothing down her hair.

"You'll be fine, Macy girl."

She nodded, wishing she believed him. *Needing* to believe him.

"You know...you can tell him to forget it," he whispered to her, voice gruff. "Your heart isn't with the sea, anymore, and that's no fault of yours."

She strengthened her hold on him as tears pricked her eyes. She'd loved the water when she was young. Loved the sea. The rhythm of the tides, the light sparkling atop the water, the boundless possibilities; it had spoken to her. Her parents could barely keep her away from it...and that had been the problem.

"I'll be okay, dad." She hoped her words didn't sound as hollow to him as they did to her.

Breckett sighed, long and slow, turned his head, and kissed her cheek. "All right." He released her, tugging his fingers through his thick beard.

She stepped back. "Tell mom I love her, and I'll see her when I get back."

"I will. You two enjoy yourselves."

"We will," Camrin said, taking Macy's hand and twining their fingers.

Just before Breckett turned to leave, Macy caught the

shimmer of tears in his eyes. Fighting back tears of her own, she allowed Camrin to lead her to his boat.

At six meters long, it was one of the smaller boats, but it was Camrin's pride. He'd dreamt of having his own boat since they were children. Its sleek, wooden hull rode the surface with a shallow draft. He was as familiar with the coastal waters as any of the more experienced fishermen and handled his boat as naturally as most people walked.

He helped her over the railing, and her heart nearly stopped as the boat swayed beneath her.

"There you go, Mace." He followed behind her.

Macy sat on the bench and clenched the rail as his weight rocked the boat. Leaning over the side, he untied the rope anchoring them to the dock, coiled it up, and turned to raise the sails. The wind filled them as Camrin adjusted the boom and sat down at the rudder.

When she was seven or eight, Macy would've given *anything* to have a boat of her own. She'd dreamt of sailing whether awake or asleep, and when she wasn't out with her father, had spent her time watching all the holos about ships and the sea she could find — not easy, when only a few buildings had fully functioning electricity, and most of the projectors were worn with age.

That had been before she learned how dangerous and unforgiving the sea could be.

The wind swept the boat away from The Watch and toward the horizon. It flowed through her hair, ruffled her dress, and caressed her skin. It had been so long…

Gradually, her grip on the rail loosed. She shifted her eyes to gently rolling water.

"Nervous?" Camrin asked.

She glanced at him; he watched her with a smile and swept his tousled red hair back from his forehead.

"Yes."

He tied off the boom, slid closer, and gently pried her hands from the railing. Massaging her stiff fingers, he lifted them to his mouth and kissed her knuckles before lowering their hands into her lap.

"I know you're scared, Mace. I honestly didn't think you'd come...but seeing you on the dock..." He squeezed her hands, and his smile widened. "It meant the world to me. You're facing your biggest fear...for *me*."

Her eyes watered, but she didn't look away.

It's not enough. You deserve more.

She blinked, and teardrops spilled down her cheek.

"Aw, Mace, don't cry." Camrin released one of her hands and brushed the moisture from her cheeks. He smiled. "I haven't told you how beautiful you look. I've never seen—" He cleared his throat and touched one of her shoulder straps. "Is this for me?"

Macy nodded. "My mom made it."

He leaned closer and cupped her chin. "I can't wait to make you mine. I've waited so long."

Camrin kissed her like he had on the dock. She curled her hands into fists on her lap, clenching the delicate fabric of her dress. His lips were soft, but demanding, and soon she felt the press of his tongue. She opened her mouth with the shock of it, and his tongue delved inside.

I can't do this.

Macy recoiled, pressing a hand to his chest to keep him from following.

Kissing him was like kissing a brother; if that made her feel ill, what would joining with him be like?

"Where are we going?" she asked, keeping her tone pleasant to mask her discomfort.

I can't do this.

Camrin licked his lips, chuckled, and returned to the rudder, giving no indication that he noticed her discomfort. "You'll see. The moment I saw it, I knew you'd love it."

They sailed in silence, and Macy's muscles eased over time. She lifted her face to the wind, closed her eyes, and enjoyed the warm rays of the setting sun on her skin. She breathed in the brine, recalling the time she'd spent on her father's boat. She…missed it.

The boat lurched in a sudden blast of wind. Macy grappled for the rail, eyes flashing open.

"Shit!" Camrin leapt to his feet.

She turned her head to look at him, and the breath fled her lungs.

Ominous clouds darkened the sky behind them, and — in the far distance — she could make out the flash of light from the lighthouse. The signal only meant one thing.

Get off the water.

The wind hit them again, bringing a chill.

"Camrin…"

"I know, Mace! Just…stay calm." He unraveled the rope securing the boom, wound it around his arm, and braced his legs.

A web of lightning spread across the clouds, followed by a roll of thunder. It reverberated through the sky, rattling the rigging and mast. Swelling waves lifted the boat and water splashed over the sides.

"W-we need to go back!" she cried, but she knew there was no turning around. You didn't sail into a storm. "Camrin, we need to get off the water!"

"I know, Macy!" His shouts were nearly lost in another blast of thunder. "We're almost there!"

She looked toward the bow which was directed at the horizon; the last sliver of daylight vanished, leaving only a faint crimson afterglow just over the water. The darkness thickened behind them as the storm was sped closer on strengthening winds. The angry ocean thrashed around the boat, and water pooled at Macy's feet.

Another clap of thunder; stinging rain pelted Macy.

She swept her gaze across the rolling waves, searching the shoreline for a safe place to land, but only steep, high cliffs were in sight.

"Hold on tight!" Camrin shouted. His wide eyes were full of fear, his face pale and strained in the dimming twilight.

Macy followed his gaze away from the land. Ice crystallized in her veins; the sea was cresting, forming a massive wave alongside them.

"Camrin!"

"Get down!"

She dove to the floor and wrapped her arms around the base of the mast. Water swirled around her, and the boom groaned as Camrin battled the wind; he was trying to turn them into the wave to avoid being hit broadside.

For a fleeting instant, everything was still and silent. Macy dared not open her eyes. Then the ship dropped and rose suddenly, sickeningly, and the crash of the wave overwhelmed all her senses simultaneously. The world spun. The sea tore her away from the mast, and the current carried her into darkness. The water surrounding her muted the cacophony of the storm.

She kicked, uncertain of which way was up, lungs burning. Finally, she broke the surface. The terrible sound of the storm and the violent waves was deafening. Macy gasped, fighting to keep her head up.

"Camrin!"

It was too dark, too chaotic. The all-encompassing sea, boundless and untamable, dominated her vision.

"Camrin!"

Lightning flashed, lighting up the water, and she saw his dark shape. Too far.

If he called her name, she didn't hear — the storm, the waves, and her own thundering heart were too loud.

More water crashed over her, forcing her under. Once again, she struggled to the surface, sputtering and gasping for air. The waves carried her away from the cliffs, away from Camrin, away from home. She was alone in the darkness. Alone in the open sea.

Just like Sarina.

Macy's limbs grew weak. She could barely take a breath without water filling her mouth.

Though it only delayed the inevitable, Macy fought.

Wave after wave battered her. Each time she went under, she surfaced a little slower. Each time, more of her strength fled. She remembered that day on the beach, so long ago. Remembered how she'd struggled against drowning.

Remembered how long Sarina had struggled.

When she was forced underwater again, Macy stopped fighting.

Her body sank deeper. Her chest was on fire.

What little air had remained in her lungs bubbled from her nose and mouth, and she closed her eyes as awareness slipped away.

The last thing she felt before blackness fell over her was a pair of arms wrapping around her torso.

CHAPTER TWO

MACY WOKE WITH A GROAN. HER ENTIRE BODY ACHED, AND HER head was on the verge of splitting in two. She pressed a hand to her temple. She hadn't felt this terrible since...

Camrin!

She opened her eyes. Bright sunlight blinded her; she squeezed her eyes shut again and turned away.

The ground beneath her was hard, and running water was splashing into a pool somewhere nearby. She flattened her hand on the coarse rock beneath her and slowly opened her eyes to slits. Sunlight filled her vision, poured over her, heating her skin and the stone she lay upon.

Where am I?

Lifting her head as her eyes adjusted, she glanced to the right and frowned. She was on a small island. All around her were storage containers — wooden barrels, metal lockers and crates, and several chests — some clearly from the time of the colonization. They were brimming with an eclectic collection of items — clothing, fishing rods, hand tools, buoys, bowls, jars, torn strips of canvas from a sail, even a few children's toys.

Beyond the island was a small waterfall, spilling from a high cliff into a nearby pool. Thick vines hung over the rock to either side of the water. She followed the run-off with her gaze to the deeper, darker water it flowed into. A few jagged rocks jutted from the depths, but it was all shadowed by the stone wall and ceiling hanging over it.

She swung her gaze around the area; the stone walls were on all sides.

She was in a cave.

Directly overhead was a large opening in the ceiling, allowing her a glimpse of the bright blue sky, but she was otherwise surrounded by rock and water.

How did I get here?

"I...I should be dead," she rasped. Gathering tears blurred her vision and stung her eyes, and her throat was dry. She should've drowned. Why had she been spared — *again* — when Sarina was never given a chance at all?

Sitting up, Macy drew her knees to her chest and hugged her legs close. Tears spilled down her cheeks.

What of Camrin? Had the sea claimed him, too?

Her sobs, though muted by the rush of the waterfall, echoed off the walls of the cavern. Shuddering breaths shook her shoulders.

Not again.

She couldn't have another tragedy on her shoulders. Couldn't bear the guilt. Camrin had taken Macy out to surprise her, to win her over...to join with her.

If I had said no, if I had told him the truth, we'd still be safe in The Watch.

A splash, different from that steady sound of the waterfall, broke through her heavy thoughts. She raised her head with a start, searching the shadows as she wiped the moisture from her eyes. The sound had come from the darkest part of the cave.

The water was in constant motion, lapping against the edges

of the island and making it difficult to determine where the disturbance had occurred.

The hairs on the back of her neck rose. She wasn't alone. Whatever was there, it was *watching* her, and she had nowhere to go. Macy was trapped, vulnerable to whoever — or *whatever* — was waiting in the dark.

Was it the stranger who'd collected all these things? Was he the one who'd rescued her?

Macy sniffled and ran her hands up and down her arms to coax the chill of fear away. She scooted closer to the island's edge.

"Hello?" she called. "Camrin? A-Are you there?"

The shadows near one of the protruding boulders shifted.

She licked her dry, rough lips. It wasn't Camrin.

"Hello? Would you…would you please come out?"

A hand emerged from the shadows and slapped against the boulder.

Macy flinched, falling onto her backside with her legs splayed in front of her, but she couldn't look away.

In structure, it was like a human hand — four fingers and a thumb, the same number of joints and comparable proportions — but the similarities ended there. The skin was gray, paler on the webbing between the long, claw-tipped fingers. Powerful tendons stood out along the back of the hand as the creature pulled itself forward.

It emerged from the shadows slowly. Macy moved her gaze up the muscled arm, over the dark, jagged stripes on its shoulder, and onto a broad, powerful chest. Its musculature was humanlike, despite its odd skin, but the creature was larger than any man Macy had ever seen.

Its build screamed *male*.

His face was surprisingly human, as well, with a broad, strong jaw and full lips. There were two slits where his nose should've been; they flared with slow breath. More stripes ran from side-to-side over the top of his head. There was a tube-like opening behind each of his cheekbones, near where his ears should be, and his eyes…

She met his gaze; her curiosity was reflected in his. Set beneath a heavy brow, his eyes were bright green with long, horizontal pupils. She'd never seen anything like them. They were unusual, but they suited him.

As unsettling and strange as this creature was, Macy didn't feel threatened by him; wouldn't he have harmed her already, if that was his intent?

"Did you save me?" she asked.

He cocked his head. His down-facing, tubular ears shifted toward her. He advanced through chest-high water. Anything below the surface was lost in the darkness.

"Can you understand me?"

His brow lowered. "Why would I not understand?" The creature's voice emanated from his chest; deep and rumbling.

Macy's eyes widened — not solely at the sound of his voice, or that he spoke English, but because she glimpsed sharp, pointed teeth in his mouth. She wrapped her arms around her legs again. "You're not going to hurt me, are you?"

His gaze dipped to her legs. "Not unless you give me reason."

Dread flowed through her, but she swallowed it back. "You saved me."

"Yes."

"Why?"

"Because I have never seen one of you up close."

"One of…me?"

His eyes roamed over her again, pupils flattening further as he moved fully into the light. His muscles rippled beneath his skin, and his torso angled forward as he approached.

Was he walking along the bottom or swimming? There was an unevenness to his movement that Macy couldn't place, an oddness to his rhythm she'd never seen.

"Human."

"You've never seen…never seen a *human* before?" she asked, trailing her gaze over his broad shoulders and chest. His skin was a few shades darker at his shoulders, sides, and waist, naturally drawing her eyes lower.

"I said I have never *seen* one of you up close. Aren't those things on the sides of your head for listening?"

Macy narrowed her eyes. "They're called ears. How do you know English if you've never been around humans?"

"What is *English?*"

"The language we're speaking."

He narrowed his eyes, mimicking her expression. "It is the language my people have always spoken…in the air."

Macy frowned. How was it this creature knew her language? The old records had reported no sapient life on Halora before the colonization; had they missed something?

"Who are your people?"

"They are of no concern to you."

Shifting onto her knees, Macy crawled closer to the water. "Do you have a name, at least?"

His wide mouth turned down in a slight frown. "I am called Jax, human. The Wanderer."

Somehow, she found a touch of humor in the situation and smiled. "My name isn't *human*. It's Macy. The Gardener."

A scintillating flash of red-brown rippled over his skin. "You mock me, human?"

Macy stared at his body in stunned fascination for several seconds before forcing her eyes back to his. "N-no. Why would you think I'm mocking you?"

"*Wanderer. Gardener,*" he said through bared teeth. The black stripes on his head and shoulders shifted to a vibrant indigo. "You are creating words to insult me."

She retreated from the edge of the island. He spoke the same language as she did, and many of his features were humanlike, but he *wasn't* human. Clearly, a communication barrier remained between them.

"I didn't make it up. A gardener is someone who tends to plants. That's what I do."

Jax eyed her with scrutiny. "Why would plants need tending? They are capable of growing on their own."

"We need a lot, for food. We plant seeds, water them, and remove dangerous plants that would kill our crops."

"For food?" His upper lip peeled back. "No wonder your teeth are so strange."

"Yours are just as strange to me." Though *frightening* might've been a more accurate word.

His expression altered, brow and mouth softening; he looked almost thoughtful. His skin reverted to gray.

"Why does your skin change color?" she asked.

"Doesn't yours?"

Macy glanced at her arm. It was tan from hours in the sun. "No. At least, not like yours."

"It just does. It is the same for all kraken."

"Kraken? Is that what your people are called?"

"It is what we call ourselves."

"Are there many of you?"

Jax's features hardened, and he moved forward, gliding through the water with that odd rhythm. The ridges of his abdominal muscles emerged first, followed by his lower half, glistening in the shaft of sunlight from above.

Macy leapt to her feet and backed away from him once she realized what she was seeing.

His torso led down to thick tentacles — black with pale stripes along their lengths — which swept forward and dragged him onto the island. He towered over her, radiating power and menace.

Macy raised her hands to warn him back, but he didn't slow. Her heart hammered against her ribs. Cold fear swept down her spine. She backpedaled faster and gasped as her calves bumped into one of the large crates behind her. Screaming, she fell, her cry cut short as she hit the water and it filled her mouth. She thrashed in panic.

It was happening all over again.

Something thick and snakelike coiled around her waist. Macy clutched the smooth skin, clawed at it, seeking purchase to drag herself to the surface.

She was lifted out of the water. She coughed, throat burning, and gulped in air with rapid breaths.

Her eyes fell to the black tentacles wrapped around her middle. She quickly removed her hands from them, snapping her gaze up to meet Jax's. Though her feet didn't reach the ground, he still loomed over her.

He leaned close. "I will not betray my people to yours."

"I'm sorry!" she said between coughs. "I wasn't... I was only curious."

He narrowed his eyes, and his pupils expanded. The tip of a tentacle brushed over her bare shoulder. Macy flinched away from it.

"Curious..." he rumbled. Lifting a hand, he moved it toward her face.

She leaned back as far as she could, staring at the translucent webbing between his fingers, at the black claws on his fingertips, at the subtle texture of his skin.

"Please. Don't hurt me." Macy turned her face away; if he was strong enough to hold her steady in midair, he could pick her to pieces with those claws effortlessly.

His hand, strangely warm, brushed the sensitive skin of her neck. Her breath quickened. He raised a clump of her wet hair and rubbed it between two fingers, separating the individual strands.

"What is this?"

"It's hair," she said, watching from the corner of her eye.

"What is its purpose?"

"I-I don't know. To keep us warm? We have it all over our bodies, but it just…grows longer there." She turned her face toward him. "You don't have any?"

"No." He tilted his head to the side and moved his hand, running his fingertip over the shell of her ear. "It is much stranger to see in the flesh."

Reluctantly, Macy lowered her hands, resting them atop his tentacle. She'd expected it to be slimy, but his skin was velvety-fine, soft over hard muscle. It wouldn't take much for him to do her serious harm; he'd just need to tighten his grip, and he'd crush her insides and snap her spine.

"What do you mean?" she asked.

"I have seen…ghosts of humans. It is different to see a human of flesh so close. To touch."

"Ghosts?" Her finger slid over one of the suction cups. It expanded, and she pulled her hand away.

His gaze dipped to her hand. "They can be seen and heard, but not touched."

"Where have you seen ghosts? Ghosts aren't real." Sea monsters weren't real, either, but here she was, talking to one…

"There are a great many things underwater."

Jax didn't elaborate; he shifted his attention to her nose, and his nostril slits flared as he leaned closer. She pressed a hand to his chest to stop him. His skin was just as soft there as it was on his tentacles. The thumping of his heart vibrated against her palm, stronger than she would've guessed, its tempo rapid and rhythm odd — it pulsed in sets of six quick beats.

"Your heart is…different," she said.

Jax glanced at her hand. He lowered his from her hair and placed it on her chest.

Macy nearly stopped breathing. Her heart raced as she stared at him with wide eyes. Part of his hand curved over her upper breast, and the tips of his claws rested against her bare skin.

"*Hearts*," he said, brow falling. "Yours are weak."

"It's not weak. Humans only have one."

"Are you all so small? So...delicate?" Removing his hand from her chest, took her wrist between forefinger and thumb and lifted her hand off his tentacle, examining it.

She tugged her hand out of his grasp. "What do you mean? Humans come in all shapes and sizes. I'm just...female. Aren't your females smaller?"

"All shapes and sizes," he muttered. "Doesn't that make mating difficult?"

"What?" Her cheeks heated.

"Do you have to find mates of the same size and shape for mating to work?"

"You thought..." She shook her head, her face burning with embarrassment. "Not *literally* all shapes and sizes. Some of us are smaller than others. Some are wider, some are thinner, but we're more or less the same."

One of his tentacles brushed the back of her knee, and the tip slid up her inner thigh. Macy sucked in a sharp breath.

"No!" she exclaimed, drawing her legs back and kicking the offending appendage.

The tentacle snapped back. His hold on her waist tightened slightly, and his expression hardened. He stared at her with alien eyes.

"Put me down," she said with a softer tone. "Please, just put me down."

She didn't think he'd listen; for the space of a few breaths, he didn't move save for the slow rise and fall of his chest and shoulders. Finally, he lowered her. Relief flooded Macy as her feet touched solid ground.

Jax withdrew his tentacles and backed away, putting a bit of distance between them.

"Thank you." Shaken, she wrapped her arms around herself and glanced past him, toward the dark part of the cavern. "How did you bring me in here?"

"Through the water."

"So, you could…could take me back. You could help me to the shore."

"No."

For a moment, she stared at him, silent, unsure if she'd heard his response or imagined it.

"Then you could show me, and I-I can find my way."

Oh, God. She didn't want to face the sea alone.

"No," he repeated. There was no malice in his voice, but his tone was firm.

"What do you mean?"

"I will not allow you the chance to lead your people to this place."

Macy dug her fingers into her arms to keep them from trembling. "I won't. I promise I won't tell anyone about you, about this cave. About *anything*. I just want to go home."

"I cannot trust the words of a human. I will not kill you, but you will remain here."

Her chest constricted; she couldn't breathe.

"Can you at least tell me if you saw my friend? He was on the boat with me. Is he…alive?"

"I saw only you, Macy."

She was relieved that Camrin hadn't been captured, too, but what were the chances he'd survived the storm?

"Please." Tears obscured her vision. "Please, let me go. I can't stay here."

"No," he said again, softer this time.

Her face crumpled, and hot tears rolled down her cheeks. He wasn't going to let her go.

Jax's eyes widened, and he approached her. Leaning close, he raised a hand toward her face.

She slapped it away and stepped back. "Leave me alone!"

Jax recoiled, red pulsing across his skin. The shocked expression faded from his face quickly.

Macy didn't care if she'd offended or angered him; he was keeping her as a prisoner. She moved farther away, sank to the ground beside a barrel, covered her face with her hands and cried. Her shoulders shook with each wail and shuddering breath as she cried.

She didn't know where she was or what she was going to do.

Would she ever see The Watch again? Would she ever see her parents or Aymee?

She didn't even know if Camrin was alive or dead. Only that it was her fault.

I should have told him!

There was a splash on the far side of the cavern. She didn't have to look up to tell Jax was gone. She was alone.

That only made her cry harder.

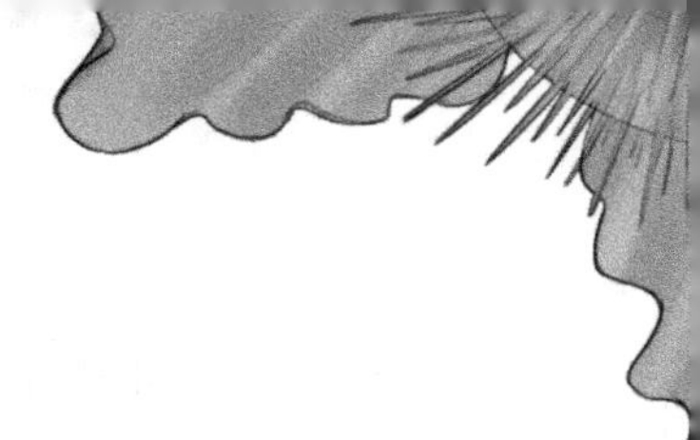

CHAPTER THREE

Senses reeling, Jax plunged into the water. The initial blast of cold did little to clear his mind.

Sorrow had saturated Macy's expression, her posture, her tone; their physical differences had not masked her emotions. Seeing her in such a state had made his chest ache, even as the water spilling from her eyes had piqued his curiosity.

Why had her eyes leaked? Was it something all humans did, or was something wrong with her?

Those questions were minor concerns compared to the sadness and desperation Macy had displayed. He'd been so close to relenting. So close to sinking down on the ground beside her and saying *yes, yes, I will take you home. I will take you anywhere you want to go.*

But he would not betray his people.

As he descended into the underwater tunnel, he changed his skin, causing it to emit a faint light. He used the uneven protrusions as handholds to pull himself through the narrow passage.

Macy was *other*; an enemy, dangerous and deceptive. Humans sought only two things — power over that which they did not control, and the destruction of what they could not control. That was what the only kraken ghost in the Facility taught, when he appeared.

Never trust a human.

But Macy's blue eyes were so full of feeling, and though they were so different from a kraken's, they held something he could not deny — a spark of life, of intelligence, of compassion. As strange as she looked, there was an exotic appeal to her features.

The feel of her, the smell, the *taste*...

His muscles burned with exertion as he sped through the tunnel. His urge to return to her was far stronger than he'd expected. For the first time in his life, Jax doubted his strength of will.

What would going back now accomplish? If he gave in, she'd be in control. How long before he gave away everything and put his people at risk?

Humans had only ever brought hardship to kraken.

She was with another human.

Within a few moments, he emerged into the all-encompassing blue of the open ocean. Nearby fish scattered at the sight of him, flitting away in all directions. Tendrils of grass swayed below, illuminated by shafts of sunlight pouring through the glittering surface above, and hard-shelled bottom feeders scuttled amongst the rocks and plants at the base of the cliffs.

Jax descended, swimming close to the rock face along the coast. From what little he'd seen of humans, they preferred the land, venturing into the water only on the floating platforms they called *boats*. Macy had thanked Jax for *saving* her, and had panicked when she fell into the water in the cave...

Perhaps the old stories were true — humans needed air to survive. If so, Macy's companion had likely been claimed by the sea; anything that might have remained of the missing human after the storm would have been eaten by scavengers already.

When Jax rescued Macy, she was being pulled into the open

sea. The current would've drawn her farther and farther from land, eventually into deeper water than most kraken dared swim. But the sea could be fickle; there was a chance the other human had been swept back to shore.

At the very least, Jax was likely to discover some sign of their boat.

He turned away from the cliffs and swam into deeper water, toward the place he'd found her the night before. When he reached the general area, he pushed up, breaking the surface.

The breeze was cool against his exposed skin. He rode the water, turning his gaze to the land; the shore was hazy in the distance, rising from the sea like a cresting wave frozen in time.

Curiosity had brought him onto land a few times in the past — as far as he knew, he was the only one of his kind to do so. The others feared it because it was the unknown. Because it was the domain of the near-mythical humans. A cursed place. Though he'd never ventured far from the sea, Jax knew the truth — everything felt different on land, the textures alien and sometimes painful, but there was nothing more to fear there than in the ocean.

He swam forward, dipping just below the surface. The likelihood of finding Macy's missing human was low, but it was an excuse to explore. An excuse to get away and sort his jumbled thoughts.

Jax lifted his eyes above water as he neared the shore. Along much of the coast, the land was a wall of rock that stood against the ceaseless battering of the ocean, impossible to traverse without climbing. But there were spots — often hidden — allowing easier access. The beach ahead was one such place.

There, the cliffs were broken up for a short span; they gave way to boulders, then to smaller rocks and pebbles, and finally the sand. Macy's boat lay on its side, between the high tide line and the surf. The large cloth the humans used to catch the wind flapped in the breeze.

He advanced slowly, fighting a current that wanted nothing more than to sweep him ashore.

When a figure rose from the sand beside the boat, Jax's hearts thumped. Macy's human was alive.

And — even from this distance — Jax knew it was a male.

The human moved to the long pole that held the wind-cloth, squatted, and lifted. He walked forward, sliding his hands as he moved, until the boat lay on its belly. The cloth billowed in the wind. Scrambling over the side, the human manipulated some ropes until the cloth hung limp.

Jax altered his color to match his surroundings as he eased closer. The human, shoulders heaving, sat in the boat with his head bowed. He remained that way for a time, oblivious to his surroundings.

Soon, Jax was close enough to make out the male's features; his short, orange hair, the reddish hue to his skin, his wide nose and thick brows. He was larger than Macy, with a heavier build. The sand around the boat was dotted with tracks leading back forth along the beach and winding up toward the rocks beyond.

The human dragged his hands over his face, dropped them to his legs, and pushed himself up.

"Macy!" he shouted into the wind. Cupping his hands around his mouth, he repeated his call, louder than before. His voice broke as he dragged out the last part of her name.

Was this Macy's *mate*?

Heat spread through Jax's abdomen. She was Jax's, now; he'd taken her from the sea, had brought her to safety, had — if she was to be believed — saved her life.

Climbing out of the boat, the human walked to its front, leaned down, and pushed. The boat began a slow journey toward the water.

Jax dug the tips of two tentacles into the soft sand beneath him, anchoring himself in place as he watched the human's progress. The risk in keeping Macy was already too great; he shouldn't allow this human to get away. If they were anything like kraken — and they seemed to be, in more ways than he was comfortable with — this one would report Macy missing. More would come, searching, and if they passed the area near the cave at the right moment, and Macy called out...

The human plunged into the water, walked alongside the boat until he was waist-deep, and swung himself up into the craft. It rocked as he moved to the pole. He tugged on the ropes, and the wind-cloth rose, filling with the sea breeze.

On land, humans were likely more dangerous, but the sea belonged to the kraken. It would be a simple thing to kill the male in the water.

Still, Jax didn't make his move. For some reason, the look of utter sadness on Macy's face came to the forefront of his mind.

The male manipulated the horizontal pole to alter the wind-cloth's direction. His boat turned, riding the wind back toward the place the humans came from. Away from the cave. Away from Macy.

As the boat grew smaller with distance, Jax hoped he wouldn't regret his hesitation.

IT WAS difficult for Jax not to see the Facility with new eyes as he approached; having encountered a living human up-close, having talked to her and touched her, he was reminded that her kind had built the place. Many, many years had passed since humans dwelled in the Facility, but their mark was all over it. Their hands had crafted the metal walls and doorways, had placed the clear windows and put up the lights, had shaped the hallways and installed the strange devices.

The Facility had always sparked Jax's curiosity, but it held only so much for him to explore. Though the Computer possessed a wealth of information, it only responded to certain requests, and generations of kraken hadn't been able to unlock its secrets. The mysteries of the Facility were alluring...but the mysteries of the surrounding sea were far easier — if more dangerous — to solve.

Was it possible that Macy held the key? Did she know how to access the Facility's secrets, would she understand the way it worked?

The place was a wonder; five individual structures nestled on the seafloor, interconnected by a series of human-built tunnels. Three of the structures had suffered damage during the Uprising and were fully flooded. They served as den space for the kraken — the safest, most secure shelter in the entire ocean.

Jax angled himself toward the glow of the exterior lights. They were beacons of hope in the vastness of the sea, a steady reminder that the kraken had a home, that the wrongs done to them in the past had not gone unpunished.

Two lights stood apart from the main building, a few body lengths from the door. When hunting parties left, they draped a net between the two posts. It signified their absence, and was meant as encouragement for those who remained — *should we not return, you have the means to hunt, and we know you will be successful.*

There was no net today; Arkon would be somewhere inside.

Jax stopped before the entrance door and pressed the buttons on the keypad beside it. Every kraken was taught the sequence from a young age, though the meaning of the symbols on the buttons had been lost to history. The light over the door changed from red to green, and it slid open.

He swam into the dim entry chamber and pressed the interior button. The door closed behind him, and the water drained from the room.

"Pressurization normalized," the Computer said; this gentle, female voice was only one of the many it used.

The inside door hissed and opened. Pure, white light filled

the hallway ahead. Jax took hold of the grip over the doorway and swung himself through. Water streamed off him as he moved down the hall, flowing into the drain channels on either side.

As infrequently as he visited since achieving adulthood, Jax knew this place well from his youth. Kraken younglings learned much in these hallways and chambers — from their elders, from the Computer, and from the ghosts.

He moved at a quick pace, pulling himself forward with arms and tentacles, and soon entered the largest — and strangest — room in this building.

The scent of old chemicals lingered in the Pool Room's humid air, fouling each breath. Large metal lockers lined one wall, and various equipment Jax could not identify was scattered throughout the space. Some of it looked like the clothing humans wore. In the center of the room was a huge pool of water.

Jax moved to one of the floor hatches and tugged it open, lowering himself into the hallway below. Huge, clear windows ran along the entire inside wall, allowing an unhindered view of the pool.

Arkon was in the water, floating above his latest work. Thousands of stones were spread on the floor beneath him, carefully arranged by color to create intricate, flowing patterns. He reached down with the tip of a tentacle to adjust some of the stones.

Reaching forward, Jax tapped his knuckles on the glass. Arkon turned in a torrent of bubbles, skin flaring yellow before shifting back to its normal blue-gray. He smiled and signed that he would come up.

Jax climbed the ladder, emerging from the lower chamber just as Arkon drew himself out of the pool.

"You must be nearly done," Jax said.

Arkon dropped his bag on the floor; the stones inside

clacked together. "I have almost finished the base layer, but it will take many more days to achieve balance in the patterns."

When they were younglings, Arkon had been fascinated by the human ghosts in the facility and had spent long hours listening to them and speaking with the Computer. He knew words the others did not understand; did he know what a *gardener* was?

Jax moved to the edge of the pool and looked down. Arkon's work was distorted by the reflection of the overhead light on the water's surface, but the overall design was clear. The large, central circle was surrounded by rings of varying size, all of which were connected by swirling patterns that reminded Jax of water current. The shifts in color from one portion to the next were subtle but unmistakable.

He'd watched Arkon work for long enough to know that each stone had been placed with purpose, following instructions only Arkon could see.

Jax was a hunter, a warrior, a restless explorer, but he envied Arkon's skill. The others called it useless, but wasn't there something to be said for a pleasing image? Wasn't there some value in something that could instill *feeling* in a single glance, even if that feeling was fleeting?

"I do not have the words to describe it, Arkon."

"Incomplete. Unsatisfactory. Ordinary." Arkon blew mist from his siphons. "Uninspired. It is missing something."

Tilting his head, Jax swept his eyes over Arkon's work. Even with the individual stones blurred by the water, the intricacy and detail were apparent. Arkon had never crafted anything on such a scale, and it was, in Jax's opinion, his most impressive work yet.

"It needs...heart," Jax said. "Something in the center, to give it life."

Arkon leaned forward and peered into the pool. His skin shifted toward blue. "Yes. A centerpiece. Something...of a different shade than all the rest. I wish you would stay for longer periods. Things are easier when you are here."

"I'm leaving again."

"I know." Arkon moved to his bag, hunched down, and rummaged through its contents.

"You know?"

"You always go, Jax the Wanderer. It is your nature. How far will you trek this time?"

"Not far. A few days, perhaps."

Lifting a smooth stone from the bag, Arkon held it in his palm and turned it, examining it briefly before he replaced it. "Good. Dracchus will likely call a hunt soon, and, though he despises you, he is displeased when you are not here to join."

"To the abyss with Dracchus."

Arkon lifted his shoulders in a casual shrug without ceasing his search. "You know how the rest are. They respect your prowess, though they distrust you because you are so often away. As strange as they think me, they at least always know where I am."

"If we wish to survive as a people, we will need to leave this place one day. Where will we go if someone like me does not find another place for us to dwell? I endanger only myself." Even as he spoke the words, Jax knew they were what Arkon would call a half-truth.

Such selfless reasons for Jax's treks were hollow justification. At heart, he could not deny the call to wander; it was in his blood. Staying too long in any single place made him restless and fouled his mood. He needed open water, needed the thrill of the unknown, needed to be away from the pointless posturing of the other kraken.

How would he react to the news that Jax had captured a human, and was keeping her as his own? If Jax had hundreds of questions for her, Arkon would have *thousands*.

"Vanishing every few days will not convince them of that, Jax. You've known this for a long while."

"I am not interested in convincing them of anything. The others can think for themselves and decide what they will. I'll continue to hunt for our food and scout new areas, regardless."

Arkon closed his bag and rose. "I know what I need!"

"What?"

"If you come across a shard of halorium — the glowing stones the ancients used to harvest — would you bring it to me?" He returned to the edge of the pool and stared over his work. "It would serve as the perfect heart for this piece."

"Those stones do strange things to the Facility," Jax said. In the presence of halorium, lights flickered, the ghosts were broken and distorted, and the Computer's voice was crackly and faint. Larger stones produced more powerful effects.

"There are still containers for them, in the Underneath. That will allow you to bring one inside without causing issues."

"But once it is removed from the container—"

"Make it a small one, then. The pool is isolated enough that a small shard shouldn't adversely affect the functions of the nearby equipment."

Jax could only stare at his friend; Arkon's skin pulsed with his excitement, and his eyes were bright, viewing possibilities no one else could see.

"I will watch for one," Jax finally said.

"Thank you. May the currents carry you where you would go, Jax."

"And may the stones fall as you would have them lie, Arkon."

As Arkon plucked up his bag and plunged back into the pool, Jax exited the chamber and made his way back to the entry doors. He entered the sequence.

"Please wait while the chamber is prepared," the computer said.

The floor hummed as unseen machines did their work. Jax

inhaled deeply; it was a short wait, but that made it no more bearable. This was the last barrier between him and the sea. The door finally opened, and he entered the small chamber; another push of a button, and the room flooded.

When he emerged, his attention was drawn immediately to the kraken gathered near the detached lights ahead. A small group ringed a pair of males who were locked in a dance.

The larger of the two was Dracchus; his skin pulsated from black to red as he moved, powerful tentacles spinning through the water in a blur. The motion created new patterns, blurs of brightness and splashes of color that whirred by with increasing speed, complexity, and ferocity. The other male struggled to keep up, but he could not match Dracchus's power and aggression.

Their dance descended into chaos as the two suddenly charged one another. The eruption of thrashing tentacles was too frantic for Jax to track, but the males separated almost as quickly as they'd attacked. The challenger slunk backward, skin pale in admission of his defeat.

Jax swam forward. Such spectacles were popular for onlookers, but held no true meaning. Dracchus was strong — everyone knew it, and required no further proof.

As he passed the gathering, Dracchus — his skin reverted to its normal black — caught Jax's gaze and held it. Crimson flared on Dracchus's shoulders; a challenge.

Jax held Dracchus's eyes for a few more heartbeats and turned away, not slowing his pace. Something far more important — and more interesting — waited for him elsewhere.

CHAPTER FOUR

MACY REMAINED HUDDLED BESIDE THE BARREL LONG AFTER JAX left, crying until she had no tears left to shed, and hated herself for it. What did it solve? What had crying ever done to help her?

She was still stuck in this cavern, more miserable than before.

She rubbed her tired eyes with the heels of her hands and released a slow, shaky breath. She needed to *do* something. Anything but sit here, waiting.

Lowering her arms, Macy looked around the cavern, halting her gaze on the vegetation hanging at the sides of the waterfall. Her eyes followed their path up the steep cliffside.

She thrust the idea aside before it went any further. Climbing was suicide. One slip and she'd plummet to the rocks below. If that didn't kill her instantly, she'd be left broken, suffering through immense pain until she finally expired — alone. When the time came, and desperation demanded the attempt, she'd try, but it wasn't yet worth the risk.

That left escaping by water.

Macy stared at the dark side of the cave. Sunlight shone on the rippling surface, casting shattered reflections on the ceiling.

Jax hadn't been specific on how he brought her in here, but there had to be some sort of tunnel hidden in the darkness.

Her legs and backside protested as she uncurled herself and crawled to the edge of the island. She leaned forward and peered into the cerulean water. Small plants swayed amidst the rocks below. It was shallow now, but the tide was receding, and it was likely deeper toward the rear of the cave.

Sharp rocks dug into her palms as she clutched the edge.

I can do this.

This wasn't the unforgiving ocean with huge, battering waves that would drag her into the abyss. It was an enclosed pool of water.

Shifting her legs around, she sat on the edge and paused. She ran her gaze over the frayed hem of her dress, over the splotches of dirt marring the once white, crisp fabric. Fingering a tear near her knee, she closed her eyes.

She had to believe Camrin was alive. She couldn't...couldn't consider the alternative.

Steeling herself, Macy slid into the water. It was chilly against her sun-warmed skin. She waded forward, and it slowly rose past her hips until it reached her chest. Her dress floated around her in the current produced by the waterfall.

Macy spent what felt like hours searching the bottom, feeling with her toes and stepping carefully. The water became too deep to stand in as she neared the shadowed area; she dove under a few times, but all she found was more rock. She stopped at the edge of the sunlight, treading water, and stared ahead. The cave wall in the back was visible, but she couldn't see the bottom of the water.

It was just a little farther. A little more to explore. She bit her lip and urged herself forward, but her limbs didn't respond.

There was no telling how deep it was, or what awaited in that darkness.

Defeated and exhausted, Macy returned to the island and

hauled herself out of the water. She wrung out her dress before she collapsed.

After allowing her limbs a rest, she forced herself up and rummaged through the various containers, removing items and arranging them around her feet. She picked up a ratty brown teddy bear; it was missing an eye and one leg, and most of the stuffing had fallen out. Lowering it, she shifted her gaze to the other items; netting, rope, shells, tools both familiar and foreign, and objects she had no name for.

She glanced up at the opening in the ceiling; the sunlight had been intense through most of the day, and even with the cooling mist from the waterfall, it was hot. If she was going to stay here, some sort of shelter would be necessary.

Macy cleared the space, returning most of the items to their containers, and shifted two of the barrels so they were a couple meters apart from each other. She stood a fishing pole in each, securing the poles by stuffing objects around their handles. As she replaced the tools, she discovered a knife.

She peered over her shoulder, as though Jax would suddenly appear and pluck the knife away, before settling her attention on the blade.

It was old; that was clear by its lack of rust and light weight. This wasn't metal forged after the colonization; it was an advanced material that couldn't be produced on Halora. And the edge was *sharp*.

Taking up a length of rope, she trimmed it into several smaller pieces. Then she unfurled the canvas, cut holes at the corners to loop the rope through, and stretched it between the fishing poles. She pulled the free end tight and anchored it with a pair of heavy crates. When she was done, she wrapped the knife in a spare shirt and set it aside.

Macy stood in front of the makeshift shelter and surveyed her work; it was crude, but it was shady, and that was all that mattered right now. She crawled beneath the canvas, thankful to be out of the sun.

The shifting shadows on the ground marked the passage of hours as the sun progressed across the sky. When would Jax return? What if he didn't come back at all? She pushed the thoughts aside, but the more she fought them, the more she thought of him.

He'd called his people kraken. The name was vaguely familiar; she'd heard stories growing up, mostly from her father and the other fisherman, about giant beasts, sea serpents, and monsters. But they were just that — stories. Myths. The sea was home to countless creatures, and long, uneventful voyages under the blazing sun could easily muddle a person's perception. A three-meter-long fish became a thirty-meter fish fairly easily, under such circumstances.

But none of those stories had mentioned anything like Jax. How had humans lived on Halora for centuries without knowing of the kraken's existence?

For all his similarities to a human, the differences were striking and unsettling; Jax was equally fascinating and frightening. But he hadn't hurt her. His curiosity had mirrored hers as they examined one another.

She settled her hand over the spot on her neck where he'd touched her. He'd been gentle. He'd even called her *delicate*. In any other situation, she might have laughed. She was slim, but she wasn't fragile; she worked as hard as any man or woman back home.

But she'd felt his strength. If he wanted to break her, he could do so with little effort.

Still, his touch hadn't been unpleasant, nor did his face repulse her like it should have. She was ashamed to admit to herself that the contact between them had elicited a powerful reaction from her body. Despite her uncertainty and fear, she'd felt something when his tentacle slid along her inner thigh. Something *there*.

Macy squeezed her eyes shut and clenched her fists.

Jax wasn't even human! How could her body betray her like that? Why would she respond to his touch when she rejected Camrin's? Camrin, who had loved her for years, who was one of her best friends? Jax was holding her captive. She should be terrified of him.

She should *hate* him.

And yet…

By late afternoon, her stomach ached, and her tongue was thick and dry. She looked at the waterfall.

What choice did she have? It was fast-running water, as fresh and safe to drink as anything outside The Watch.

Macy grabbed a cup and a piece of cloth from one of the crates and lowered herself into the pool. She was just tall enough to stand on her toes and walk across, her chin brushing the surface. When she arrived at the narrow stone ledge beneath the waterfall, she set the cup down and hauled herself up. She rinsed the cup out and filled it through the cloth; without any way to boil it, it would have to be enough.

Pulling the cloth away, she brought the cup to her lips and drank. The water was heaven in her mouth; crisp, fresh, and cool. She drank three cups full before refilling it a final time. As she returned to the island, she held the cup of precious water high over her head.

She lay down under her shelter. Time passed slowly, and she was just drifting off when she heard a splash.

Jax made no attempt at stealth as he emerged from the water with three fish wriggling in the unyielding grip of his tentacles. The first thing to catch his attention was the makeshift shelter she'd constructed on the island. His eyes dropped as Macy, who lay beneath the raised canvas, lifted her head.

Her hair hung loose over her shoulders; it was fuller now that it had dried, and he imagined it would feel even softer. Seeing it brush over her skin made him long to touch her again.

She held his gaze as he approached, betraying no emotion. Jax was the first to look away; he pulled himself onto the land and stopped in front of the shelter, leaning forward to run the tip of a finger over the tight, neat knots she'd used to fasten the wind-cloth to the poles.

Macy had so easily repurposed these items to fit her needs. Was that one of the reasons these otherwise weak creatures were dangerous?

"You have been busy," he said.

"I needed to get out of the sun." She sat up. "Not like there was anything else for me to do."

He tilted his head back. Only a sliver of light shone into the cave; soon, it would be full dark. But during most of the day — when the sky was clear — the island bore the brunt of the sunlight. Was it as uncomfortable to humans as it was to kraken?

Jax studied Macy. Perhaps it was a trick of the light, but her skin appeared pinker than it had before. She'd said human skin didn't change like a kraken's. "Your color is different. Does it take a long while for you to make such changes?"

She furrowed her brow and glanced at her shoulder, touching a finger to it. "It's burned."

"Burned? How?"

She stared at him in silence. After a few moments, she sighed and reached for the cup on the ground beside her. "I told you a human's skin doesn't change color. Not—"

"You lied."

Her eyes narrowed. "I didn't *lie*, and if you wouldn't interrupt me, I'd tell you why."

"You said a human's skin does not change color. Your skin has changed color."

"I said it didn't change *like yours.*"

"Perhaps you must learn to couple your words with more accuracy."

"You know what? I don't have to talk to you," she snapped, turning her back to him.

Jax lowered his brow and tightened his grip on the fish. He was curious to learn about humans — about her — but he had no patience for deceit.

"As you'll have it." He separated one of the fish from the trio and tossed it onto the ground before her. "You can eat in silence."

The fish thrashed and flopped, gills flaring and mouth gaping. The glowing tendrils protruding from its head bobbed with its movement. She cast a single, fleeting glance at the creature.

Heat flared in Jax's gut. He'd hurried back from the Facility to see her, to speak with her, to share a meal with her, and now she was ignoring him. If all humans had the potential to be so frustrating, he understood why his ancestors had risen against them.

He moved closer to the water and bent down to eat his share. The meat was tender, and the fish struggled only briefly.

"That's so gross," she muttered.

Jax twisted to look at her. She raised the cup to her lips and poured the contents into her mouth.

Placing the fish bones aside, he turned toward Macy fully. "What are you doing?"

She twisted, too, giving him *more* of her back, and maintained her silence.

He slithered over to her, and as he came alongside her, he leaned forward to see her tongue slip out of her mouth and wipe moisture from her lips. Without looking at him, she lifted her chin and turned away.

Jax reached around her with a tentacle and snatched the cup from her hand.

"Hey! Give that back!" She leapt up and reached for it.

Retreating to the shaft of sunlight, he angled the cup to look inside. Water. Was that the purpose of such objects? There was water everywhere. Why would anyone need a container to carry so small an amount?

He poured a bit of it over a suction cup. The humans called it *fresh* water, but to the kraken, it was foul. A waste of water.

"You are putting this inside your body? Is it your wish to die?"

Macy grabbed the cup out of his hold. She remained near, posture rigid, and glared at him. "Why should I bother answering your questions? You'll just call me a liar."

"Speak plainly, and I won't have to."

"Are all kraken rude, or is it just you?"

"Empty that before you hurt yourself, then eat."

Macy raised the cup and gulped down the remainder of the water.

Cold flowed through Jax's veins; his stomach twisted, and his skin involuntarily pulsed yellow. He had treated her poorly while she'd been in his care, but he hadn't known it was possible to push a human to self-harm.

"You have doomed yourself," he said quietly. "Why?"

"I haven't done anything. I'd die if I *didn't* drink it."

"I...what does that mean? Fresh water is deadly."

"To humans, salt water is deadly. We need fresh water to live." She gestured to her arm. "Our skin changes color if we are ill or if we're in the sun too long. It also changes if we're angry or embarrassed, but it doesn't change like yours."

He shifted his gaze along her arm, following it to her shoulder. The single strip of pale flesh there — near the strap of her cloth covering — was in stark contrast to the angry red surrounding it. Would the same happen to a kraken after being in the sun for too long?

"You still need to eat," he said; however pronounced the differences between them, all creatures needed food.

She glanced at the fish. Only its mouth moved now, opening and closing as it gulped air.

"I can't eat that."

Jax's skin darkened. "I hunted for you. Do you reject it?"

"I said I *can't*. I can't eat it like that."

Anger flared in his gut; success was never guaranteed on a hunt, making any catch precious. To see his effort — to see good food — so disrespected was appalling.

He clenched his jaw and forced his skin back to neutral.

If he wanted to learn about her people, about their artifacts, he needed to keep her content. Thus far, he'd failed miserably.

"Explain. If you would."

"It's raw."

"It is fresh."

She scrunched her nose. Jax didn't know how to interpret the expression.

"It needs to be cooked. If I eat it raw, I could get sick and possibly die."

Cooked. The word was familiar to him, though only vaguely. Perhaps it was one of the many words most younglings learned and promptly forgot — a word that had no meaning or use in the life of a kraken. A word from a different world.

"So...you can only eat plants?"

"I can eat the fish, but it needs to be cooked."

"What is *cooked?*"

Macy tilted her head. "Do you know what a fire is?"

"Yes. The Computer uses strange smoke to put it out, when—"

"Computer?"

He snapped his mouth shut. It was more than he'd meant to give away, more than he should have said. "I know fire, Macy. That is all that's important."

"Oh no. You're not dodging this question. I've answered yours, now you can answer mine. What computer?"

Frustrated, he expelled air through his siphons. Macy jumped back and stared at him with wide eyes.

"What is wrong?" he asked, his irritation dampened by confusion.

"I thought those were your ears!"

"They are my siphons." He turned his head and pointed to the small hole behind his siphon. "These are my ears…*earholes*, if it is more accurate."

She studied it intently for a moment before she looked away, scratching her arm. "Sorry for assuming."

He frowned at her posture and tone. "I am sorry, as well, Macy."

Her eyes met his. "For what?"

"Have I not done the same, many times?"

"Yeah. I guess you have." She stepped away, placed her cup on the ground beneath the canvas, and went to one of the numerous containers nearby. After emptying its contents into the other bins, she walked to the edge of the island and dunked the container into the water. She carried it to her shelter and set it down.

Using both hands, she picked up the fish and dropped it into the container.

"You need fire to cook the fish, so you may eat safely," Jax said.

"Yes." She settled her attention upon him. "But you still haven't told me about this computer."

Jax inhaled deeply. If he wanted her to answer his questions truthfully, he would have to extend her the same courtesy. But he couldn't endanger his people.

"There is a voice in the walls, in the place my people dwell. It is called the *Computer,* and it speaks to us. Sometimes, it will answer questions, and sometimes it will give us warnings. Often, we do not understand what it means."

Macy stood, her eyes widening. "You mean down there?" She pointed toward the tunnel. "In the sea?"

"I can tell you no more, Macy."

"But you just told me you have a computer down there! That's…that's human technology!" She paused, eyes darting from side to side as though in thought. "What do your ghosts look like?"

If Macy chose to act against the kraken, what information would prove damaging? "Like humans," he replied finally. "Sometimes we can see through them. Sometimes they flicker, or look…fuzzy."

"They're holograms. Recordings."

"Holograms." *Ghosts* seemed simpler and more fitting. "You are excited by this?"

"Yes! We never knew there was a settlement underwater."

"I did not say it was underwater."

"You didn't have to. What do the holograms say?"

"What do you need to make your fire?"

"What do they say, Jax?"

"I can tell you no more, Macy."

"But—"

"No more," he growled.

Macy shut her mouth, pressing her lips tight, and curled her hands into fists. She took in a deep breath and released it slowly. "Right. I'm your prisoner."

Her anger and resignation struck like a blow.

"Such information is not mine alone to give, Macy."

"Right," she repeated, and sat down in her shelter.

The uncertainty that filled Jax was foreign to him; he could do nothing but watch her, for a time, with no idea of how to proceed.

"What do you need to make fire, Macy? I will not allow you to starve."

"So just let me go."

"And what will I tell my people, when yours come to hunt us?"

"I said I wouldn't tell anyone!"

Jax moved to the crates. He picked through their contents, unable to keep the history between humans and kraken from the forefront of his mind. It was too dark and bloody to be ignored. "If I gave you my word that no harm will come to you while you are here, would you believe me?"

"You already said you wouldn't kill me, and you're going through a lot of effort to keep me alive."

He looked at her over his shoulder. That shadows were thickening; night would be upon them soon. "That doesn't answer my question, Macy.

She sighed. "Yes. I believe you."

Nodding, he turned back to the human artifacts. "That is more than I expected. For now, let it be enough."

"It's not enough for me! I didn't choose to be here!"

"Tell me what you need to make a fire, and I will obtain it for you."

She growled. "Wood — *dry* wood — and something to create a spark. Flint and steel, or one of those little fire starters."

Jax sorted the Facility's strange collection of items in his mind. He knew a few pieces of equipment that could start a fire without a doubt, but they were all tied into the buildings themselves; even if he could remove them, he doubted they'd work with that connection severed. But there was another possibility...

"Would heat work?"

"It'd have to be extremely hot."

"I know of something that may help, but I'll have to leave to obtain it."

Macy was quiet for a time. When he glanced at her, she was staring at the sky.

"It's going to be dark," she said.

"Yes."

"Is it…safe here?"

"Safer than anyplace out there."

She nodded and dropped her gaze to her lap.

"I'll be as fast as I can, Macy."

He counted his heartbeats; she hadn't yet replied by fifty. Moving quietly, he picked up her cup and filled it under the waterfall. She watched as he placed it on the ground beside her, but said nothing.

Her silence followed him into the sea.

THE WATER WAS dark as he hurried to the Facility, and he saw no other kraken when he entered. He moved through the halls with more caution than usual; when he set his heart on being away, the place put him in strange moods. There was a tightness in his chest and a restless energy in his tentacles. He itched to move on.

He found the room he was looking for without encountering anyone.

The humans had kept many weapons in the Facility — a variety of guns, spears, knives, and harpoons. Though the kraken preferred the simpler tools, they'd always remained mindful of the weapons their old foes had wielded. They'd stand the best chance in using such devices, should the age-old conflict spark again.

Jax removed a heat gun from the charging rack. It was relatively small, fitting in one hand, and its case was sleek and glossy, but he knew better than to be fooled by its appearance. This was a dangerous weapon. He checked the charge and made sure its operation was disabled before exiting the Facility.

He saw no one on his way out. Nonetheless, he kept low and matched his skin to the bottom. That he'd returned so soon would be strange to most kraken; that he'd taken a heat gun would rouse true suspicion.

Moonlight — silvery and faint —shone through the surface by the time he reached the tunnel entrance. His hearts beat rapidly. He was bringing a weapon into the presence of a human. Perhaps he was as foolish as some of the others thought. Perhaps this would be his end.

He wanted to trust Macy. Wanted to believe her. But his people had made a point of *remembering*; the kraken would never forget the cruelty of humanity. She could guide him as necessary, but he would not allow her near the gun.

The cave was dark save for the weak light cast by the stars directly overhead when he emerged inside. His eyes didn't adjust until he'd climbed onto the island. He paused midway across it.

Macy was curled in her shelter, wrapped in the cloth coverings from his collection. Her breathing was slow and steady; she was fast asleep. She'd stacked the driftwood that had been spread throughout the numerous containers in a pile beside one of the barrels.

Jax crept closer, lowering himself near to the ground. She seemed so tiny and serene. So distant from the frustration and sorrow she carried while awake. Holding his breath, he reached forward and brushed a strand of hair out of her face.

For all her oddities, she was fiercely alluring; heat stirred in his veins. Females were rare amongst his people — so few remained that the survival of their species depended upon keeping the females safe. Macy wasn't kraken, but she seemed no less precious.

His gaze roamed over her features, and his hearts quickened.

He would be the one to protect her.

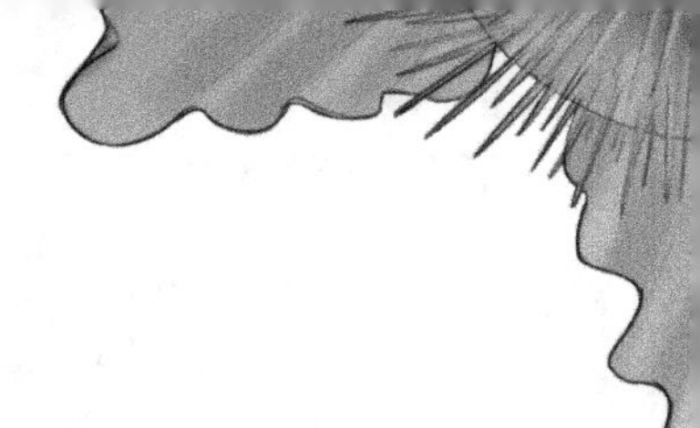

CHAPTER FIVE

MACY OPENED HER EYES BEFORE THE FOG OF SLEEP LIFTED FROM her mind. She only vaguely registered the presence of a large, blurred shape ahead. Her vision cleared as she blinked away the grogginess and her eyes adjusted to the dim light. The dark form moved; it seemed to unfold, rising from the water with a series of soft splashes.

Her brain was slow to determine what she was seeing.

"Are you awake now, Macy?" Jax asked.

She furrowed her brow; he'd left just before dark. Macy had gathered as much driftwood as she could find in the containers and collected an armful of extra clothing before the light died. She'd draped herself in cloth and sat down under her shelter to await his return…

A wave of dizziness hit her as she lifted her head. She groaned and shut her eyes, dropping her cheek back into the crook of her arm.

"Yes," she replied, voice muffled.

There was another splash, followed by the strange slithering sound that meant he was on land, drawing closer to her.

"Do you feel unwell?"

"Hungry and lightheaded, but I'll be fine." Macy raised her head again and looked up. The sky was stained with the soft pinks and golds of sunrise. She'd been more tired than she'd realized.

Jax stood a couple of meters away, water running from his gray and black skin to pool on the ground beneath him. Her eyes followed one of the droplets as it rolled down his chest, over the muscle of his abdomen, and past his pelvis, catching the light from different angles as it moved. For the first time, Macy wondered where his *equipment* was. She'd seen a few younger boys as they ran naked through town on occasion, and had seen Camrin's once when they'd gone swimming. As they'd grown older, it would sometimes become erect when he was with her — visible despite his pants — and she'd pretend not to notice.

However minimal, none of that experience helped her imagine what Jax's might look like, much less where it was.

When she realized she was staring, her face heated, and she forced her eyes to his. "How long have you been there?"

Jax shrugged. He made the gesture with such ease that she was briefly overcome by how surreal the situation was — a sea monster with both human speech and mannerisms.

"I returned when the larger moon was in the center of the sky."

Macy straightened her arms and pushed herself up, brushing aside the clothing piled atop her. She ran her hand through her hair and winced as her fingers caught in several snarls. "I meant to stay awake."

"Weren't you tired?"

"Yes." Hungry and scared, too.

"Then no harm has been done." He dipped his chin toward the driftwood. "That is for your fire?"

"Yeah." She found her cup nearby and picked it up, peering inside. It was empty.

Jax came forward and held out a hand. She hesitated before placing the cup on his waiting palm and draping a piece of cloth atop it.

"Let the water flow through the cloth. It'll help keep it clean," she said in response to his questioning expression.

He nodded. "Do you need anything else for the fire, or is the wood enough?" he asked as he crossed the island.

Macy watched, fascinated by the way he moved. Though his body remained upright, he didn't so much walk as drag himself along with his tentacles. It created an undulating rhythm to his movement; dipping, sliding, rising, tentacles in constant motion.

She tore her gaze away and got to her feet, ducking out from beneath her shelter. No more gawking at her captor. She had a fish to cook.

"Macy?"

"Oh, um…" She cleared her throat; what had he asked? "Oh! Kindling. Something that'll easily catch fire."

Brushing debris from her legs, Macy stepped around her tent and surveyed the crates. Some were metal with slits along their sides; she picked up the emptiest of them and dumped its contents into another bin.

Jax sauntered up alongside her. He handed her the cup; she passed him the crate.

"Bring that to the vines by the waterfall," she said, sipping the water, "and keep it dry, if you can."

He nodded. In the water, he moved with an otherworldly grace, arms raised over his head to hold the crate well above the surface. He was across the pool in seconds.

Setting her cup down, Macy entered the water and swam to the other side. It was cold, raising goosebumps on her arms and legs. She turned away from the waterfall as it misted her face; during the heat of the day, it would be refreshing, but it was too chilly now.

Jax leaned an elbow on the narrow ledge that ran along the length of the rock face, the crate perched beside him. Macy climbed onto the ledge nearby. She shivered immediately.

Shaking her hands dry, she forced her attention to the vegetation on the cliffside. The mass of vines clinging to the stone began at the top of the cliff — about fifteen meters up — and hung nearly to the water. Tufts of scrubby grass had sprouted from some of the cracks, with more growing along the base of the cliff.

Macy gathered all the grass within reach, piling the green handfuls to one side and the brown to the other. Once that was done, she went to work on the vines, shifting the glossy leaves aside to reveal the webs of branches and roots beneath.

The dead growth eventually gave way when she grasped it with both hands and leaned back, but the living vines were far more stubborn, clinging to the cliff face with silent desperation. She settled for tearing off some of the larger leaves, piling all of it into the crate.

After plucking the final leaf, she tilted her head back, trailing her gaze up the cliffside.

The vines are strong...

"Macy?"

Jax's voice cut through her thoughts, and she turned back to the crate.

"There's not much else I can get, right now." She frowned down at her harvest. "Would you bring it back to the island, please? And again, try not to get any of it wet."

He lifted the crate over his head and swam back to the island.

Knowing what to expect didn't dull the chill of the water when Macy slipped back into the pool. She hurried after Jax, though there was no way she'd ever be able to keep up with him. He carried the crate to her tent, set it on the ground, and turned toward her as she pulled herself out of the water.

She shivered again, and when she looked at Jax, he made no attempt to hide the way his eyes roamed over her body — from head to foot and back again, lingering on her chest.

Suddenly self-conscious, Macy glanced down. Her soaked dress was plastered to her breasts and hardened nipples. Mortified, she crossed her arms over her chest, shielding herself from his gaze.

Jax shifted closer and tilted his head, brow creased. "Why do you cover yourself?"

Was it possible that her nipples tightened further under his scrutiny?

"W-we need to build the fire," she said.

"What does the fire have to do with it?"

"It doesn't."

He held her gaze for several seconds, but didn't press any further. Instead, he moved aside and hunkered down beside her when she knelt before the crate. She felt him watching her, and couldn't ignore how tightly the dress clung to her body.

Keeping an arm over her chest, Macy removed some dried grass and vines from the crate and piled them on the ground. She arranged several pieces of driftwood over the pile, leaving room for airflow, and leaned back.

If they could get it lit, it would do well enough with the fish, but the relatively small fuel supply wouldn't last very long. It was enough to cook three or four meals — maybe a bit more, if she was conservative.

One problem at a time.

"Okay. You said you had something to spark this, right?" she asked.

"Yes." Jax twisted slightly, shifting his tentacles, and moved something into his hand. When he brought it forward, Macy widened her eyes.

"You have a gun."

Jax raised the gun, tilting it nonchalantly. He didn't point it at her, but that did little to ease her concerns. "For the fire."

"How is a gun going to help us make a fire? Have you ever even used one before?"

"This gun creates heat."

Macy stared at the weapon. He had to have taken it from wherever his people lived. There were similar weapons in The Watch, but they were rundown from centuries of use and increasingly improvised repair. Jax's gun looked like it had just been manufactured.

"Okay." She extended her hand, palm up.

He looked at her waiting hand, brow falling. "Have *you* ever used one before?"

"I've been taught to handle them."

"More reason not to give it to you. Move back."

Macy frowned, but she obeyed. Why would he hand her a weapon that could totally alter the power balance between them?

Turning toward the pile of fuel, Jax fiddled with a control on the gun; Macy guessed it was some sort of power setting. In one fluid motion, he dipped his torso forward and slid his tentacles backward, leaving him nearly on his belly. He held his upper half suspended just over the ground.

There was a soft, high-pitched whine, barely audible over the waterfall. He held the gun with both hands, pointed at the base of the kindling, and pulled the trigger.

At first, nothing happened. She was about to ask if something was wrong when a wisp of smoke rose from the pile. Within a moment, the fire ignited. Jax released the trigger and shifted into an upright position.

"It worked!" Macy grinned as the flames grew.

He watched the flames with slitted pupils. "It has a strange way of moving."

"Just don't touch it." Macy rose and slid the crate to stacked driftwood, adding the remaining grass and vines to the pile. Then she flipped the crate over and scrubbed its bottom clean with a cloth. "Would you bring me the fish?"

Turning back to the fire, she set the crate over it, upside-down. The slits on the sides and base acted as vents, allowing air and smoke to flow freely, and provided a grill-like cooking surface.

Jax entered the corner of her vision. He held the fish in one hand, his clawed thumb hooked in its mouth. It curled its tail to one side, gills flaring.

Macy ducked into the shelter and removed the knife from its hiding place, unwrapping it. The grip was comfortable in her hand. She knew people in The Watch who would've killed for such a fine-quality blade.

"Where did you get that?" Jax demanded.

She stood and turned to face him, hiding the knife behind her back to keep him from grabbing it. "I found it in one of the crates."

He extended his arm, holding his palm up. It was fast becoming a popular gesture between the two of them.

"I'm keeping it," she said, lifting her chin. "I need it."

"Why do you need it?"

"I need it as a tool. Not a weapon."

"When I have more reason to trust you, you may have it as a tool."

"Damnit, Jax! What do you think this is going to do to you? It'd be stupid for me to even try."

His brow fell low, and his pupils expanded to a strange hour-glass shape. Macy held her ground — and his gaze. Finally, he lowered his arm in silent acceptance.

"Thank you," she said softly and glanced at the fish. She raised her empty hand.

Jax passed the fish to her without a word and followed when she went to the edge of the water. He eased down beside her to watch; she wasn't sure if it was an extension of further trust, or if he'd realized she truly didn't pose any threat to him, knife or not.

She worked quickly, slicing open the fish's belly to gut it before cutting a slab of meat from each of its sides. Her father had taught her the motions when she was young, and her hand moved with confidence and familiarity. Whenever she cleaned a fish, she couldn't help but remember those days spent with him, before they lost Sarina. Her father often sang when he performed such tasks, making up the words as he went and never missing a beat in his husky baritone.

Her chest ached, and she paused. Her parents were likely worried sick if they didn't already believe her dead.

One problem at a time.

After she'd stripped the skin from the two fillets, she rinsed the meat and her knife in the water.

"Are you not going to eat the rest?" Jax asked.

Macy glanced at the discarded pieces — skin, guts, bones, head, and tail — and wrinkled her nose. "No."

"That is a waste of good food."

"All yours," she said, getting to her feet.

He gathered the scraps, leaving only the bones, and drew his tentacles together to raise his torso.

Macy entered the shelter, turned, and sat on the ground before the fire. She set the knife atop its cloth. Jax lowered himself into his version of a sitting position to her left as she selected the largest of the leaves from her pile. She folded them around her fillets.

The wraps sizzled when she laid them atop the crate, releasing a surprisingly sweet smell. She glanced at Jax and immediately regretted doing so; he was slipping fish guts into his mouth and chewing them slowly.

"That's still gross," she muttered, keeping her attention on her hands as she wrapped her knife in its cloth and tucked it away.

"Is that what you think of me, Macy? That I am *gross?*"

She looked up at him with a frown. Their differences were stark, but they didn't matter; she'd grown accustomed to his appearance during their short time together. He was more intriguing than anything. There was undeniable beauty to his form and the way he moved.

"No, Jax. I don't find you gross. Just..."

"Just good food."

"It's uncooked, and you're eating its bowels."

"There are no fires underwater, and all the soft bits are good. Perhaps humans don't appreciate it because you have so many *plants* to eat." He curled his lip slightly, giving her a glimpse of a pointed tooth.

"I doubt you've ever eaten the plants we do, so you can't say anything about it. And humans don't appreciate the parasites that come with eating raw meat." She carefully flipped the meat, drinking in the aroma of cooking fish.

The sky was rapidly shifting to its normal blue, and the air was warming as sunlight streamed through the opening.

Jax's nostrils flared. "The smell is...not unpleasant."

The corner of her mouth lifted.

After giving them a bit longer to cook, she plucked both bundles off the crate and lay them on the ground beside her. She opened one, barely allowing it time to cool before she tore into the juicy, flakey fish. It was hot; she inhaled through her mouth to keep from burning her tongue as she chewed, but it was damned good.

"Its color is unnatural," Jax leaned closer and studied the meat with unmasked curiosity.

Macy stopped her hand just before she slid another chunk into her mouth. She glanced down at it and held the piece out. "Want to try it?"

He accepted the offered morsel, lifting it close to his face to examine with narrowed eyes. After turning it from side to side and giving it a few squeezes, he brought up his other hand and, delicately, tore off a smaller piece with the tips of his claws.

"If you're not going to eat it, give it back," Macy said after swallowing another bite.

Jax swung his gaze to her. Without breaking eye contact, he opened his mouth and placed both pieces onto his tongue. His brow furrowed as he chewed. "This no longer tastes like fish."

"It does. Like *cooked* fish. The leaves add some flavor to it, too." She nibbled on another chunk; only a few tiny bits remained on the first leaf. "At home, we use spices to alter the flavor of our food and create variety in the tastes."

He ran his tongue over his teeth. "Like the smell, the taste is not unpleasant. But it seems like too much trouble when it already tasted fine as it was."

She shrugged and picked up the other bundle. It had cooled enough not to burn her fingers. Unfolding it, she ate in silence.

"Still, it would be interesting to try these...*spices*," he said after a while.

"Spices come from plants."

Jax frowned, dropping his gaze to the charred leaves she'd used to wrap the fish.

"My dad loves his food spicy. He makes things so hot it feels like your mouth is on fire. I don't know why he enjoys it, but he does, even if it makes him turn red and pour sweat."

"So...spices make your mouth burn?"

"Not all of them. There are all kinds, and if you use them right, they can enhance the natural flavor of whatever food you use them on. There are even sweet spices we use to make treats." She tilted her head. "You probably don't know what most of that means, do you?"

"I don't fully understand. I have heard some of the words

before…but they have never held meaning to my people. Still, I think I understand enough."

Macy finished her fish and slid the leaves into the fire through a slat on the crate. She sat quietly; only the ceaseless burbling of the waterfall broke the silence. This was the second day since she'd been brought here. She didn't know if Camrin had survived, didn't know if anyone would even consider them missing, yet.

How long before her parents thought they'd lost another daughter to the sea?

Here, Macy had no one. Jax came and went, and they were two different people from two different worlds. She felt…lost.

Warm tears slid down her cheeks. She hurriedly wiped them away.

Jax leaned toward her, gaze intent on her face. "Why are your eyes leaking, Macy? Is it some sickness?"

Macy got on her knees. "I swear I won't say a word about you or your people."

"I will not argue with you on this again." He turned away and moved toward the water, his skin darkening.

"Where are you going?" she asked, brushing away more tears.

He didn't answer, didn't slow his movement.

"Jax?"

He continued forward. Macy's heart quickened, and she scrambled to her feet. She didn't want to do it again. Didn't want to spend endless hours alone, caged in with nowhere to go, with no one to talk to. All she'd have were her thoughts, her guilt.

Her fears.

"Jax, please!" She raced after him, and — without thinking — plunged into the water.

He finally turned toward her. His features were hard, but he watched silently as she waded toward him.

"Please. D-don't leave me. Don't leave me alone here again." Macy sagged forward, despair sapping her strength. This was all too much.

Jax was there suddenly; rather than falling face-first into the water, she fell into the solid, velvet-draped planes of his muscles. His tentacles brushed her legs, unseen beneath the surface. She threw her arms around him and squeezed.

The thundering of her heart filled her ears. After ten beats, Jax embraced her and lifted her from the water. He cradled her against his chest. She slipped her arms around his neck and buried her face against him, letting her tears flow freely as she sought comfort in his nearness.

CHAPTER SIX

MACY'S SKIN WAS WARM AND SMOOTH, THE FEEL OF IT strengthened by the desperation of her hold on Jax. His hearts pounded in rapid succession and his chest was tight. This was a thrill not unlike that of a coming hunt, but it was a different sort of excitement, a new heat in his blood. Her body was soft; it molded to his, melted into his embrace, and his flesh tingled where it met hers.

He desired her. There was no hiding from the fact, no denying its truth.

Kraken females had pursued him for his prowess and ability to provide, but their numbers were few, and they'd always pushed for him to change. To deny his nature. That was not what Macy sought in his arms now.

She doesn't want to be alone.

The realization struck him hard; he understood her loneliness, related to it, because he felt it, too. Years of wandering alone crashed up him like a wave battering the shore.

Her scent — a combination of salty and sweet, with a hint of earth and stone — washed over him. He tasted it through his tentacles, smelled it through his nostrils, and it permeated him.

The only barrier between them was the wet cloth she wore. His memory of how it had sculpted to her body, accenting her tantalizing curves, sparked something in his gut.

A fire burned inside of him, and it was for Macy.

It took all his will not to extrude as his arousal grew; his emotions had never been so conflicted, his desires never so misaligned. He longed to take her but needed to comfort her. Macy's sorrow flowed into him.

The water from her eyes — her *crying* — was hot against his chest. Her shoulders trembled with shaky breaths, and he smoothed a tentacle over her back, rubbing gently. She tightened her hold on him.

Instinct demanded he do anything he could to make her happy; her sadness was a blade twisting inside him. But he couldn't give her the one thing she wanted. He couldn't let her go. He knew it now, more than ever, and protecting his people was only one reason.

Jax held her until her crying subsided. By then, his hearts had slowed, but his blood hadn't cooled. He doubted it ever would while she touched him.

Macy's grip loosened, and one of her arms slipped away. Her palm smoothed down his shoulder to settle over the center of his chest. She curled her fingers, brushing one back and forth over his skin.

He held his breath; would she realize, soon, the way they were touching? Would she fight out of his grasp? She viewed him as her captor, and her feelings on the situation weren't likely to have changed so suddenly.

"Do you have a family?" she asked softly.

Jax knew what family was, what it meant, but he'd never thought much about it. "I had a mother. I do not know my father's name, or if he spawned other young."

"Did your father leave you and your mother?"

"Leave? He was a hunter and would have served our people

until his death. I likely swam with him when I was old enough to hunt."

Her finger stilled. "So…he never knew of you?"

"Why do you sound so sad when you ask that?" Jax glanced down at her; despite the angle, her downturned lips and creased brow were clear.

"You grew up never knowing your father. Haven't you ever wondered who he was? What it would have been like to be raised by him?"

"I was raised by all the males. That is how I learned to hunt, scavenge, and survive. If my father lived, he took part in it. I see nothing sad in that."

"And your mother?"

"Females… They have their own matters to attend. I knew her. Our lives rarely met while she lived."

Macy raised her head and looked up at him. The whites of her eyes had reddened, making her irises brighter in comparison. "I don't understand. She didn't raise you? Only the…males? Did you have a home?"

"I remained with her until I could be taught by the hunters. Then, I sheltered in various dens until I was old enough to claim my own. How are human children raised, if our ways are so strange to you?"

"By our mother and father, in *one* home. We stay until we're joined…and, a lot of times, even after."

Jax couldn't imagine three or four kraken sharing a den; they'd tear one another apart after a few days.

"What do you mean by *joined*? Join a hunt, or…do you mean *mated*?"

Macy's cheeks darkened. She dropped her eyes and pulled her hand away from his chest as though it burned. "Would you… Put me down, please."

He frowned; she felt so good against him, fit so perfectly. Water sloshed around him as he swam back to the island. Reluctantly, he lowered her onto the ground and released his hold, the tip of a tentacle lingering briefly on her back.

"Thank you." She stepped back and tugged the fabric of her covering, pulling it down so it didn't cling to her body, and crossed her arms over her chest.

"It is the same as mating?" he asked.

"No. I mean…it's not *just* sex. When two humans decide they want to join, it usually means…forever. Until one of them dies."

"Why make such a bond?"

"Why wouldn't we? If you love someone, and can't stand the thought of being apart from them…" She paused; her expression became drawn, and when she spoke again, there was sadness in her voice. "Why wouldn't you join your life with theirs? Why not build a home together, a family?"

It was a concept wholly alien compared to ways of the kraken. Mating had little to do with emotion; the kraken needed to reproduce to survive, and the females would choose the males they thought most likely to father strong children.

His thoughts turned to Macy's loneliness — to his own loneliness. To the man on the beach, calling Macy's name.

"I saw a male on the beach yesterday. He was in your boat, calling for you. Are you *joined* with him?" His chest burned at the thought of her with another male; the feeling was both unfamiliar and startling in its intensity.

Macy met his gaze. She took a step closer, eyes wide and full of hope. "He's alive? You saw Camrin?"

Her expression strengthened the flaring emotion inside Jax. He remembered the terms for what he felt — possessiveness. Jealousy. He'd never cared about what other kraken had, never felt hurt when females left him for another male. But Macy being mated to *Camrin* was too much to bear.

And he *had* to know for sure.

"Are you joined with him?" he repeated.

The light in her eyes dimmed, and she looked away. For a moment, she was silent, staring aside with a deep frown.

"Macy—"

"We were on our way to join."

Jax clenched his fists, and his entire body tensed. Beneath the water, his tentacles thrashed restlessly. "Until the storm. Until *me*."

She looked at him. "Yes."

Everything inside him halted, and searing heat flooded his veins. Jax had saved her life and taken it in the same action. He'd caused her sorrow, and he was the reason it continued. But he would not relent, *could* not; she was his, now, just as much as any of the objects he'd found in the sea and brought to this place.

Macy dropped her gaze, fingers restless along the bottom of her covering. "Everyone knew he was going to ask. I knew, too. My mom and dad were hoping for it. We've been friends for so long, and he's always cared about me... He never kept that a secret. He waited, gave me plenty of time, but I think he knew he had to be the one to make the move because I...just *couldn't*."

Jax eased slightly, unclenching his fists.

"He wanted it to be a surprise, so he was taking me somewhere special. A place we could join, become husband and wife, without anyone else around. And I was going to." Her lip quivered, and a sheen of water filled her eyes. "It was *wrong*. I should have told him, years ago. He deserved to know. But I felt so guilty, and I didn't want to break his heart. I thought my feelings would change, that I would grow to love him. I mean...I *do* love him. As a friend. A brother."

The water fell from her eyes as she met Jax's gaze. "I would've gone through with it and lived a lie. Now, he probably thinks I'm dead, and...and I... I never told him."

He considered her words, thrusting aside his own roiling

emotions. She was not joined with Camrin. Jax had prevented that from happening when he rescued her.

"Isn't that better for him?" His voice was cold, even to himself, but it was the only way to keep some distance between them. The only way to fight the urge to take her into another soothing embrace.

He guessed she wouldn't be so accepting of his touch, now.

Macy flinched. "I...don't know. I know what it's like to hold onto something and not let it go. You just...stop *living*."

Though he didn't want to talk about her almost-mate anymore, Jax sensed that Macy needed to. She needed to sort through her feelings.

"You think he will hold on to you that way...and you feel guilt for it?" he asked.

She nodded.

"You are not responsible for what he does with himself, Macy."

"I *will* be responsible for his guilt, though. If I'd told him sooner, told him *no*, we would never have gotten on that boat. If I had told him years ago, he'd probably already have a family of his own by now. But I didn't. I was too scared, and he'd always been so kind, and after all this time, I felt like...I owed him. And now...now he'll blame himself for my death.

"If you'd just take me ho—"

He raised a hand, and she snapped her mouth shut.

"There is a rule my people follow; hunters eat first. Do you know why?"

She swallowed and brushed the moisture off her cheeks. "Because without the hunters, there would be no food."

"Yes." Something new flared within him — pride. There were fully grown kraken who still didn't seem to understand the rule. "You have not been feeding yourself, Macy."

Her brow lowered. "I-I don't understand."

Jax brought his fists to his chest and swept them outward,

throwing his fingers open. "You give of yourself. To your people, to your parents, to Camrin. You worry for them; you concern yourself with how they will feel. You speak as though you only worked to accomplish what they expected."

She turned her face away.

He pulled himself up onto the island and approached her. "Look at me, Macy."

Swallowing again, she obeyed, her lips pressed into a tight line.

"What have you done for yourself? If you do not *feed* yourself, you will not have anything to give to the others. Do you understand?"

"Yes." Her response sounded forced.

"If I followed the wishes of some of the kraken, my every moment would be spent obtaining food for them. Even some who are capable of hunting for themselves. I would never be able to explore, would never enjoy new places, because there would be nothing left for me. That is like dying inside.

"Let your people think you died in the storm. You already let them kill you within."

A crease appeared between her brows, and she stood in silence for a time.

"And you?" Macy finally asked, looking at him.

"What of me?"

"How much do you intend to take? I'm your damned prisoner here; it's not like I have a choice in...feeding myself, or whatever you want to call it. I can't explore and enjoy new places. I'm *trapped* here."

Jax's nostrils flared; there was still sorrow in her tone, but it was reinforced by an undercurrent of anger. She was right. How could he speak to her of such things when *he* was the obstacle preventing her from controlling her own life?

I'm trapped *here.*

Those words echoed in his mind, resonated to his core. He

understood her pain — he'd felt it himself, time after time. Since he'd come of age and claimed his den, he had spent his time running from that feeling, seeking his own life, his own places.

He'd told her many times that he'd not risk his people's safety by letting her return to her home, and he nearly said it again. He clenched his jaw to keep the words from escaping; they'd begun to sound hollow, even to him.

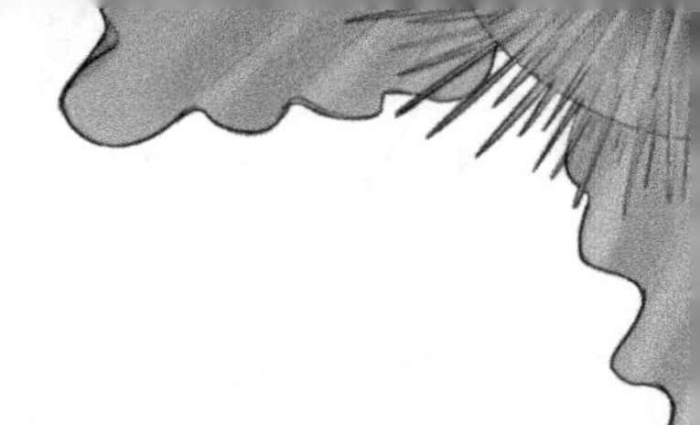

CHAPTER SEVEN

THEY SPOKE LITTLE THROUGH THE REST OF THE DAY AND INTO THE next morning. Thick, palpable tension filled the air between them. Macy knew Jax wanted to talk, but he'd kept his distance. He'd meant well in his attempts to comfort her; there'd been truth in his words, but hers held truth, too. Guilt was clear in his eyes when he looked at her, and she hardened herself against it. Even if she knew his reasons, even if she understood them, keeping her here wasn't right.

Still…he'd saved her. He'd saved a human he knew nothing about when he could easily have let her drown.

Despite the words they'd exchanged, Jax had only left Macy when she said she was hungry. With little to occupy her apart from her own thoughts while he was gone, Macy found her eyes wandering to the vegetation on the cliffside repeatedly.

Camrin is alive.

Her heart had soared at the news. He'd be frantic, heartbroken, desperate, but he was *alive*, and she could find him.

If Macy owed Camrin anything, it was closure. The truth of her feelings would cause him pain, but she couldn't allow him to spend the rest of his life believing himself responsible for her death, longing for what they might've had...

She stared at the cliffside until Jax returned. She needed to try — for herself.

There would only be one chance.

Around midday, she crawled out of the shelter and stood up. Jax was drifting in the shadowed water, barely moving, his eyes fixed on nothing.

"Jax?"

He lifted his head and swung his gaze to her.

A pang of guilt constricted Macy's chest; the eagerness and anticipation in his expression suggested he'd been waiting for her to speak to him for a long while.

"Would you..." She bit her lip and shifted her weight. "I'm hungry."

He brightened slightly. She couldn't be sure if it was because she'd spoken, or because she'd given him an excuse to leave this awkward silence behind.

"I will bring you something to eat."

"Thank you."

Jax seemed torn as he left, hesitating and glancing over his shoulder.

Fear gripped Macy's insides; did he suspect her true motive?

His pupils expanded, his siphons widened, and he disappeared under the surface.

Macy held her breath, counting the seconds to ensure he was gone. He hadn't been gone for long the last two times he'd hunted for her. There was only a tiny window of opportunity.

She used some scraps of cloth to tie her wrapped knife to her thigh and ran across the island, leaping into the pool. The chill only pushed her to the ledge faster. Hauling herself up beside the waterfall, she tipped her head back.

The cliff was higher than anything she'd ever climbed, a sheer wall of rock and vines. This wouldn't be like climbing a tree. But the vegetation was secure, and this was her only shot. Jax wasn't going to take her home. If she wanted to ease her loved ones' grief, to confess everything to Camrin, she had to climb.

Taking a deep breath, she reached up as high as she could and slipped her fingers into the mess of vines, wrapping the loose ends around her hand. She tugged and then leaned back with her full weight.

The vines held.

She released a tremulous breath and jumped, grabbing another handful of vegetation. Pressing her feet to the rock, she found whatever purchase she could with her toes, and climbed. She held her gaze on the top as she moved higher and higher.

Time was limited — Jax could return at any moment — but she kept her pace slow and steady. There were only three possible outcomes for this. He'd come back to find her part way up the cliff, he'd come back and find her missing...

Or he'd find her broken body floating in the pool below.

The thought made her dizzy. She pressed her forehead against the vegetation and closed her eyes.

Focus. Just keep looking up.

Perspiration beaded on her skin, and her muscles screamed with exertion. Long hours of labor in the fields had kept her fit, but she was unused to these motions. She was lifting her own bodyweight each time she moved higher.

By the halfway point, her limbs were trembling, and doubt had infested her mind. She halted, clinging to the cliffside, and forced herself to take deep, even breaths.

Let your people think you died in the storm.

"No."

You already let them kill you within.

"I didn't," she rasped.

Her denial didn't make Jax's words less true.

Think of Camrin. Of Aymee. Of mom and dad, and how they must feel. First Sarina, and now me...

But mom has always blamed me for Sarina's death.

"Don't cry. Don't you dare cry." She squeezed the vines, hands aching, and looked up. "Almost there."

Bracing her feet against the rock, she stretched one arm, reaching high above her head to resume her climb. She'd made it another meter when dead vegetation crumbled beneath her foot; she slipped and clutched the vines desperately. The sweat on her palms made her hands slick.

Macy dropped, stomach lurching, and clawed for a handhold. A scream caught in her throat, frozen by fear.

She came to a jolting halt when she caught a thick, tangled mass of vegetation, and her arm felt as though it would be torn off. She wound the vines around her hands and wrists and closed her eyes, trying to calm her pounding heart and slow her frantic breaths.

It was a close call, but she had to press on, had to fight through her fear. Time was running out.

She moved her feet carefully, securing one before seeking a spot to brace the other. She needed to relieve some of the strain on her arms.

The vines loosened. She slipped a few centimeters.

Her heart stopped.

Jax was uneasy, leaving Macy alone; there was a sinking feeling in his gut, and his throat was tight. He couldn't shake the sense of blind, nervous anticipation. Something was going to happen.

He kept his hunt short, gathering a few of the hard-shelled bottom-dwellers scuttling amidst the rocks and vegetation below the tunnel opening. He slid a claw between the armor segments behind their eyes to kill them; their underbellies were unprotected, the meat sweet and easy to access. Hopefully, humans could eat them without getting sick.

Though collecting his prey was a simple task, his hearts were racing by the time he finished. He hurried to the tunnel and dragged himself through rapidly. Perhaps she'd talk to him again, as the food cooked, and he'd be granted another glimpse of the female behind the sorrow and anger.

I am the reason she is sad, the reason she is angry.

The truth was unavoidable. He was keeping Macy against her will. It was just as damaging as her need to give everything to the other humans without leaving anything for herself, if not more so.

Arkon had a word that seemed fitting now; Jax was a *hypocrite*.

Though he railed against being contained, though he resisted the commands of others and sought his own path, he'd stolen Macy's freedom without a second thought. What did it matter that she was a human, or that their peoples shared a violent history? She was a thinking being, an emotional being, and seemed to possess many of the same yearnings as Jax himself.

He emerged from the tunnel, lifted his head over the surface, and swam to the island. As he laid the hard-shells on the ground, he glanced at her shelter. Even through her anger, she'd cast appreciative glances at him each time he'd returned with fresh food; he longed to see that expression now.

She wasn't there.

Jax pulled himself onto the island and moved to its center. She wasn't looking through the containers, and he didn't see her in the water. It was only when his hearts resumed their pounding that he heard a rustling of leaves.

He turned to the waterfall just as a small rock fell from the cliffside. It clacked noisily on the ledge and rolled into the water.

Jax tilted his head back. The breath fled his lungs when he saw Macy clutching the vines, halfway up the cliff face.

Surging forward, he plunged into the pool and called her name as soon as he had air enough to make the sound. Though he spent little time outside the water, he knew things worked differently in the air. Things *fell* differently.

Macy gasped and looked down at him. Just as their eyes met, the plants she held tore free. She screamed and fell backward. The vine caught with a jolt and Macy slammed into the cliffside before the plants snapped. She dropped.

He heard nothing but her scream and his thundering hearts as he leapt onto the ledge. Cold fear flowed through him, but his chest burned. He couldn't tell if his lungs were too full or too empty.

She hit him in the chest. He wrapped his arms around her as the impact knocked them into the water, reaching out with his front tentacles for some purchase on the rocks. Macy thrashed, kicking wildly and swinging her arms. They were under for three heartbeats before Jax gained a strong enough hold to pull back onto the ground. He kept her in his arms.

Macy coughed, spitting up water. Her soaked hair hung around her face, and her fingers clutched his arms tightly enough for her blunt fingernails to feel like claws. She sagged against him and breathed raggedly.

She was frightened, but he didn't think she was hurt.

If he'd returned even a few moments later...

Jax's relief was swept away on a tide of fury. If *he* understood the danger of what she'd done, Macy had undoubtedly known the risk.

"Were you trying to kill yourself?" he demanded.

Macy stiffened and reared back. "I had to try!"

Her response should have cooled him. He had offered similar reasoning in his youth when his early explorations had resulted in injury or near-death. But it only angered him further.

He caught her wrists with two tentacles and pressed her against the wall, pinning her with his body.

She arched her back and strained to pull free. "Let me go!"

He took hold of her face, forcing her eyes to his. "So you can die? If I wished you dead, I would have let it happen during the storm!"

"Why didn't you?" She glared at him and bared her teeth. "If I'm going to die in this damned cave, why not let it be now? Why are you keeping me here?"

"Because you are a treasure I plucked from the sea, and you are *mine!*" he roared.

Macy gasped, staring at him with wide eyes. She'd gone completely still.

Only her shocked expression made him realize what he'd said. It was the truth, the heart of his motivation, the thing he'd denied — even to himself. He desired her, was drawn in by her allure, and she roused his curiosity...but it wasn't enough. He needed to claim her. Had needed to since his first glimpse during the storm.

"You are mine," he repeated, "and I will not let you go."

She struggled to free her arms, holding his gaze with hers. "You're a monster."

Jax's chest constricted. Hearing that from her, spoken with such fury, was more painful than he could have imagined.

He released her, and she fell to her knees.

Vision clouded by rage, he lashed out, tearing the vines off the cliffside with claws and tentacles and throwing them into the pool behind him. Brittle, dead growth snapped and poked at him, and bits of rock and dirt tumbled down, but he didn't stop. He attacked them like they were his most hated foe.

They had nearly taken Macy from him.

When there were no more vines within reach, he turned to Macy and leaned over her, chest heaving.

Shock and fear had replaced her anger.

"Kraken are *exactly* what humans made us to be," he growled.

Jax plunged into the water before either of them could say anything more. He had never known such fury, had never allowed it to so fully drive his actions. A small part of him — a part that had somehow maintained a semblance of control — insisted he leave before he turned his rage upon her. Whatever she'd said, whatever she'd done, she didn't deserve his wrath.

If anyone deserved that, it was Jax himself.

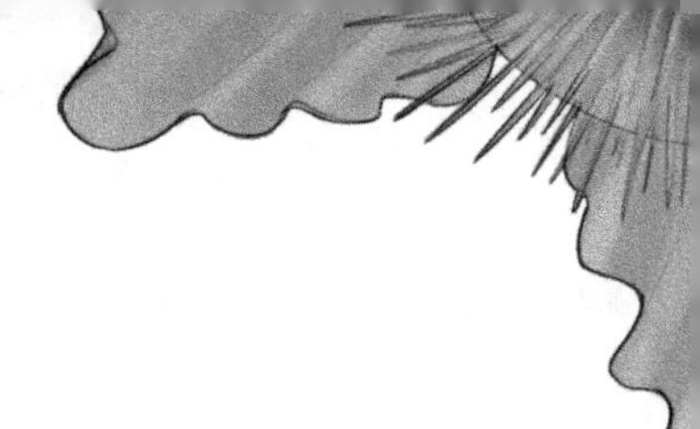

CHAPTER EIGHT

YOU'RE A MONSTER.

Each time the words echoed through Macy's mind, she saw the hurt in Jax's eyes, the flicker of pain on his face that preceded his rage.

I didn't mean it.

She stared at the dark water he'd disappeared into, willing him to come back so she could apologize. But he didn't return.

Macy staggered to her feet, braced a hand on the cliffside for balance, and looked around. Torn vines lay everywhere. She glanced up, reminding herself just how tall the cliff was. Just how far she'd fallen.

It had been foolish. *Dangerous* and foolish. If Jax hadn't returned when he did, she would've died. All because of guilt… and pride.

She stepped through the vines and dropped into the pool. Her body made her aware of every ache and pain as she swam. She pulled herself onto the island with weak, shaky arms, and for a time could do little more than lie on the ground with water pooling around her.

Macy felt more alone than ever.

She shifted her gaze, and her chest ached; three Halorian lobsters were piled nearby.

The fishermen back home often set traps for the bottom-dwelling creatures, but the lobsters were cautious. The traps needed to be left undisturbed for days at a time before they'd catch anything. As difficult as they were to obtain, they were one of Macy's favorite foods.

And Jax had caught these for her.

She looked back at the shadowed portion of the cave.

Macy had always thought of herself as practical and hard-working — *one problem at a time*, just like her father always said. She woke early every morning, put in long hours tending the fields and greenhouses, and helped her neighbors however she could. Weaving baskets, cooking meals, sewing clothes, repairing roofs; anything. Whatever urges to wander and explore she'd felt as a child had been quashed by Sarina's death.

Everyone had a part to play in The Watch…and people rarely left.

There were other settlements out there, but the nearest was weeks away by land, and what would be different in any of them apart from the people's faces?

You have not been feeding yourself, Macy.

Jax's words had hurt because he was right. After Sarina's death, Macy thought she needed to make up for her sister's absence, that she had to be the best daughter she could be. She'd done the work of two people. All to ensure the people around her were happy and wanted for nothing.

She'd tip-toed around her mother, who'd never forgiven Macy for what had happened, and performed every chore without complaint, held her tongue through every hurtful comment. Despite her misgivings, Macy would have done everything to keep Camrin content after their joining.

Macy hadn't been living. The people around her had slowly

drained her life, a little at a time. There'd been no maliciousness in it. They kept taking because she kept giving.

Her father and Aymee had tried, in their own, subtle ways, to steer her away from that behavior. She saw it now. But they'd been too gentle — or Macy too stubborn — to change anything.

The choice had never been theirs to make. It had always belonged to Macy; she was the only person who could've altered her course.

Would it be so bad? To...to remain here with Jax?

Could it even work? They were from different worlds. She had needs that he didn't; he lived in water, and she on land. He was...*other*.

What would she be to him? A belonging, a prisoner?

Or...a friend?

Despite everything, she enjoyed her conversations with Jax. She took delight in the wonder and curiosity he exhibited. He awoke the same in her; Jax was fascinating, and she wanted to know more about him and his kind.

Let your people think you died in the storm.

Could she? Could she go on, knowing that her family and friends mourned her?

It was insane and selfish, but it was also...*freeing*. Her *death* would allow Camrin to move on. He had friends and family to comfort him through his grief, and, in time, he'd find someone to love him as he deserved. To love him like Macy couldn't.

Ultimately, what choice did she have? Jax refused to let her go. It angered her, but she understood. His need to protect his people superseded all else. She could continue to fight against him...or, she could accept her circumstances and work within them.

If she wanted to eventually get out of here, perhaps the best route was to befriend Jax. To earn his trust in the hope that, one day, her word would be enough for him.

Though she was sore from head to toe, Macy stood up and

went to work. She laid new grass and driftwood on the ashes of her last fire and covered it with the empty crate. After refilling the metal bucket with water from the pool, she hauled it back to the shelter and set it atop the container.

It wasn't until she dropped the lobsters into the bucket that she realized she had no way to start the fire. Jax hadn't allowed her to touch the gun.

She settled down under her shelter to wait. Soon, her eyelids grew heavy, and she gave in to sleep.

A splash startled her awake. She sat up, heart thumping. It felt like she'd only closed her eyes for a moment, but the cave was dim, with no direct sunlight coming through the opening.

Macy searched the water. "Jax?"

Movement caught her attention; Jax emerged from the shadows and swam toward the island.

Relief spread through her, paired with something more. She was wary, yes — what would he say, after what she'd called him? — but it didn't explain the warmth spreading through her belly.

He'd come back.

He stopped at the edge of the island, eyes fixed on hers. They stared at one another in silence.

"Macy, I—"

"I'm sorry," she blurted; she needed to get the words out, needed him to know. "I didn't mean it. I don't think you're a monster. I should never have said that."

Jax closed his mouth, brow furrowed. He searched her face. "You said it because of the way I've acted toward you. I am sorry for the way I've treated you, Macy. For taking away your choice."

His guilt was plain on his features. He had as little choice in the matter as she did. What would his people do if they knew he had her? That he'd revealed himself, revealed his existence, to a human? They clearly considered humans a threat, and there was something he'd said before he left...

"I know. I understand." She folded her hands in her lap and dropped her gaze to them. "What did you mean, before, about kraken being as humans made you?"

"You truly do not know?"

"Know what, Jax?"

"Kraken were created by humans, long ago."

"What? I don't…" She shook her head. "You can't mean…*made* you, right?"

"That is exactly what I mean," he replied, gaze unwavering. "Humans used their technology to make kraken, in the ancient times."

"But…there are no reports, no stories, nothing!"

"There are, in our home. The ghosts speak of it, and the Computer. We were created by humans to do work they could not."

Macy's mind raced, but she could barely comprehend what he'd told her. If it was true, it explained how his people existed, despite the pre-colonization scans of Halora — public record to this day — indicating the planet was devoid of sapient life. But why was there *nothing* in The Watch about them?

Why was there no record of wherever it was the kraken lived?

"How? How were you made?" she asked.

"I do not understand the words the ghosts use when they speak of such things."

Macy stood and approached Jax. She knelt on the edge of the island, just in front of him, and held out her hand.

He looked at it and raised a questioning gaze to her. Hesitantly, he took her hand, but she turned her palm to press flat against his, lining up their splayed fingers. His hand was larger, but — apart from the webbing between his fingers and his sharp claws — was just like hers.

She studied his face next. There was so much *human* in him. Did he realize it? Could it really be a coincidence? She brushed her fingers along the ridge of his brow and trailed them down the side of his face.

His nostrils flared, and his shoulders rose with a deep inhalation. Slowly, he lifted his free hand and touched his fingertips to her cheek, running them downward to trace the line of her jaw. Her skin tingled in the wake of his touch, and heat rippled through her, pooling in her belly. She locked eyes with him.

"Your skin has changed again." His voice was rougher, huskier, seeming to rumble into her through the points of contact between them.

Her heart fluttered, and she felt a sudden *need* for more. Instead, she pulled back, breaking away from him. Nervously, she tucked her hair behind her ear and stood.

Jax caught her calf before she could retreat. Her breath hitched; his touch burned sweetly.

"What are these marks, Macy?"

"What marks?" She angled her leg to see. He didn't remove his hand, maintaining that light, fiery contact.

Her leg was a patchwork of scrapes and bruises from the top of her foot to her knee, undoubtedly the result of slamming into the cliffside during her failed climb. She lifted the hem of her dress, revealing more bruises on her thigh. Based on the way her side felt, she was sure there was bruising there, too. It was minor compared to what she might've suffered.

He leaned forward, and his eyes trailed fire over her skin. It was ridiculous; there was nothing sexual about it, and she didn't understand why she was reacting in that fashion.

"They are wounds, aren't they?" he asked.

"Yeah. They're bruises. You don't...bruise?"

"Are they...tender? When pressure is placed on them?"

"Yes, and they change color as they heal."

"I think we bruise, too," he said. "Skin in such spots will not change color properly for a day or so, and touching them causes minor pain."

He slid his hand down the back of her leg, following the curve of her calf and cupping her heel before allowing her to lower her foot. Their eyes were locked the whole time; Macy's heart beat rapidly, her breasts ached, and her sex clenched.

What is happening to me?

Macy stepped away. She felt detached from her own body, no longer in control of it. Camrin's touch had never elicited such responses.

"Would you start the fire, please?"

Jax was silent for a few seconds, brow creased — he was studying her again, searching her. She moved back as he pulled himself onto the island. Water sluiced down his skin. She watched the play of powerful muscles beneath his flesh, and the heat at her core was, for an instant, hotter than any flame.

He twisted, and a splotch of color caught her eye — the gun was strapped to the upper part of one of his tentacles with a piece of rope. He untied it and took the weapon in hand. Grasping it by the barrel, he met Macy's gaze, and held the gun to her, grip-first.

Macy frowned. "I…don't understand."

"This is the power setting," he said, pointing to a knob on the side. "And here, behind the trigger, is the on and off button." He extended his arm fully. "This…is my trust. Do you understand now?"

"Even after what I did? Tricking you so I could escape?"

"I would have done the same if our places were reversed. I do not want you to be my prisoner."

Her chest tightened, but it wasn't from pain or sadness; it was elation. She smiled and took the gun.

"Thank you. I…" Her smile faded, and she bit her bottom lip.

"What is wrong, Macy?"

She walked to her shelter, running the words through her

mind as she crouched to light the fire. She felt Jax's eyes on her; he was awaiting an answer. Lowering herself to the ground, she placed the gun aside, took a deep breath, and looked at him.

"I thought about what you said."

"About which thing I said?" He moved closer, but only a little.

"About letting my family — my people — believe I'm dead."

"I pushed too far. I didn't mean to upset you."

She folded her hands in her lap, running her thumb along the tops of her knuckles. "I understand why you can't let me go back, that there's more than just me and you, and…and even though it feels selfish and wrong to want them to believe I'm *gone*, I do think it's…it's for the best."

Macy shifted her gaze to the fire. "I don't want to be your prisoner, and I don't want to be caged here."

"I…don't understand. You think it best for them to believe you are gone, but you do not want to stay here?" He shook his head. "I cannot take you back."

"I'm not asking you to."

"What are you asking, then?"

"I want to see things. Want to explore the world. I don't want to be confined by The Watch, or this place, or anywhere again." She met his eyes. "You're Jax the Wanderer, right? And you said I'm…that I'm *yours*. So. Take me with you, out there. Not back home, but beyond. Then…then I'll be yours, and stay with you willingly."

JAX STARED into Macy's eyes. Though her voice was filled with conflicting emotions, her gaze was steady, unwavering, devoid of hesitance. If only his thoughts were as steady as her eyes.

The weight of her words was immense; did she understand what they meant to him? Could she possibly mean them in the way he wanted her to?

It was a Choosing. Despite their conflicts, despite their differences, Macy had looked upon him and decided to give herself to him. Decided she'd be *his*. That was far more powerful than the claim he'd laid upon her.

His pounding hearts pumped searing blood through his veins. He wanted Macy more than he'd wanted anything. Their slightest contact was a thrill to him; he ached with longing, itched for another touch. Her reactions displayed equal intensity, but each time, she'd pulled herself away.

Offering herself was only one part of it. Did she want Jax in return?

He crossed the island and sank down before her. She didn't flinch when he slid a tentacle over her lap and wrapped it around one of her wrists, didn't pull away as he raised her arm and pressed his palm to hers.

Her warm, smooth skin sent a delightful pulse through him, and her scent suffused his suction cups. All the while, she held eye contact with him.

"This is what you want?" he asked. "Truly?"

"Yes. I want to feed myself, to take what *I* want for once."

A hundred warnings flitted through his mind. The dangers of the sea were too great; she belonged with her people; their attraction was unnatural. All true, to some extent, but he rejected them. He'd given her little choice, but the choice was still hers to make.

"And if I said I would take you back to your home? Back to your old life?"

Her brows fell, and she looked away. "Then I would go home...and part of me would regret it for the rest of my life. I love my friends and family, and I should go and let them know I'm alive, should take that pain away from them. I know I'll have shelter, food, and security there. But...I wouldn't be happy."

The raw honesty of her answer struck Jax hard. He bent his fingers, pressing their pads to the tops of hers.

"You think you will find happiness with me?"

Macy brushed her thumb along his webbing. "I do."

He had never cared much for the company of other kraken, apart from Arkon, and he'd never known one who shared his desire to journey to unfamiliar places. Solitude had suited Jax well. It wasn't until Macy that he realized his own loneliness. What would it be like to have her with him as he pushed the boundaries of the known world? What would it be like to have her share in the wonder and the thrill?

He dropped his gaze to watch her thumb move. The gentleness of her touch was pleasurable against the sensitive skin, but it reminded him of something more pressing.

"I cannot stray far from the sea, Macy."

"I know, and I'm okay with that."

"If you want to explore with me, it will have to be in the water." He shifted his fingers, sliding them between hers. She had no webbing to help her swim, no siphons or gills, and being wet made her cold.

"I-I know that, too."

"You said I saved your life when your boat overturned. Was it the water that nearly killed you?"

Macy attempted to withdraw her hand, but he held it.

"The ocean is unforgiving, Macy."

"I know." She looked away from and laughed, humorlessly; she was crying again. "I know that more than some."

"And I need to know that you will be able to handle yourself in the water. I need to know why you fear it."

"I...I need to get the bucket off the fire."

Jax pressed his lips together, siphons flaring, and released his hold on her wrist. He watched as she wrapped cloth around her hands, lifted the bucket of bubbling water off the crate, and set it down nearby. Though it had been removed from the heat, steam continued to billow from within.

She picked up a tool from inside her shelter — a long metal

handle with a shell-shaped piece on the end she'd called a *spoon* — and used it to fish out the hard-shells and deposit them on a scrap of cloth spread on the ground. Their shells had changed to bright red. Did *everything* change so drastically when it was cooked?

She turned toward him, hesitated, and retook her place beside him. She sat in silence, looking everywhere but at him.

"Macy. We cannot avoid speaking of this."

"I'm not…not trying to avoid it. It's just…" She inhaled shakily, and when she finally met his eyes, hers were leaking again.

He raised his hand and brushed the water from her cheeks before settling his palm over her knee. "Tell me."

"I've never cried this much," she laughed, offering him a sad smile, gone as quickly as it had come. "Probably hard to believe. I've been crying since you brought me here, it feels like."

"It is okay, Macy. Tell me."

"My father is a fisherman, just like his father, and his grandfather…so he started teaching us almost before we could walk. As far back as I can remember, I *loved* the sea. They couldn't keep me away from it. I sailed with him, helping out as much as I could, and we were both happy. His pride in me felt good, but that wasn't what called me back. It was the water.

"Standing on the shore, or in his boat, the sea went on forever. There was no end to it. And swimming was like… flying. It was so freeing. *Nobody* knew what was out there…it could've been *anything*."

Jax wasn't sure what flying was, but he understood the sense of freedom, of possibility. The call of the unknown. He'd chased it for most of his life.

"What changed, Macy?"

"Something happened when I was nine." She dropped her gaze. "It was during the wet season. The water is always treacherous that time of year. My dad used to say it'd turn on you just to see you flounder. He and my mother told me to stay away from the shore, but…I couldn't. I wanted to swim. *Needed* to, I guess. So, I snuck out when they weren't paying attention."

"I understand. When I was a youngling, I yearned to wander and explore, and I was scolded by the adults for it." Jax gave her leg a gentle squeeze. "That did not stop me from going."

Macy stared at his hand; he was about to remove it when she placed her own atop it. "You wouldn't be The Wanderer if you had listened."

"Yes. And I could no more deny who I was than you could deny who you were."

"Who I was nearly destroyed my family." Her tongue slipped out to wet her lips, and she squeezed his hand. "My sister, Sarina, was three years older than me. She saw me sneak out and followed me. For a while, she tried to convince me to go back, but, in the end, she relented. Sarina loved the sea as much as I did. If I promised to stay close, she'd go with me and wouldn't tell our parents.

"We had so much fun. The sun was hitting the water just right, and it *glowed*. It was so beautiful. We kept cupping it in our hands, pretending we were holding liquid gold. But we didn't realize how late it was getting, or how far out we'd gone. The tide was rising. That…that's when a huge wave hit us. I went under and got turned upside-down, and then I was being pulled away from shore."

Though he didn't often venture near the coast, Jax was familiar with the powerful, ever-shifting currents that pervaded those shallow waters. They were difficult even for kraken to travel, at times.

"I screamed for Sarina when I resurfaced. I remember the fear, the panic… I heard her calling for me, and saw her fighting to keep her head above the water, but no matter how hard we swam, the current pulled us farther and farther apart. More waves hit me and sent me under. I struggled back up every time, gasping for air, growing weaker and weaker.

"I kept calling her name, watching her get farther from me... And, when another wave pushed me under, I must've been turned around, because I lost her. I couldn't hear her anymore, and I spun in circles looking, but I couldn't see her. My nose, chest, and throat were burning, and I was so scared. I couldn't *breathe*. Couldn't keep myself above the surface for much longer."

Jax watched the subtle but unmistakable play of emotions over her features — flashes of fear, panic, desperation, guilt, and sorrow — and frowned. This confirmed the old stories. Humans *couldn't* breathe underwater. The thought of her struggles tore at his insides, and the pain was given claws by her expression.

She wiped tears from her face with the back of her hand. "My dad found me. After they'd realized we were gone, he and some of our neighbors came looking for us. He guessed where we snuck off to, and was sailing his boat along the beach. He found me...but he didn't find her. He never...never found Sarina. And it was all *my* fault.

"I never went back to the water until..."

"Until the day I found you?"

Macy nodded and offer a strained smile. "The sea seems to have it out for me."

Jax's chest ached; sorrow flowed from her every word and permeated her expression. She had cared for Sarina deeply — and still did. He could never truly know the suffering Macy had endured, but he understood the depth of her feelings. Understood the bond. Though his people didn't treat family the same as hers, he had a brother, of sorts, in Arkon. And the mere thought of losing Arkon so suddenly was devastating.

This was an old pain Macy carried, but it was no less intense for its age. If anything, it had been strengthened by the passage of time, had become a wound that never healed.

"You cannot blame yourself for the..." He paused, searching his memory for one of Arkon's words. "...*fickleness* of the sea. It takes what it desires, and we can do little to stop it. And you were a youngling. When we are young, we know fear, and we know danger, but we do not *understand* them for what they are."

"It could have been prevented," she said, glancing up at him. "My parents told me to stay away. They knew how dangerous the tides were that time of year, and I didn't listen."

"As I said, Macy, you were too young to *understand* the danger. Your sister was, too. You learned a harsh lesson that day — harsher than anyone should endure at that age — but her death was an accident."

Her eyes — glistening and bright — searched his. Suddenly, she threw herself upon him, wrapping her arms around his neck. Her weight was solid, but slight. Her body shook with her cries.

Jax held her, brushing his claws lightly through her hair. Macy had cried often in the short while he'd known her, and it had affected him deeply each time. But the sounds she made now were agonizing. Raw emotion poured out of her and flowed directly into Jax, demanding he acknowledge it, that he feel it himself.

He was helpless but to hold her.

Slipping two tentacles around Macy, he drew her closer, welcomed her heat, her pain, her vulnerability. If he knew how, he would have taken her suffering away. Would have welcomed it into himself to spare her.

Her cries gradually quieted, leaving only occasional, shuddering intakes of breath. Jax waited for her to pull away once she realized they were holding each other.

She brushed her palm over the back of his head and down his neck before moving it back up again. It was a soothing, intimate caress, and despite the circumstances, it heated his blood. He tightened his embrace.

"Thank you," she whispered, her breath warm on his skin.

"For what?" He lightly ran the tip of a tentacle over her back.

She buried her face against his neck. "After Sarina's death, no one wanted to talk about it — about *her*. It hurt too much for everyone. Whenever I was in town, I felt everyone's pitying stares on me...even my dad looked at me that way. My mother was the only one to voice it, though. She blamed me. I know...I know she didn't mean to, but it was there, even as years passed. She never forgave me." Her hand cupped the back of his head. "I think I just really needed to hear what you said."

"Perhaps it is with humans as it is with kraken — we cannot control how others think or feel. All that matters, Macy, is that you forgive yourself."

"I know." Macy inhaled deeply and sighed, lifting her head to look up at him. Her eyes were red, the flesh around them irritated and puffy, and her cheeks were pink. But she smiled.

She was beautiful.

Macy leaned forward and pressed her lips to Jax's cheek. Their lingering touch sent jolts of pleasure across his face, running just below the surface of his skin.

When she finally pulled away, he raised a hand and pressed his fingertips to the spot she'd touched with her lips. The slowly fading sensation pulsed outward.

"What was that?" he asked.

"What I just did?"

Jax nodded.

She smiled, and this time, it lit up her eyes. "You've never been kissed?"

"*Kissed*. I have known nothing like it."

"The kraken don't kiss?"

"We do not. Do your people do it often?"

Her skin brightened, and she averted her gaze. "Yes. There are...many ways to kiss. It's a way to show affection."

Possibilities raced through Jax's mind, but he couldn't make sense of his thoughts. The feel of it had been so overwhelming, so *amazing*, despite its simplicity, that he couldn't imagine why humans would spend their time doing anything else.

He wanted to experience it again and again.

Allowing himself no hesitation, he leaned down and pressed his lips to her cheek. Her scent enveloped him, and he tasted a hint of her sweetness.

Macy laughed, leaned back in his arms, and rested her hands on his shoulders. Their gazes met, and he saw his desires reflected in her eyes.

"We should eat," she said, glancing at the hard-shells. "I never said thank you for getting those."

As quickly as it had come, the moment ended. It was for the best; who was to say their bodies were even compatible?

But it would be pleasurable to determine if they are, regardless.

He released her reluctantly and followed her to the waiting food. "You've already spoiled the meat."

"You say that about everything I cook, but you enjoy it anyway." She smirked, retrieved her knife, and folded her legs beneath her. Taking a hard-shell into her lap, she wedged the tip of her blade between the shell sections on its underside and pried it open. The meat inside was white and puffy.

Jax picked up one of the remaining hard-shells and took it apart, using his claws the same way she used her knife. As they were, humans seemed ill-equipped for survival, but their capabilities were immensely enhanced by even the simplest tools.

He hesitated before taking his first bite; the meat was softer and more flavorful than he was used to, though it felt strange on his tongue.

"I told you." Grinning, she slipped a piece of meat between her lips.

His eyes dipped to her mouth; she'd said there were many ways to kiss. How would her lips feel on different parts of his body? How would her skin taste on her neck, her shoulder, her thighs?

"You did." He lifted one of the jointed legs and sucked the meat from within. Allowing himself to think of her lips, her warmth, or the softness of her touch would only cause him discomfort. "We need to speak of your...proposal, Macy."

It hurt to watch her smile fade.

She lowered her gaze, picking at her food nervously. "What about it?"

"As much as I want to take you out there—"

"I can't stay here, Jax!"

"And we can find some solution to that. But your story... humans cannot breathe in the water. How long can you hold your breath? I might have nearly killed you merely by bringing you here, Macy."

She frowned, her eyes roaming over everything around her — the hard-shells, the fire, the knife — settling, finally, on the heat gun. Her brow creased.

"The place you found the gun...are there more things there? If...if people once lived down there, they must've had *something*."

There were more *things* than he could count in the Facility, and the kraken knew little about most of them. "What sort of device could help with this?"

"There's a suit in the little museum back in The Watch. It covers the entire body, and there's a mask that goes with it. The first colonists used those suits for deep sea diving. I've only ever seen the one, but... Is there anything like that down there?"

He'd explored every accessible part of the Facility as a youngling, had searched through all the containers and storage areas and examined objects he would never have a name for. That had been so long ago...the weapons were important to keep track of, as they could be used for hunting and protection, but so much else was beyond his people's understanding.

"I do not know, Macy. There may be, but I will have to go and search."

She raised her head and looked at him with wide eyes. "You will?"

He nodded. Yesterday, he would've called himself mad to even consider equipping her with a potential way to escape. Now he was excited over the prospect. Excited at the thought of having someone to share in the wonderment of exploration.

Someone to chase away his loneliness.

"Thank you, Jax!"

It was difficult not to smile at her gratefulness and enthusiasm; he didn't fight the urge. He settled the end of a tentacle on her leg. Keeping it still afterward was even more difficult. "It may be well into the night before I return. Do you require anything before I leave?"

Macy looked down and set her hand over his tentacle. She curled her fingers around it lightly, brushing them over his suction cups. A thrill coursed through him.

"No. As much as I'll hate being alone, I'll be fine."

He hoped she was being truthful. He slid his tentacle off her slowly, turned, and moved to the water. "Eat the rest. So it is not wasted."

Macy chuckled. "I'll leave the heads for you to pick at later."

Jax smiled and dove into the pool.

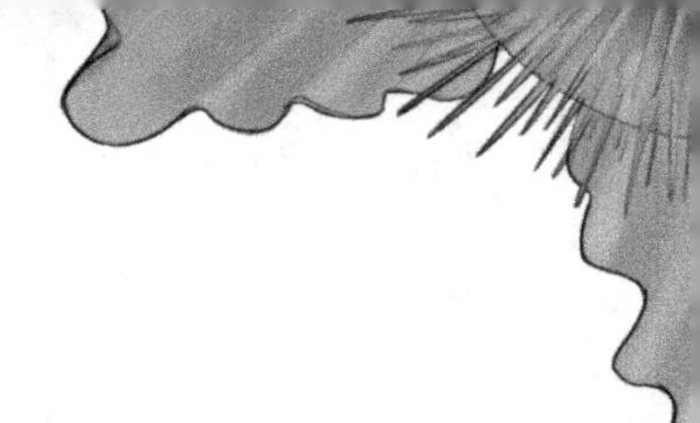

CHAPTER NINE

JAX'S RETURN TRIP TO THE FACILITY WAS THE FASTEST HE'D EVER made. He was sped on by the image of Macy, skin aglow in the soft orange firelight as the cave darkened. Sped on by the memory of their kisses.

He couldn't understand how such a simple form of contact had left such a strong impression upon him. Another mystery to consider; another aspect of his inexplicable, undeniable attraction to Macy. She should have appeared alien to him. Should have, at best, left him feeling indifferent. Instead, she called to him with an exotic allure stronger than anything he'd experienced with his own kind.

How did humans mate? If kissing was any indication, their ways were stranger than he could imagine.

As he neared the Facility, he slowed and dropped to the seafloor. This was his second return in only three days. By this point, the others wouldn't be overly suspicious to see him back, but they might question his activities if he gathered some old human items and left again immediately. Ultimately, they wouldn't do anything unless he put their home in danger, but he had no desire to endure the tedious interactions that would arise from the curiosity of the other kraken.

He paused amidst a cluster of rocks overlooking the Facility's main entrance, counting his heartbeats as he watched for movement.

Nothing stirred outside; the floor illuminated by the structure's lights was undisturbed, but a net hung, swaying in the current, from one of the detached light posts. Not a hunt, but a sign that someone — most likely Dracchus — meant to gather a party and set out soon.

Jax gritted his teeth. The hunters usually met in the Mess, a large chamber in the main building that must've served as a gathering place for the humans of old. It was mostly cleared of debris and furniture, so he'd always assumed it had received its name because of its state immediately after the Uprising.

He wasted no time reviewing his options; the main building was the best preserved, containing the largest amount of functioning human items. If any of the suits existed, they'd be there. He would simply have to move quietly and avoid the hallways around the Mess.

Keeping out of the light as best he could, Jax swam to the main door, entered the sequence, and slipped inside. The Computer welcomed him after the water drained from the entry chamber.

There were so many rooms; where best to start?

Jax entered the first hallway cautiously. The overhead lights flickered in places, casting strange shadows on the walkway and walls, and the metal beneath his tentacles thrummed faintly. One of the hunters who'd raised Jax once told him it was the Facility's heartbeat.

As he advanced along the corridor, he slipped into the likeliest chambers. Many of them had been left in disarray after the Uprising, and years of disuse hadn't been kind in the wake of such chaos. Some of the rooms held decrepit furniture — tables of varying heights and dimensions, many built directly into the walls; broken structures called chairs; containers of more shapes and sizes than Jax could count. All designed for human bodies.

Other rooms harbored ancient machinery, humming and clanking in banged-up shells. He couldn't guess the purpose of any of it, but if he opened the casings and examined the insides, he could describe them to Macy. Perhaps she would know…

There was no time for such worries; the task at hand was already likely to keep him here far longer than he wished. He didn't want to prolong his time away from Macy by chasing the whims of his curiosity.

He pushed onward, rummaging through the containers he could open, delving as deep into his memory as he could for anything that might direct him to what he sought. He recognized some of the unknown objects as tools, but couldn't imagine what they were meant for.

The cruel humor of the situation became clear to Jax as he moved into the next hallway and began through a new set of rooms. Macy knew exactly what he was looking for, and likely bore insight into how the old humans might have stored such items. The most efficient way to locate the device would be to have Macy here to help in the search.

But Jax couldn't bring Macy to the Facility. The potential hostility with which the other kraken might greet her was unimportant beside the true issue; she wouldn't survive the journey. He needed her here to locate the suit and mask, but he needed the suit and mask to bring her here.

It was a strange path of thought for him; another new experience opened by Macy. Was his time with her changing him, or simply awakening things that had always been inside?

The sound of a door closing deeper in the building echoed

through the corridor. Jax darted into a side-chamber and pressed himself against the wall, hearts pounding.

Voices drifted to him, too distorted by distance and reverberation for him to identify either the words or their speakers.

He was skulking through the halls of his home like a tiny, helpless creature in a den of predators. He'd lived most of his life without allowing fear to control him. Why was he succumbing now? Why was he afraid?

Because if the others learn about Macy, they may seek her out...but she is mine, *and mine alone.*

It was for her protection; the others would not necessarily be persuaded toward mercy by their curiosity as he had been. Humans were the first and oldest enemies of the kraken. Without weapons, Macy was helpless — even the heat gun would be a poor defense if she were set upon by multiple foes.

After a hurried search of the room, he forced himself back into the hall. He was driven to protect her, yes, but he knew his motivation was drawn as much from possessiveness. Jax had no desire to share her. Macy had given herself to him; the others had no right to so much as look upon her.

After searching a third hallway and discovering nothing of use, he stopped. He hadn't expected a quick, easy search, but this was taking too long. The fluttering in his gut urged him to return to Macy.

How could he return without anything to show for the time away? Seeing disappointment on her face would crush him.

But he'd have to shift his search to the other side of the building, soon, which would put him close to the Mess. Close to the other kraken.

He closed his eyes and tore through his memory. What had he seen here over the years, and where? The suit and mask were meant to help humans survive underwater; if Jax were human, where would he keep such devices?

Near the exits.

Logical, yes, but he'd found nothing in the chambers nearest the main door save empty containers. If such equipment had once been stored there, it was moved or destroyed in the time since. There were two other such doors, but he would have to pass the Mess to reach either.

Where else? He ran through the rooms in his mind, sorting them as best he could; there was a room for storing nothing but weaponry, many rooms meant as dwellings, rooms housing nothing but machinery…everything had a place, a purpose, even if he was unable to determine what that purpose was.

There were a few rooms that contained only ghosts, and, in a couple of them, more chairs. One chamber held nothing but screens, displaying strange symbols none of the kraken understood.

The Pool Room.

He hurried through the halls toward the Pool Room; no one had ever agreed on why the humans had built it, but Jax knew now that humans could not survive underwater without the aid of special equipment. The ghosts often spoke of testing. Testing on kraken, testing on the glowing rocks…and testing on things with names that held no meaning to the kraken.

Would they have tested their diving equipment, too? If the environment outside the Facility was too extreme for humans, wouldn't it make sense for them to have a place where they could conduct their tests free of danger?

It was a wild hunch, a stretch, but he had little else to act upon.

Jax closed the door quietly behind him and crept to the edge of the pool. Arkon was nowhere in sight; Jax's relief was followed by a pang of guilt. He couldn't keep Macy secret forever, but he wasn't ready to tell his friend, yet. Best to avoid the conversation for now.

The overall pattern Arkon had created on the floor of the pool was little changed, but the refinements were clear — the earlier symmetry of the design was slightly off now, but it only added to the sense of movement created by the entire thing. Jax was even more impressed than he'd been initially.

Another wave of guilt flowed through him when he realized he'd forgotten about the glowing centerpiece he'd promised.

He crossed to the lockers on the far wall, and his heartbeats quickened; he'd seen the objects inside of them before and should have thought of them immediately when Macy described what she needed.

Reaching into a locker, he removed the item hanging within. It was a black suit, like the other human clothing he'd found only in that it was clearly meant to cover a human body. A *small* human body…

Raising the suit, he studied it. Macy wasn't large — Camrin was easily the bigger of the two — but this suit appeared to be designed for someone half her size. The black material had a strange texture to it, and a faint hexagonal pattern over its entirety. Jax pinched it between his finger and thumb. It was oddly resistant despite its thinness.

When he took it in both hands and pulled, the fabric stretched easily. It maintained its large size for a few heartbeats before reverting to its original shape. A sleek, white piece was attached at the wrist, and another on the chest. Jax wasn't sure if they were metal or plastic, but neither came off when he tugged on them.

He set the suit aside and resumed his search. Four lockers later, he found the other piece she'd mentioned. It was a thin, curved piece of glass with a metal frame. At the bottom corners were two attachments that reminded him of gills. The mask had no straps or fasteners of any kind; he didn't know how she was meant to put the thing on, but this had to be it.

The remaining lockers each held one of the suits, and he found six more masks. He moved back to consider them. There was no guarantee they'd all function properly; he'd be best served by taking them all. The devices were wasted hanging here, forgotten, especially when someone had use for them.

Besides, Macy would never enter the Facility. No human would.

Jax frowned.

It didn't feel right, taking all of them. Perhaps they'd never see use, like most items in the Facility, but this was where they belonged. They were as much ghosts as the holograms.

He laid one of the suits on the floor, placed a second suit and two masks atop it, and tied it into a bundle around one of his tentacles to ensure it would be close during his journey to the cave. As he turned to leave, the door opened.

There was nowhere — and no time — to hide; he was exposed. Straining for a natural way to begin a conversation with Arkon, he swung his attention to the doorway.

Jax clenched his jaw. Arkon had not come.

Dracchus halted just inside the room. His eyes met Jax's, and he pushed up with his tentacles, raising himself high. He was slightly longer and broader than Jax, and heavily muscled; that struck fear into some of the others. Dracchus wasn't hesitant to make use of his size and strength.

They stared at one another, locked in a silent struggle for which Jax had no patience. Dracchus's normally black skin had a crimson undertone.

"You saw the signal outside." Dracchus's jaw muscles bulged as he rolled his shoulders. He looked over the room before settling his gaze back on Jax. "Where is your friend?"

"Somewhere else, Dracchus. His den may be a good place to begin the search."

Brighter red seeped into Dracchus's skin. "There is no time for these games, Wanderer. We mean to depart soon."

"Do not allow me to delay you." Jax lifted his hand, palm up, and gestured to the door.

Dracchus advanced. Jax rose up to meet him, holding his position.

The challenge was clear in Dracchus's posture, coloring, and expression; his directness had always been admirable. There were no secrets with him, no attempts at subtlety. He always made his feelings clear — as often through actions as through words.

"We need our best out there, Wanderer. I will not deny you and Arkon your due as hunters."

"I've other matters to attend." Jax's hearts thumped rapidly, and heat rippled through his limbs; his body was preparing for a battle, and he didn't resist.

Eyes flaring, Dracchus moved closer, stopping just in front of Jax. "Do you mean to abandon our people entirely, now?"

"I have not abandoned our people. But I will not swim with you on this hunt."

"Because you do not trust my judgment. Would you prefer to lead this hunt?"

"You are hunt leader, Dracchus, and I will not challenge you for it. I have other concerns to occupy my time." Jax's muscles felt like coiled springs, near trembling with the need to expend the stored energy.

Macy is likely asleep, by now. If I must take the time to remove Dracchus from my path, so be it...

"You have a duty to the kraken, Wanderer. We hunt together, we thrive together, as it has always been."

"I ask for no share in your bounty. I will sustain myself during my absence."

But, if the suits worked, and Macy could travel safely underwater, what reason would Jax have to return — apart from Arkon?

Dracchus narrowed his eyes and swept his gaze over the room again. "If Arkon is not here, why are you in this chamber?"

"For the same reason you've come."

"Did you not say his den would be the best place to search?"

"Now that I know he is not here."

The air between them buzzed with tension; Dracchus was just as on-edge as Jax, just as ready to act. This rivalry between them had started many years ago. Jax had been tired of it since the beginning.

Dracchus leaned close, nostrils flaring. Confusion skittered across his features. "There is an odd scent on you, Wanderer."

Macy. Jax's skin tingled with the remembrance of their contact.

"There are many scents in the ocean unfamiliar to you, Dracchus, because you do not venture beyond the hunting grounds."

"You owe this duty to your people, Wanderer. We all do. Gather with the others in the Mess."

Jax leaned in and locked his gaze with Dracchus's. It would be simple to initiate a brawl. Despite both kraken anticipating it, Jax was just a little faster, and the first strike could be the one to turn the tide in his favor. "No."

The cords on Dracchus's neck stood out. "You betray us. Face my challenge, Wanderer, before our people. It is time you were made to answer to your selfishness."

A formal challenge; it meant witnesses, a gathering outside, and the intricate, delicate motions of the dance. And it would end in physical combat because neither would back down. Dracchus wanted to best Jax before a crowd because no one would quite take his word if he claimed to have defeated Jax without anyone to support his claim.

"I refuse your challenge, Dracchus. Our people need food more than they need entertainment." Jax moved around Dracchus and toward the door. "You need your strength for the hunt."

Dracchus remained in place, shoulders rising and falling

with his deep breaths, bristling with anger. "The things you could accomplish, Wanderer, if you cared…"

Jax pushed through the door, dropping a hand to ensure the bundle was still secure. He cared deeply about the kraken, despite the way they'd treated him and Arkon over the years, but they would survive, whether he helped or not, just as they always had.

Macy *needed* his aid, and he was beginning to suspect he needed her just as much.

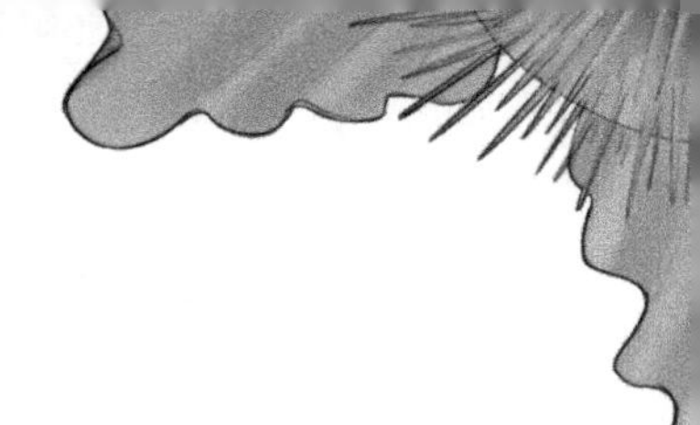

CHAPTER TEN

It was still mostly dark when Macy opened her eyes. She wasn't sure what had woken her — a noise, perhaps, or a dream already faded from memory — but she knew instinctively that she wasn't alone. She turned her head to see Jax nearby.

He lay on his stomach, arms folded under his cheek, breath slow and deep in his slumber. One tentacle was stretched toward her, its tip only centimeters away.

Macy rolled onto her side and cradled her head in the crook of her arm. This was the first time she'd seen him sleep. He always seemed to be awake and doing something, so she hadn't been sure if kraken slept or not. It reminded her of an old conversation with her father.

They'd been out on the water, riding the waves in his boat, when Breckett had insisted to seven-year-old Macy that fish slept. She hadn't been able to hide her skepticism — how could anything sleep, with water in its eyes? — and demanded to know how he was so sure. Even at that age, she knew his response — *because I just know* — was grown-up talk that really meant *I don't know, but I'm right so be quiet.*

Macy smiled sadly. She missed those days. Missed her family

and friends, but this was for the best — for both Macy and the kraken.

With his face relaxed in sleep, Jax appeared more human; it was likely because his unusual pupils were concealed.

Her gaze settled on his lips. She touched her fingers to her own, and — not for the first time — wondered what kissing him would feel like. Not a peck on the cheek, but a *kiss*, like Camrin had given her on the dock. She'd longed for Camrin's kiss to end; from Jax, she yearned for *more*.

Macy's eyes continued their slow trek over his body; first over the well-defined muscles of his shoulders, back, and arms, and then down to his inhuman lower half. His skin darkened below his waist, but the stripes that ran along his tentacles — the same pattern from his head and shoulders — were clear in the gloom.

Though it was difficult to distinguish one tentacle from the next in the dim light, she knew them well from their days together. They were thick at their tops, tapering gradually to narrow tips. She followed the flow of the one he'd stretched toward her. It was twisted slightly, exposing the lighter, suction-cup-lined skin on its underside.

Had he reached out to her before or after he fell asleep?

She moved a hand toward his tentacle, stopping only to watch his face and ensure he was still asleep. Lightly, she touched her finger to the skin on his tentacle's underside, running it along the edges of his suction cups. His flesh was different there. Softer.

The tentacle twitched, its end curling.

Macy grinned. He was ticklish.

With another glance to make sure he hadn't woken, she slid her finger around the rim of a suction cup. It twitched. She released a muffled laugh.

"Macy?"

She yanked her hand back and met his gaze. Jax had lifted

his head and propped himself up on an arm, pupils large. She tried — and failed — to keep the amusement from her face.

"Good morning," she said, biting the inside of her lip to curtail her smile.

Jax furrowed his brow and twisted to look up at the opening; the sky displayed on the earliest gray of approaching dawn. When he turned back to her, the end of his tentacle flicked back and forth. "That felt strange. What were you doing?"

"I wasn't doing anything."

"I felt your touch. Tasted your skin."

"You *what?*"

"Tasted you. Or smelled…perhaps both. They are the same, in many ways."

"You can *taste* with those?" She pointed at his tentacle.

His eyes followed her gesture, and a smile — as amused as hers had been a moment before — spread across his lips. He shifted his position, torso upright but tentacles coiled beneath him. "With the cups, yes."

Macy immediately thought of their first encounter, how his tentacle had slithered up between her legs, brushing her inner thigh…

She'd been shocked, then, just as she was now, but the memory kindled something more. Fire blazed in her core. Macy pressed her knees together, suddenly aware of just how short her dress was.

Clearing her throat, Macy smiled and sat up. "Did you know they are ticklish?"

"Ticklish? What is that?"

She held out her hand. "Give me one of your tentacles."

He extended one and lowered it onto her waiting palm. It was heavier than she would've guessed. The suction cups moved against her skin, and she raised her gaze to his, arching a brow.

His smile didn't falter.

"So, that's how you're going to play." She turned his tentacle over into her other hand and curled her fingers around it firmly. Then she ran the tip of one finger along the underside in a long, light stroke.

The tentacle's muscles contracted, and it naturally recoiled from her touch. Jax flinched. His pupils narrowed as he looked at her. "That was a strange sensation. Not unpleasant, but...strong."

"Mhmm." She repeated the motion, but this time, she didn't let up, brushing her fingertip back and forth and wiggling her fingers against the sides of his suction cups.

His tentacle writhed in her grasp, and she felt a shudder ran up its length and spread through his entire body. He tugged his limb out of her hold. Macy laughed, dropping her hands.

Jax shook the end of his tentacle, as though the sensation lingered, and examined its underside. "What was that?"

"I was tickling you. You're ticklish. Haven't you been tickled before?"

"Kraken do not often come into such contact." His expression was questioning, but not suspicious. "Are humans also *ticklish?*"

"Most are." Macy frowned. She couldn't imagine a child growing up without such little tastes of affection, without experiencing something as simple as being tickled. Jax had said he was brought up by a group of males, who taught him to survive and hunt, but had he ever been held, ever been soothed?

Had he ever laughed?

She was jarred from her thoughts by Jax's sudden movement; he pulled himself forward and wrapped a tentacle around her ankle. Macy yelped as he tugged her leg straight, lifting it slightly off the ground, and leaned over it.

"Jax, what are you—"

He lifted another tentacle and lightly ran its tip along her sole.

Macy's leg jerked, and she widened her eyes.

The look of concentration on his face shifted into one of amusement.

"Jax, don't you—"

Holding her leg fast, he brushed his tentacle over her foot a little more firmly, up and down, from heel to toe. Peals of laughter escaped her. She yanked her foot, but Jax wouldn't relinquish it, wouldn't cease his relentless tickling.

"Jax! Stop!" she begged, thrashing on the ground.

He stopped abruptly, though he didn't release her leg. "Is tickling dangerous to humans?"

Strands of hair hung in Macy's face as she lay there, taking in great gulps of air. Her stomach ached from laughter. "Yes. And you just killed me."

Leaning over her, he brushed her hair back. The mirth he'd worn a moment before had been replaced by deep concern.

Macy met his gaze, trying to appear solemn, but she couldn't hold back a chuckle. "I'm fine. I just...need a moment to recover. Tickling can get to be...too much."

He frowned at her and straightened. Slowly, he ran his gaze down, over her body, settling it on her legs. Leaning back a little more, he tilted his head. His tentacle wound around her calf as it crept up her leg. A moment later, he settled a hand on her bare thigh.

Macy's breath hitched, and her heart fluttered.

His eyes met hers as he slid his palm up her leg with tantalizing slowness. His fingers kneaded her flesh "This does not tickle?"

Macy could only shake her head. All her focus was on that hand — on the warmth of his touch, the tiny pricks from his claws, and his firm, but gentle grip on her flesh. Heat pulsed in her belly and her sex clenched with need.

Jax stilled his hand when it hit the hem of her dress. His tentacle brushed her inner thigh and halted, as well. "Your scent has changed. It is...sweeter."

A different heat flooded her. Macy sat up and broke out of his grasp. Unable to meet his gaze, she scooted back, putting some distance between them, and tugged her dress down over her thighs.

How could something as innocent as tickling turn into...*this*? She'd been so mesmerized by his eyes, so enthralled by his touch, that she'd been tempted to part her thighs and allow him to explore her fully.

Was there something *wrong* with her, to have spurned Camrin's touch, but crave Jax's? Even the thought of his tentacles caressing her made her shiver — not with repulsion, but with want.

Jax didn't pursue her. He eased down, his eyes never leaving her. He clenched and relaxed his jaw several times, as though he wanted to speak and didn't know how to begin. Finally, he twisted his torso and fiddled with something behind him.

Curious, Macy lifted her head and watched.

When he turned toward her again, he held a black bundle in his hands. He took it in his tentacles and stretched them forward, placing the bundle on the ground before her.

"I think these are what you spoke of, Macy." His tentacles withdrew.

She crawled forward, sat on her heels, and peeled the wet fabric back. Once each side lay flat, Macy recognized the item — it was the same sort of suit she'd seen in the museum. A second suit was folded up inside, tucked between two masks.

Macy's excitement overcame her discomfort, and she flashed Jax a wide smile. "You found *two* sets?"

"I only *brought* two," he said, "in case one does not work."

"That's incredible!" She inspected the suits. They were in even better condition than the one from home, despite how old they had to be. "I can't imagine what else might be down there."

"I could not tell you what most of it is."

Macy looked at him. "Do the...ghosts not tell you?"

"Each of them speaks about something different, but it is always the same words," he replied. "Sometimes, the Computer will give information, but we usually do not know the right things to say to make it speak freely."

"Was there no one around, in the beginning, who knew how to speak to it?"

"The humans. Apart from them...I do not know."

Macy couldn't imagine the wealth of information hidden away down there.

Jax dipped his chin toward the suits. "Are those the right things?"

"Yes. Thank you!"

"And...you know how to make them function?"

"Not...really."

"Aren't they human technology?"

"Yes, but I didn't grow up using this stuff, either." Macy leaned forward touched the white, circular attachment on the chest of the suit. It was the size of her palm and had no visible buttons or screen. She shifted her attention to the rectangular piece on the right wrist. There were small grooves running across it lengthwise; she traced them with her fingers.

Macy and Jax both retreated as light erupted from the wrist piece. It flickered for an instant and coalesced into a glowing orb.

"There is a ghost in the suit," Jax whispered.

Macy chuckled and shook her head. "A hologram."

"Hello!" The hologram pulsed with each syllable. "I am your system assistant and monitor, Sam. How may I be of service?"

"Sam, tell me about the suit," Macy said.

"The Tureon Personal Diving System — or PDS — is the most advanced diving suit in use today, designed and manufactured by Tureon Industries, Incorporated! Through the use of innovative energy field technology, your PDS will automatically adjust to changes in pressure, temperature, and lighting in underwater environments, ensuring your safety and comfort at all times."

"It speaks like the other ghosts…using words with no meaning," Jax's pupils were narrowed in the light of the hologram.

"They have meaning, Jax. Maybe not to us, but they do."

Setting the extra equipment aside, she studied the suit spread on the ground. It was much smaller than the one on display in The Watch. This looked child-sized. "Sam, how does the PDS work?"

"The PDS uses a patented Tureon Industries field generator — the circular piece on the chest — to create a thin but powerful energy field between the wearer's skin and the inner layer of the suit. This field will automatically adjust to compensate for any pressure changes outside the suit up to depths of ten thousand meters. All force is absorbed by the field and dispersed harmlessly into the surrounding water. The dispersion can be used intuitively as a means of supplemental propulsion through the water. Temperature control will also adjust the field to keep the wearer's body temperature regulated.

"The PDS integrates fully with the included oxygenator mask. The mask filters oxygen from the surrounding water, providing the wearer with a constant stream of fresh, breathable air. The mask is also equipped with a number of popular features, including advanced sensory systems, a headlamp, and an integrated HUD including temperature and depth gauges, a rangefinder, and GPS navigation. Your PDS allows full voice-activated operation of internal systems through the mask, and will automatically interface with all other PDS systems within range for underwater communication."

Macy picked up one of the masks. It was so lightweight, looked so simple, that she couldn't imagine how it was anything more than a piece of glass. She ran her thumb along the edge and frowned. How was she even supposed to put it on, without any fasteners?

With her other hand, she unfolded the other suit. It was the same size as the first. She turned it over and searched it, but she couldn't find any buttons or seams in the fabric.

Jax moved around the hologram and positioned himself behind Macy, watching over her shoulder.

"Sam, does the PDS come in different sizes?"

"No. The PDS is designed as a one-size-fits-all device for ages six and up."

She set the mask and spare suit down and picked up the first PDS. The hologram remained in place. "Sam, can you show me how to put it on?"

"Sure!" The orb expanded and swirled, reshaping itself into a man — naked except for his underpants. His body was athletic and toned, his jaw squared, his teeth white and straight. The hologram's eyes fell on Macy as he extended his hands and a PDS suit appeared in them. "Would you like to follow along through the process, or view a demonstration?"

"Do the...holograms amongst your people respond to what you say, Macy?" Jax asked.

"Yes, why?" Macy glanced over her shoulder.

Jax was staring at the hologram with a scowl. "It seems unnatural."

"This is how technology used to be. Most of the holos in your home are probably recordings of real people."

"So, *this* was once a living human?"

"Sam? I don't know. Maybe."

Jax's frown deepened.

Sam didn't move save for the occasional blink of his eyes, suit dutifully extended before him.

"Should I put the suit on now?" Macy asked.

"If you are ready to venture out of this place."

She was more than ready to see something other than stone walls, but she was also terrified of what awaited beyond them.

Fear must've shown on her face, because Jax eased himself down to her eye level, placing a hand on her bicep.

"I will not allow anything to happen to you, Macy."

She searched his eyes — his strange, beautiful eyes — and nodded. She believed him. Trusted him.

"Sam, I would like to follow along."

"Great! Please remove all clothing before we proceed."

Jax's grip on her arm tightened.

"What?" Macy asked, eyes wide as the hologram's underpants vanished.

"Is that always…extruding like that?" Jax asked.

Macy stared at the hologram's genitals. "Um…" Her brows lowered as Jax's words registered. "Extruding?"

"Why are you staring like that, Macy?"

Her face warmed, and she quickly looked away. "I…wasn't expecting that. And if you mean, um…"

"Does it always hang out?"

Macy covered her eyes with a hand. She was supposed to be figuring out how to use the suit, not explaining human anatomy to Jax. "Yes." She removed her hand and looked at him. "Where else would it be?"

Without meaning to, she skimmed her gaze down Jax's body. Why wouldn't he be curious? Whatever his upper body looked like, his lower half was anything but human. Macy cleared her throat and stood up.

Jax's hand fell from her arm.

She clenched the suit's fabric. "Jax…could you turn around, please?"

"Why? Is there something behind us?"

Laughing, she shook her head. "No, I just need to undress."

"Why does that require me to turn around?"

"Because…because I'll be undressing."

"That means you will remove your clothing, does it not?"

"Yes." She lifted a hand, pointed her index finger down, and twirled it in a circle.

Though his expression clearly indicated his confusion, Jax turned away. She waited a moment longer — to make sure he didn't peek — before she faced the hologram and quickly removed her dress and undergarments.

She felt exposed. She'd never been naked in the open before, and with Jax immediately behind her, able to turn around at any moment...

It thrilled her.

"Sam, I am ready to proceed."

"Please hold your PDS like so—" he held his by the shoulders in front of him and moved one hand to the circle on its chest "— and move your fingers counter-clockwise around the field generator unit."

When Macy did so, a seam opened down the back of the suit, running from the lower back up to the neck, where it split the hood in half.

"Now, step into the legs and pull the PDS on. Don't worry! It will stretch to accommodate your height and body shape."

Macy slipped one foot into the legging, followed by the other, and sure enough, the fabric stretched to cover the length of her legs. She tugged it up over her hips and slipped her arms through the sleeves, spreading and flexing her fingers to get the gloves on snugly.

"Once you have it on comfortably, move your fingers clockwise around the field generator unit, like so."

Raising a hand, Macy did as it said. She felt the suit close along her back, breaking her bare skin's contact with the open air. The suit molded to her body, but she felt no discomfort; it fit perfectly.

"Now that your suit is sealed, please reach behind your head and find the hood. You'll need to have it up if you want your mask to properly seal and integrate with your PDS's internal systems. If you have long, hair, you'll want to pull it back out of the way for this part. Let me know when you are ready to proceed."

"You can turn back now, Jax," Macy said, gathering her hair.

JAX HELD his breath as he turned; it had been surprisingly difficult to keep from looking at her as she undressed. Kraken wore no clothing, and nakedness was simply a natural state. He could no more understand her aversion to it than understand his attraction to her. It shouldn't have affected him at all, but the mystery of what lay beneath her clothes had only been strengthened by the hologram — if male humans were so different from kraken, what were female humans like?

Macy was pulling her hair back. The suit — the *pee dee ess* — fit her perfectly. His blood heated at the sight; it had sculpted to her body, covering her curves with a thin layer of fabric, teasing him by barely hiding the secrets he'd yet to discover. It took no small amount of concentration to keep himself from extruding.

Holding her hair in a bundle, she took hold of the excess fabric around her neck and pulled it over her head, covering her hair and ears completely. It was as close as she'd looked to a kraken in the time he'd known her.

He didn't care for it.

Jax shifted his gaze to the hologram. It was now covered, as well, wearing a suit just like Macy's. There was a bulge in the fabric between its legs.

Macy didn't have a bulge. He'd expected, after seeing the protruding shaft of a male human, that female humans would be similar — always *out*, always *open* — but Macy's suit gave no hint of the unfurled petals of a female kraken.

"Jax?"

Jarred from his thoughts, he met her eyes. "Yes?"

Macy was silent for a moment. "Um...nothing."

She turned back to the hologram. Jax couldn't keep his gaze from dipping. The suit hugged the curves of her backside; the anatomy of her lower body was strange, but tantalizing.

"Sam, I am ready to proceed," Macy said.

"Great! It's time to get your mask on. Please place your hands on the sides of the mask and lift it toward your face. Remember, the bottom of the mask is the part with the small vents — that's how you'll receive your air! Make sure your fingers are away from the edges and move the mask into place around your face. Your PDS will do the rest!"

Macy picked up one of the masks and held it between her hands, uncertainty creeping into her expression. "Okay. Here's hoping it works…"

She lifted the mask near her face, aligned it, and pulled it close.

Jax clenched his teeth; the suit seemed to *move* — the fabric around her head shimmer, and the seam between the mask and hood vanished. Macy's face was pale, her eyes wide.

The hologram flickered and disappeared.

Muscles tense, Jax moved closer, ready to tear the mask off Macy's face, to rip the suit from her body.

"Okay," she repeated. Her voice was different, somehow. She sounded more like the ghosts.

"Are you all right?" he asked.

Macy's eyes shifted to Jax. A soft light inside the mask illuminated her face.

"I'm fine." She offered him a large smile. "Just…surprised. It's strange, but I think it'll work."

She lifted her left arm and touched the white piece on her wrist. A small hologram appeared in the air over it, filled with shapes and symbols. The symbols moved when she touched them with her fingers; after a few swipes, the mask released with a quiet hiss of air. She took it in both hands.

"Yeah, it'll work. Just wanted to make sure it came off." She brought the mask up to her face, and it resealed. Then she paused, eyes drifting upward, and nodded. "Okay, Sam. Thank you."

"What?" Jax asked.

"You can't hear him?"

"Hear who? The ghost?"

"Yes. Sam. He's talking to me in the suit." She tilted her head. "You can hear me, but not him?"

"I have not heard him since he disappeared, Macy." The ghost was speaking to her in her head? It made Jax uneasy, but if she trusted it, so would he...though he'd remain wary.

"I guess his voice doesn't project like mine does."

She walked to the edge of the island and lowered herself into the water; with the receding tide, it only reached to her middle. Her hands skimmed over the surface.

"It's so different. Like I'm not even in the water at all," she said, looking over her shoulder at Jax. "It's not even cold."

Jax moved into the water as well. Macy bent down, submerged her arms, and swung them slowly back and forth. He eased himself as deep as his shoulders and swam backward, toward the underwater tunnel.

"This way, Macy."

The water rose as she followed. She didn't stop until it reached her neck, head tilted back to keep her chin above the waterline. Her rounded eyes were locked on the dark water before her.

"Macy?"

"I'm...I'm scared."

He swam to her side and placed a hand on her arm; the suit felt different, now that she had it on, and seemed to vibrate faintly beneath his palm. "What is there to fear?"

She laughed. "*Everything*. Humans aren't meant for the sea."

"And kraken are not meant to *exist*," he replied gently, "but that hasn't stopped either of our people."

She stared at him, her gaze unwavering. "Will you...will you keep hold of me?"

"Yes." He moved to her front, facing her, and put an arm around her waist. She hugged his neck and didn't struggle when he raised two tentacles to support her legs and lift her feet off the bottom.

Slowly, Jax swam backward. Her body tensed. The suit's low thrum pulsed through him.

"I will protect you, Macy. I will keep you safe. Trust me in this."

Macy encircled his hips with her legs, holding herself that much closer, and searched his face. She nodded. "I do."

"Good." His chest swelled with pride and, something more.

Their position was very near the tangle of limbs that was two kraken mating. His shaft, still hidden, was pressed between her legs. It ached to be released.

Their relationship had changed so much in so short a time; a few days ago, she would've slapped him if he laid a finger upon her. Now, she clung to him like he was her rock during a storm. But his physical attraction to her was only a small part of his desire for Macy.

He longed for her companionship. To hear her voice, and listen to everything she had to say, to share his meals with her, to share a den with her.

Jax wanted Macy to claim him as her own.

He wanted to be the *one* she chose. The one she *joined* with.

"Are you ready?" he asked.

She inhaled deeply and slowly released the breath. "I'm ready."

Though her features were drawn, displaying her fear, her eyes remained steady.

She has the heart of a hunter.

Jax smiled and dipped underwater.

CHAPTER ELEVEN

Macy tightened her hold on Jax as they submerged. She waited for water to fill her ears, nose, and mouth, to drag her to depths that couldn't be penetrated by light, but she was met with only silence. Her lungs filled with fresh, clean air.

The light in the mask made it difficult to see through the dark water surrounding her.

"Sam, could you turn off the inside light?"

It turned off instantly.

Ice flowed through her as she was plunged into darkness. Her heart thundered, and her breath grew shallow. The ocean was terrifying enough, but the ocean in total darkness?

"Would you like the external lamp switched on, or would you prefer to activate night vision?"

A gentle glow filled her vision. It took a moment for her eyes to adjust, and another few to understand the source of the illumination — Jax. His stripes emitted soft, blue light.

"I...don't need anything right now, Sam."

She stared at Jax in wonder as they descended toward an opening on the cave wall, near the floor — a tunnel. Her hold on him strengthened while he guided them through the opening.

Keeping an arm around her, he pulled them along with his free hand and tentacles, maneuvering around the turns and avoiding jutting rocks.

Macy was glad she hadn't been brave enough to attempt this route on her own. She had no doubt she would've drowned.

Soon, she saw a light ahead; Jax's skin dimmed as they neared. They emerged from the tunnel soon after.

The ocean was as she'd never seen it before. Rays of morning sunlight streamed through the surface at harsh angles, lighting up the sea floor below — swaying seagrass, sand, and colorful bits of coral. In the shaded spots, the plants gave off their own light, all in various shades of blue. Fish and other sea creatures — some that she'd never seen before — swam alone and in schools or scuttled along the bottom.

She raised her eyes and looked straight ahead. It was so open and blue, so *beautiful*, so *terrible*, and she was an insignificant thing that could be swallowed up at any moment.

Except she had Jax. Jax, who'd sworn to keep her safe. This was *his* world, and she trusted him.

Admitting that to him — and to herself — had eased her fears. She didn't have to carry it on her own. Jax was strong, and he was here to lessen her burden, to ensure she wasn't crushed beneath it.

Macy turned her head toward him. He was watching her intently, and hadn't loosened his hold on her.

"I'm okay," she said.

He shook his head and gestured to the side of his head — where his ear hole was located.

He can't hear me.

She released her hold on his neck and placed a hand on the center of her chest. With her other hand, she pointed down.

Jax nodded and swam toward the bottom. His movement was strange, in open water; he'd fan out his tentacles and bring them all together, thrusting himself forward. Each thrust propelled them far, their speed diminishing just before he spread his tentacles again. They reached the seafloor within seconds. Various creatures scurried away, kicking up clouds of sand as they sought shelter amidst rocks, pieces of coral, and clumps of grass.

Macy grinned and lowered her legs from his hips, patting his arm. He hesitated, eyeing her skeptically, but released his hold on her.

She dropped the last bit of distance. Her feet touched the bottom lightly, and though she couldn't feel the grains of sand through the suit, it was an amazing experience.

She was *walking* on the ocean floor.

The joy she'd known as a child came roaring back. It had been so long since she felt such exhilaration, such delight, so long since she'd reveled in discovering something new.

Jax remained close as she stepped around the plant life. She bent down and brushed her fingers over a shell tucked in the seagrass. Picking it up, she raised it for inspection, releasing a yelp when at least a dozen legs sprouted from the opening. Macy dropped the shell and stumbled back.

A tentacle wrapped around her waist, halting her backward momentum. She glanced at Jax first — he wore an amused smile — and then behind her. Jagged rocks jutted from the seafloor just centimeters from her heel.

He righted her, and she patted his tentacle. When he released his hold, she turned her attention down, searching for the shelled creature. It was about a meter away, sending up puffs of sand as it dug a hole to bury itself in.

Jax caught her attention and waved for her to follow as he swam away. She felt a moment of alarm — he was her safety, her rock, and walking on solid ground wasn't nearly the same as *swimming* in open water, dealing with currents and riptides and...

He won't let anything happen to me.

Keeping her eyes on Jax, Macy kicked off the sea floor. She swam after him, and any lingering worry faded away; with the suit, she *glided* through the water and caught up with him quickly.

He increased his pace gradually, swimming just to the side and ahead of her. She pulled ahead briefly between each of his powerful thrusts — and she'd been right, it *was* like flying, now more than ever. But her attention returned to Jax over and over; he moved with undeniable strength and grace, and seeing him here — in his natural environment — was as wondrous as the ocean itself.

Jax glanced at her over his shoulder. Macy smiled, her stomach fluttering with excitement. She hadn't felt so giddy since her childhood. When he returned the smile, her excitement took a different turn; the sensation in her belly spread until she was warm all over.

"I have detected a fluctuation in your body temperature. Do you—"

"Not now, Sam," she said, blushing.

As Jax drew alongside her, he caught her hand and pulled her close. He slipped his arms around her; she wrapped her arms and legs around him without conscious thought.

Their momentum slowed, and for a moment, they seemed to drift on the current. Then they darted forward, faster than she'd thought possible. Water rushed by; Jax spun, giving Macy a dazzling show of light as the sparkling surface tumbled around her, alternately above and below, until she wasn't sure which way was up. She laughed, pressing her head to his shoulder.

His spin gradually ended, and they came to a stop. Macy pulled back to look at Jax. He grinned at her, displaying his sharp teeth, and it didn't unsettle her. There was genuine delight in his expression.

He shifted so they were both upright, and Macy withdrew her legs from his waist. His gaze flicked to something over her shoulder, and he nodded in the same direction. Macy turned her head to see what he had gestured toward.

Huge stalks of seaweed swayed in the current behind her, anchored to the seafloor by thick stems. Sunlight beamed through the large leaves, granting them delicate violet and crimson glows. The plants stretched as far as she could see, so dense in some places that they appeared impenetrable, and a variety of creatures swam in and out of the leaves.

It was an underwater forest.

"Wow." She looked back to Jax and pointed toward the seaweed.

He released her, and once there was a little space between them, he pointed at her and then down at the ground. She nodded and allowed herself to sink to the sea floor. Jax cast her a glance over his shoulder and disappeared into the seaweed forest.

Macy frowned, sweeping her gaze over the stalks for any sign of him. What was he doing?

"Jax?" she called, before remembering he couldn't hear her. She stepped closer.

The fish continued their business, and small creatures scurried along the bottom, darting from stalk to stalk. The leaves cast tinted shadows on the seafloor around Macy's feet. She raised a hand and pushed aside the seaweed to peer beyond.

Macy crossed the boundary, brushing leaves as she moved farther in. Seagrass was thick around her feet. Creatures fled at her approach, seeking shelter in the surrounding seaweed.

"Jax?"

Something grabbed her shoulder.

Macy shrieked and spun around.

It took her a moment to realize she was looking at Jax; his skin matched the seaweed — a blend of red and purple — right down to its apparent texture. He frowned, eyes narrowed.

She'd seen him change color before and assumed it had

something to do with his emotions, but she'd never seen his skin like this. If he hadn't touched her, she would never have noticed him. He was almost perfectly camouflaged.

And he didn't look happy.

He took her hand and led her deeper into the forest. The color of his skin rippled, reverting to normal. She touched his shoulder just to see if it would change again.

Jax glanced at her, brow lifted in question, but he continued forward, keeping close to the bottom.

Macy smiled and squeezed his hand. "Don't be mad at me."

He squeezed her hand back, gently, and pointed up.

She tilted her head back, and her breath hitched in her throat. Here, amidst the seaweed, the light was even more intense. The surface broke it into shafts, like the beams of sunlight that sometimes penetrated the clouds after a storm. The backlit, ever-shifting leaves reminded her of the panes of the stained-glass window back in The Watch — the one that had been put together in the lighthouse to commemorate the fallen colonists of years gone by.

The result was an array of dancing color — whites, blues, greens, reds, and purples — unlike anything she'd ever seen.

Macy lowered her gaze to watch Jax as they swam. The multicolored shadows on his skin seemed fitting; he could change into any of those colors, she was sure; perhaps even all of them at once.

They spent hours exploring the seaweed forest and the surrounding area. It wasn't until Macy felt hollow pangs of hunger that she caught Jax's attention, rubbing her stomach.

He nodded, and they swam back toward the cave.

Before they reached the underwater cliffside, he gestured to her again — just a bit more forcefully than before — and pointed at the floor. She guessed that he had meant for her to stay put the first time. She smirked and made to move forward.

He didn't gesture or point again. Instead, he *glared* at her.

Macy chuckled and moved back. "Okay, okay. I get it."

He'd left her on the edge of a shallow drop-off. She watched as he moved to the rocks and grass below. Fish darted away from him, but he didn't pay attention to any of them. He perched himself atop one of the larger rocks, and his skin changed instantly to match the stone. If she didn't know any better, she might've thought he'd vanished; he looked like part of the rock itself.

She was hungry, but her hunger didn't outweigh her curiosity as time passed. Jax had brought her a lot of food over the last few days, and she was eager to see how he hunted, eager to see him in action.

Little by little, the fish returned to the area around Jax. He remained so still that she almost doubted he was there.

A school of large, orange fish — gulpers, to the people of The Watch, because their mouths opened wider than their bodies — swam near the rock.

The sudden movement was too fast for Macy to fully register. Jax's tentacles flared out, enveloping the gulpers like a large net. In a blur of frantic motion, dozens of the fish scattered in all directions, regrouping several meters away.

Jax returned to his normal coloring. For several seconds, he was a mass of writhing tentacles. Then he swam back toward her. The three bright orange fish he'd caught, each wrapped in a tentacle, were easy to spot against his dark skin.

"That was amazing!" Macy grinned at him as he neared.

Smiling, he pointed toward the cave.

She glanced back at the tunnel and bit her lip. The thought of braving the dark, narrow passage on her own sent a chill along her spine.

One problem at a time.

The open ocean had pushed her courage far enough, for now. She turned back to Jax and extended her arms. He embraced Macy without hesitation and swam into the tunnel with her.

When Sam asked if she wanted light, she declined, preferring to bask in Jax's glow.

They exited the tunnel and broke the surface soon after.

"Sam, release the mask," she said.

"All right. Field generator deactivated," Sam said.

There was a soft hiss as the seal was broken. She yanked off the mask and tugged her hood down as Jax carried her through the water. As they reached the island's edge, Macy tossed the mask atop the spare clothing. She turned to Jax, threw her arms around him again, and rested her cheek on his shoulder.

"Thank you, Jax!" Lingering exhilaration thrummed through her.

She would never have thought it possible to feel that way, especially after she'd given up the sea, but this had been more than she could've imagined. The guilt of her sister's death had weighed down Macy's heart for years. She'd suffered stares of pity and accusation, had tormented herself with *what-ifs*. Today, for the first time in so long, Macy had *lived*.

Because of Jax.

"It's been a long time since I've had that much fun. It was wonderful!" Macy lifted her head and pressed her lips to his.

Jax tensed. She only registered what she'd done when his eyes widened.

Macy quickly pulled back. "Oh."

He searched her face, his brow drawn in confusion, and — before she realized what he meant to do — he leaned down and kissed her.

She clenched his shoulders as his mouth pressed against hers; his lips were soft and firm at once, and heat spread across her face and sparked fire in her belly.

This was what Camrin's kiss had been missing. This unfamiliar, unexpected, overwhelming sensation that stole the breath from her lungs. She forgot everything around her; she and Jax may well have been the only two people in the world. Jax's lack of skill was meaningless, because his slightest touch sent pleasure spiraling through her.

Macy closed her eyes and gave herself to the kiss. It was a whispering caress, a soft brush of mouths, and their breath mingled as they explored one another.

Jax's tentacles slid up her legs and over her back, rubbing gently. He drew her against him, and she felt the rapid thumping of his hearts, melding with her own heartbeat through their chests.

The prick of his claws on her hip and the graze of his teeth heightened her awareness of him; something sparked within Macy, something dark and forbidden. Liquid heat pooled between her legs, and her sex pulsated with need.

Macy opened her mouth and touched her tongue to his lips.

Jax's entire body jolted. He pulled away abruptly, sat her on the edge of the island, and sank into the water to his shoulders.

Confused and aroused, Macy stared at him. Her lips tingled from the kiss while her skin cooled in his absence. She pressed her fingers to her mouth briefly.

"Jax?"

His eyes were large, pupils dilated, but he held her gaze. His nostrils flared. "We should tend the fish."

"Are...are you okay?"

"Yes. Kissing is...overwhelming. It feels good, but it is... intense." He pressed his lips together and lifted three of his tentacles out of the water. The fish writhed in his hold as he swam around the island and deposited them in the empty bucket near her shelter.

She stood on unsteady legs, only now aware of the weariness in her limbs. Their ache wasn't as pleasant — or as dire — as the one between her legs. She pressed her thighs together, hoping to relieve it, but it only strengthened.

Macy didn't know what had driven her to kiss Jax, but she knew things between them had changed drastically.

JAX LAY on his back beside Macy, tentacles in the water, and gazed up through the cave opening. Countless stars glittered against the deep violet of the night sky. The fire had burned down to little more than a few spots of glowing orange Macy called *embers*. It still produced pleasant warmth, and she remained nearby.

When she'd been ready to remove her suit, Jax turned around without argument; his self-control after their kiss had been tenuous enough that he didn't trust himself to so much as *think* about her naked body. The touch of her tongue against his lips had forced his shaft to extrude like he was an adolescent.

As much as he wanted her, the decision was Macy's. When she was ready — if ever — she would make it known. Until such a time, he needed to be the master of his own body, needed to control his desires, and needed to respect her right to choose. It didn't matter how strongly his cock throbbed.

He'd remained in the water as she cleaned and cooked the fish, waiting until long after his arousal had cooled before daring to venture close.

They'd lapsed into companionable silence.

Now, as they watched the stars, they were treated to the music of the waves outside, a song backed by the constant flow of the waterfall. Jax had spent his life underwater, and would never have guessed at the abundance of beauty above the surface.

Jax turned his head to Macy. Her skin and hair were pale in the starlight, her eyes bright with its reflection.

He couldn't *possibly* have imagined the beauty of the surface world.

What would his people say about her, about his attraction to her? Would they find it unnatural, distasteful, a betrayal to their kind? Or would they understand her appeal?

The questions did not long remain on his mind; he didn't care what they thought. Macy was his. A treasure he would keep to himself. She had given him a taste of something he'd sought for years, something he'd never discovered during his wanderings — contentment.

As though sensing his gaze, Macy looked at him and smiled. "What?"

"I have never encountered anything like you, Macy."

She chuckled. "Because I'm human?"

He smiled; he enjoyed the sound of her laughter. "I doubt there are other humans like you."

"Hmm...I'm not quite sure what to say to that. I mean, there are probably plenty of people like me. I'm nothing special." She rolled onto her side and propped her head on her hand. Golden hair fell around her arm, and Jax longed to touch it again. "Why are you called the Wanderer? Despite the obvious."

"It is because of the obvious. I've always pushed boundaries, since I was a youngling, have always sought new places. I had explored every accessible part of our home by my tenth year, and a few places thought to be sealed forever. The adults attempted to break my curiosity, but they never could. Once I was an adult, I set out on my own, farther than the others would dare, because I had to know what was out there. I couldn't confine myself to my den and do nothing between hunts."

"Are there others like you?"

Jax shook his head. Arkon understood, but his calling was different, his urge to explore focused within himself rather than on the enormity of the sea. "That is why *I* am the Wanderer. Kraken venture out to hunt, sometimes quite far, but always in groups, and always to places they know."

"Do they still try to stop you?"

"They see no point in it, anymore. So long as I contribute as I can, they are content to allow me my strange behavior. I am an accomplished enough hunter that most of them show me respect, regardless."

"How often do you need to contribute? You've been *here* for a while…are they going to wonder where you are?"

"If a hunt is called when I am there, I go along."

Except for the last one…

"Some might wonder where I am," he continued, "but they know well enough by now…I will return when I do, and if I do not return, it is because I am dead. Some would think me deserving of it for my foolishness."

She frowned. "Do you have any friends? Anyone who would worry?"

"Yes. There is one."

Her lips lifted into a smile. "Are you going to tell me?"

"He is called Arkon," he said. "We became friends as younglings. He was considered…odd by the others."

"Like you."

Jax nodded. "For different reasons, but yes. We became friends because we were different from the rest, and we defended each other from other males who sought to challenge us."

"Why would they challenge you?"

He flicked his tentacles through the water. "Because they thought *different* meant *weak*. Most learned their lesson, in time. I was stronger and faster than most of them, and Arkon was the cleverest of us. When he fought, he held his own, but he'd often confuse the others into backing down before it ever came to that."

"How would he do that?"

"He knows words the rest of us don't understand. And when he couldn't talk…he has his own way of moving, and it throws many off-guard because they cannot easily predict what he will do. As we got older, he showed little interest in such contests, and he simply stopped acknowledging challenges. Eventually, everyone left him alone."

"What does he do now?"

Jax turned his head to look back at the sky. In some ways, the stars, with their barely perceptible patterns, reminded him of Arkon's work, but that didn't help him describe it to Macy.

"When he isn't trying to draw new information out of the Computer, he makes...patterns. Designs. With rocks and anything else he can find."

"An artist."

A whisper of movement called his attention back to her briefly; she'd shifted onto her back and returned her gaze to the stars.

"I think my friend Aymee would like Arkon," she said. "She's an artist, too, and even though people don't need art like they do food and water, the things she creates make people smile. She works, just like the rest of us — she's one of the doctor's apprentices — but she really comes alive when she's *creating*."

Macy raised her hand with one finger extended, moving it as though she were tracing lines between the stars. Jax's eyes followed.

"When we were young, Aymee and I would look at the stars, just like we are now, and we'd connect them to make pictures. Dogs, or sailboats, or spoons, anything we could imagine." She let her hand fall to her stomach.

"I think Arkon would like our people to enjoy what he creates," Jax said. "He is often unsatisfied by his creations, always looking to the next thing. But most of the kraken do not understand it enough to enjoy it...or they simply do not try. He would like your Aymee."

"I think he would, too. I think she feels as trapped in The Watch as I did."

"Do you feel trapped, now?" Jax's throat tightened, and he

stilled his tentacles; the question spawned fear in him because he couldn't predict her answer with any certainty.

After a long silence, Macy shook her head. "No. Had you not agreed to take me out with you, I would, but now... I think I'm happy." Her brow furrowed. "I miss them, and that won't change, but I can live with it."

Jax rolled onto his side, leaning on his elbow in an imitation of her earlier position. From his slightly higher vantage, he was granted a full view of her; she'd put on a pair of loose pants and a long-sleeved shirt with buttons down the front, but he couldn't forget the body that'd been teased by her dress and the diving suit.

Quiet stretched between them; Macy watched the stars, and Jax watched her, marveling at the play of starlight on her smooth skin. Though he'd seen living humans from afar, and the holograms in the Facility up close, he hadn't been prepared for the wonder of Macy — her look, her feel, the sensations she stirred in him.

"Do humans dream, Macy?"

Macy turned to mirror his position. "You mean while sleeping?"

"Any time."

"Like daydreaming? Hopes? Thoughts of the future?"

"All of them," he replied, but he hadn't asked her the right question. "What do *you* dream of?"

"I...don't know." She glanced at the ground between them, brow drawn. "I dreamt of sailing and fishing with my father when I was younger, but after Sarina..." Her shoulders lifted and dropped. "I expected to join with Camrin, but I don't know anymore."

"But Camrin was never your dream. What...were your hopes? Your *daydreams*?"

"I had none. I'd resigned myself to the reality of my situation...to the consequences of my choices." Her eyes met his. "Dreaming would only lead me to disappointment."

"What about now?" He held her gaze. "You've made a different choice than you intended. Has your situation changed enough for you to have hope?"

"Honestly, Jax...I don't know. In a way, I've resigned myself to this, too." She turned her face toward her shelter. "I accepted this as my only choice because you wouldn't...you wouldn't let me go. I decided to make the best of what I got."

He'd known throughout, had known he denied her true choice. Even now, their closeness — their developing relationship — couldn't be taken as it seemed, because he had forced her to choose this situation. The dull thump of his hearts rose over the sounds of moving water.

"But if I would have been given a choice," she continued, "if I had known, I would have chosen this. It's...weird, really, because I'm pretty much trapped in this cave, but I feel freer than ever. That's because of you. I know my decisions — and my silence — were my own fault, but if I'd know, I would have chosen this, Jax."

His nostrils flared as he drew in a deep breath and slowly expelled it. "I was wrong when I said I only had one friend."

Macy smiled and brushed the tips of her fingers over his cheek. "What about your dreams, Jax?"

Her touch was warm, gentle, soothing; he craved more of it.

"In my dreams, I swim farther than I have ever gone. Farther, maybe, than is possible. To places that must exist only in my mind. To...cities below the surface, built for kraken, cities in which my people can thrive. But they never go to those places in my dreams, just as they will not journey with me while I am awake."

"Why don't they go with you?"

Jax lifted his gaze and swept it across the stars. "Because most kraken fear what is unknown to them. I *know* we cannot forever remain in our home, and we must seek new places to den, new places to hunt…and I do not fear the unknown."

"And no one will go with you? Not even Arkon?"

"His focus is within himself. He struggles with things I do not fully understand…though I know they are somehow important. The others are too set in their ways. They were taught that straying too far meant death, and that I was not of my right mind."

Macy lowered her head into the crook of her elbow. "I'd go with you. It may not mean much, but I would."

He lowered himself into a similar position to keep his eyes at the same level as hers. "It means more than I can say."

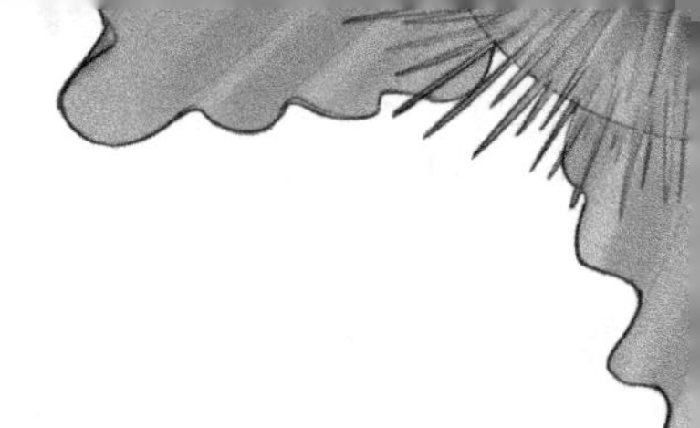

CHAPTER TWELVE

Nine days had passed since Jax brought Macy to the cave. Nine days of eating nothing but fish and Halorian lobsters. She was grateful that he provided food, but she was beginning to feel the effects of an all-meat diet. Her body needed variety, needed nutrients she could only get from plants, but she wasn't sure how to explain it to him.

She needed to go to land.

Five days ago, their first trip into the ocean had marked the turning point in their relationship. Conversation flowed between them easily, now; they enjoyed one another's company. Macy eagerly anticipated their trips, and her fear diminished with each one. The two of them grew a little closer every day.

But they hadn't kissed again.

In fact, Jax seemed very careful about physical contact between them. He took her hand when she offered it, but whenever he took her through the tunnel, he'd release her immediately after emerging and put distance between them. If she hadn't caught him staring at her with open want on several occasions, she might have thought their moments of passion figments of her imagination.

She craved contact with him, and used any excuse to have it — the *accidental* brush of her hand against his, having him hold her as they passed through the tunnel, or sliding a little closer to him at night in the hope that one of his tentacles would settle over her as they slept.

Her mind returned to their kiss often; she wanted to relive it. What would have happened, had he not pulled away? How much further might they have gone?

Macy glanced down at the wadded shirt between her hands, still held beneath the waterfall. She might've scrubbed it twice without realizing while she'd been lost in thought; ever since Jax asked her about dreams, she'd caught herself daydreaming with increasing frequency.

Her daydreams usually involved Jax.

Pulling her arms back, she wrung the shirt out and spread it on the dry section of the ledge in the sunlight. None of the clothing would be truly clean without soap, but this was better than nothing.

She looked over her shoulder. Jax was stacking a fresh pile of driftwood beside her tent. They'd discovered, through trial and error, that a few of the containers were waterproof when sealed. He'd used them to gather more dry fuel for her fires.

Her eyes dipped to watch the play of muscles along his shoulders and back. She'd felt their movement beneath her palm, and longed to feel it again; all she could do now was look away and suffer through her yearning.

After cleaning the rest of the clothes and laying them to dry, she returned to the island.

"Jax?"

He turned, and his muscles shifted again, and she *still* couldn't touch. "Yes?"

"I need to go onto land." There. She'd said it.

"For what?" His tone and expression were free of the suspicion she'd expected.

She sat down on one of the overturned crates. "Do you remember when I told you that humans ate plants?"

"A difficult thing to forget."

Macy smiled; they both ate things that disgusted the other. "Well, I haven't had any, and I kind of *need* to."

"Have I not been bringing enough food?" he asked, brow creased.

"You have, but I need more than meat. Humans need a variety of nutrients, and some of those nutrients come from plants."

He removed the last piece of wood from the container, added it to the pile, and turned to face her fully. "If you say you need them, we will go and find what you require."

Macy lifted her eyebrows. "You do realize we will have to go inland?"

Jax nodded and brushed his hands together, wiping away sand and debris. "You will be our guide."

"I could go alone if you want to remain near the water."

"I do not know the dangers on land, but I'm sure there are many. I cannot leave you alone. It will be...an adventure." Despite his serious tone, his eyes lit up.

"Yeah," she said, grinning, "it will be."

MACY REMOVED her mask as she walked up the beach. Her body felt heavy after leaving the water, turning the trip across the sand into a trudge. Was this what Jax experienced when he went onto land?

He followed her with an empty container in his arms, leaving wide, confused tracks in his wake. Had she not known their source, she might've guessed they'd been left by some massive sea serpent.

The beach continued for another nine or ten meters before

giving way to rockier ground; to either side, those rocks grew into the seaside cliffs dominating most of the coastline, but here they were tame enough to cross. The thick jungle vegetation was visible just beyond — dark green, violet, and crimson growth. Just like the woods around The Watch.

Tugging her hood down, Macy turned to Jax. "If we're lucky, we won't have to go too far inland."

Out in the sunlight, the gray of his skin was muted, but he displayed no discomfort. "I'll follow wherever you lead, Macy."

They made their way over sand and stone until they reached the first vegetation — tendrils of crimson creeper and short stalks of capeweed with bowl-shaped, indigo leaves. She glanced back at Jax; he'd slowed amidst the plants, his expression drawn.

"This feels strange," he said.

"Good strange or bad strange?" Macy brushed aside a red vine as she reached the taller vegetation.

"For now, just strange. And the taste... You do not eat *these* plants, do you?"

"No, I don't. But the capeweed — the little blue ones — make good dyes."

He was silent for a time; leaves rustled and crunched with their passage, and the waves sighed against the shore behind them.

"Do you have another meaning for that word?" he asked.

"Which word?"

"*Dyes.*"

"Dyes are mixtures that can be used to change the color of fabric or make paint. A lot of them can be extracted from plants."

"What about the red plants?"

Macy wrinkled her nose. If she never had to tear up another crimson creeper, she could die happy. "No. Even though their pigment is bright, it changes to a muddy brown when you try to distill it, and it *stinks*."

The shadows thickened as Jax and Macy ventured farther into the jungle, the thickening canopy blocking out more of the sunlight. She quieted, splitting her attention between the search for edible plants and the search for safe passage. She pointed out poisonous vegetation to Jax, warning him to keep away, and avoided the worst of the tangled roots and uneven ground as best she could.

Macy stopped when she spotted something familiar up ahead — a plant with huge, layered green leaves at its base. The leaves narrowed toward their tops, and a two-meter-long stalk jutted from their center, with several smaller, thorn-like protrusions toward its tip. Four tendrils hung from the end, glistening with some sort of nectar.

"Do you see that one? It's a snatcher."

"A snatcher?" Jax furrowed his brow.

"Watch." Macy crouched and snapped a branch off a nearby bush. When she stood, she threw the branch as hard as she could. It landed in the undergrowth in front of the snatcher.

The stalk snapped down — almost matching the speed she'd seen from Jax underwater — and the thorns turned inward, catching the branch and piercing several fallen leaves. The tendrils at the end of the stalk had retracted. After a few moments, the thorns parted again, and the stalk straightened. Slowly, the tendrils extended, dangling their beads of nectar.

"How much else is like that up here?" Jax swept his eyes over their surroundings warily.

"There are a few different species of carnivorous plant native to Halora. That one's the most dangerous. If it doesn't get enough sustenance, it can actually uproot and drag itself to a new hunting ground."

Jax frowned and moved closer, positioning himself between

Macy and the snatcher. One of his tentacles curled briefly around her calf. "I will remain watchful."

They continued onward until Macy found thick shoots of naba growing around the base of a tree. She drew her knife and cut them into small enough pieces to lay in the container. Rather than store the last one, she split it down the middle and scooped out a chunk of its spongy center. She stuck it in her mouth and moaned, squeezing her eyes shut at the sweet burst of juice.

"*So* good. Here," she said, offering a piece to Jax. "Try it."

"I have tried cooked meat. Let that be enough for now."

"Please?"

His eyes lifted from the naba to meet her gaze, and he hesitated, frowning. "You need it, Macy, not me."

"You're not curious at all? Where's that sense of adventure, Jax?"

"If I eat this...plant, and it makes me sick, what then?"

Macy lowered her hand. "I...didn't think of that."

"It is an experience I will survive without knowing," he said gently, adjusting his hold on the container.

After eating the remainder of the open naba, she collected a few more stalks and led Jax onward. She found some bitterstock vegetables — which tasted exactly as the name implied — soon after. Though she didn't want to eat them, they were nutritious, and she couldn't afford pickiness.

"Oh, look!" Macy exclaimed, pointing up above their heads. The branches of a nearby tree were laden with bunches of winefruit — round, violet-skinned fruits with pulpy centers. "Could you pick those?"

He eyed her skeptically, set the container on the ground, and rose up on his tentacles. Reaching over his head, he tore down a cluster of fruit. "What are these?"

"Winefruit. You peel the skin and eat the inside."

"The same way you remove the meat from inside a hard-shell?"

She smiled and plucked the individual fruits off the branch when he held them to her, stacking them in the container. "Yeah, kind of. They use them in The Watch to make wine, which is a strong, sweet drink that makes you…feel and act differently if you drink too much."

"Different how?"

"It makes you…looser, mentally and physically. The more you drink, the hazier your mind becomes, and you lose control sometimes."

He scowled. "Why would anyone drink something that dulls their senses like that? Do they mean to endanger themselves?"

Macy shrugged. "To feel good. It's not as bad as I'm making it sound. Some people abuse it, and it becomes a problem, but mostly people drink to loosen up and have fun. Being in The Watch isn't like being out here, or in the sea. It's safe. We don't have to all be on our guard every moment."

Jax frowned and closed the container, bending to lift it. He stopped before he touched it, wide-eyed gaze focused on something behind Macy.

"What is it?" She turned to look behind her.

A krull stood twenty meters away, staring at Macy and Jax with small, dark eyes.

It was a large creature, its head twice as high as Macy, with a long, powerful neck and slender horns extending forward from its narrow head. The neck was nearly half its height; in comparison, its body and legs were thin and frail-looking. Apart from a splash of red just beneath either side of its jaw, its fur was the deep violet of most of the vegetation.

Jax inserted himself between Macy and the krull, spreading his arms and raising several of his tentacles — making himself look even larger. His skin shifted to crimson, his stripes pulsing indigo.

He's protecting me.

The thought made Macy smile. She placed a hand on his shoulder. "It's okay. They're harmless."

"It does not look harmless."

"It's so they can protect themselves from predators, or fight each other during mating season." She trailed her hand down his back, over tense muscles. "Sarina and I used to feed them as kids, until we found out that made them easier targets for the hunters."

The krull turned its head and bit off a large leaf, keeping one eye on Jax while it chewed.

Jax relaxed, if only slightly, and glanced at Macy over his shoulder. "It is a creature your people hunt?"

"Yes."

He looked back at the krull. "What do they taste like?"

Macy laughed. "I don't know how to explain it. Like meat, I guess, but different than fish meat."

"If it is not dangerous…we should continue."

"I think I have plenty for now. We can go back."

"How long do these plants last, now that we have gathered them?" he asked, retrieving the container.

"Some last longer than others. Not much more than a week, probably, but I'll eat it all before it spoils."

Jax nodded; his people lived on raw meat, so she guessed they were used to eating soon after obtaining food.

He led the way on their return trip, retracing their path with startling accuracy. Several times, she stepped in her own footprints in the few patches of soft, exposed ground they crossed. Being on land didn't seem to hamper his sense of direction.

The air changed immediately when they emerged from the vegetation — the cloying, earth scent of the jungle was replaced by a cool, briny ocean breeze.

"Thank you." Macy gathered her hair and pulled her hood

over it. "I wasn't sure if you'd agree to bring me onto land, much less come along."

He smiled at her; he seemed more at ease now that they were returning to the water. "You have faced the sea with me. This is the least I can do, for you."

He'd brushed it off as unimportant, but this trip was another extension of his trust — more than ever before. Jax had taken her ashore, followed her into the unknown, into an environment he wasn't made for, and relied upon her to warn him of potential dangers.

Macy watched him, lost in thought, as he moved toward the water.

When he realized she wasn't following, he turned toward her, tucking the container under an arm to extend a hand to her. "Come, Macy."

She grinned and brought the mask to her face as she went to take his hand.

TOGETHER, they fought the tide and entered the open ocean, swimming slowly toward the cave. Jax's tentacles felt odd; the discomfort of crossing plants, roots, dirt, and rock lingered long after he'd left land. Moving up there hadn't hurt, but the alien textures had made him long for the sea.

He led Macy to the bottom, placing the container on a rocky shelf near a large coral growth. The area was full of life and color, home to more creatures than he could count.

After gesturing for her to remain with the container, Jax pulled himself along the seafloor, altering his skin to match his surroundings as he went. He slowed as he neared the coral. A few fish hurried away, driven by instinct. Their movement spooked other creatures into fleeing.

Pressing himself into the sand, he willed his hearts to slow and waited. Hunting was often a matter of patience.

Macy wasn't far; he *felt* her eyes on him, watching.

Patience; it wouldn't help either of them if he caught nothing.

Before long, the fish emerged from whatever hiding places they'd found. Small creatures with segmented shells hurried around Jax in the sand, but they would provide little meat, and he wasn't likely to catch more than a few before they fled.

Had Macy ever hunted? She'd mentioned hunters amongst the humans, but it wasn't likely that she'd been one of them. Not because she was incapable, but because her role had simply been different. She had provided food for her people in a different way.

Could she learn to hunt? There were likely tools in the Facility that could compensate for her lack of natural weaponry, and she was intelligent. Though Jax took pride in providing for her, he had a sense that she'd be more content if she were able to contribute.

This, however, was no time for such thoughts; he shifted his attention back to the surrounding waters. Small fish darted through holes in the coral and moved in and out of the nearby plants. Occasionally, a larger fish drifted past, but none came near enough to grab.

Something pressed down on his back.

Jax shoved himself up and spun, tentacles splayed to strike. Through the cloud of sand, he made out the dark shape of Macy's suit; his hearts skipped, and he halted. The fear on her face was apparent as the sand settled.

She was speaking and gesturing frantically toward something behind and above Jax. He looked over his shoulder.

His blood went cold.

It was a razorback, easily as long as six kraken from its mouth to the tip of its tail. With skin the same blue as the surrounding water, the powerful beasts were difficult to spot despite their size. Slightly darker spines crested its head and ran along its back and belly, and two sets of large fins propelled it through the water, aided by the motion of its long tail.

They ate whatever they chose, kraken included. And this one was moving directly toward Jax and Macy.

There was no time for thought — they had no adequate weapons, and the razorback had already spotted them. Jax wrapped his arms around Macy, hugging her to his chest, and darted forward. She clung to him as he sped along the bottom, toward the more pronounced rocks near the coast.

He risked a glance over his shoulder; the razorback was closing the distance rapidly.

Jax moved as fast as he could; swimming, clawing, dragging, desperate to remove Macy from danger. The skin on his back burned, and he felt the razorback gaining, expected its attack at any moment. He kept as low to the increasingly rocky floor as possible without causing Macy harm. The irregularity of the bottom was the only protection they had until they found real shelter.

There was a rush of water behind him. Jax spun aside just as the razorback lunged. Macy squeezed him, burying her masked face against his chest, as the razorback's blunt snout hit the bottom.

Swinging his gaze away from the beast, Jax surveyed the terrain ahead. They were quickly approaching the shoreline, where the coastal cliffs met the ocean. Amongst the rocks were two massive boulders tipped against one another. A dark, narrow space was left between them.

He didn't know if they would both fit, and it didn't matter.

So long as Macy was safe.

Water churned as the razorback righted itself. Trusting Macy to hold on, Jax released his hold on her to use his hands for extra speed. Her grip was tight enough to be painful.

A little farther.

The razorback's shadow fell over Jax. It would attack again within a few heartbeats' time.

With a final thrust, he propelled himself toward the opening between the rocks, hurriedly prying Macy's arms and legs off to shove her into the gap first. He flattened himself as best he could to fit behind her, his shoulders nearly too wide to fit.

He curled his tentacles beneath him and changed his skin to match the rock.

The stone shook with the razorback's impact. Jax's eyes were wide and unseeing in the darkness, and Macy's hands were frantic upon him, trembling. He sucked in water through his siphons, struggling to get enough oxygen.

He found one of Macy's hands and took it in his, holding it as he counted the beats of his hearts. The sound of the razorback's movement was muffled in the enclosed space. Was it swimming around the boulders, waiting out its prey, or would it move on? Would it try to fit its snout into the opening?

Releasing her hand, he slowly twisted himself around, scraping his shoulders on the stone, and peered out of the hole.

The belly spines of the razorback passed the entrance, dipping for a moment to brush the sand on the seafloor.

Jax reached an arm back, and Macy grabbed hold of his hand again. Though the razorback passed only twice more, they remained in that position for a long while.

Patience.

Eventually, Jax pulled away from Macy and crawled forward, poking his head out of the shelter. He counted to one hundred before exiting completely. Gesturing for her to stay, he crept up along the boulder, and from the higher vantage, checked his surroundings.

Convinced that it had gone — unlike the kraken and some other predators, razorbacks did not lay in wait for their prey — Jax returned to the hole and helped Macy out. Her eyes were wide, darting about in a desperate search for the beast.

He took her in his arms, and she clung to him again, the desperation of her hold little diminished. As he swam back to the cave, he scanned the water frequently.

Macy held him while they passed through the tunnel, held him when they emerged inside the cave, held him as he climbed onto the island.

"Sam, r-release the mask," she said.

There was a now-familiar hiss. She removed the mask with one hand, keeping her other arm around Jax.

"You are safe now, Macy." He eased a tentacle down her back.

"What *was* that?"

"A razorback. The most dangerous hunter in the sea."

Her trembling lessened, and the tension in her muscles gradually faded. "Why haven't we seen one before?"

Jax carried her to the tent and sank down on the floor, curling his front tentacles to support her as she leaned into him. "Because there are not many, and they do not tend to hunt in shallow waters. I do not know why that one ventured so near the land..."

"Where is it from?"

"The deep sea. Most prey in the shallows is not large enough to sustain them, and they cannot easily move amidst the rocks and reefs. But in open water, especially at night...they eat whatever they want."

"Have you hunted them before?" Unlocking her legs from around his middle, she set the mask aside, pulled her hood back, and shook out her hair. It was damp with sweat. He'd not smelled it on her often, but it was oddly enticing.

"Yes. Sometimes, a razorback gets a taste for kraken and claims the area near our home as its territory. All able-bodied kraken take part in those hunts." He lifted a tentacle, bending it to show her the jagged scar ringing it about halfway up. "I lost a tentacle to a razorback, during one such hunt. I was lucky."

Macy traced the scar lightly with her fingertips; Jax's skin heated beneath her touch, and it took all his concentration to hold himself still.

"It grew back?"

He tilted his head. "Of course it grew back."

"You say that as though I should've known."

"You asked as though it were strange to you."

"Humans limbs don't grow back."

Jax pulled back enough to take gentle hold of her wrist and lift her arm. The upper bodies of humans and kraken were remarkably similar. Though her hand was concealed by her diving suit, he knew its details well; apart from webbing and claws, it was the same as his.

But hers wouldn't grow back if it were torn off.

Pressing their palms together, he gazed into her eyes. Humans came from a different world, a world of air, filled with strange beasts and predatory plants, and it seemed unlikely they should have survived for so long. They were fragile creatures, based on what he'd seen.

"I will protect you, Macy."

Macy settled her free hand on his chest. "I know."

Her eyes dropped. Slowly, she slid her hand over his chest and ran it along his shoulder stripes before moving it back down.

Jax inhaled, drawing in her scent, and only then realized the truth of their position. Her legs were to either side of his waist, and the spot between her thighs — the mystery he longed to solve — was poised over his slit. Faint but unmistakable heat radiated from her.

Her hand hesitated at his middle before venturing farther down, moving past the point where his skin darkened. His breath quickened as her fingers neared his slit. His shaft throbbed.

Jax caught her wrist with his free hand.

She gasped, eyes wide, and her cheeks pinkened.

"Macy," he said through his teeth. His body ached for her; his need nearly overwhelmed him. Did she realize what she was pushing him toward? Was she motivated by attraction, or simple, innocent curiosity?

Jax withdrew his tentacles from beneath her, letting her onto the ground gently, and released his hold on her. He moved back toward the water. After their escape from the razorback, his emotions were too amplified; he couldn't resist her for long.

His body was different from a human male's. There was too much of a chance she'd be frightened if his cock extruded without warning.

"Jax?"

"I…just need a little time." He glanced at her over his shoulder and forced a smile to his lips. "After the razorback… It came too close to harming you, Macy."

Macy frowned and rubbed her arms. "Okay. You won't be gone long?"

He shook his head and entered the water. "Just going to check outside. Make sure it did not follow our scent."

"Please be careful."

Dipping under, he propelled himself toward the tunnel.

CHAPTER THIRTEEN

MACY STARED AT THE DARK WATER THAT HID THE TUNNEL. HER heart pounded, and unease twisted her insides. They'd waited a day to ensure the razorback left. One day. Despite Jax's confidence — he insisted it had moved on to a better hunting place — Macy was a wreck. She hadn't wanted him to go. She could do without the food they'd left behind.

But Jax had insisted because he knew she needed it.

Macy clenched the fabric of her dress in her fists and bit her lip.

I can't lose him, too.

She closed her eyes, drawing a deep breath.

"Jax will be fine. He's a hunter. He's fast. He'll...he *will* be back."

She opened her eyes and waited. Hoped. One minute led to the next, and the next, and there was still no sign of him.

Macy got to her feet and paced. "I can't do this. I can't sit here and...and...worry. I need—" she stopped and stared at the barrels she'd used to create her tent, "—a distraction."

Walking to the closest barrel, she lifted the fishing pole and carefully set it down on the ground. The canvas created a gentle breeze as it sagged. She hadn't searched these containers yet — not thoroughly. Her priority had been to get out of the sun.

She bent down and removed the items within, setting them atop the nearby crates and on the ground around her feet.

There were a few more pieces of driftwood; she added them to her respectable pile. She had no immediate use for many of the other items — more cups, scraps of clothing, a dented metal sign with only the letters *CAU* readable on its rusted face, bits of tangled fishing line, a small net, and a wooden smoking pipe.

Near the bottom of the barrel, she discovered a square metal container. She reached in with both hands, leaning against the rim, and after a few seconds of struggling, grasped the box by its sides. It was heavier than she'd expected, and her arms strained as she lifted it. Something rattled inside when she tilted it.

Crouching, she set the box on the ground and checked the latches. They were locked.

Macy scowled, huffed, and shoved herself up to rummage through the assortment of tools in the other bins. She found a flathead screwdriver and tossed it down beside the box before moving to the edge of the island. Laying on her stomach, she reached into the water and felt around on the bottom until she found a fist-sized rock.

She returned to the box, knelt, and angled it so the latches were faceup. Picking up the screwdriver, she wedged its tip into the narrow seam between the latch and the casing. She hammered it in until the first latch popped and repeated the process for the other one.

Setting her tools aside, she laid the box flat and opened the lid.

An eclectic collection of items lay within. She took them out one by one, studying each individually. First was a small, pink bottle. She removed the cap; the contents were dry, but an unfamiliar floral scent lingered inside.

Next was a flat piece of plastic. When her thumb touched the corner, a hologram flickered on, displaying a man and a woman standing together, arms around each other's shoulders. They were smiling. Macy brushed her hand through the image, and it changed — the same woman from the first, this time with two other women and a man, all dressed in the blue jumpsuits.

The hologram flickered again, distorting the image before it vanished completely. Frowning, Macy set it aside and turned her attention to the other items. In a small, fabric-lined box she found a necklace with a thin, golden chain and a tear-shaped gemstone in a delicate setting. The stone was clear, but when she turned it toward the light, it broke the rays into a rainbow of color.

After the necklace were four glass vials, all the same size and shape. Each contained a bit of dirt. One was labeled *Earth*; the next, which had a red tint, was labeled *Mars*; the third was nearly black, marked *Tau Ceti III*. The last of them held the rich, familiar brown soil she'd worked in for years, and was labeled *Halora*.

It was clear these objects had belonged to a woman — and that woman must've been one of the original colonists. Macy didn't recognize *Mars* or *Tau Ceti*, but she knew about Earth. That was the human homeworld. A place she'd only seen in pictures. The owner of these items had traveled impossible distances to get to Halora.

Carefully setting the vials back inside the container, Macy picked up the last object. It reminded her of the wrist attachment on the PDS, though this was a bit larger. She slid her thumb over its surface.

A small, soft light came on, and a hologram materialized above the device. The rectangular projection was a list of some sort; when Macy flicked her finger up and down, the items cycled. Little of it made sense. Some of the listings were clearly names, but she didn't know any of the people, and they were always paired with some sort of title. She pressed one.

Sound blared from the device. Startled, Macy nearly dropped it. She stared at the hologram, which had morphed into a small orb of light that pulsed and changed colors with the beat of the music.

Macy had never heard anything like it. Music was popular in The Watch, serving as a primary means of entertainment — drums, fiddles, and flutes, mostly, and there was even a guitar that had been passed through one family. But the sounds and tones coming from the hologram were alien to her. She couldn't imagine what instruments had produced them. The music was upbeat, and the rhythm vibrated through her.

She grinned, fascinated, and bobbed her head to the beat. Was this what music used to sound like when the colony was new? It was…amazing.

Macy set the device down and rose. It had been a long while since she'd danced; since she'd let herself go. She closed her eyes and let the beat wash over her. Though it was foreign, the sound flowed through her; she rocked her hips, raised her arms, and let the music sweep away her conscious thought.

The song ended, and another began immediately; the differences between the two were clear, but she didn't stop moving, easily transitioning into the new rhythm.

"Macy?"

She spun at the sound of Jax's voice. "Jax!"

He was on the island with the retrieved container on the ground before him. Rivulets of water ran down his muscled form, pooling on the ground. She ran to him, shoved aside the container with her foot, and hugged him.

"You're back!" She pulled away and grabbed his hands, tugging him along. "Come dance with me!"

His brow furrowed, but he didn't resist as she led him to the center of the island. He glanced at the music device. "Where did you get that?"

"It was in a locked container at the bottom of the barrel."

"What is the noise it is making?"

"Music." She laughed, releasing his hands, and swayed to the sound. "Dance with me, Jax. Just move to the sound."

Jax's eyes dropped to follow the motion of her hips.

Macy chuckled and guided his hands to her waist. "Like this."

He watched for a few more seconds before mimicking her movement, swaying his hips from side to side. She settled her hands on his shoulders, and their gazes met. Soon, he fell into Macy's rhythm, and their bodies moved in unison; push and pull, back and forth, lost in the beat.

Macy couldn't contain her joy. Jax's tentacles curled and twisted, waves of movement pulsing through their lengths to match the waves of sound. Any hesitancy he displayed in the beginning was gone.

The music changed again; the next song had a slower beat, but it was deeper, *sensual*; the notes repeatedly built toward a climax and dropped off before reaching it.

Her eyes locked with Jax's. His face was serious, focused, his gaze intense. The way he looked at her sent a thrill through her body, making her pulse quicken.

He slid his hands along her sides, first up toward her ribs and then down, over her hips and to her outer thighs. His tentacles brushed her calves and the backs of her bare knees.

Macy's smile faded, and her laughter died. She was consumed with *want*. Days of unquenched desire rushed back, flooding her core with heat.

Suddenly, her dress was rough and constricting against her skin, rasping over her hardened nipples, adding to her discomfort.

Her breath grew ragged as they moved to the new rhythm, and Jax drew increasingly closer, his touch more desperate and insistent with every passing moment. He drew back with each fall in the music. He was hypnotic, carnal, luring her in, mesmerizing her.

She stepped closer, breaking their rhythm to wrap her arms around his neck.

Jax enfolded her in his arms. His tentacles slipped around her thighs and lifted her off the ground, pressing her against him. Macy's legs reflexively encircled his hips. He leaned his head down, and she rose to meet him.

Their lips fused.

Neither of them held back. They branded one another with their mouths. It was everything it had been before, and more.

Macy flicked her tongue over his lips, savoring the salty taste of his skin. Instead of pulling away, Jax opened his mouth, allowing her to delve in.

Tentatively, he touched his tongue to hers, and that was all it took. He seized command of the kiss, deepened it, and stole her breath. It was raw. Demanding. Scintillating.

Lust surged through her.

Macy's thighs squeezed his hips, and she dug her heels into his lower back to pull him closer. She needed *more*; more heat, more contact, more skin against skin. She slid a hand down his back and the other to his neck. It wasn't enough, wasn't *nearly* enough.

She pressed her chest against his.

Jax's hand slipped into her hair, taking hold and guiding her deeper into the kiss. His other hand dropped to her backside and squeezed.

Her hips jerked, and she gasped into his mouth. She tilted her head back, and he grazed her throat with lips and teeth. Delight rushed along every nerve in her body.

"Jax," Macy said with a throaty sigh.

He growled her name; it rumbled from his chest and into her, stronger and more provocative than the music. He tensed, kneading her flesh, and Macy heard the clack of his closing teeth near her ear. Something hard and slick jutted out beneath her, nestling against the crevice between her ass cheeks. It felt like no other part of his body. She knew enough about males to guess what it was.

She raised her head. His features were drawn, his lips pressed tight.

"Jax? What's wrong?"

He held her gaze for a few moments, and then she felt him pulling away, hand falling from her hair to shoulder, attempting to put space between them.

"Don't," she said.

Jax stilled. Macy cupped his jaw and brushed her thumb over his cheek.

"Don't," she repeated gently.

"This is not what you want," he rasped.

"Isn't it?"

His brow furrowed, and his pupils expanded as he searched her face.

The music thumped, distant and forgotten, overpowered by the heavy, quick beat of Macy's heart. She wanted Jax more than she could express. Perhaps it was wrong, or unnatural, and part of her was scared…but she didn't care about that.

She'd told him she was his; now she wanted to *be* his.

And she wanted Jax to be hers, too.

Without releasing her hold on him, she leaned to the side. Jax slipped his other hand to her ass, supporting her, as she turned off the music. The familiar roar of the waterfall returned to prominence, backed by the quieter cries of the sea from outside. It was music that suited Jax far better.

She righted herself and looked at him. The urgency of her lust had waned, but its strength was undiminished. With her skin overly sensitive, her breasts heavier, and her sex wet with need, Macy felt like a stranger in her own body.

That lent a new sense of excitement to the experience.

Jax tipped his head down, pressing his forehead to hers, and inhaled. He slid a tentacle up each of her legs. They coiled lightly around her calves and brushed her inner thighs.

Macy gasped at the sensation.

"Your scent is maddening, Macy." His shaft throbbed against her backside.

She flushed; knowing he could *smell* her was unsettling and arousing at once. Closing her eyes, she moved her hand from his face to the back of his head.

"I've never done this," Macy said. "I'm...not sure what to do, but I'm not...I'm not uncertain of you, Jax."

His clawed hands flexed. "I don't want to frighten you. We are...different. I am not like the man your suit showed you."

"I know, and I don't care." Macy laughed softly and shook her head. "Maybe I should, but I don't. I...I want to see. To know you. To...explore you." She brushed her lips against his. "I want you."

Jax's shaft slid along her thighs and stomach as he lowered her, and he shuddered. When she was on her feet, he moved back.

Macy watched his face, noting the vulnerability in his eyes. She understood his concern — that she'd find him repulsive, that she'd truly think him a monster — just as she knew it was unfounded. She lowered her eyes to his broad shoulders and their markings, along his torso, over ridges of muscle draped in velvety-soft skin.

Catching her lower lip between her teeth, she forced her gaze lower, past the darkened skin, stopping on his jutting shaft. Her eyes widened, and she exhaled in a rush. It was long, thick, and glistening with a sheen of moisture, its color lightening toward its rimmed tip.

But she wasn't shocked by his lack of a scrotum, or that he secreted his own lubrication; no, it was the thin, two-centimeter-long feelers around the base of his shaft that caught her off guard. She knew *exactly* where those would touch.

"Macy…"

She looked up. The vulnerability in his eyes now warred with the tension in his posture. His hands were fisted at his sides, shoulders squared, chin angled down. Macy stepped closer.

Jax held his ground, nostrils and siphons flaring.

Dropping her gaze again, she reached for him. His erection twitched as she held her hand over it until she finally wrapped her fingers around his girth. It was warm and hard, his soft skin made slick by its coating.

A tremor coursed through Jax, and he released a shuddering breath.

Encouraged by his reaction, she slid her fist to the base of his shaft, where the small tendrils moved over her hand with surprising strength. She stroked one with her finger.

Jax groaned. The feeler ran along Macy's finger with an almost rhythmic, undulating flutter.

Exhaling, Macy squeezed her thighs together. No, she didn't feel repulsion toward him. There was only pure, undeniable desire; she saw him, felt him, *wanted* him.

He wrapped a tentacle around her wrist and withdrew her hand from his shaft, guiding it to his chest and releasing it. Before she could react, his hands fell onto her thighs and slid up, hooking the hem of her dress.

Macy caught his wrists. He paused, meeting her gaze, and resumed the upward motion of his hands. She didn't resist. A tentacle followed in the wake of each of his palms, suction cups brushing lightly over her outer thighs before curling around to trace the curve of her backside.

She shivered when his touch flowed over her hips and along her sides, the air cool against her heated skin as more of it was gradually exposed. The tip of a tentacle crossed the flat of her stomach and caressed the underside of her breasts. She raised her arms as his hands moved up their lengths, pushing the dress up and off, and her hair fell around her naked shoulders.

Instinct demanded she cover herself, but Jax held her arms apart, keeping her bared to his hungry, gleaming gaze.

JAX SETTLED his gaze on Macy's face and followed the lines of her jaw, down over her chin and along the column of her neck. He lingered at the hollow of her throat, nearing the edge of the familiar; her dress had hidden most everything below this point. The unknown, as ever, called to him.

He lowered his eyes and took in the swell of her breasts; they were more defined than those of female kraken, which were less pronounced when not nursing young. The erect buds of her nipples were deeper pink than the rest of her skin.

Lower still; his gaze slipped over her stomach, past the slight dip of her belly button and the flared curves of her hips. He paused his attention briefly on the triangular patch of golden hair between her legs, which coaxed his eye downward a little farther.

Coiling his tentacles more firmly around her thighs, he spread them wider, allowing him a glimpse of the pink flesh of her slit.

How had he resisted for so long? How had he touched her, been touched by her, and not yet given in to the consuming fire of his needs?

"You are beautiful." His voice was husky, nearly a growl. He looked up and met her half-lidded eyes.

"Jax…"

He slid his hands up her arms and over her shoulders, then back down to cover her breasts. Her smooth, firm flesh yielded to his touch, and Macy closed her eyes and arched into his palms. He kneaded gently before he took her nipples between the pads of his fingers and stroked them.

Macy grasped his biceps and moaned.

Jax moved his tentacle down from her stomach, over the patch of hair, and ran the tip slowly along her folds.

She gasped, opening her eyes wide. Her legs jerked, squeezing against his hold.

Her arousal coated his tentacle with moisture; its sweetness on his suction cups was unlike anything he'd ever experienced. His mouth watered with the desire to taste her on his tongue.

Panting, Macy tightened her grip on his arms and subtly tilted her hips into his touch. Jax moved his tentacle again. Her entire body reacted, and she whimpered his name.

He dropped his hands to her backside and lifted her, drawing her legs against his sides with his tentacles. She undulated her hips against his abdomen as he carried her to the edge of the island.

"Where are we going?" Her confusion didn't seem to affect her desire.

When he reached the end of the land, he turned and slipped into the water, sitting her on the edge. He sank down until his face was level with her pelvis. She propped herself on her elbows and watched as he placed his hands on her knees, spreading them wide, and guided her legs over his shoulders. It granted him a full view of her glistening sex.

"Oh," she breathed.

He glanced up, and Macy averted her eyes. Her face was red, and she caught her lip between her flat, white teeth.

"Macy…"

Despite her hesitance, her gaze was bright with need. "I've… I don't know what to…"

"You do not have to do anything." Jax raised his front tentacles out of the water, running them up her legs and around her waist to cradle the small of her back. He moved a hand to her sex and slid the back of a finger along her folds.

She shivered and made a soft sound, lifting her hips.

With a second finger, he parted her sex, revealing the hidden petals within. Lured by her scent, he leaned closer, extended his tongue, and licked.

Macy bucked, digging her heels into his back, and put a hand on his head. "Jax!"

Her taste swept through his mouth and overwhelmed his senses; he needed *more*. His cock throbbed with aching need, his hearts pounded, and he longed to sink into her heat, but the discomfort was a small price for another taste of her.

He pressed his lips to her sex and kissed, flicking his tongue along her soft, smooth flesh and over the small nub at the top of her cleft. Macy dropped her head back with a cry, and her entire body jolted.

Curious, he did it again; the moment he brushed the nub, she came to life, pulling him closer with her legs as she sagged onto the ground. She withdrew her hand from his head, grasping handfuls of her hair.

Releasing a growl, Jax closed his eyes and delved into her, licking, nipping, sucking; *drinking* in her essence. She writhed beneath him, hips undulating against his mouth. He held her fast, allowing her no escape. The air was redolent with her scent and filled with her throaty whispers and moans.

He'd never heard such sounds from female kraken; his kind mated in the water. Macy's passionate cries urged him on and aroused him so much it hurt, but he couldn't stop.

Jax latched onto the small nub and sucked.

Macy screamed, quivering, and lurched up to wrap her arms around his neck. Her blunt fingernails grazed his skin as nectar flowed from her sex. He drank greedily, not relenting until he'd lapped up every drop, until her arms fell away and her trembling subsided.

He guided her legs off his shoulders and kissed the patch of hair on her pelvis, kissed over stomach, her breasts, easing her down as he worked his way up. Bringing more of his tentacles forward, he latched onto the island and pulled himself up. Macy cupped his face.

Jax braced himself with a hand to either side of her and stared down, sliding his hips up until his shaft pressed against her folds. Her heat flowed into him; he gritted his teeth, suppressing a shudder of pleasure. He didn't know how long he'd last. Before he'd seen her naked body, before he'd known if they could mate, he'd dreamt of this. Of her.

He held her gaze; they both knew that nothing would be same after this moment. Whatever relationship they'd formed would be forever altered. She'd chosen him. She was claiming him as her own.

Macy raised her knees, opening to him. She smiled.

Inhaling her scent, Jax closed his eyes. Her body was soft, awaiting his touch, welcoming their *joining*. And he couldn't wait any longer.

He pulled back and grasped his cock in one hand, guiding its head to her sex. His secretion combined with hers and eased his entrance as he slid into the tight heat of her channel. She tensed. Her inner muscles gripped him, and her hands fell to his shoulders, nails biting into his skin. He stilled.

"Keep going," Macy wrapped her legs around his waist.

The pressure was almost too much, and it took everything to keep from spilling in those first few moments. She was stretching to accommodate him, to draw more of him in, but could he hold out long enough for it to matter? His entire body tingled with the feel of her; he smelled nothing but her; Macy was the very air he breathed.

Steeling himself, he withdrew slightly — unable to suppress a groan — and thrust in, burying himself until their pelvises came together and the feelers at the base of his shaft caressed her sex. Macy let out a choked cry.

Incredible heat surrounded him, squeezed him, consumed him. Excruciating need surged within him.

Jax gazed down at her and knew that he was lost.

MACY WAS ON FIRE. Every bit of her skin burned with the longing to be touched, kissed, caressed. The pain of his entrance had been fleeting, swept aside by the feel of him filling her. Her inner walls pulsed deliciously around his shaft. She tightened her legs, pulling him even deeper.

Jax bared his teeth in a growl and closed his eyes, his face a mask of agony and pleasure. He ground his hips against hers. Macy moaned as one of the tendrils flicked over her clit. They moved constantly, brushing the sensitive folds of her sex.

"Jax," she breathed. Her body strained against him, and she whimpered as the sensations built within. Her nipples grazed his chest as she arched her back. "Please."

He groaned and pumped his pelvis back and forward, intensifying the friction, forcing her pleasure to new, impossible heights. Each thrust was deeper, harder, and faster than the one before.

A tentacle trailed along her leg, starting at her toes and sliding up to her knee before moving down again.

It started with a spark. When it ignited, it roared through her in a flash of light. Macy came with a series of cries, clenching Jax as she convulsed, and her consciousness shattered. Waves of pleasure crashed through her, powerful and potent, and she was lost in their depths, left with nothing but pure sensation. She writhed beneath him. She was no longer Macy; a wild, fiery thing had replaced her, bucking and clawing, fueled by pleasure and torn apart by it, its hunger insatiable.

Jax's growl reverberated through Macy, heightening her

climax as a new heat — *his* heat — flooded her. He pistoned his hips, slamming into her with fierce, desperate speed. A tentacle grasped each of her thighs, pulling her against him with more force.

Another orgasm ravaged her, more forceful than the last, and she screamed in rapture. Her sex quivered and clenched. She clung to Jax, drawing their bodies somehow closer as she rode it out.

Finally, they stilled, breath ragged and raw. Macy released him and eased onto the ground. She stared into his alien eyes, and her heart leapt.

He wore a faint smile, but the depth of emotion in his eyes was immense. They were filled with satisfaction, joy, possessiveness…and something more. He leaned down and kissed her.

Macy returned the kiss, brushing her fingers over his siphons and down his neck to settle on his shoulders.

She'd accepted Jax into her body, and she had no regrets.

CHAPTER FOURTEEN

Jax swam along the seafloor, matching his skin to the terrain. He kept his eyes in constant motion; it was unlikely the razorback had lingered in the coastal shallows for two days, but the attack had caught him off-guard, and that was unsettling. When it came to Macy's safety, he couldn't allow himself any degree of carelessness.

Despite his dedication to alertness, he couldn't prevent his mind from repeatedly returning to the prior day. What they'd shared had proven more fulfilling and meaningful than he could've imagined. Even thoughts of prowling razorbacks couldn't overcome his elation. He didn't know if Macy considered them *joined* in the manner of her people, but she had *chosen* him.

They were mates.

To kraken, it was an incredibly important — if fleeting — concept, a state that could change as suddenly as the tides during a storm. Because of that, he shouldn't allow himself such excitement. Shouldn't allow himself such attachment.

But Macy had said humans didn't view such relationships in the same manner. When they chose, they did so for life.

He halted and flattened himself to the bottom as he approached a potential hunting area. Each moment away from her was a new sort of suffering, a unique agony, but it was his duty to provide for her, and he'd not yet obtained tools to allow her to assist on hunts. Today, she would rest.

As he observed the nearby sea creatures, his mind conjured images from yesterday. After their joining, Macy had gone to the waterfall to wash herself; he supposed such behavior was another human oddity, one beyond his understanding. Jax had watched the water caress her bare skin. Had watched droplets roll down her breasts and gather, briefly, on the tips of her nipples before falling. He'd watched rivulets run to the hair between her legs, and lower. It had been no surprise when his willpower failed.

Jax had joined her, and soon their closeness led to touching, then kissing, and finally to another joining. They'd eaten afterward, and laid side-by-side as the stars eventually came out. Their quiet conversation had continued until well after the moons passed across the cave's opening.

When he'd woken at dawn, he was still on land, with Macy enveloped in his arms and tentacles.

Now, he watched spinefish glide by with their long, flat tails, watched armored grayfish sink down into the sand to bury themselves with flapping fins, likely digging nests for their eggs. Silver, reflective fish drifted over the seagrass, using the light bouncing off their scales to attract smaller creatures. Schools of brightly colored fish with oversized, flowing fins swam by with irregular rhythms; their slow, nonchalant pace broken by seemingly random bursts of speed. A few hard-shells — Macy called them *lobsters* — trundled along the bottom, long feelers sweeping in front of them.

Jax crept closer. Most of these creatures did not stray far from the cover of rocks, coral, and seagrass; open water left them vulnerable. They wouldn't come to him.

Though he wouldn't dismiss an opportunity for any significant catch, his attention returned to the spinefish. Most of them were large enough, individually, that one would provide a satisfying meal for Jax and Macy both — especially since she had plants to eat with the meat.

Movement farther out caught his eye; a dark shape approached the area from the relative gloom that always lingered in the distance underwater.

No matter how well you can see, the old hunters had said, *the sea never reveals everything.*

As the dark shape drew nearer, he recognized it for a kraken — its tentacles flared and flattened, flared and flattened. Jax would recognize that uniquely graceful manner of swimming anywhere; Arkon glided along with seemingly little effort, tentacles always extending to straight lines whether they were trailing behind him or splayed in all directions.

Arkon drifted, turning his head from side to side as he searched the environment. He was clearly alone — when hunting parties traveled, they stayed close together, spreading out only enough not to hinder one another's movement. They were less likely to be attacked in a group, and that closeness meant no one was completely undefended.

Why was Arkon this far from the Facility by himself?

Jax pushed up from the bottom, rising to Arkon's level, and flashed orange over his skin.

Arkon spotted him and matched Jax's brief coloration, but sent a pulse of green through it. He was agitated by something. Slowing, Arkon moved his hands and front tentacles in a series of gestures.

Need to speak. Surface.

Signaling his understanding, Jax scanned his surroundings for a final time and swam toward the glittering reflections that marked the barrier between water and air. They'd be totally exposed up there; Arkon would not take such a risk lightly.

Jax emerged first, and Arkon broke the surface a moment later.

"We must be quick. There was a razorback hunting these waters two days ago," Jax said.

"You have been absent eleven days, Jax. I did not expect to find you so close after such a time. In fact, I hoped I would not find you at all." Arkon's pupils shrank to slits in the morning sunlight.

Of all the things Jax might've expected Arkon to say, he couldn't have guessed anything close to those words. That was Arkon — he had his habits, his *obsessions*, as he'd say, but once he broke from them, he was entirely unpredictable.

"You hoped for my death, then?"

Arkon shook his head, brow falling. "Your brain must have been addled. Dracchus claimed you have returned at least once to the Facility since you and I last spoke, and that you departed immediately. When I called him a liar, he simply restated in his claim — without taking offense. I feared he was being truthful. I knew if I came looking for you, and couldn't locate you, Dracchus was speaking false."

"You came out here because of something Dracchus said? You've never much cared about what he thought one way or the other, Arkon."

"And you, Jax, know of his persistence better than anyone. He must have demanded I tell him your whereabouts a dozen times, and insisted that your behavior when he encountered you was suspicious."

"I've returned twice, Arkon."

"And departed immediately both times?" Arkon blew air out of his siphons.

"Yes. I was retrieving old human devices."

"For your collection?"

Jax clenched his jaw. He'd avoided Arkon because he didn't want to lie to him. The trust they had in one another was strong, deep, unshakeable. Jax had never intended to endanger it, but he'd done so by deciding to withhold the truth. And even now, after everything, how much could he bring himself to say? If any kraken would understand — if any could accept what Jax was doing — it was Arkon.

He'd told Macy once that he couldn't give her much information because he needed to protect the other kraken. This was no different; the choice was not Jax's alone. She had a part in it. She'd be affected by it.

"In a way, yes."

Narrowing his eyes, Arkon swam closer. "You have never been one to speak cryptically. What is it you are hiding, Jax?"

Jax's stomach churned. Of course, Arkon would be suspicious; little escaped his notice. "I cannot explain it to you. Not yet."

"Why?"

"Because…it is better understood if I show you, Arkon, and showing you is not my choice to make."

Arkon held Jax's gaze. They floated in silence for many heartbeats.

"Is it worth the trouble you are stirring up?" Arkon finally asked.

"What trouble?"

"Dracchus. He distrusts you, and in this instance, I cannot blame him. You've given him good reason. You declined a hunt, Jax? For all your wandering, you've never once done that, and Dracchus knows it well."

"As I have said before, to the abyss with Dracchus."

The corner of Arkon's mouth lifted in a half-smile. "I do not believe there is a hole big enough to swallow him."

Jax couldn't help his own smile. "And if there was, he'd likely want to fight it."

Arkon's expression brightened with humor briefly before reverting to its prior seriousness. "I don't think he will back down this time. He's wanted to prove himself against you since we were young, Jax, and for some reason, your recent behavior has pushed him to new levels."

"I have deferred leadership of most hunts to him. I do not challenge him publicly, I do not attempt to sway the others in any way. What reason have I given him?" Jax's hearts thumped, and anger poured heat into his veins.

"Dracchus's concerns are...foreign to me, in many ways," Arkon said, dropping his gaze, "and I cannot pretend to understand him any more than I can pretend to truly understand you. If I were to venture a guess, it would be an oversimplification, and that would avail us nothing."

"It does not matter. I will deal with him when I must." Part of Jax was tempted to return to the Facility now and issue a challenge to Dracchus. If Dracchus suffered another defeat against Jax, he would settle for a time, but it would never stop. Not until one of them was dead.

"That is what I am trying to explain, Jax. This time, it may well be more than you can deal with, if you leave it for too long. He has made no attempt to keep his opinions to himself. For all the respect they have for your abilities, you are no more normal to the others than I am. If Dracchus convinces them of your betrayal, the truth will make little difference."

Jax tilted his head back and stared, unseeing, toward the soothing blue of the cloudless sky. Even as part of him wanted the fight, the rest of him — stronger by far — wanted nothing more than to return to Macy and never concern himself with these affairs again. He knew, had the situation involved anyone other than Jax, Arkon would have paid it no mind; he held no interest in social struggles.

Could Jax live without seeing the Facility again?

His immediate answer was *yes*. He wasn't sure how to feel about his lack of shame for it.

"For now, I will not worry about Dracchus or the rest of

them." Jax returned his attention to Arkon. "I have betrayed your trust, and for that I am sorry. If you take the chance of trusting me one more time, I ask ten days of you. On the tenth morning, I will meet you at the Broken Cavern, and I will reveal the secret I have kept."

Arkon searched Jax's face and, after a short while, nodded. "You have my trust, Jax, as always. Ten days. But please…do not ignore the situation with Dracchus. It will grow worse the longer it is disregarded."

"Warn the others of the razorback. May the stones fall as you would have them lie, Arkon."

"And the currents carry you where you would go, Jax."

"You're quieter than normal." Macy slipped a piece of fish into her mouth.

Jax picked at his food with the tips of two claws; he'd eaten little, thus far.

She had woken to find him gone, but it couldn't have been more than twenty minutes later when he emerged from the tunnel with a meter-long spinefish dangling from an extended tentacle.

Macy set her food down and crawled toward him. She brushed her fingers over his tentacle before settling her hand over his. "Jax?"

His eyes fell to her hand. "I have something to ask of you," he finally said, "but the choice is yours."

Something in his voice — his uncertainty, perhaps — made her heart skip and her stomach clench. She was used to him lapsing into companionable silence from time to time, but this…she'd never seen him so withdrawn, so…*off*.

Was he…was he going to send her away? Send her back home?

The thought stung. She hadn't realized how much it would hurt...but she hadn't expected to care for him so deeply, either.

Jax lifted his gaze. "Why do you appear so troubled, Macy?"

She drew away. "Are you...are you giving me up?"

"What do you mean?" He tilted his head, brow creased.

"Are you giving me the choice to go home?"

He slid his tentacles toward her, wrapped them around her back, and pulled her close. Raising his hands, he cupped her cheeks. "Why would you think that?"

Macy put her hands on his shoulders and searched his face. In it, she saw sincerity, desire, confusion. "You're not acting like yourself, Jax. So, when you said you had something to ask me, that it would be my choice, I just thought..." She licked her lips and inhaled deeply. "You're not letting me go, then?"

"I don't ever want to." He smoothed back her hair, and his thumb brushed over her ear. "I am sorry that I've not behaved like myself this morning. My thoughts have been...burdened."

All the fear and panic that had welled inside her vanished, leaving a vast space to fill with concern. She settled a hand over his and pressed her cheek into his palm. "What's wrong?"

"Arkon came searching for me this morning. He was troubled...in part because I betrayed his trust."

"How so?"

"I have avoided him the last few times I went home because I did not want to lie to him."

Macy frowned. "What would you have lied to him about?"

The tip of his thumb claw lightly grazed her cheek. "You."

"Me? Why would I— You don't want him to know about me."

"I don't want any of them to know about you."

To keep his people safe, he'd refused to tell her much about their home. To keep Macy safe, he'd hidden her from the kraken.

"What…what would they do if they did?" She pressed her palms to his chest.

"I…do not know, Macy. They are all aware of the history between our people. How that would affect their reactions, I cannot guess. If they came to know you, I do not think any would wish you harm."

"You didn't harm me, even before you knew me."

There was a sorrow in his smile that she'd not seen before. "I am not like most of them."

She nodded and took his hands in hers, settling them on her lap. "And Arkon?"

"He would not hurt you."

"You said this is only part of the problem. What's the rest?"

"I have raised the suspicions of another kraken, and he seems determined to convince our people that I have betrayed them."

"Betrayed them how? Because of your absence? That's normal for you, isn't it?"

"When I went back to find your suit, Dracchus confronted me. He had declared a hunt. I refused, which I have never done. I have missed hunts during my wanderings, but I have never refused one while I was present. Our people rely on the hunters to bring in enough meat to keep them fed, especially those who are unable to go out on their own."

How could she not feel responsible for that? He'd gone back because of her, and had refused because of her.

"Is that all it takes? You refuse a single hunt, and it means you're working against them?

He squeezed her hands gently. "In your home, you grow food for your people, and you have men who hunt on land and sea to bring home meat, don't you?"

"Yes, but if someone doesn't work for a day, it doesn't mean they're betraying us."

"Because you have plenty already. For kraken, there is *only* the hunt. It is our survival. There is nothing more important, except protecting females and younglings."

"What will they do?"

"I cannot say." One of his tentacles brushed up and down her back slowly. "But it makes little difference to me. My place has never truly been there."

The melancholy in his voice was undercut by a strange confidence. She didn't know how to respond to him, didn't understand how he felt about it; he likely didn't understand, himself.

"What was it you wanted to ask me, Jax?"

"I have betrayed your trust, as well, Macy." His jaw muscles ticked. "I told Arkon I would show him what I have been hiding in ten days. It was not right for me to speak for you, to take your choice, so know that you do not have to agree. You don't have to come with me and meet him."

Withdrawing a hand from his, she traced the dark stripes on his head and pressed a kiss to his lips. "You trust him, and I trust you. I'd like to meet your friend."

Jax leaned his forehead against hers and slipped his arms around her. "You are certain?"

"Yes." Macy smiled and rubbed her nose against his face. "It will set your mind at ease, and maybe his... Well, maybe not so much his."

"I think he will be more...curious, than anything."

She chuckled. "I remember someone else being curious."

"I still am." The tip of a tentacle slipped between her thighs and the hem of her long shirt.

His touch sent a thrill through her. Her sex clenched, and she rose to her knees, bracing her hands on his chest and parting her thighs. He settled his hands on her hips.

"What is it you're still curious about?" she asked.

"I want to know every little piece of you, and learn how you respond when I touch each one."

"So touch me, Jax," she begged. His words made her ache for more.

He bunched her shirt in his hands and drew it over her head. She returned her hands to his broad chest, and he cupped her breasts, caressed them, teased their hardened tips.

Macy arched into his palms with a sigh.

When the tentacle between Macy's thighs stroked her slit, she gasped and parted her legs further. The tip of his limb slid along her slick folds. She closed her eyes and let her head fall back, surrendering to his ministrations. She rocked against him, jolts of pleasure sweeping through her as he moved his suction cups, one at a time, over her clit.

She came quickly. He took hold of her hips, forcing her to ride out the waves. Liquid heat flooded her core and flowed from her, coating his tentacle and her thighs. Before she'd recovered, he lifted her and pressed the tip of his jutting erection to her sex, lowering her onto him with deliberate slowness. Her inner muscles quivered, drawing him deeper.

Jax slid his hands to her legs, guiding them to encircle his hips, and she locked her arms around his neck.

Breath ragged, she opened her eyes.

The two of them remained still, their bodies intertwined, and Macy felt the beat of his pulse echoing through her. She'd never felt so close to anyone in her life; her bond with Jax transcended physicality, extending into her heart, her *soul*.

She hugged him closer, kissed him, rose and fell to take him fully into her body. His tentacles ran up her back and curled over her shoulders as he broke the kiss and pressed his lips to her neck.

"Macy," he rasped, moving in time with her, his thrusts pushing deeper and deeper.

Macy closed her eyes and tilted her head back. "Love me, Jax."

He growled and returned his hands to her hips, lifting her up and slamming her down on his shaft. She took him to his base, and his feelers writhed, flicking along her folds and over her clit. All the while, his lips trailed heat over her face and neck.

She lost herself in a whirlwind of sensation and pleasure, in Jax's scent, feel, and intensity. Short breaths escaped her with his thrusts, each one striking a cord within her that pushed her higher and higher until she finally erupted.

She came with a cry, clawing at his back with her nails.

Jax roared as her sex clamped on his shaft, and his body shook with the force of his climax. His heat flooded her. She rode him until neither of them had anything left to give.

He held her when she sagged against him, as they both caught their breath, and continued to place gentle kisses on her skin.

Macy smiled and rubbed her cheek against his shoulder. She was on the verge of dozing when he spoke softly.

"Always, Macy."

CHAPTER FIFTEEN

THE WATER WAS STILL DIM WHEN JAX AND MACY LEFT THE CAVE; the sun had only just begun cresting, and the gray-blue sky bled first to pink, then to golden as it approached the horizon. They held hands as they swam. Though it slowed their pace, it was a comfort to them both. They hadn't seen the razorback during their excursions over the last several days, but Jax would never forget how close they'd come to tragedy.

He was reluctant to allow Macy beyond his reach.

Jax kept close to the coastal cliffs as they moved; the rocks had been their salvation when the razorback attacked, and he'd not risk another chase to reach cover.

They saw a variety of fish on the way — grayfish, spinefish, gulpers, and dozens more Jax had no name for — but it was the basketmouths that caught Macy's attention. Longer than razor-backs, the basketmouths glided near the surface, their long, flat bodies flowing behind him as they held their wide mouths open. Despite their size, their only prey were creatures so tiny they were nearly invisible.

Finally, they reached the Broken Cavern. It had been years since Jax's last visit, and he'd forgotten the strangeness of the place. When he'd first found it, he'd thought — in his inexperience — that it was a natural cave, somehow overlooking the perfectly shaped planes of the walls and floor. It seemed, from outside, to be part of the cliff face.

He knew now that it had been built by humans.

Macy's eyes were wide as she looked from side to side. The floor was flat and deep — as deep as seven or eight kraken, stretched end-to-end — and the walls extended over the water level. It was dark inside, and as they left the last of the meager daylight behind, Jax cast his own glow.

Smiling, Macy moved her gaze over him appreciatively, just as she had two nights before when they joined beneath the starry sky. Though this was neither the time nor the place, his blood heated with arousal.

When they were far enough inside to see the huge chunks of crumbled stone on the bottom, he brought Macy to the surface, blinked the water from his eyes, and swept his gaze about.

The Broken Cavern was the largest cave he'd ever found; the ceiling was so high that it was lost in darkness, but a huge crack allowed the still-gray morning light to filter through it. At some point in its existence, the roof had broken open, dumping stone into the water.

To either side, the walls jutted a body's length over the surface, like perfectly flat, symmetrical cliffs. Two metal bridges spanned one side to the other. The center of one of the bridges was missing, its edges twisted and bent. Massive chains hung from thick posts set into the tops of the walls.

"All this time, we never knew... How do we not know about these places in The Watch?" Macy's voice, though soft, echoed off the walls.

"I cannot say, Macy. All of this was made many years ago, and the people who walked here are long dead."

They swam to one of the ladders set into the wall. Jax

allowed Macy to climb the metal rungs first and hauled himself up behind her. The metal groaned under his weight.

Macy stood on the stone walkway, mask in hand and head tilted back as she surveyed the huge chamber. She stepped to the second wall, leaning forward to examine the fading, flaked paint upon it, and pulled back her hood.

The painting had been the only reason Arkon agreed to come here after Jax discovered it years ago. It was in slightly worse condition, now, but the basic shapes were still clear — stretching from one end of the wall to the other, it depicted humans of various shapes and sizes. Time had largely obscured their features, but their joy was apparent. Arkon had said someone created the image by hand in the ancient days.

Jax had always harbored doubts about that… Before meeting Macy, at least.

"This is amazing. What was it used for?" She turned and walked to one of the posts, running her hand over one of the huge chain links.

Jax moved closer to her, glancing up at the broken ceiling. When was the last time a piece had fallen?

"I don't know, Macy."

"This stuff is almost like mooring…but I've never seen ships big enough for this."

"There are some, on the seafloor," he replied distractedly. "You should move back for now, out of sight. Until Arkon has come."

Macy met his gaze. "Okay. You're…*sure?*"

Jax nodded and gestured to the steps cut out in the wall behind them; they led up to the next level, from which the bridges connected the two sides.

Macy climbed the steps and settled herself as far back as she could, leaning against the wall. She placed her mask beside her and folded her hands in her lap.

Positioning himself between Macy and the ladder, Jax

crossed his arms over his chest and rested his elbow on a nearby post. An unfamiliar, restless energy flowed through him; he willed his limbs to still.

He was so unused to the feeling that he didn't immediately recognize it: *nervousness*.

Soon, he heard movement in the water and shifted his attention toward it.

Arkon's glow was unmistakable as he swam to the ladder. He climbed swiftly, stopped atop the walkway, and looked at the faded painting. "It has been a long while since I came here."

"I know. This place is fitting, though."

Meeting Jax's gaze, Arkon frowned. "No more vagueness, Jax. It doesn't suit you. What do you wish to show me?"

Jax turned to the painting. The people it depicted wore clothing that looked nothing like Macy's, and many of them had different coloring and features, but they were all clearly human. Her people, for better or worse, had made this place, had made the Facility, had made the kraken.

"A human," Jax finally said.

"Your attempts at humor are strange, Jax."

"I'm not being humorous. I've been away for so long because I rescued a human female from the sea during the last storm and have been living with her since."

"This…" It wasn't often Arkon was speechless; Jax couldn't help feeling a pang of satisfaction at it, despite his nervousness. "Have you gone mad, Jax? You…you're serious?"

Jax twisted to look behind. "Macy, please come and meet Arkon."

Her footfalls were quiet as she stepped into the open. She looked into Jax's eyes before she turned toward Arkon, smiled, and raised her hand in greeting. "Hello, Arkon."

Features slack, Arkon looked from Macy to Jax. A tiny crease appeared in the center of his brow. "You have a human," he said, flatly.

"Her name is Macy."

"Macy." Arkon tilted his head and parted his lips as though to speak, but it was several moments before he produced a sound. "My apologies if I'm… You must understand, this…this is…"

She laughed; the sound was amplified by the cave, but was no less beautiful for it. She stopped beside Jax. "I understand very well."

"Of course. Typically, I'm somewhat more articulate. Jax has a reputation for pushing into the unknown, but this is unprecedented, even for him." Arkon moved a little closer. "You're wearing one of the suits from the Pool Room."

Macy settled a hand over her stomach. "Jax gave it to me."

"What function does it fulfill? I've been curious about those suits for a long while."

"It goes with the mask," she gestured behind her, though the mask was out of sight, "and together they protect me underwater. Otherwise, I can't be under for more than about thirty seconds, and anything below a certain depth could kill me."

"So humans *can't* survive underwater…"

"Apparently not," Jax said.

"You're a different color than Jax."

"Yes." Arkon spread his arms to the sides and glanced down at himself. "Most of us are, even if variations are only slight. Is it not the same for your kind?"

"It is," Macy replied. "My friend Aymee is tanner than me, and her hair is brown. Some humans have lighter or darker skin, and different colored eyes and hair. I guess it's just not something I think about much because it's normal to me. The colors I see on you and Jax are different…and we don't *change* colors, either."

"They do," Jax corrected, "but it is much subtler, and they cannot control it."

Arkon moved closer still, stopping immediately in front of Macy.

Jax tensed for a moment. His instinct was to protect, but he trusted his friend.

Lifting a hand, Arkon brushed his fingertips over Macy's hair. Jax recalled his own curiosity and fascination all too well; neither had truly diminished, but it didn't make it easier to watch another male touch her.

Arkon's nostrils flared, and he met Jax's gaze. "Your scent…"

Jaw clenched, Jax nodded. He hadn't anticipated this reaction in himself, couldn't have guessed he'd feel this way, but there was no denying it. Macy was *his*, and he wasn't comfortable with *anyone* touching her.

Arkon dropped his hand and backed away. "You mated with a human?" His expression was too conflicted to decipher.

Jax waited for a flash of shame, for the sense that he'd betrayed his people, the guilt of committing an unspeakable wrong. All he felt was contentment. What shame was there in what he and Macy had shared?

"Um…he can *smell* that?" Macy rubbed her reddened cheeks. "Of course he can," she muttered.

"This…" Arkon's eyes darted between Jax and Macy. "This is *amazing*. Everything…everything worked? It all fit together?"

"Wha…? Oh god." Macy hid behind Jax.

"Arkon," Jax growled, baring his teeth.

"Take no offense, please. This is simply fascinating."

"I'm not offended," Macy said. "It's just… People don't usually talk about that so openly. But, um, yes. We…fit."

Jax glanced at her over his shoulder, brow low. "If you answer him, it will only encourage him to ask more."

"My silence didn't deter you."

"So you are willing to answer questions that make you uncomfortable?" Jax asked. When she nodded, he moved away, allowing Macy and Arkon full view of one another, and leaned against the wall. "Consider yourself warned."

Arkon grinned. "Jax, what—"

"*She* has agreed to answer your questions, Arkon. Not me."

"*Some* of them," Macy said.

A thousand questions flitted across Arkon's face, but he gave voice to none of them immediately. The tips of his tentacles writhed ceaselessly on the floor. Jax had rarely seen him so excited.

After a long hesitation, Arkon turned to the wall and swept his eyes over the painting. "How did your people create *this*?"

"With paint and brushes. Something that size, with that much detail, would've taken a long time to finish."

"But...how?" Arkon reached forward, trailing a fingertip over the paint. "When you look at it in little pieces, it's a mess. A jumble of uneven colors, lacking precision. But when you step back, it somehow comes together to make something...*real*."

Macy tilted her head and smiled. "You almost sound like Aymee. She sees more detail in everything than I ever could, especially when she paints."

"You know someone who can do *this*?"

"Yeah. She could probably even teach you." Macy's smile faltered. "She's back in The Watch, though."

Jax didn't miss the sorrow on Macy's face, or the way her shoulders drooped. She'd given up everything she'd known for him. This was another reminder that her old life was over, that she'd never see the people she cared about again.

Something splashed in the water below.

"I wish I could—" Confusion halted Macy's words and creased her brow. She glanced down; a pair of black tentacles were wrapped around her ankles.

Alarm burst through Jax, but before he could move, Macy's feet were yanked out from beneath her.

Her scream was cut off when her body slammed into the walkway. She clawed at the ground as she was dragged toward the water. Her desperate, terrified eyes found Jax just before she disappeared over the edge.

She called his name, but a loud splash swallowed her voice.

Jax darted forward and leapt off the walkway. He landed in churning water. Bubbles obscured his vision as Macy struggled against her attacker, granting Jax only glimpses of her golden hair and the black skin of a kraken.

Dracchus.

Chest burning with rage, Jax charged into the writhing tentacles.

Macy kicked and thrashed as her captor attempted to subdue her. Jax forced his tentacles between them and sank his claws into Dracchus's limbs, tinting the water red with blood. Arkon entered the fray a moment later, attacking Dracchus from behind, and together they pried Macy away from his grip.

Skin crimson, Dracchus shifted his effort to Jax.

To the surface, Jax signed to Arkon, thrusting Macy toward him.

Arkon hurried away with her.

Dracchus wound a tentacle around Jax's throat, dragging him back into the fight.

Rather than pull away, Jax pushed himself toward Dracchus, slamming into him. Their limbs became a tangled mess, tentacles coiling and grabbing, claws slashing, each vying for the advantage. Dracchus sliced open Jax's cheek; Jax retaliated by jabbing his claws into Dracchus's ribs.

Jax couldn't see much, between the dim light and flowing blood, but it didn't matter. Dracchus wouldn't back down; he was everywhere, exerting his superior strength, crushing and tearing. Jax didn't try to overpower his foe. He moved *with* his foe's effort, twisting and redirecting momentum, attacking through every opening left by the larger kraken.

In Jax's rage, the pain of his wounds was distant. Years of rivalry and challenge made no difference now — Dracchus had laid hands on Jax's mate, might well have done her harm, might have *killed* her. This wasn't about who was the strongest, or who was best suited to lead. Their people were not here to witness this battle.

Thick tentacles wrapped around Jax's abdomen and dragged him close. Before he could escape, Dracchus clamped his hands over Jax's throat, cutting off the path of his siphons. Jax buried his claws in his opponent's forearms, but Dracchus didn't relent.

Jax clenched his teeth. He would not allow Dracchus to touch Macy again. Would not allow her to come to further harm. He needed, more than anything, to get back to her. To know she was safe.

He dropped his hands to the tentacles encircling his waist as the edges of his vision darkened.

If Dracchus meant to have his victory today, there would be a steep price.

MACY BROKE into a coughing fit the instant her head broke the surface. She hacked up water, her nose and throat on fire. Once her coughing subsided enough, she took in a ragged, burning lungful of air. Her vision — which had been failing due to lack of oxygen — cleared slowly.

The strong arms holding her were not Jax's.

She called his name, searching for him, but she couldn't see him in the thrashing water. She only knew he was fighting, and that she was being moved away from him.

"I have you, Macy," Arkon said. "Please calm down."

"Where's Jax?" She tried to turn in Arkon's arms, but he held her tight.

"Jax has faced worse. His concern is for you, now."

Macy gulped air desperately as Arkon swam to the wall. He removed an arm from her without loosening his hold and pulled himself up the ladder with seemingly little effort. Only when they were on solid ground did he release her.

Ignoring the trembling in her limbs, the ache in her chest,

and the sting in her nose and throat, she crawled to the edge and stared down into the water.

Where is he? Where is Jax?

Arkon sank down beside her. "Are you all right, Macy?"

"I'm fine."

The water darkened with a huge, fresh cloud of blood, and Macy's heart seized.

"Jax!" she cried.

Before she could dive in, Arkon wrapped his arms around her waist. She latched onto the edge and pulled against his hold; he grunted with exertion, but she couldn't break free.

"There's nothing you can do for him right now, Macy!"

Macy turned her tear-filled eyes upon him. "So why aren't you helping him? He's your friend!"

His brow furrowed, and he shifted his head back. "What is wrong with your—" He shook his head. "Do you promise to remain here?"

"Yes! Yes! Please, just help him!"

Arkon's eyes lingered on her for another second, and then he released her and dove off the edge.

The water was still now, save for the slowly dispersing blood.

Macy blinked away her tears as they blurred her vision, praying for some sign of Jax. She bit her lips to hold in a cry of distress.

The water stirred. She clutched the stone hard enough to hurt her fingers.

Arkon surfaced first, facing away from her. Dracchus's black head came up next. Fresh cuts glistened on the side of his face in the weak light streaming through the broken ceiling. Macy's breath caught in her throat.

As more of Dracchus emerged, she realized there was a gray arm wrapped around his neck. Jax surfaced behind Dracchus, his other arm looped beneath one of the larger kraken's armpits, and he'd grasped his own wrist to lock the hold.

He wasn't dead.

Relief urged moisture down Macy's cheeks. Her heart slowed to its normal pace, and the fear that had gripped it eased. It took everything in her to remain still; she'd given her word to Arkon.

Jax swam backward, dragging his captive toward the ladder. Somehow, between himself and Arkon, they managed to drag the large kraken up onto the walkway, though Dracchus seemed to put up no resistance.

Without releasing his hold, Jax turned toward Macy.

Arkon hurried to her side and offered her a hand. She took it and pulled herself up onto shaky legs. Arkon imposed himself partially in front of her.

"You have truly betrayed us, Wanderer," Dracchus said. His voice was deeper than Jax's, rougher.

"I have done no such thing," Jax replied. "But you have attacked someone I care for. Should I kill you now, after you almost killed her?"

"I was not going to kill her." Dracchus's amber eyes were fixed on Macy. His expression was hard, betraying none of the pain he must have felt, given his numerous open wounds.

Macy ran her eyes over him. He was bigger than Jax, broader, perhaps slightly taller. Blood oozed from cuts and punctures all over his body, and one of his tentacles lay limp on the floor, sporting a gash so large and deep that it had nearly been severed.

What wounds had Jax taken? There were slash marks on his cheek, scratches on his arms and tentacles, but the rest of his body was hidden behind his captive.

"You dragged her into the water," Jax said.

"And? She came here by sea."

She couldn't tell if it was just the last shred of pride playing on Dracchus's features or his hatred for her.

"Humans cannot breathe underwater." Jax's tentacles coiled tighter.

"Then they should stay away from the water." Dracchus's jaw muscles bulged, but he didn't look away from Macy.

Arkon shifted, breaking her eye contact with Dracchus, and frowned over his shoulder.

"She has as much right to it as any of us," Jax said, "but *you* have no right to touch her."

"And what right do you have to forsake your people for a human, Wanderer?"

"He didn't," Macy said.

"What reason would I have to take the word of a human? The Wanderer has refused to hunt, so he has forsaken our survival."

"One refused hunt is *not* a betrayal." She placed a hand on Arkon's arm and peered around him.

"Humans must be foolish, to believe such. Without food, the kraken will die, and no hunter is more skilled than Jax the Wanderer." Dracchus bared his teeth as he spoke. A few of them were smeared with crimson.

"And I have *always* given, despite what you and all the rest think of me," Jax growled, tugging back on Dracchus's neck. "I have taken for myself, for once, and it is immediately a betrayal?"

Dracchus grimaced. "What have you told her? Have you already betrayed our home? Our younglings?"

"Jax has told me nothing to endanger your people or your home," Macy said.

"He has mated with you; you wear each other's scents. What will come of that? When humans come to seek revenge for the past, will Jax say he did not mean for it to come to such?"

Macy stepped around Arkon, shrugging off his restraining hand, and approached Dracchus. "I never knew of your existence, not until Jax saved me. No one knows. Jax has refused to let me go back, despite his guilt, because he cannot — and will not — betray you. And I *chose* to stay with him." She met Jax's eyes for a moment.

Silence settled over the chamber as Dracchus stared down at her.

"It may not mean anything to you," Macy continued, "but as much as he cares for your people, he also took responsibility for me. He knows I can't survive without him, just like you say the kraken cannot survive without hunters, and he has selflessly provided for me. He didn't have to save me. He didn't have to keep his word to me. But he has…he's protected me, just like he's continued to protect the kraken. With honor."

Dracchus narrowed his eyes, flared his nostrils, and clenched his jaw. He leaned his head back, finally breaking eye contact with her.

"You speak true. The Wanderer keeps his word…but he has also chosen to mate something *other*. A human. It is unnatural."

Macy refused to react to the disgust in his voice, refused to be ashamed for what she and Jax shared.

Jax moved suddenly, swinging Dracchus around and slamming him face-first into the wall. His tentacles wrapped around Dracchus's arms, pulling them back, as he pressed his forearm against the back of his captive's head.

"You will not speak of her in that way again," Jax growled.

Dracchus's cheek was on the stone, his expression a blend of anger, pain, and stubbornness.

Macy touched Jax's shoulder. "Don't."

"It is less than he deserves, Macy."

"Didn't you think the same of me, in the beginning?"

Jax turned his head toward her, frowning. The fury on his face faded.

She ran her hand down his back, careful to avoid his wounds. "You've been taught to hate humans your entire life. It's not something you can stop immediately, and no amount of punishment will change that."

"You would have died, Macy." His voice was low, raw, desperate.

Macy glanced at Dracchus. "I...I don't believe he meant to hurt me. At least to that extent. You didn't know humans could drown either."

Jax's posture was tense with conflict, and Macy couldn't guess what he meant to do, couldn't guess at what he'd choose. She had no doubt that he'd kill Dracchus if he deemed it necessary.

"What was your intent toward her, Dracchus?" he finally asked.

"To bring her before our people. As proof of your treachery, and as a warning that we must remain aware of the humans nearby."

"She will not be brought to the kraken for judgment," Jax said.

"As I said, Wanderer, you have bested me. I will not defy your will in this. But I will not keep it from our people, either."

"They will demand an explanation from you, Jax," Arkon said.

"They will demand justice." The intensity in Dracchus's eyes was unwavering. "Whether she is a threat on her own or not, her people have always been a danger to us. Our people deserve to know."

"I will *not* bring her before them. They have no say in my choice, no say in her life!" Jax snarled.

"I'll go," Macy said, despite her fear. Jax and Arkon hadn't hurt her, and while Dracchus hadn't necessarily been gentle, he'd not meant her true harm. If he'd wanted her dead, she wouldn't have survived her sudden trip into the water. She had to believe the other kraken would act the same.

The chamber was silent, and the gazes of all three kraken weighed heavily upon her.

"You're not going," Jax finally said.

"There is enough strain between you and your people. You don't need this. You don't…don't need to keep me secret."

"I do not know what they will do, Macy. I cannot protect you against all of them."

"It…doesn't matter. What would happen if you didn't bring me? Would you be hunted, banished, imprisoned? I need to go to them, Jax, and…we'll figure out what to do from there."

"No. I do not need that place. Do not need them. I will face the consequences, but I will not bring you directly into danger."

Macy stepped closer and cupped Jax's cheeks. "I'm going."

"Do not dishonor her courage, Wanderer," Dracchus said. "I cannot work against the will of our people, but I give you my word that I will help protect her from unjust harm."

Jax clenched his jaw, teeth bared, and searched Macy's face. A faint tremor ran through his limbs. With a grunt, he released Dracchus.

"Whatever may come, Jax, I am beside you," Arkon said.

Dracchus pushed away from the wall and rolled his neck and shoulders.

Jax turned to face Macy, settling his hands on her upper arms; his grip was just a bit too tight. "You are certain of this?"

Macy nodded, flattened her palms against his chest, and leaned forward to kiss his lips. "I am."

His frown didn't fade. He drew her into his arms, holding her head against his shoulder, and wrapped a pair of tentacles around her waist. Macy returned his embrace.

"We are not beholden to them," he rasped.

"But they are your people, and they are all you have."

"You gave up your people."

Macy glanced at Arkon and Dracchus; the two stood silently, watching. Lifting her head, she looked up at Jax. "I have you."

Tortured emotions played across his face; pain, sorrow, confusion, guilt. "I will do everything to keep you safe."

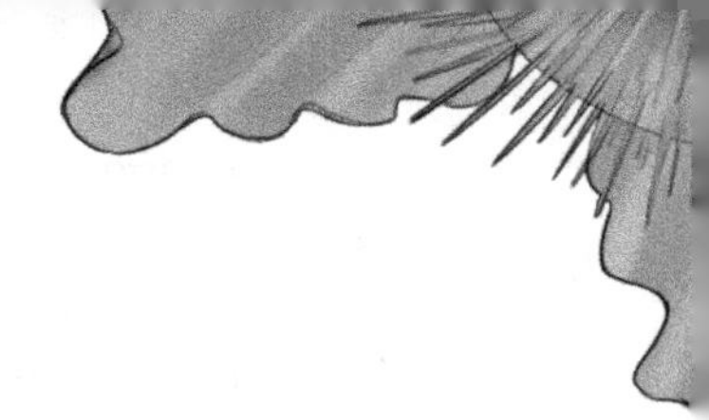

CHAPTER SIXTEEN

The kraken surrounded Macy as they swam, with Dracchus
— seemingly on high alert — in the lead. Their eyes moved
ceaselessly, undoubtedly scanning the water for signs of razorbacks and other predators. Macy's attention was torn between
the scenery, the sea life, and the kraken themselves.

Dracchus looked back only rarely, but Arkon and Jax seemed
to glance at one another often; each time, they made strange
gestures with their hands and tentacles, and a variety of colors
flashed over their skin. They had an entire language without
words! Dracchus took part, too, though he seemed to have
comparatively little to say.

They continued away from shore. Jax had never taken Macy
in this direction, and never quite so far. Gradually, they
descended, and the sunlight shining through the surface grew
more distorted and faint.

The seafloor around them became relatively flat and open,
broken only by a few clusters of rock. Despite her kraken
escort, Macy couldn't help but feel exposed; would three be
enough to fight off a razorback?

Her eyes shifted to something ahead. Light. It was diffused

by the haze of distance, but there was no mistaking it — there was light on the bottom of the sea.

It grew more distinct as they neared, and the dark shape behind it slowly took form. Macy's jaw hung agape. She'd thought the place they'd just been was a lost wonder; this surpassed anything she could have imagined.

They were swimming directly toward a huge building — *several* buildings — all constructed on the seafloor. White lights shone at intervals along the exterior walls, bathing the surrounding terrain in their glow. Dracchus led them to a large door and halted, turning to face the others.

The kraken ran through another series of gestures and color-changes. Even if Macy had known what it all meant, she wasn't sure she could've kept up with it — they signaled with speed and ease, and had probably been doing so their entire lives.

Their communication ended. Dracchus swam off without a backward glance. Jax moved to the door and glanced at Macy, waving her over. She swam closer.

"Do you require entry?" Sam asked, startling her after such a long period of quiet.

"Umm...yes?"

Jax had been reaching for a keypad beside the doorframe; his hand halted when the keys flashed. A few moments later, the light over the door turned green, and the door slid open, revealing a chamber with another door inside.

Both Jax and Arkon stared at Macy in bewilderment. Their confused expressions lingered as the three of them entered the chamber, and the door closed behind them.

"Re-pressurization sequence initiated," Sam said.

The water in the room drained, gently depositing Macy on her feet. The red light over the interior door switched to green.

"Pressurization complete," said a feminine voice from somewhere overhead. "Welcome back, diver three-seven-nine."

"Sam, release the mask," Macy said. She pulled it off as soon as the seal was broken.

"That was…different," Arkon said, glancing at Jax.

"The suit?" Jax asked.

Both kraken looked at Macy expectantly.

"What?" she asked, confused. "What was supposed to happen?"

"We've always had press the buttons outside in a certain sequence to enter," Arkon said, "and I have never heard the computer say anything like that before."

"Oh. Sam asked if I required entry."

"Sam?" Arkon's brow furrowed.

"The ghost inside her suit," Jax replied.

"Those suits have hologram projectors integrated into them?" Arkon asked.

Jax drew back and stared at his friend. "If you knew they were called holograms, why do you always let me call them ghost?"

"*Ghost* is simpler. *Hologram* just earns a blank stare from most of the others here, so there's little point in using the term."

Macy smirked as Jax — now glaring at Arkon — pressed a button on the wall. The interior door slid open. The corridor beyond appeared to be constructed of metal, and the overhead lights were bright and clear, though some of the farthest flickered.

The walls and floor were covered with dried sand and crusted salt, and here and there lay pieces of withered seaweed and the empty shells of various sea creatures. Somehow, despite the mess, there was no sign of actual damage to the structure — no spots of rust or corrosion, no broken panels, no dangling wires.

Surprisingly, the air smelled fresh. She'd expected it to be stuffy, or at least smell strongly of the sea, but it was odor-free.

"I will inform the others," Arkon said.

Jax nodded. "I'll take her to the Mess."

"The mess?" Macy asked as Arkon left.

"It is a large room we use for gatherings. Usually when a hunt is forming."

"Oh." Now that they were here, her apprehension reared back and made itself known. Her awe at this place's existence, at its functionality, couldn't distract her from the uncertainty of what was to come.

Jax took her hand in his, drawing her attention to his face. "We could leave." There was an almost pleading tone in his voice. She couldn't imagine him getting any closer to begging than that.

Macy shook her head and squeezed his hand. As much as she feared what his people would think of her — and *do* to her — she needed to see this through. Not just for Jax, but for herself. She'd chosen to join his world, to become part of his life…and she'd already run away from her own home. How would she live with herself if she was responsible for his ostracization?

His chest swelled with a deep inhalation. He exhaled through his siphons and nodded. Without further word, Jax led her through the corridors, taking several turns and passing dozens of doors. There were signs on the walls in numerous places — *OPERATIONS, ADMINISTRATION, LABORATORY, INFIRMARY, RECREATION* — most accompanied by arrows pointing down the various hallways.

She followed Jax into a room with a faded plastic sign on the wall outside — *CAFETERIA*. It was spacious, the floor surprisingly clean and open. There were several folded tables standing to one side, and to the other was a counter that connected to a dark room beyond, but it was otherwise empty.

"Over here," Jax moved to the tables and slid a few aside, opening a narrow space.

Macy stepped past Jax and entered the spot he'd cleared. With the tables — each standing half a meter taller than her —

to either side and the wall behind, she felt caged-in; the feeling only worsened when he moved in front of the opening.

He must've seen something on her face, because he frowned down at her. "It is best they do not see you until it is time. After that, remain close."

"Okay."

However anxious she was, she trusted him. He wouldn't let anything happen to her.

Voices drifted to her from the corridor. Jax looked over his shoulder before turning fully, giving her his back. His wounds were easier to spot in the light; the bleeding had stopped, but the cuts and punctures on his back were an angry red. She clasped her hands together to keep from touching him.

All she could do now was wait.

As more kraken entered the Mess, Jax forced his breathing to steady and his hearts to slow. He'd always cared about the well-being of his people, and despite his strained relationship with them, he'd never had cause to distrust them.

But the other kraken had no reason to view Macy as anything other than a threat, an enemy.

Though Macy had insisted on doing this, he'd entertained thoughts of simply grabbing her and fleeing back to the cave since they'd left the Broken Cavern. There was a chance they'd be hunted, but it was the safest option. The most likely to succeed. Here, Macy and Jax were both vulnerable. Out in the open sea, however, he was unrivaled.

Arkon arrived and maneuvered through the others to approach Jax. He wore a deep frown.

"Some have already come in from the water. Dracchus will arrive soon, I think, and I doubt he'll wait to begin this affair," Arkon said.

"The sooner done with, the better," Jax muttered.

The others cast curious glances at him. Before Dracchus, Arkon, and Jax split up, they'd agreed not to tell the others the reasons for the gathering. There was no need to work the kraken into a frenzy beforehand.

"I meant what I said, earlier." Arkon moved beside Jax and turned to face the crowd.

"I know. Thank you."

By the time Dracchus entered, fifty or sixty kraken had gathered. They parted to allow him through. With his wounds — and Jax's — on full display, the others wouldn't have to guess there'd been a fight. Their only question would be who had won. Without witnesses, it was meaningless, but that wouldn't stop them from speculating.

Jax nodded to Dracchus. He hated that they were doing this, hated that Macy was here, at the mercy of his people, but if it was to be done, this was the proper manner. He could not begrudge Dracchus that.

"What is this about?" asked Ector; he was one of the few remaining elders, a hunter who'd taught Jax and younglings of a similar age.

Dracchus positioned himself a body's length away from Jax and faced the crowd. "I have called this gathering to present proof of Jax the Wanderer's treachery against our people, that we all may know his true nature." His words were measured and carefully spoken; he took a deep breath before continuing. "We have long allowed his wandering, as his skill as a hunter has brought our people great bounty, but his interest has never been with us.

"Seventeen days ago, he refused to join a hunt. He acted strange, but I could not tell what he was hiding. Today, I have discovered the truth of it, the reason that he has forsaken his people. He has chosen a human female over his own kind."

Many kraken spoke at once, their words indecipherable, but

their expressions clear. They looked between Dracchus and Jax with a mixture of anger and disbelief.

"There have been no humans since the uprising," shouted Kronus over the din. The crowd quieted.

"If any of you had listened to me," Jax said, "you would know there are humans, less than half a day's swim away."

"Why have they not come, then?"

"Because they are as ignorant of our existence as you are of theirs."

"How do you know this?" Vander asked.

"Part of Dracchus's claim is true. I have spent better than two weeks in the company of a female human." Jax's hearts pounded against his ribs, and his skin was ablaze, but he held his ground against the other kraken's outbursts.

They shouted amongst themselves, arguing whether humans were even real, whether Jax's word could be trusted. The kraken were nothing if not individuals; each had his or her own opinion on the matter and was convinced it was correct.

"Enough!" Jax yelled over their noise.

The kraken fell silent. Jax looked over his shoulder. Macy's eyes were wide, her face pale; fear was written upon her features. "I will be right beside you, Macy."

Twisting, he extended a hand to her.

She swallowed and took his hand, slowly stepping forward. Jax moved aside to allow her out of the nook.

The silence in the room was broken by several exhalations through siphons, and numerous kraken retreated reflexively.

"Though it was against my wishes, this human — Macy — insisted she face you. To show that she means no harm and that she is not an enemy to our people," Jax said.

"Humans are forever enemies to our people," Dracchus insisted.

"I'm not your enemy, Dracchus," Macy said, then looked toward the others. "I'm not an enemy to any of you."

"We should do to her as we did her ancestors!" one of the males shouted.

"She is not her ancestors, any more than we are ours." Jax moved forward and stopped in front of Macy, raking his gaze over the crowd. "She has done *nothing* to any of us. The wrongs of the past are not hers to answer for."

Kronus advanced. "She is *human*! She doesn't belong here. Not anymore. I say we throw her out to sea and let the razorbacks have her."

Macy's hands fell on Jax's back, and a tremor ran through them.

Arkon drew up on Jax's right side.

Dracchus dragged himself into place to Jax's left. "There is no cause to do her harm, Kronus."

"You made these claims against the Wanderer, and now you defend his human?" Kronus's skin darkened.

"She is not the one who has done wrong." Dracchus folded his arms across his chest and stared at Kronus.

Jax was grateful for Dracchus's defense of Macy, but he knew what those words meant — *Jax* had committed the crime. He was the one who deserved punishment.

Perhaps he did deserve it, for allowing Macy to come here.

"We cannot simply let her out," another kraken said.

"Why not let the razorbacks have her? Kronus is right; humans have no place here."

"She knows this place, now. What if she makes it back to her kind and leads them here?"

"I won't speak a word about this place, or about any of you," Macy said. "And I'm not returning to my people. My place is with Jax."

My place is with Jax.

Those words sent a wave of warmth through Jax and nearly stopped his hearts. He would have turned and pulled Macy against him, would have crushed his mouth over hers to taste her, would have reveled in all that was *her*…if not for the threat posed by the other kraken.

"We cannot trust the word of a human!" Kronus snarled, moving forward, raising himself high on his tentacles. A red undertone crept into his skin.

Jax shifted to block Kronus's view of Macy. "If you mean to challenge me, do so. But you—" he ran his gaze over the others "—*none* of you — will lay neither hand nor tentacle upon her."

Kronus thrust a clawed finger at Jax. "That *thing* does not belong here, and if we cannot risk it telling others, it needs to be killed!"

"I will kill anyone, human or kraken, who means to harm my mate*!*" Jax roared. His skin flared red as he lunged forward; Kronus fell back, fear in his eyes.

The room was utterly silent. The other kraken stared at Jax, and he met each of their gazes one at a time, unwavering.

"She is *mine*," he growled.

Ector dragged himself closer, past the stunned Kronus, and slowly looked from Jax to Macy. His demeanor was calm, his coloring neutral.

Fire flowed through Jax's veins. He would fight any of them, all of them, without a second thought.

"Dracchus is correct," Ector said, meeting Jax's eyes. "The human is not at fault here, and she has not yet proven worthy of either our scorn or our punishment. But Jax the Wanderer has forsaken his duty to his people."

Jax searched for sorrow in Ector's expression, or anger, or disappointment — for *anything*. But he couldn't read the old kraken's face.

Ector turned to the others. "If Jax has taken her as his mate, she has a place here, like any of us. As strange as it may be, we must honor his choice in that. But she cannot leave."

A confused combination of relief and resentment struck Jax with the nods and calls of assent from the other kraken. They were sparing her life and stealing her freedom in a single decision.

"Jax trusts this human, Ector," Arkon said. "Should that not be enough for us? He has always served our people selflessly, despite his wanderings."

"His judgment cannot be trusted, now that he has mated a *human*." The fear in Kronus's eyes had been overcome by disgust.

"Do we have an agreement on my terms?" Ector asked. "She stays, and is not to be harmed."

Most everyone seemed to agree. Kronus didn't look away from Jax, and didn't offer an answer. Were he not already flooded with emotion, Jax would've been amused at himself; he'd thought Dracchus would prove the biggest obstacle.

Kronus turned and left. Several other kraken — all males — followed.

Ector twisted back to look at Jax. "She is not our enemy. Unless she leaves."

Jax clenched his jaw, grinding his teeth together, and held any response he might have given. Ector had diffused a situation that may well have ended in bloodshed, but the cost... There had to be another way.

As Ector departed, Jax faced Macy.

"I'm sorry," she said quietly. "I should have listened to you."

Shaking his head, Jax raised his hand to cup her cheek and wrapped his tentacles around her waist to draw her close. "You are safe. That is enough, for now. We will figure out what to do, from here."

"They've trapped you as much as they've trapped me."

"Is it better to be alive and caged, or dead and free?" he asked. The answer should have been simple, but he realized he didn't have one. "They've wronged you, Macy."

"I did not intend for their judgment to be passed upon you, human," Dracchus said.

"What *did* you expect, bringing her here?" Jax demanded. "That they would welcome her with open arms and slit me open to pay for my supposed crimes? They might have killed her, were it not for Ector."

Dracchus frowned, studying Macy. "I want what is best for our people. Nothing more nor less than that. Our numbers are few, Wanderer, and you are needed as much as I, or Arkon."

"I refused a single hunt, Dracchus. And you play it as the ultimate betrayal."

"You refused a single hunt, yes," Dracchus said through bared teeth, "but you have been missing during countless others! Your whims do not change our need for food and protection."

"I am not responsible for all of us!" Jax released his hold on Macy and turned fully toward Dracchus. "You have ever sought to prove yourself against me, to show everyone you are better than me, and you have finally won. Does it satisfy you?"

Macy grabbed hold of Jax's arm, tugging him back, though he didn't budge. "Jax..."

"It gives me no satisfaction," Dracchus shouted. "You have been gifted more so than any of us, and you waste your skills by wandering aimlessly. For what? What good does it do our people? What good does it do you? That the best of us should be so selfish brings shame upon us all!"

"What makes me better than you, Dracchus?" Jax's hearts thundered. He clenched his fists at his sides and forced his tentacles to still; Macy's touch was cold compared to the heat in his blood. "*You* lead the hunts that sustain our people. *You* give everything of yourself to protect them and feed them. I am no better than any of us, and my place has never been here. Is that enough to earn your hatred?"

Arkon took hold of Jax's other arm. "There is no more reason to fight, my friend."

"You are the one who should lead, Wanderer." The fury was gone from Dracchus's voice.

More than the restraining hands upon his arms, Dracchus's tone broke through Jax's anger. They stared at each other for a long while.

"I cannot," Jax finally said. He dropped his gaze to Macy's hand and clasped it in his own. Without further word to Dracchus, he led Macy out of the Mess and into her new life.

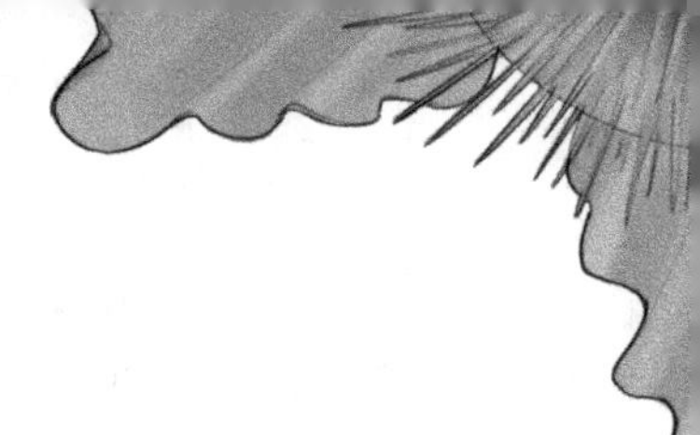

CHAPTER SEVENTEEN

THEY DIDN'T ENCOUNTER ANY OTHER KRAKEN AS JAX LED MACY into the hallway, and for that, she was grateful. Were it not for Jax and Arkon — and even Dracchus, to some extent — she would have had trouble viewing the kraken as people rather than monsters. Some of them had been *eager* to kill her.

She'd never seen such behavior from the humans back in The Watch, even at their worst. She didn't expect Jax's people to welcome her with open arms, but she hadn't been prepared to experience their loathing firsthand.

I should have listened to Jax.

Though she believed coming here had been the right decision, she hadn't realized the potential cost, hadn't realized how hard it would be to pay it...

And it could have gone *far* worse for them both.

Jax set an easy pace as she followed him through the empty corridors. He stopped frequently to show her the various rooms; many had signs on the walls and doors that defined their function, but he never used their names. If the kraken had obtained most of their information from holograms and a talking computer, it was likely they didn't know how to read.

Many of the chambers were in a state of disarray, with furniture scattered and overturned. The lights flickered in some of the rooms, and others were totally dark, but most of the place was well-lit and appeared in working order, if somewhat dirty.

"Do you have a…room here?" she asked after a while.

"I have a den, but it is in another building." His frown had only deepened since the meeting.

"Oh." They entered a tunnel-like hallway with windows on either side, allowing Macy view of the sea beyond. "Will you be staying there, then?"

"No. I will stay in the den you choose for yourself…if you want me to."

"I do! Or…I could stay in your den?"

He stopped and turned toward one of the windows, looking out into the water. "It is in a flooded building. Kraken do not tend to den in the air."

Another thing she was taking him from.

Macy frowned and wrapped her arms around herself. "What did you mean when you said I was your mate?"

Jax glanced at her. His rigid posture didn't ease, nor did his expression soften. "You chose me. *Joined* with me. And said you would be mine."

He spoke the truth, but…he didn't seem happy about it. And why would he be? Because of her, he'd been brought before his people to face judgment, and now he was trapped here.

"I did." She couldn't bring herself to look at him; she didn't want to face his anger.

"It is none of their concern. I did not want to say it aloud, because it is for us alone. I wanted to hear it from you. Not speak it to them in hopes it would sway their judgment."

Macy furrowed her brow. "From…me?"

"Your people treat such things differently. You seem to take your time with them, to consider them carefully so that when you make the choice, it is a lasting one. I wanted to give you the time you needed."

She lifted her eyes to meet his. "You *want* me...as your mate?"

"I do. In *your* time."

Macy stepped closer to Jax. She licked her lips, hesitating before she put her hand on his chest. "And if I choose now?"

He settled his hand over hers. "Why are so quick to choose me, when it took so long for you to decide about Camrin?"

"Because I didn't love Camrin."

Macy stilled once the words were out; she hadn't needed to consider them, she just *knew*.

His grip on her hand tightened, and she felt his heartbeats strengthen beneath her palm. "But...you love me?" he rasped.

They'd filled their short time together with genuine emotion. She thought back on all those shared moments — the way he'd comforted her and eased her into the water when she'd first donned the suit, and how secure she felt once she'd given herself to trusting him; his reaction to his first taste of cooked meat, or when she'd tickled him. She recalled the firm set of his features when she'd followed him into the seaweed forest against his wishes. Recalled the fear in his eyes when the razor-back had attacked, and the way he'd shielded her with his body.

The intensity and passion with which he'd looked upon her while they danced — and when they made love — gleamed in his eyes whenever their gazes met.

And this morning, after he'd wrestled her free of Dracchus's clutches... Not knowing if Jax was okay, if he would survive, knowing he was so close but still out of sight — it had been a new sort of agony. She was terrified of losing him.

She cared for Camrin, and was concerned for his well-being, but her feelings toward him had never been this strong, never this deep. She'd never felt as though she couldn't breathe without Camrin in her life. But Jax...

Macy searched his face. There was a small crease between his brows, and the corners of his lips were downturned, but there was something in his eyes... Hopefulness? Longing? Could it even be *love*?

Dropping her mask, she moved even closer and hooked her hand around the back of his neck. "I do. I love you, Jax."

The words came even easier, now, without any hesitation. They felt *right*.

For a moment, he held her gaze in silence. When his answer came, it was swift and left no room for question. He slipped his free hand into her hair, encircled her with his tentacles, and drew her against him.

Jax kissed her with a tenderness, a *need*, that made her knees weak and her heart flutter.

She wound her arms around his neck and pulled herself into the kiss. Her tongue stroked his, flicked over his sharp teeth, and if she tasted blood she didn't care. She wanted only to touch him, to be as close as possible. The suit was an unacceptable barrier between them...

But this wasn't the place.

Breath ragged, Macy pulled back and pressed her forehead to his. She caressed his jaw, stilling when her fingers ran over the gash on his cheek. Frowning, she pulled back, looking over the cuts on his shoulders and chest. She knew there were more elsewhere.

"We should clean those," she said.

"I will be fine, Macy."

"You're covered in wounds."

He raised one of his arms and turned it, displaying at least three gashes and two puncture wounds. "I have suffered worse. This is nothing."

"What if they get infected?"

"I do not know what that means."

"It's when a wound festers and doesn't quite heal."

"Why wouldn't a wound heal?"

"Well, they do, eventually..." Macy stared at the cut on his cheek. "Are you sure you're fine?"

"Yes, Macy." He brushed a lock of her hair back from her face. "I am sure. But...what about *you*?"

"What about me? Am *I* hurt? I'm probably already bruised, and I'll be sore tomorrow, but I'm okay." She settled her hands on his shoulders.

His hands fell to her hips, and he appeared to wrestle with something internally, lips parting as though to speak before snapping closed. Finally, he released her. "Come. You need to choose a new den for us."

Jax picked up her mask and continued down the corridor, leaving Macy to follow. She frowned. What had he been about to say?

As they reached the end of the tunnel, Macy glanced up at the sign near the entryway: *CABINS*. The hallway beyond was lined with identical doors spaced at regular intervals. She peered through one of the open doors as they passed and was reminded of the oldest homes in The Watch; there was a small living space, with a bed, a dresser, and a table with three chairs. The next open room was the same as the first, right down to the color of the bedding and walls. Their only difference was in the miscellaneous items strewn about.

She stepped inside and looked around, noticing an open door in the corner. As she moved closer, she realized the doorway led into a lavatory. She *almost* held in a squeal of delight; when she pressed the button on the toilet, it actually flushed, and she couldn't contain herself.

"You have running water here!" She turned on the faucet at the sink. It sputtered, spraying brownish water, but soon flowed clear. Cupping her hands, she took a sip.

It was fresh.

"Fresh water," Jax scoffed. "Useless for kraken." He stood in the entrance to the room, sweeping his gaze slowly about. "What is that device for? The first one you touched?"

"It's a toilet. It's for, um…going to… When you have to…you know. Get rid of…waste." Her cheeks burned. After all they'd shared, why was *this* embarrassing to explain?

"I see." There was a hint of skepticism on his face. "Humans need a tool for everything, it seems."

"We're not talking about this anymore." She rubbed her cheeks.

Jax shrugged, moved across the living space, and stopped in the lavatory doorway. "What of that, then?" He pointed at the stall in the corner.

"A shower. It's for bathing, like I did in the waterfall in our cave…"

She frowned; they wouldn't be going back to the cave. *This* was their home now, not because they'd chosen it, but because it had been forced upon them.

Turning away from Jax, she occupied herself by turning the dials in the shower. Water sprayed from the nozzle overhead; like the sink, it cleared after a few seconds. Steam gathered in the air.

Not just fresh water, but *hot* water.

It couldn't eliminate her sorrow, but having a working toilet, clean water, and hot showers was an unexpected upside to the situation.

"Jax, this is amazing!"

He leaned past her and turned the water off. "I burned myself playing with these as a youngling. You should be careful."

Macy chuckled and kissed his uninjured cheek. "That happens with hot water."

She turned to the cabinet built into the wall and opened it. Her smile widened; it held towels, washcloths, and little bottles of soap. Twisting the cap off a bottle, she held it under her nose and sniffed. Whatever scent it may have once emitted was gone, but when she poured some of the liquid into her hand and rubbed, it lathered immediately.

Clearly, the things the colonists had brought to this place had been made to last.

After rinsing her hands in the sink, Macy rummaged through the other items. There were bottles of teeth cleaner, a brush and several combs, cans of some sort of cream, and sticks with thin, horizontal blades at their ends. Though these blades were rather different than the straight razors men used to shave in The Watch, she guessed they served the same purpose.

She picked up one of the cans and read the label.

Removal of body hair? Wasn't that what the razors were for?

After replacing the can, Macy returned to the main room and searched the dresser. The clothes in the drawers were plain — pants, shirts, undershorts, jumpsuits, and even an overcoat, all in shades of white, gray, and dark blue. They were clearly tailored for a man.

Macy stepped back and looked around the room. There were no personal objects in sight, no further clues as to who had lived here. "Do you know if your people removed anything from these rooms?"

Jax watched her from the doorway to the lavatory. "I do not know. The likely have, over time, but it's been many, many years since humans lived here."

She walked into the hallway and entered another open room. It was in the same condition as the last, but the clothing stored in the dresser was closer to Macy's size.

"I can choose any room?" Macy asked.

"Out of what's accessible. Some of the doors are locked, or stuck." Jax leaned his shoulder against the doorframe.

"You've never tried opening them?"

"I've tried opening each one, many times. But I have never been curious enough to try breaking them open."

Macy grinned and approached him. "You've never been

curious enough? Aren't you the same Jax who's filled up a cave with interesting things you found in the ocean? Who has spent his entire life seeking out new places, even when it puts your life at risk?"

"Kraken larger and stronger than I have tried to open some of those doors. It is sometimes used as a test of strength, and the result has always been the same for everyone who has tried." His eyes shifted, following the border of the door up and around. "Arkon once spent four days asking the computer to open them, when we were younger. My curiosity was better directed elsewhere."

She brushed her fingers over the markings on his shoulder. "Do you have anything in your den you'd like to bring here?"

"Is this the room you have chosen?"

"Yes."

Jax nodded and cupped her cheek, brushing the pad of his thumb over her skin. "All that I need is here already."

Macy placed her hand over his and turned it to kiss his palm.

"Then I suppose we should get settled in." She walked toward the lavatory, glancing back as she slowly drew the suit off her arms. At the doorway, she paused, wriggled the PDS down over her hips, and kicked it aside.

Jax straightened, pupils dilating, and approached her. That now-familiar hunger had entered his gaze. "When you say *get settled in...*"

She stared at him from over her shoulder, trailing her gaze down his body and back up again. "I suppose we could *really* get settled in before I take a shower."

He stopped just behind her and ran his hands down her back and sides until they came to rest at her hips. His tentacles caressed her legs with tantalizing, feather-light strokes, sending waves of pleasure and anticipation straight to her core. She closed her eyes and sighed.

His tentacles stopped their teasing and wrapped around her

legs, widening her stance. He tugged her hips back and Macy's eyes flashed open as his shaft slid along her folds.

"Jax!" She flattened a hand on the wall to brace herself.

He slid one hand over her belly and cupped her breast. Macy moaned, leaning into his palm. Her heart raced as Jax shifted his other hand to cover her sex. Carefully, he parted her and stroked her clit with the pad of his finger in small, leisurely circles.

Macy bucked her hips; between his hands and the slide of his erection over her folds, it was nearly too much. She tried to rise, but her back met his solid chest, and his arms caged her in. His tentacles held her legs firmly in place.

"Macy," Jax growled, his breath tickling her ear. "My mate."

"Yes," she rasped. With her free hand, she clutched his forearm, urging his finger to keep moving. The sensation swirled and flourished, dominating her senses. An explosion of pleasure drew nearer as he built her higher and higher. She strained toward it, rocked against his touch, but she needed more. "Please, Jax."

"Say it, Macy." He brushed his lips along her neck, down to where it met her shoulder, and increased the pressure on her clit. "Say that you are mine."

He'd never been so vocal during their lovemaking; the low, seductive tone of his voice, paired with what he was doing to her body, ignited an inferno inside her.

"Yes! I'm yours! I'm yours, Jax!" she cried as rapture blazed through her.

He lifted himself and hooked an arm around her middle. Body thrumming, Macy barely perceived the head of his shaft against her quivering sex before he thrust into her, filling her, stretching her, sending her into another frenzy.

. . .

JAX GRITTED his teeth as Macy's inner walls gripped his cock, their fluttering nearly pushing him over the brink. He held her against him, stilling her hips; the slightest movement would be the end for him, and this was too soon.

He skimmed his gaze over her slender, arching back, over the golden, shimmering hair swept over her shoulder. Her eyes were shut, her lips parted in ecstasy. She was beautiful. Radiant.

His.

"Mine," he said, drawing his hips back, "and mine alone."

Jax slammed into her. He kept a hand on her hip, fingers flexing as he hissed through his teeth. From this angle, her sex was tighter, and drew him into her very center.

Pleasure surged through his limbs with each slow, measured thrust. Every time he pushed forward, he pulled her against him, sinking deeper and deeper into her heat. The room was filled with nothing but the sounds of their flesh meeting, her high, ragged panting, and his low, grunting breaths.

One of her hands clawed at the wall; she trembled around him as though she was about to come undone.

Suddenly, Macy reared up and wrapped an arm around his head, twisting to capture his mouth in a fierce kiss. Jax moved his hand down to stroke her swollen nub. She came instantly, her sagging body held upright only by him, her cries muffled by their unbroken kiss.

Macy had surrendered to him, given herself to him, become *his* in all ways. He would not allow her gift to go unanswered.

For a fleeting, agonizing moment, the pressure within him was too much; it would destroy him, tear him apart, leave nothing in the aftermath. Macy's sex clamped around his shaft. His feelers trailed over her slick flesh, stimulated by her vibrations, and forced his overwhelming pleasure higher and higher. He braced two tentacles against the doorframe.

He would give himself to her, without regret.

Jax exploded.

He growled against her mouth, quickening his thrusts as his muscles tensed and his seed flowed into her. He didn't stop until only the echoes of his climax remained; even then, he didn't withdraw from her body, wanting to maintain their connection for as long as possible.

Macy tilted her head to one side, eyes shut, and smiled. Jax leaned down and grazed his teeth along her throat, to her shoulder.

His interests had often been fleeting — he'd chase them until his curiosity was sated and move on. He'd left behind countless places, countless objects, but Macy… The more he had of her, the more he craved. The more he *needed*.

"Mmm…I don't know if I can move," she mumbled.

"Do you want to?" He slid the tip of a tentacle along her inner thigh.

Releasing a soft moan, she lowered her arm, brushing her hand along his cheek before dropping it to caress the base of his shaft. Her light touch teased his feelers.

"Do you?" she asked, and there was laughter in her voice.

"Very much." Jax pulled back, withdrawing from her, and turned her to face him. His tentacles coiled around her legs, raising them to either side of his hips. He slipped back into her welcoming heat.

Macy looped her arms around his neck, and Jax lost himself in the passion of her half-lidded gaze and the ecstasy that was her body.

MACY SLEPT in Jax's embrace, their limbs entwined. He watched the steady rise and fall of her chest, marveled at the serenity upon her face. She'd used the *shower* after their joining. It was too small for them to fit in together, so he'd contented himself with observing.

His eyes had repeatedly shifted to the bruises on her chest.

She had said they were from her fall — when Dracchus first tugged her toward the water. While Jax was grateful that the bruises seemed to be the full extent of her injuries, he was still furious.

He could no longer direct all his anger at Dracchus alone, and that only added to his rage. Macy didn't deserve this — she didn't deserve the pain, the anxiety, this imprisonment. Jax's throat constricted when he recalled how she'd begged him for freedom, how she'd bargained for it. Though Dracchus had set into motion the events that ended with her freedom stolen away, he hadn't been the one to ultimately take it.

No, that decision belonged to the others.

Jax lifted a strand of golden hair with the tip of his claw and wound it around his finger. He couldn't understand why she seemed more beautiful to him with each passing day.

She loves me.

He didn't fully understand that, either, but he'd recognized the weight of her admission, the power of her words, their depth of feeling. Just as *joining* held a different meaning for humans, *love* likely meant something more.

Looking at her in that moment, he knew the truth in his hearts. He'd do everything and anything to keep her safe. He'd never tire of her, would never cast her aside, would never betray her. Jax couldn't imagine his life without her anymore. Every taste of Macy, no matter how minor, made him want more. Now, he was sure — he would give up *anything* for her, his people included.

Macy sighed, brushing her hand over his chest and up to his jaw.

"You okay?" Her voice was soft and slurred with grogginess.

"I am fine, Macy. Rest. I will be here."

She hummed. Her hand relaxed, and her breathing slowed.

He unwound her hair from his claw and held her, leaning his

face close to take in her scent. After so many years of wandering, he'd finally found his place — not the Facility, but Macy. Anywhere she went would be his home.

And he wouldn't remain idle while she was forced to dwell in this place.

"I love you, too, Macy," he whispered.

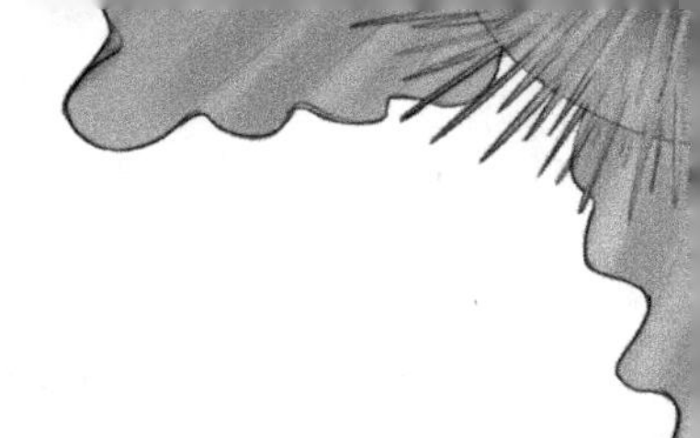

CHAPTER EIGHTEEN

THE DAYS PASSED SLOWLY FOR MACY. AT FIRST, SHE'D BEEN content to linger in the housing area, using her time to search the accessible rooms. Apart from a few personal items scattered here and there — the most exciting of which was another music player — the rooms were identical. Even the clothes were the same — the sizes varied, but the cuts, colors, and fabrics were repeated in every chamber.

She'd attempted to enter the locked rooms, but every PIN she punched in was denied, and Jax hadn't been wrong about the doors — they weren't going to budge.

Jax forbid her from venturing out of the cabin area on her own, and Macy had been too wary to disobey. Though the elder kraken had declared Macy one of them, she couldn't forget the animosity they'd directed at her. The best way to avoid trouble was to stay out of sight.

By the sixth day, their new home felt like a prison.

It was clearly worse for Jax. He stayed with her for hours every day, making love and idle conversation, but he'd grown increasingly withdrawn as time passed. He'd leave for long stretches, and Macy understood why.

Wanderer.

In the cave, they'd been free. Jax could take her out whenever either of them wanted to go, could show her places he'd discovered and see them anew through her eyes. The world had been open to them. All that had been taken away from him.

It had been her choice — against Jax's wishes — to come here. She knew he was unhappy, resentful of his people, but how much blame did he place on her? If she'd listened to him, if she'd just agreed to return to the cave, how different would things be now?

Her recent illness hadn't helped ease his nerves. For the last several days, she'd woken up feeling nauseous, and vomited two or three times in a morning. During those periods, she'd been unable to keep food down. Even the slightest whiff of fish sent her running to the toilet. By midday — which she only determined thanks to the clock in her room — her stomach would settle, and she'd feel fine.

She played it off as nothing; Jax was already out of sorts, and she didn't want to add to his distress. But she couldn't assuage her concern. At first, she thought it was the food they'd gathered in the jungle, but she'd consumed plenty of it in the cave without getting sick, and had eaten the same vegetation while she lived in The Watch.

Macy's mind shifted to the building next. What if there was a problem with the air filtration system? Perhaps it didn't affect the kraken because their respiration was so different, or simply because they were a hardier species. Humans hadn't lived here for so long that there was no way to be sure it was still a safe environment — at least not before it was too late.

But the nausea only struck during the morning. If the air was somehow contaminated, wouldn't she be sick all the time?

By the fifteenth day, she'd had enough. She wasn't going to allow fear to prevent her from making the most of her situation.

Jax was gone again; his absences had grown longer and

longer, and though he always returned by the evening, she missed him terribly during the day. It felt like they were drifting apart. A seed of doubt had taken root inside her, twisting its way through her being — one day, he might not return at all. Their lovemaking was as intense as ever, and her connection to him during those times was soul-deep, but when they finished, she felt the rift tear open again, threatening to swallow her up.

Today, she refused to sit and wait.

Macy strapped on the knife and gun Jax had given her for protection — each had a thigh holster, and though she was unused to wearing weapons, they were comfortable enough — and exited the cabin area. She wandered the corridors barefoot, peering into darkened rooms here and there. She neither saw nor heard any kraken.

When she spotted the sign indicating the pool, she stopped and stared down the hallway at the closed door. Jax had mentioned Arkon often spent time there. She didn't know if Arkon accompanied Jax to wherever it was he was going every day, but it couldn't hurt to check. She needed a friendly face.

She approached the door, pressed the button beside it, and entered when it slid open. The overwhelming stench of chemicals assaulted her immediately. Her stomach churned, and she doubled over.

The sound of the door closing behind her was whisper-soft.

"Are you all right, Macy?"

Macy jumped, lifting her eyes to Arkon. He was at the edge of the pool, frowning at her.

She took two deep, slow breaths through her mouth — not that it helped much with the smell — and nodded. "I'm fine. I just…need a moment. The smell in here is…"

"It can be overpowering when one is unused to it." As though in response to his own words, his nostrils flared. "But I think you will grow used to it in time."

Macy didn't share his confidence.

She stepped farther into the room, moving her gaze along the lockers lining the far wall, over the dormant pieces of equipment and machinery scattered around the floor, and finally to the large, rectangular pool in the center. The water within was totally clear; if it weren't for the light reflecting on its surface, she might not have known it was there at all.

As she neared the pool, she realized there was something on the bottom. She gasped when it came into full view. The floor was covered with countless small stones, arranged in swathes of color to create intricate, swirling patterns.

"Did you make this?" Macy asked, looking at Arkon. His arms were folded over his chest, fingertips drumming his bicep. "I'm sorry. If I'm…interrupting, or intruding, I can go."

"Not at all. I've refined the patterns to my satisfaction — if only barely — but it's still missing the centerpiece." When he turned his head to her and smiled, the warmth of his expression eased the tension. "Jax was supposed to bring back a glowing stone, but he's been understandably distracted for the last few weeks."

She returned her attention to the design. "It's beautiful."

"Thank you for saying so."

"I'd guess you don't hear it often enough. Our people are alike in that way. Most of them like to look at art, but think making it is a waste of time when you could be focusing on something more practical instead."

"Jax tells me, in his way, and though he claims not to understand it or have any capacity for it…his insights are often enlightening. As for it being a waste of time…I find that a short-sighted notion."

"Aymee said something very similar to that." Macy turned her head and studied Arkon. "I think she would love to know you."

"The more I hear of this Aymee, the more I would love to know her." He met Macy's gaze, and his smile faltered. "How have you been, Macy? Though it could have gone worse, the gathering didn't end how I'd hoped. What faith I had in my kind was, apparently, misplaced."

"I…don't blame them. They acted in fear, and even knowing as little as I do about the history between our peoples, I think the kraken were within their rights here." She sat down on the edge of the pool, rolled up the legs of her pants, and dipped her feet in. It was colder than she'd expected. "I'm pretty sure humans would've reacted the same way if the roles were reversed."

"There are always more extreme elements, it would seem, who make up for their lack of numbers through sheer aggression. Kronus and his group do not speak for all of us, no more than Dracchus, Jax, or Ector do." Arkon eased himself down beside her; his position looked awkward, with his tentacles folded beneath him to hang into the water, but he made no indication of discomfort. "You didn't answer my question, though. How are you?"

"I'm getting by, one day at a time." She searched his eyes; their violet hue reminded her of the sky immediately after sunset. Compared to Jax and Dracchus, Arkon was lean, his face narrower and more refined, but he seemed no less powerful. "You've been Jax's friend for a long time. How often does he normally remain here between his wanderings?"

Arkon lifted his hands, palms up, and shrugged. "Days, sometimes. This is the longest I recall him being here in many years… He's out of sorts. Restless. Not his usual self…"

Macy's eyes stung with tears, and she turned her face away. "I trapped him here."

"You cannot blame yourself for this, Macy. I know without a doubt that Jax does not."

"How can you be sure?" she asked, wiping the back of her fingers across her cheeks. "He is rarely here."

"I have known Jax for most of my life. And the way he looks

at you… He blames the others. Dracchus, yes, but the rest even more so. For him, being caged is worse than death, and they caged his mate. He won't easily forgive any of them for it. Kronus is lucky you managed to calm Jax down."

Macy managed a small smile. "How can I help him?"

The tips of Arkon's tentacles flicked slowly from side to side, gently splashing. "Patience. Though I won't deny that he could benefit from being slapped around a bit, too."

She laughed; it felt surprisingly good. "He doesn't like that very much. I've done it a couple times."

He grinned. "Honestly, Macy… I think he's so caught up in what has been lost, that he's losing sight of what he has."

"Thank you, Arkon." She settled a hand over his. It was clear why Jax considered him his closest friend; of all the kraken — Jax included — Arkon had been the kindest, the most accepting.

"It is no trouble." Though his movement was subtle, she noticed his gaze drop, and he furrowed his brow. He lifted his arm to get a closer look at her hand. "The similarities are as pronounced as the differences…"

"They are." Macy allowed him his inspection and lowered her hand to her lap when he was done. She kicked her feet through the water. "Jax told me you often speak with the computer?"

"As dull as it typically is, yes, I do."

"Are you able to access it?"

"In what capacity? There are vocal commands and interactions that seem to function normally, but I know I've uncovered only a fraction of the information it must hold. I believe access beyond that may require use of the screens, but the kraken never learned to read, and the Computer itself hasn't been helpful in that regard."

"I could teach you."

Arkon's face brightened; his smile returned, and his eyes sparkled. "I will hold you to your word on that, Macy."

She'd smiled more in this short time with him than she had in the last week. "You have my word, Arkon."

"Was there something specific you wanted from the computer?"

"I guess…*everything*. There must be a wealth of information here. Even…even what they did to your people. How they created you, and why."

"What few answers we have for those questions are unsatisfactory and incomplete, at best." He stared down at the little ripples on the surface of the pool. "If I bring you to a room with working screens, do you think you could find that information?"

"I'll try my best."

Arkon nodded and pushed himself up, water sloshing with the sudden movement of his tentacles. "Let's go, then."

"Really?" Macy pulled her feet out of the pool and rolled down her pant legs. "You can take me now?"

"I do not think either of us has anything more pressing to attend at the moment," he said with a smirk.

Macy chuckled as she stood up. "I'm quite tired of staring at the walls."

"Perhaps we'll figure out how to paint them, at some point. One matter at a time, though." Arkon moved toward the door; at its core, his dragging gait was similar to the way Jax moved on land, but Arkon was somehow more graceful.

She followed him out of the pool room. "Arkon?"

He slowed and twisted to look at her over his shoulder. "Hmm?"

Catching up to him, she glanced down at her hands. "I know we've only just met, but you are so easy to talk to you and…and I would like it if I could call you my friend."

"Of course, Macy." He dipped his head. "I have never had a female friend…it is not the way of our people. But I can now boast that my number of friends has doubled."

Something inside her chest warmed. She missed Aymee, and Jax's frequent absence had left her lonelier than she'd been since their first few days together. Arkon's friendship was a balm for the wounds her heart had suffered.

"The others don't deserve you, Arkon."

Water still dripped from Jax as he entered the area Macy called the *Cabins*. He'd waited an eternity for the water to drain from the entry chamber and had considered trying to force the interior door more than once. Macy had been sick, as of late, and leaving her alone made him anxious.

He wished he didn't have to.

The door to their den was open, as it usually was when they were awake and not otherwise engaged. He entered; Macy wasn't on the bed, at the table, or in the shower. He called her name and returned to the hallway, calling again.

There was no answer, no sign of movement.

He hurried through the nearby corridors, shouting for her, checking every open room. His hearts pounded, their pace increasing with each empty chamber.

What if she had wandered off and fallen ill? What if another kraken had come, knowing Jax was gone, and taken her?

The surface of Jax's skin prickled like it was on fire, but he was cold inside.

He left the cabin area, pulling himself through the tunnel with arms and tentacles, and reentered the main building. All was silent save for the gentle hum of the Facility itself. His calls echoed off the walls.

Along the way, he leaned into every room, both hoping and fearing that he would find her in one.

She was nowhere.

He found nothing to indicate the recent passage of other

kraken, but he'd been out for a long while; any such trails might have dried up already.

"Macy!" he shouted as he reached the intersection of two main corridors.

"Was that Jax?" Macy's voice was unmistakable, though it was distorted by distance.

He rushed toward it, finally stopping in the doorway of a large room full of screens and controls. Macy and Arkon both looked at Jax from their place at the central console.

"You're back!" she exclaimed.

Relief rushed through him, a soothing tide washing over the beach. "You're all right." The receding tide left anger in its wake. "Why are you here? You shouldn't wander far from our den; it is not safe."

She frowned. "I needed to get out of there for a little while."

"What if Kronus had come across you, alone in the hall? What if you had fallen ill in some room that is rarely visited, and I couldn't find you?" His hearts hadn't slowed, and the heat on his skin only intensified.

"I feel fine, Jax. I was with Arkon."

Jax's gaze flicked briefly to Arkon, whose expression was unreadable. "You will not leave the cabins again," he growled, moving into the room.

"What?" For a moment, her eyes were wide, and her lips parted in shock. Then she straightened, her body going rigid. She glared at him. "I am not an object, Jax! You can't keep me like I'm some trophy you pulled out of the ocean. I'd think you of all people would understand that!"

He clenched his jaw; her words struck to his core, twisted inside him like a blade. His voice nearly failed. "I *need* you safe."

Jax was no better than the rest of them; he was pushing her into a smaller cage, even though he sought to free her from the one his people had created.

The anger on her face slowly faded. She held his gaze and

sighed. "I know, Jax. I know. But I can't stay in there all day, every day. I need—" her eyes drifted to Arkon, "—someone to talk to."

"You can talk to me, Macy," Jax said.

"You haven't been here!"

He gritted his teeth and released a long breath through his nostrils. She was right. He'd been gone often, and for long periods of time; why wouldn't she be restless, staring at the same walls every day?

Closing the remaining distance between them, he stopped in front of her and looked into the unfathomable depths of her eyes. "I am sorry."

Macy placed her hand on his chest. He covered it with his own and leaned down, pressing his forehead to hers.

"Don't pull away from me, Jax," she said softly.

"I'm not trying to." He closed his eyes and took in her scent, letting it wash over his senses and permeate him. It had changed subtly over the last few weeks, and, somehow, had become only more alluring to him.

She drew back and smiled. "And I was safe. I've been with Arkon since I left the cabins, and I have the weapons you gave me."

Arkon nodded when Jax glanced at him. He trusted Arkon to risk his life in defense of Macy, but it was still hard to accept that he'd allowed her protection to fall to someone else.

"She is quite openly appreciative of my work," Arkon said. "Perhaps you should have her teach you how to properly compliment me."

The high, sweet sound of Macy's laughter shattered Jax's lingering worry; here, now, all was well, and Macy was safe and happy. Even if it was fleeting, it was precious enough not to be ignored or dismissed.

"What are the two of you doing in here anyway?" Jax asked.

The room wasn't often visited by kraken — not that many of them were.

"Macy knows how to read." Arkon's smile was broader than Jax had seen in a long while.

He looked from Arkon to Macy and back again questioningly. "What does that have to do with your being here?"

"She thinks she might be able to access new information on the Computer. About our kind, about this place…about *everything*."

"Can you?" Jax returned his attention to Macy.

"I can try. You got here right after we did, so I haven't done anything yet."

Jax and Arkon moved to watch over Macy's shoulder as she brought up a projected screen full of symbols. The images moved when her fingers touched them, sliding aside or vanishing altogether, only for new symbols to appear.

"Welcome," said the Computer. Its voice, emanating only from the console, seemed smaller. "Please enter your authorization code to proceed."

"A code? Hmm…" Macy tapped at the screen.

"Access denied."

She touched several more symbols.

"Access denied."

Macy stared down at the console, drumming her fingers atop it. She raised her hand to the projection, finger extended, and stopped, glancing at Jax. "What's the code you use to get into this building?"

Jax leaned forward, and Macy stepped aside to allow him a closer look at the symbols. They were all meaningless to him, but a few were familiar — he realized suddenly they were same as those beside the entry door.

"This one first," Arkon said, pointing to one. Macy pressed it.

Slowly, Jax and Arkon ran through the remaining symbols. They were arranged in a different order on the projection, and it was difficult to piece together a sequence that had long ago become second nature. His hand knew the keypad's buttons by touch, remembered the distance between each, the order in which they needed to be pressed.

"Access granted," the computer said, and the screen changed abruptly.

"I can't believe that actually worked." The screen cast a soft blue glow upon Macy's smiling face as she read. "Halorium Project?"

"Halorium is a stone found on the ocean floor," Arkon replied. "It emits blue light. Our ancestors were tasked with gathering halorium for the humans who dwelled here."

"It does strange things to human machinery." Jax frowned; the stuff was rare, but it was out there… Would it interfere with Macy's suit like it did everything else?

Macy swiped her finger across the screen, and an image appeared. It was a shard of halorium, spinning in place and pulsing light, so real that Jax wondered if he could reach out and touch it.

"Computer, what is the Halorium Project?" Macy asked.

"The Halorium Project is a joint venture between Tureon Industries and the Interstellar Defense Coalition with the goal of harvesting a rare mineral on Halora. It was founded when scouting ships discovered halorium deposits after first landing on Halora, in 2455 SGY."

"What is SGY?"

"Standard Galactic Year. A system put in place so colonies across the galaxy could operate on a unifying measure of the passage of time, regardless of local planetary orbits and rotations."

"So how long ago was 2455?"

"Three hundred and seventy-seven Halorian years ago."

"What did they want with halorium?"

"Halorium emits a form of radiation that has not been found

anywhere else in the known galaxy. This radiation has proven harmless to living creatures during tests conducted in this laboratory. Because of its unique properties, halorium can be used as a powerful and extremely long-lasting source of energy. This facility is powered entirely by halorium."

Macy lifted her hand and touched the tip of the shard; its movement altered, and it tumbled slowly, end-over-end. "Jax said it does strange things to human machinery."

"Specifically, the energy fields emitted by halorium interfere with electronics. It must be kept in specially shielded containers to protect such devices from its effects. The halorium reactors of this facility are shielded at three times the recommended standard to protect the facility's operations."

"Why did the kraken mine it?"

"I do not understand your question," the computer said.

Macy looked at Jax and Arkon.

"Who are the kraken?" she asked.

"The kraken was a mythological sea creature from ancient Earth legends," the computer replied. A new picture flashed up, this time flat. It was black and white, a series of lines that came together into a coherent image — a huge, tentacled creature dragging a ship with three masts into the water. "It was believed to be a cephalopod of immense size, and ancient sailors believed it was capable of pulling men overboard, breaking ships in half, and dragging vessels into the sea."

"It is the name our people took," Jax said, "to make humans fear us."

"What did they call you before that?"

He shook his head, staring at the image. He'd never seen anything like it. Arkon was even more intent, leaning so close his face nearly touched the projection, eyes roving over every line. There were clear similarities between the kraken of Halora and the one depicted in the picture. It made Jax proud, for some reason, but also sorrowful. "We don't know. The kraken cast off the name given to them by humans many years before my birth."

Macy tilted her head. "Computer, who harvested the halorium?"

"Initially, it was harvested by human divers. After several fatalities connected to electronic and equipment failure, halorium harvest was shifted to octopoid laborers."

"Octopoid," Macy mumbled, glancing down at Jax's tentacles. "Tell me about the octopoids."

"*Octopoid* is an unofficial term used to designate a genetically modified, aquatic race of humanoids. They were created by an integrated team of Tureon and IDC scientists, using a splice of human and cephalopod DNA as their basis. The octopoids were designed to be intelligent enough to follow orders and are adapted specifically to Halorian oceans."

"What does that mean?" Jax asked, looking from the screen to Macy. "Human and cepho-pod?"

"Computer, show me a cephalopod."

The screen changed, displaying a creature very much like the kraken it had before. But — like the halorium shard — this creature looked like it was there. It had eight tentacles, all covered with suction cups along their undersides, and a bulbous head attached directly to its lower half. Its eyes were familiar; they were the same as Jax's, or Arkon's, or any of their people's.

"I think..." Macy turned her face toward Jax, "you're part human and part cephalopod."

Jax's hearts thumped as he exchanged a glance with Arkon. He didn't understand much of what the Computer had said, but Macy's summary was clear. The kraken had always known they'd been created by humans, but had never known — with any degree of certainty, anyway — they were *related* to humans.

Macy grasped his wrist, lifted his hand, and pressed their palms together. "It would explain why we're so similar."

He bent his fingers over her fingertips. "And yet so different."

"Tell me more about the octopoids," Macy said, shifting closer to Jax.

"The octopoids were designed to possess heightened strength, speed, and reflexes. The regenerative capabilities of their cephalopod cousins were also enhanced, allowing them to heal from wounds at an accelerated rate, averaging eight-point-three times the speed of the natural human healing process. The IDC had intentions to use similarly modified beings in potential military scenarios, but the octopoids in this facility were used only to harvest halorium. They were designed to exhibit low fertility rates and a low occurrence of female chromosomes in the overall population, counterbalanced by a relatively short gestation period of seventeen weeks. The average life expectancy of octopoids is believed to be comparable to humans, though conclusive data has never been obtained."

"Our numbers dwindle because this is how they made us?" Jax asked.

"It is no wonder there are so few females, and younglings are so rare," Arkon said. "It is no blight on our people. It was designed into us from the beginning."

"But why?" Jax asked. He looked back at the screen, as though it would show him an answer he could understand. "Why were kraken...why were *octopoids* made with low fertility and few females?"

"Those features were included as a means of population control," the computer explained. "In order to save on space within the facility, it was more practical to allow the octopoids to reproduce naturally and keep the labor force populated. Low fertility and fewer females resulted in far more manageable and even population growth."

"So, we were not merely their slaves, they controlled our young, too? They...restricted our ability to continue our race?"

Jax's stomach twisted, and his muscles were tense; the wrongs had been committed hundreds of years before, but their effects had never ceased.

"We existed only to fulfill a specific purpose for them," Arkon said. "And even after they were gone, we never broke out of their shadow. We exist, and nothing more. Even that has been threatened by the very beings who created us."

"Why did the humans leave this place?" Macy asked them. "No one in The Watch knows of it, or about any of you, so where else would they have gone?"

"They didn't leave." Jax met her gaze; the first hints of fear broke through her confusion.

She turned her attention back to the screen. "Computer, what happened to the humans in the facility?"

"Macy..." To his own ears, Jax's tone was strange, sad, reluctant.

"Official records are incomplete. At the time of the incident, several IDC guardsmen reported that the octopoid population had gone into open revolt against the facility's human inhabitants."

The screen changed. Jax had never seen images from the uprising — none of them had — but he knew it for what it was immediately.

Another set of ghosts.

A human male appeared in the projection. The room behind him had to be one of the cabins, just like the one Macy had chosen as a den. Droplets of water rolled down his face; he wiped at them absently with the back of his hand and smeared blood over his cheek from a cut near his eye.

"This is Ensign Matherson of the Interstellar Defense Coalition, officer number three-two-seven-alpha-nine. If anyone is in range to pick up this transmission, this facility is being over-run. The—"

Frantic shouts echoed from the hallway behind him. He

turned quickly, lifting a gun and pointing it toward the door. "We are being overrun by those...those *things* the scientists made. Those fucking octo-freaks or whatever the hell they call them. Word is they've already blown a hole in the side of the sub bay and flooded it."

The human — Ensign Matherson — turned back toward whatever device had captured his image. "We have the few surviving civvies and scientists hunkering down in their cabins, but we don't have the supplies to last long. We need immediate support and evacuation. Please, we ne—"

He jumped as a series of booms erupted from the hallway.

Another human in the same clothes as Matherson entered the doorway. "They're coming, Mathers! We gotta fall back!"

Matherson looked back at the recording device. "Send help ASAP!"

He ran into the hallway and glanced to his left. There was more shouting, and the two humans raised their weapons and fired, producing more of the booms, even louder now than before. Something hit the other human — it looked like a harpoon, to Jax — and the man fell, knocking Matherson to the floor face-first.

Before Matherson recovered, a large, dark figure leapt onto his back. A kraken.

The kraken wrapped his tentacles around Matherson's wrists and yanked them apart, the gun clattering away. Matherson struggled to turn and face his opponent as the kraken reached for something beyond the doorframe. A moment later, its hand reappeared, clutching the harpoon.

Matherson screamed. His screams continued for many heartbeats as the kraken jabbed the harpoon into his back repeatedly, splattering himself with blood.

Macy's hands flew up to cover her mouth.

More kraken moved past the doorway. Distant pops and screams echoed through the hall.

The screen flickered and reverted to its previous state.

"That was the final transmission sent from this facility before the communications array became nonfunctional, sent only on secure military channels," the computer said. "Contact was maintained with human survivors in cabins two, ten, thirteen, and twenty-six following the incident. Communications ended twenty-one days later, and the residents of those cabins have remained unresponsive in the time since."

Macy had gone pale, her expression a blend of shock and horror. Jax had known what happened here, but he'd never *seen* it. This was the first time he felt shame for the actions of his ancestors.

"Macy, are you all right?" he asked, placing a hand on her shoulder. She flinched; his chest constricted.

"They would have done that to me." She pressed a hand to her stomach.

"I would not have allowed it. I would have done everything in my power to protect you, and beyond."

"I...I don't—" Macy turned and ran, crossing the room before she doubled over and vomited in the corner.

Jax hurried to Macy's side. He eased down beside her, put his arms around her shoulders, and brushed her hair out of her face. Was this another bout with her recent illness, or a result of what she'd seen?

"I need to lie down," she whispered.

"Anything." Jax gently scooped her into his arms and rose, holding her against his chest. She curled into him.

"There are dead bodies in those rooms."

"Just more ghosts." He smoothed back her hair as he carried her into the hallway, glancing over his shoulder. Arkon nodded, his expression troubled.

Jax turned his attention forward. He wouldn't think about the dead bodies, or the Uprising. Macy was here *now*, alive...and he would keep her that way.

CHAPTER NINETEEN

MACY REMAINED IN BED FOR THE REST OF THE DAY AFTER THE computer's revelations, overcome with shock and nausea. She ate nothing that evening, and very little through the following week.

She was as worried as Jax; each time he came with food, already filleted and cooked, it sent her stomach into revolt. All she'd been able to keep down was a bit of naba. She hated that Jax had to venture onto land by himself to obtain it.

Arkon visited her several times throughout the week, relaying new information he'd gleaned from the computer. Now that he knew how to access it, he spent hours questioning it, delving ever deeper into its data.

Finally, as the week ended, Macy woke without queasiness. She rose cautiously and slipped out of bed. Jax was nowhere to be seen; he must've left while she slept. After relieving herself and showering, she felt better than she had in a long time. Her middle seemed rounder, as though — despite eating almost nothing for days — she'd gained weight.

As she dressed, she nibbled on one of the last pieces of naba. Had Jax gone out to find more? Wherever he was, she couldn't sit here and wait; this was the first time she'd felt well in weeks. She strapped on the thigh holders for her knife and gun and left.

Macy had just stepped into the main building when she saw movement from the corner of her eye. Startled, she retreated, fixing her gaze on an open doorway down the hall. No light came from within the chamber.

The hairs on the back of her neck rose.

"Hello?" she called.

No answer.

Frowning, Macy approached the doorway. Her hand fell to the butt of her gun. Something slid across the floor inside.

"Hello?" she repeated.

A small, bald head poked out from the doorway, around the height of Macy's waist. Two big, silver eyes met her gaze.

It took Macy a moment to realize what she was looking at — a kraken, but far smaller than any she'd yet seen. This was a child. A *female* child, if its delicate facial features and body structure were any indication.

Crouching, Macy smiled at the kraken. "Hello."

The girl's eyes dipped, and her lips twitched into a smile.

"Do you know who I am?" Macy asked.

"Human."

"Yes, but I won't hurt you. My name is Macy. What's your name?"

The kraken child hesitated, glancing over her shoulder nervously. "Melaina."

"That's a beautiful name. What brings you here, Melaina?"

"I was curious."

"About me?"

Melaina nodded.

"What would you like to know?" Macy asked.

The girl moved forward until she was before Macy, raised her hand — her claws were short and dull compared to Jax's — and touched Macy's hair.

"It's so soft," Melaina whispered.

Macy chuckled. She understood the kraken's fascination with her hair, but Melaina's innocence leant her curiosity a certain charm.

The girl lowered her arm. "Is it true you are Jax's mate?"

"It is."

"How long will you mate him for?"

"What?" Macy's brows lowered. "What do you mean?"

"How long will you be mated to Jax?"

"Forever, I suppose. For as long as I live if he'll have me."

Melaina tilted her head. "Even after he gives you a youngling?"

"A…youngling? You mean a baby? No." Macy shook her head and smiled. "No, no. I'm human. We can't have… It doesn't work like that for us."

"If you cannot have young, why does he choose to stay with you?"

Macy inwardly flinched. This was just a child's curiosity, with no malicious intent. As far as Macy knew, female kraken chose to mate only to produce young and moved to new males frequently. It made sense, given what the computer had said — babies were so rare that the kraken had to join often to sustain their existence as a species.

"We just really care for each other," Macy said.

Melaina looked at her skeptically.

The idea of choosing a single person to join with for life had been strange even to Jax, and he was one of the most open-minded of his people. Of course it would be difficult for other kraken to imagine.

Macy smiled; she needed to steer their conversation else-where. "Would you like to play a game?"

The girl's face brightened. "What game?"

"It's one I used to play with my sister. Have you ever played hide-and-seek?"

"What is hide-and-seek? Is it like hunters-hiders?"

"How is that played?"

Melaina's tentacles twitched and curled in her excitement. "One team is the hunters, and the other team is hiders. The hunters have to find all the hiders."

"Yes! It's exactly like that. Would you play with me? I haven't played in a long time, not since I was little."

Melaina clapped her hands. "Can I hide first?"

"On two conditions — no camouflage, and we stay in the cabin area." Macy gestured to the tunnel behind her.

"Camouflage?"

Macy touched Melaina's arm. The girl recoiled slightly. "Changing your skin color. My skin doesn't change like yours, so it would be unfair."

The girl inched forward and reached out tentatively, pressing her fingertips to Macy's forearm. "It doesn't change at all?"

"Only a little, but I can't match it to my surroundings like you." Macy stood. "Okay, I'll count, and you hide. Ready?"

"Yes!"

They played for an hour. Melaina's initial distrust quickly evaporated as their laughter echoed through the corridors.

Though Macy thought herself and Sarina had been good at hiding as children, Melaina's skills were superior — even without camouflage. The young kraken was able to squeeze into spots that should've been too small to fit in, and proved surprisingly adept at climbing into high places Macy hadn't initially expected her to reach.

When they tired of the game, they went to Macy's room and turned on the music player. After she overcame her startlement, Melaina was thrilled. She danced around the room with Macy and laughed until they were lying on the floor, breathless.

It was between two songs when they heard the calls from

somewhere in the corridor. Melaina perked up, and Macy turned off the music.

"Melaina!"

"Oh no," Melaina groaned, scurrying across the room and into the hallway.

Macy followed. "What's wrong?"

The question was answered once Macy stepped through the doorway. Another kraken was approaching, and its features contorted with rage when it met Macy's gaze. This was another female — an *adult* female. She was built lighter than the males, with a narrow waist and small breasts, her dark nipples bare.

As soon as she was in reach, one of the kraken's tentacles darted out to take hold of Melaina's wrist, pulling the girl back. The female imposed herself between Macy and the child.

"What are you doing with my youngling, human?" she demanded.

Melaina poked her head out from behind the female. "I was cur—"

"Silence!" The female twisted to look at the girl. "What have I told you about wandering?"

For a moment, Macy pitied the child; was this how Jax had been treated in his youth?

"We were only playing," Macy said.

The kraken turned her narrowed gaze on Macy. "My daughter will not *play* with humans, or *talk* to humans, or have *anything* to do with humans."

Whatever joy Macy had felt moments before fled from the female's animosity. "She was only curious, and I enjoyed her company."

The female's lip curled in disgust. "Such curiosity leads to kraken like Arkon and *Jax*. I will not have my child follow that path."

Anger pulsed through Macy. "There's nothing wrong with either of them."

The kraken dropped her gaze, sliding it over Macy's body, and smirked. "Jax's wanderings took him to my den, and led him away from me. Do you think he will not leave you? A human with no limbs? A human who cannot dance, who cannot defend herself, who cannot bear young?" She swept her hand down to her waist, where her slit unfurled like a blooming flower, revealing her open sex. "Do you think you can please him like his own kind can?"

Macy's eyes widened, and she lifted her gaze to the female's. Though she tried to push the kraken's words aside, they lingered, taking root in Macy's mind to build upon her doubts. "Jax cares for me."

"For now. You are a...*curiosity* to him. He will tire of you soon enough. He always does." The female turned away.

"How long did Jax stay with you? A week?"

The kraken whipped around with a growl, baring her teeth.

Macy lowered her hand, draping her fingertips over the grip of her gun.

"Jax has betrayed us again. Arming a human."

"I am one of you while I'm here."

"You will never be one of us, *human*." The female gathered Melaina and led the child away.

Macy stared after them, lifting a hand to wave when Melaina glanced backward with rounded, sad eyes. Once they turned a corner, Macy went back into her room. She released a long, shaky breath; the adrenaline that had pumped through her veins was already wearing off.

How much of what the female had said was true? Could Melaina be *his* child? Jax didn't know who his own father was, and if he had mated with that female...there was a chance.

Her fingers trembled as she unstrapped the gun and set it aside. She'd come so close to drawing it, and what would that have accomplished? How would Jax react to Macy shooting a kraken? How would the rest of them react?

You are a curiosity to him.

What could she do for Jax? What would make him happy, what would make him feel like she was worth giving up the freedom he so coveted?

ARKON PAUSED ON THE BEACH, setting down the sealed container in his arms. "Fascinating, how varied the environments are up here. I knew there was more beyond the shoreline, but I suppose I've never really imagined anything other than cliffs and patches of sand."

"Macy said there is land enough that a human could walk for weeks before nearing the other side." Jax lowered his container and looked over his shoulder toward the greenery they'd just left. "As much as I crave to explore, I do not think I could venture much farther than we've already gone. It is…unsettling, to be so far away from the sea."

"Yes, it is. But she is a human, Jax. They are land creatures, and that may call to her, even as the sea calls to us."

"She is a human, but I don't think there is anyone like her — human or kraken." A pleasant breeze flowed over his skin, and the sand was warm; he'd never expected to find so many little things to enjoy on land. Everything above the surface was so dry, hard, and heavy, but there were many new sensations to experience.

"And she really eats these plants?" Arkon patted the lid of the container.

"It seems to be all she can keep down, lately." Jax frowned, staring at the container before meeting his friend's gaze. "I worry for her, Arkon, but she acts as though I shouldn't be concerned."

"She doesn't want to cause you any more trouble, Jax."

"What trouble has she caused me?"

Arkon huffed through his siphons. "You truly don't see it?"

"See what?"

"She sees how unhappy you are," Arkon replied with a frown. "She counts the hours you're away, and she blames herself. Macy thinks she is the reason you feel chained to the Facility, and that you will come to resent her for it."

"That is foolish."

"Is it, Jax?"

"Yes, it is, Arkon. Why would she think she could cause me such distress, or that I would hold her responsible for things she has no control over?"

"Because you are not yourself when you are in that place, and you're gone more often than not. What is she meant to think of it?"

"I love her!" Jax shouted, whirling toward Arkon. Sand flew around his tentacles.

Arkon recoiled slightly at Jax's sudden outburst, eyes wide. He tilted his head. "You *love* her. What does that mean? Not to her or her people, but to you?"

"You know what it means, Arkon. You know what *everything* means." Jax turned away and looked out over the rolling blue waves.

"I have some idea of what it means to humans. But I want to know what it means to *you*."

Jax gritted his teeth and clenched his fists; he didn't have to answer to Arkon. Didn't have to explain himself, or open himself up to judgment.

"She…is my home," Jax finally replied, closing his eyes. "I would never wander again, so long as she were safe. Anything I have, anything I can give, I would give to protect her, to see her smile. But she is not safe in the Facility, amongst our people. And she is not happy living in a cage."

"And your answer is to stay away as much as you can?"

Though there was no malice in Arkon's voice, the words cut deep.

Taking a deep, steadying breath, Jax turned to Arkon. Their friendship had never been one of secrets or mistrust. "I have been away because I have been gathering supplies and searching for suitable dens."

Arkon's expression slackened. "You mean to take her away."

"I do."

"You're the foolish one, Jax."

Anger swept through Jax's chest like fire, but Arkon spoke again before he could open his mouth.

"You should have told me. Anything I can do to aid you, simply ask. Along the same lines, why haven't you told *her*? Do you know how much that would have eased her worries?"

Just as quickly, Jax's anger was snuffed out, replaced by a deep, gnawing guilt. Arkon had always been the clever one; Jax was a hunter, an explorer, and secrets and subtleties were unnatural to him.

Jax bent down and lifted the container full of greens. "I will tell her upon our return. She needs to know...the only one at fault has been me."

"It will do you both well."

MACY WAS NOT in the main room of their den when Jax returned, but he could hear the shower running. He placed the containers on the floor near the table for her to sort through later.

His hearts pounded as he approached the lavatory. The door was open, and steam hung near the ceiling, making the air warm and thick. He should have realized the things Arkon told him long before, should have noticed the effect he was having upon her, should have shared his plans with her *weeks* ago. He'd only refrained because he didn't want to give her false hope.

There had to be someplace farther than the other kraken's willingness to follow, a place beyond the reach of humans, where Jax and Macy could make a den. He just needed time to find it.

Her body was a dark shape through the foggy, curved glass of the shower stall. She had her fingers in her hair when she turned around.

"Jax?" Macy asked, rubbing away a patch of condensation to peer through at him. She smiled when she met his eyes.

"Perhaps you could wipe the rest clear," he said with a smile of his own.

Macy laughed. Instead of wiping away the rest, she ran a finger through the condensation, making two large circles below her face. He didn't realize what they were meant to be until she made a smaller circle at the center of each.

Jax grinned. Despite everything, she still found it in herself to joke, to laugh, to play little games that made them both smile. Her personality brought him as much joy as their physical connection — even more.

"I missed you," she said, turning the water off.

"And I you."

She cracked the door and reached out to grab the towel hanging on the wall nearby, providing him a glimpse of her bare shoulder. She wrapped the towel around her body, slipped one leg through the shower opening, and angled her foot to flex her shapely calf.

Though the conversation he needed to have with her weighed heavily upon Jax, he didn't think he could resist her teasing for long.

"I have a surprise for you," she said.

His curiosity had always been easily provoked, but her words were particularly tantalizing — what could she mean?

"And?"

She opened the door fully and stepped out of the shower, her fingers gliding over his chest as she neared him. Her touch sent tingles across Jax's skin and heated his blood.

Macy leaned forward and kissed him. He opened his mouth to her, kissing her back in a slow, sensual caress of lips and tongues. She bit his lip.

Jax started, eyes flashing open. Had a female kraken done that, his lip would have been torn to shreds, but Macy's bite only excited him further. He growled and reached for her.

She laughed and retreated out of his reach. "You have to find it."

"Find what?" He extended a tentacle and brushed it along her inner thigh, skimming it around the back of her leg to tickle the sensitive skin behind her knee.

"Your surprise," she said, voice husky. She swayed toward him.

Jax advanced, and she didn't back away this time. He cupped her cheeks, and ran his hands down her neck, over her shoulders, and to the top of her towel. "Is it...under here?"

"Maybe."

He gradually loosened the towel. Her eyes gleamed with anticipation and desire. Jax parted the fabric with deliberate slowness, allowing it to caress her breasts. His eyes moved over her flesh as it was exposed bit by bit.

When the towel was open, he released it; it was forgotten before it hit the floor. He slid his palms over her nipples and down her sides, trailing them over her slightly rounded belly to her pelvis.

"Where...where is the hair?" He brushed the backs of his fingers over the smooth, bare skin that had once been covered by a triangle of soft, golden hair, and down across her exposed slit.

"I shaved it off."

"Why?" Confusion and arousal vied for supremacy within him, but neither was strong enough to overpower the other. He lifted his gaze to hers; there was something in her eyes he couldn't place, and she quickly looked away.

"I…thought you might like it."

He hooked the side of his finger beneath her chin and lifted her face. "There was nothing wrong with it. Why do you think I would like this better?"

Her eyes met his fleetingly. Jax frowned.

"Your females don't have hair to…to cover themselves. So, I thought you might like to see it better, without…"

He stilled at those words; he'd never described what female krakens looked like to Macy, had never explained the differences.

Who had approached her? Who had *shown* her?

"Macy. Look at me."

She did, but now her eyes glistened with unshed tears. "Y-You don't like it."

"I don't like *why* you did it," he said, too harshly; she flinched at his tone. He exhaled through his siphons. "Do not ever think, Macy, that you need to change yourself to appease me. I love you as you are."

She searched his face and blinked. Tears slid down her cheeks. "You love me?"

"Yes. I do."

Her face crumpled, and she threw her arms around his neck. Jax smoothed back her wet hair as he embraced her, gently grazing the tips of his claws over her scalp.

How could he have missed her vulnerability? How could he not have realized he was starving her of companionship? He'd never intended for her to feel inadequate, or less than the female kraken, or…alone.

"I am sorry, Macy."

She sniffed and pressed her cheek to his chest. "For what?"

"For not being here for you. For not making you feel as loved and important as you are. And…for not telling you why I have been gone so often."

She pulled back and looked up at him. "You can tell me now."

He lifted her and laid her upon the bed, climbing in after to draw her against him. His throat was tight; once he spoke of his plans to her, they were as good — in his eyes — as a promise. "I've been preparing for us to leave this place."

"What?" She raised her head, damp hair falling onto his chest.

"When you agreed to stay with me, your condition was that you be allowed the freedom to venture out with me. I've failed you in that because of our situation here."

"You didn't fail. You've never failed me, Jax. This…this is beyond our control."

He tucked her hair behind her ear and twined a strand around his finger. "No, it's not beyond our control. My people will only venture so far. We just need the right place to go, and we can leave here and never worry about them finding us."

"But they're your people. What about Arkon?"

"I will miss him…just as you miss your Aymee and your family. But the rest of them…they mean nothing, next to your happiness. If they feel I have betrayed them, they have certainly betrayed me, as well. I owe them nothing more."

Macy brushed a hand over his cheek, his jaw, down his neck. "All this time you've been gone, you were doing it for us?"

He nodded, brow furrowing. "If I had told you, it would have saved you much worry. That is no one's fault but my own."

"I forgive you." She pressed her lips to his; her kiss had never tasted quite so sweet. "You truly love me?"

"You are my home," he rasped, tightening his hold on her. "I will always return to you."

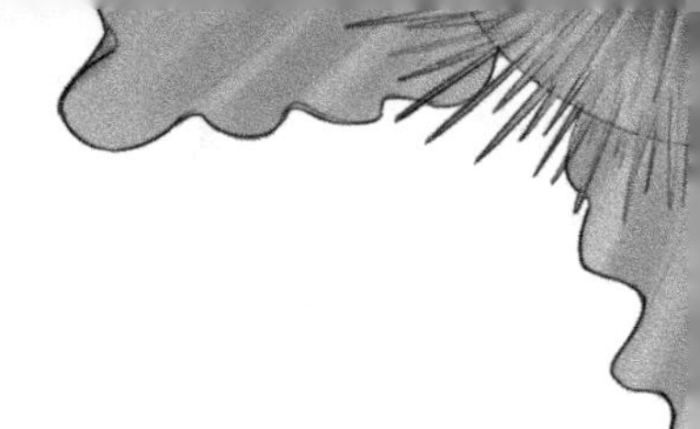

CHAPTER TWENTY

Macy laughed and leaned over Jax, struggling against his strength despite the futility. He had her wrists trapped in his hands and a tentacle around her waist, preventing her from moving the piece of naba any closer to his mouth.

"One bite. Just *one* bite," she begged.

"I will not allow you to poison me, human," Jax said, his playful smile belied his serious tone.

"You're part human, so I doubt a little piece is going to kill you."

"The smell of it alone may be enough to kill me."

"It smells sweet! If you try it, I'll—" she lowered her head until her lips were near his ear and whispered, "—take you in my mouth again."

The humor fled from his face, and his brow fell low. "That is cruel, to offer something I cannot decline in exchange for my life."

Macy rubbed her bare leg along his body, feeling the push of his shaft against his slit. "Your life isn't in danger."

With lightning speed, he flipped her onto her back, pinning

her wrists to the bed and propping himself over her. "You are worth it, either way."

She spread her legs, welcoming him, and wiggled her eyebrows. "You know what you need to do first."

Jax held her gaze for a long while. Finally, with a frustrated grunt, he dipped his head and moved his mouth toward the naba in her hand. His tongue slipped out and licked her finger.

"I can think of some other things you ought to do with that tongue." She lifted her hips, rubbing against him.

"So can I," he whispered, his breath tickling her skin, "and none of them involve eating a pla—"

There was a sudden commotion in the corridor — a raised, frantic voice echoed off the walls. Jax shifted into an upright position and twisted toward the door.

"Jax!" someone called from the hallway. It sounded like Dracchus.

Leaping off the bed, Jax positioned himself between Macy and the door. She sat up and scooted to the edge, adjusted her clothing, and stood.

"Where is my youngling?" shrieked an unfortunately familiar voice. "I will kill that human if she has Melaina!"

The female kraken from the day before — Melaina's mother — darted through the doorway, her eyes blazing. Jax blocked her path; for a moment, Macy was certain the kraken would claw him apart and advance.

"Where is Melaina?" The female stopped in front of Jax and didn't remove her eyes from Macy.

Dracchus filled the doorway a moment later, his shoulders nearly spanning the frame.

"I haven't seen her since yesterday," Macy said.

"This is our den, Rhea," Jax growled. "You cannot enter in this fashion."

"Melaina is missing," Rhea hissed. "Yesterday, I found her here, in your den, with your human. Where is she? Melaina!"

Macy's stomach twisted; the same desperation had been in her parents' voices when Sarina was swept out to sea and lost forever.

"This is foolishness, Rhea," Dracchus said. "The youngling is not here."

"I swear, she's not here." Macy held the female's gaze.

"Liar!" Rhea launched herself at Macy.

The males reacted faster than Macy could register; Jax grabbed Rhea's wrists, shifting to place his body directly in front of her, and Dracchus looped his arms around the female's waist and lifted her off the floor.

"Enough of this!" Jax wrestled the thrashing female; knowing how strong he was, Macy was impressed by how much effort he exerted in stilling Rhea. "Melaina is not here, and has not been here since I returned yesterday. Macy does not have her!"

Rhea's struggled for a moment longer then let out a pained wail. Her body went slack.

Jax looked at Dracchus. Neither of them released their hold on her.

"She has been missing all morning," Dracchus said. "We've searched all the buildings and have found no sign. Rhea flew into a rage when she found out we had not searched this area, and claimed that Macy had taken Melaina."

Jax didn't react to Rhea's cries. "Is everyone capable helping in the search?"

Dracchus nodded. "Even most of the females."

"Melaina told me she liked to venture outside the facility and explore," Macy said. "Maybe she's out there."

"That is where we're going next," said Dracchus. "I need you to lead a party, Jax. There's been a razorback sighted nearby."

Fear skittered along Macy's spine. She couldn't imagine Melaina out there, defenseless, *helpless*, against one of those things.

"Of course." Jax dropped his eyes to Rhea. "We need to go now to find your youngling. You are needed in the search."

Rhea nodded. Cautiously, Jax and Dracchus released her, keeping their wary gazes upon her. She didn't so much as glance at Macy and was quiet as Dracchus led her into the hallway.

"I want to help," Macy said when they were gone.

Jax shook his head. "You are not going out there."

"I want to help find her, Jax."

Macy pictured Melaina's sweet little smile and large, curious eyes. How could she do nothing? How could she sit by and allow another innocent life to be taken by the ocean?

"Even with your suit, you cannot move as quickly as a kraken, and I will not risk another attack from a razorback." He closed the distance between them and placed his hands on her shoulders. "It is best for you to remain here."

"I don't want to be useless, Jax. I can help."

"You are not useless, Macy. But I cannot allow you to come."

"If I were kraken, you wouldn't deny me."

"Human or kraken, I would do anything to keep you safe."

Macy pressed her lips together. She took a deep breath and released it slowly. "You mated with Rhea, didn't you?"

His jaw muscles bulged. "Yes. Briefly."

She dropped her gaze and pushed aside the flare of jealousy that had erupted inside. It was in the past. "Could...Melaina be yours?"

"No. Melaina had already been birthed when I mated with Rhea."

Hearing that eased some of her tension. "Okay."

Jax leaned down and kissed her forehead. "I must go. I will return as soon as I can."

Macy brushed her hand over his arm, nodded, and watched him leave. She counted the seconds; how long would it take for him to gather with the others and exit the building?

When she was sure he wouldn't come back, she ran across

the room and to the dresser. She tugged off her clothes, opened the bottom drawer, and hurriedly donned her PDS.

Jax would be furious when he found out, but that wasn't important. All that mattered was finding Melaina. Macy wasn't as fast or maneuverable as the kraken, but she had something none of them possessed — Sam.

Once her mask was sealed, she strapped on her gun and her knife, making sure they were within easy reach. She left the cabins and made her way toward the exit cautiously, checking around every corner before she proceeded, but saw no one. Still, she couldn't stop glancing over her shoulder as the pressurization chamber drained.

She entered the chamber. The door slid shut behind her, and she drummed her fingers on the gun holster while the room filled.

"Re-pressurization sequence initiated," Sam said. The light over the exit door turned green, and it opened.

Macy swam out and stilled. The endless, lonely sea surrounded her, and her breath was suddenly short. Those old, familiar feels rushed back and coiled around her heart. Every time she'd been in the water, Jax was by her side, anchoring her with his presence.

Now she was alone.

"Irregular respiration detected. Do you require assistance?"

She closed her eyes and forced herself to take several slow, deep breaths.

No, not alone. She had Sam. And Melaina needed her.

She reopened her eyes. "Sam, do you have...heat vision, or something like it? Something that will make living creatures stand out?"

"Thermal and infrared vision are limited in the water, but living creatures can be detected through a combination of—"

"I don't need the details, Sam. Just...turn that on, please?"

"Scanning for living creatures now."

For a moment, her vision was unchanged, and then a soft, barely perceptible wave of light spread outward from her location. As it advanced, spots of brightness appeared. It took her a moment to realize what they were — sea creatures. Fish swam amongst the rocks, and little, many-legged creatures scuttled along the bottom, their forms highlighted by the mask.

"Sam, can you show me only creatures the size of a human toddler and larger?"

"Filtering."

Most of the highlighted shapes vanished.

One problem down. On to the next.

Where had Melaina gone?

Several small arrows hovered on the left side of her vision; Macy turned her head to see a group of kraken, their bodies highlighted by the mask, swimming in the distance. If they saw her, they'd likely send her back inside. Worse, her violation of the kraken's terms would provide individuals like Kronus with reason to renew their efforts against her.

She swam away from the Facility, glancing behind only once. She could *feel* the distance between her and the door growing.

Her heart pounded, but she kept her breath even.

I can do this.

The seafloor was increasingly rocky and uneven as Macy proceeded. She swept her gaze from side to side; large fish drifted near the bottom, and whenever one of them moved out of her field of view, a little marker appeared on the edge of the mask. Sam was detecting creatures all around, whether she was looking at them or not.

She looked back again. The Facility was little more than a hint of light in the distant gloom, and no kraken had followed her. Macy took another calming breath. She'd be fine; the building was back there, somewhere, and Sam probably knew the way...

Jax will find me.

She swam farther, banking to the right. Melaina wouldn't have gone too far. The girl was young, but she was intelligent.

More markers appeared on her left; she turned toward them and stopped when she saw something slide from between two rocks. A tentacle! A hand followed, and then a head.

Melaina's wide, frightened eyes fell on Macy. The girl shook her head frantically and pointed up.

A large marker was on the upper edge of the mask. Larger than any she'd seen so far.

Macy tilted her head back, and the air fled her lungs. The massive, highlighted creature flowing through the water overhead was an image from her nightmares.

A razorback. And it was turning toward Macy.

She swam forward, putting herself between the monster and the child.

"Go!" she screamed, and waved back toward the Facility.

Macy turned toward the razorback and waved her arms. It seemed to fixate on her; she moved away from Melaina, away from the Facility, and the beast followed.

She kicked her legs and used her hands to pull herself along the rocks on the bottom, much like Jax had done.

"Irregular vital signs detected. Do you require assistance?"

"What kind of assistance?" she asked, panting, arms already burning from exertion.

"Would you like me to send a distress signal?"

"That doesn't do me any good now, Sam." Macy looked behind her and her eyes widened. The razorback was gaining. "Can you track that thing's movement?"

"Are you referring to the eighteen-meter-long sea creature behind you?"

"Yes!"

The large arrow that marked the razorback changed to bright green, and a number appeared below it — 13.6M. Within the space of a heartbeat, it dropped to 11.1M.

Macy searched the rocks ahead, but the shadows and irregularities made it difficult to determine whether any openings were large enough for her to squeeze into.

"Sam, I need a spot to hide!"

"There is a crevice straight ahead, in eight-point-five meters." The spot was suddenly highlighted in yellow.

Gritting her teeth, she pushed onward, driven by the deafening pounding of her heart. The distance between Macy and the crevice shrank rapidly; her lead on the razorback dwindled faster.

Please! Please!

The crevice was just within reach when the water behind her shifted. Grasping the edges, she dove into the shelter.

Something powerful clamped down on her leg, and her momentum halted. Macy screamed as the pressure increased and searing pain lanced through her calf.

"PDS exterior compromised. Energy field unstable," Sam said far too calmly. "Redirecting power to compensate."

Macy clawed at the rock around her. For a moment, she held herself in place. When the razorback tugged, it felt as though her arms and leg would be torn from their sockets. She clenched her jaw to hold in her scream as a fresh wave of agony blasted through her.

Her hold slipped, and the razorback dragged Macy out of the crevice. Water rushed around her. The beast snapped its head to the side, swinging her, shredding the muscles of her calf.

Information and alerts appeared on the inside of the mask, and Sam was talking, but she couldn't focus on any of it.

She reached down to take hold of her wounded leg, hoping to alleviate some of the pressure, when her fingers brushed over the knife. Clenching her thigh, she stared at the razorback through the blood misting the water. The way it was moving, she'd never reach its head with the knife.

The gun!

She drew her other leg up, knee to her chest, and struggled to get a hold of the gun. When she finally pulled it from the holster, the razorback changed the direction of its swing.

Screaming through clenched teeth, she slammed her free foot into its snout repeatedly. Her heel connected with its eye and the beast released her abruptly and swam away, snapping its head from side to side. It wheeled around.

She didn't waste a moment; she aimed and squeezed the trigger several times in quick succession as she sank toward the bottom. The sound of the gun firing was strangely muted in the water — she felt its power, more than heard it.

The razorback twisted and thrashed as its blood clouded the water. It reared back, opening its jaws.

Macy fired until the gun was empty. Her feet touched the rocky seafloor; it was strangely comforting to have solid ground beneath her, despite the flaring pain in her leg.

As the razorback charged again, Macy released the gun and drew her knife. The beast's movements were slower now, but seemed no less powerful.

Just before the razorback reached her, she pushed off the bottom. The razorback's snout missed her by centimeters. Macy used her momentum to spin, swinging her arm around and slamming the knife into the beast's eye. She held on as it flipped and tumbled through the water, grabbing hold of one of its spines with her other hand.

The beast twisted its head to the side and snapped his jaws over her injured leg and swam forward.

Macy screamed, but she didn't let go. Tightening her grip on the knife, she tore it free and slammed it into the razorback's head again and again. She looked over her shoulder to see the large rock just before the razorback slammed her into it.

❲❳

JAX SWAM higher above the bottom than he normally would, granting him a wider view of the area. Melaina wasn't likely to have gone far, but if she'd changed her skin to hide, it would be incredibly difficult to spot her.

He led his party in a wide arc around the front of the Facility, slowly expanding their search area; despite the danger of attracting predators, the kraken kept their skin glowing, creating a beacon for the youngling to swim toward.

Movement to the right caught his attention. He halted and turned toward it, altering his grip on his harpoon gun, and his party fell in around him. Something was fast approaching them. Jax tensed, preparing to defend himself.

As the creature neared, its features grew clear — it was a kraken, skin pulsing with warning flashes.

Melaina!

Jax slung the harpoon over his shoulder and rushed forward to meet her. The youngling nearly collided with him. Her eyes were wide, and her skin flashed frantically. She hastily signed, but her movements were difficult to understand, made imprecise by her fear. He signaled for her to slow down.

Danger. Go help. Need help.

He scanned the water for any signs of danger, for a razorback or a sandseeker, but saw nothing.

Melaina grabbed his hand and tugged, waving for him to follow. Before he could react, she swam off, back in the direction from which she'd come.

Despite his confusion, Jax set off after her; the rush of water behind meant his party had done the same. He caught up to Melaina and sped alongside her, gaze darting between the youngling and the seafloor ahead.

His hearts skipped when he saw it; *there*, where distance made everything murky, loomed the shape of a huge razorback. The water surrounding it was clouded with blood.

Jax increased his pace, surpassing Melaina, and swung the

harpoon gun into his hands. There was something wrong with the scene ahead; the razorback was moving, but only barely, its long tail and fins swaying gently. He'd never seen one so still.

The other kraken spread out, weapons in hand, and encircled the beast. But Jax knew there'd be no need for weapons as he came around the razorback's front.

Its head was a mangled mess. One eyeball protruded from its socket, and the other was missing entirely. The handle of a knife jutted from its ruined skull. The spines protruding from the creature's head had snagged on the rocks below, anchoring it in place, and its body — twisted at an odd angle — moved in with the current.

The kraken remained cautious as they closed their circle, until one of the others flashed his light and gestured toward the bottom.

The alarm on the other kraken's face urged Jax forward. His veins filled with ice as his position afforded him a clearer view; pinned beneath the razorback's shoulder was a figure in a black suit.

Macy turned her head toward Jax when he arrived. Her skin was pale and beaded with sweat in the glow of her mask, her features strained. She mouthed his name.

For a moment, terror froze him in place. In all their time together, through all her bouts of illness, he'd never seen her look so worn, so pained...so close to death. He shook it off and signed to the party. They rushed to the razorback, and — moving quickly but carefully — broke the spines that held it in place.

Macy squeezed her eyes shut, bared her teeth, and arched her back as the kraken shifted the creature.

Jax dropped to Macy's side the instant the beast was free. He swept his eyes over her; they were drawn immediately to the wisps of blood flowing from her leg where her suit — and her calf beneath — had been torn to shreds.

He leaned forward and gathered her in his arms. She clung to him with surprising, desperate strength. Their eyes met; he pressed his forehead against her mask and held her gaze as he wound a tentacle around her leg to stop her bleeding.

Her scream was loud enough that he felt its vibration against the glass.

Leaving the others to tend to the razorback, Jax lifted her off the bottom. Melaina looked from Macy to Jax, her features drawn with worry and fear. The youngling swam beside him as he raced toward the Facility.

Though they hadn't been far away, it was the longest, most difficult swim of his life; he pushed as fast as he could without jarring her, without putting any more strain on her wounded leg, without allowing more of her blood to flow. The water in the entry chamber had never drained so slowly. He wished, for a fleeting moment, that the Computer had a physical form he could rake his claws across after it spouted a cheery welcome.

"Will she be okay?" Melaina asked once the water was shallow enough to speak.

"Yes," he said with a confidence he did not feel.

When the interior door opened, he rushed through.

"What do you need, Macy? Where do you want me to take you?"

"The infirmary," Macy said through the mask.

"I don't know that word. Describe the room."

"White. Lots of tables. Beds. Red sign—" she sucked in a sharp breath through her teeth "—with two crossed lines."

He moved as quickly as possible through the corridors, twisting his torso to ensure she didn't bump into anything. Though he'd never heard the word she used, he knew the room she'd described, and he hit the button outside the entry with his elbow when he arrived.

The double doors slid apart, disappearing into the wall, and he hurried inside. He laid Macy atop one of the tall, narrow beds.

"Sam, release the mask." She turned her head to the side, letting the mask fall to the floor, and dropped her hands to grip her leg just below the knee. Jax kept his tentacle tight. "Need something to slow the bleeding. A bandage. Cloth. Anything."

Melaina was at the side of the bed, peering over the low railing. "I am sorry."

"It's okay. I'm glad you're safe," Macy's smile was strained as she looked at the youngling.

"Gather cloth to soak up the blood," Jax said to Melaina. The youngling hurried to do so, and Jax shifted his attention to Macy. "You are going to be fine."

He wasn't certain whether his words were meant to assure her, or himself.

Melaina returned with a bundle of folded cloth in her arms.

Jax took a piece from her — it looked like the sheet from one of the beds — and tore it into a more manageable strip. He took Macy's foot in one hand and lifted it higher. She hissed; her knuckles paled as she dug her fingers into her leg.

"Just wrap it. Quick," she said.

Clenching his jaw, he withdrew his tentacle. Blood seeped from the wounds, spilling onto the bedding beneath and staining it. Fast as he could, he wrapped the cloth around her leg and pulled it tight. Crimson blossomed across the fabric.

Macy's breath was ragged, and tears leaked from her eyes to mingle with the sheen of sweat on her face. Her tears didn't stop her from curling forward, taking the ends of the cloth from Jax, and tying them together. She sagged back onto the bed once she was done, chest heaving.

Humans didn't heal like kraken did — Jax knew that much, but it wasn't enough to help her. Had her body already suffered more than its limit? Helplessness roared inside him, an insatiable fire devouring everything, threatening to consume him. What if he did something wrong?

What if he made it worse?

"Melaina," Jax said. The youngling shifted her wide-eyed gaze to him. "I need you to find Arkon and send him here. You know him?"

She nodded.

"Good. Do not stray from the Facility. If you see others, pass the message on and remain inside."

Melaina turned and hurried away.

Jax leaned over Macy and cupped her face. "Tell me what you need, Macy," he rasped.

"Need to clean the wounds," she said. "Disinfect them."

"I do not know what *disinfect* means."

She laughed, despite her obvious pain, and lifted a hand to his cheek. "Then look for something to seal the wounds. Might look like a small gun. Or…a needle and thread. Check the cabinets."

Jax nodded, though his body refused, at first, to move away from her.

"Go on. I'll be right here." She returned her hand to her leg.

He opened the nearest cabinet and ran his eyes over its contents — dozens of bottles, glass jars, and plastic pouches and boxes. Each item had human symbols on its face, and some possessed the same crossed lines that were on the sign beside the door.

"What happened?" Arkon asked from the entry.

"We need to…*disinfect* her wounds," Jax said without turning away, "and seal them. Do you know anything of this?" There was so much in this cabinet alone, and most of it looked the same apart from the symbols.

"I have seen a device in some of the holograms that appeared to be used to seal wounds." The sound of Arkon crossing the room was pronounced in his haste. "It looked like a heat gun, but it was smaller, with a long, cylindrical protrusion at the rear."

The two searched the cabinets frantically; Jax brushed objects aside to see behind them and opened the little boxes to pour out their contents, creating a clamor. But he found nothing like what Arkon and Macy had described.

Moving backward, he swept his gaze across the room; there had to be something, somewhere, to help her. His hearts thundered against his ribs. He'd seen a few kraken bleed out during hunts, when the severity of their injuries outpaced their ability to heal.

Time was against Macy.

Jax hurried to the long counter against the wall and searched its drawers rapidly. Most were full of tools he had no name for. One of the upper drawers was larger than the rest; he tugged it open.

It contained something familiar to him, though its scale was smaller — a charging rack, like the one where the heat guns were stored. This one had four guns docked within, each with a long protrusion extending behind its narrow grips.

Jax pulled one out and turned to Arkon. "Is this it?"

Arkon nodded, and the two moved to Macy.

What little color had remained in her face was gone now. She lay with her eyes closed, her lips caught between her teeth. The cloth on her leg was so saturated that blood slowly dripped from it.

"We found something to seal the wounds, Macy," Jax said.

"Okay. Need to take off the bandage."

Jax wasted no time; he passed the gun into a tentacle and tore the knot apart with his claw. Macy grunted through gritted teeth, squeezing her eye shut, as he peeled off the fabric.

Arkon wiped away the freshly welling blood with another cloth. There were several jagged tears in her skin, the worst of which was as long as Jax's finger. The shredded material of the suit lay across the wounds.

"We need to cut away the suit," Arkon said.

Jax slipped his claws beneath the fabric and tugged up; it stretched, but did not tear. When he exerted more pressure, Macy hissed through her teeth; his knuckles were digging into her leg.

"We need to take it off," Jax said.

He touched the plastic piece on her chest and slid his fingertips around the edges, releasing the seal along the back. Despite his care when he tilted her onto her side, Macy cried out in pain. With Arkon's help, Jax pulled the suit down, rolling it off her arms. They lifted her lower half to pull it past her waist. She bent her uninjured leg to help remove it from the suit.

There was no way to remove the suit from her injured leg without causing pain, so Jax did it as quickly as possible. Macy writhed on the bed, limbs trembling, and clutched one of his arms. Her fingers bit into his flesh.

Once the suit was off, she eased back onto the bed, breathing heavily. Jax tossed the suit aside as Arkon draped a sheet over her torso and thighs.

Jax picked up the gun and stared at Macy's ravaged leg. It didn't look nearly as bad as the razorback's head, but that counted for nothing.

"How do I use it?"

Arkon held his hand out. "I've seen it in use."

Without hesitation, Jax handed the gun to Arkon. "Quickly."

Nodding, Arkon leaned over her leg. With two fingers, he pushed one of the gashes closed. Macy whimpered. Arkon pressed the tip of the gun to her skin and pulled the trigger.

Macy's entire body tensed, and her mouth opened in a scream that was, for several terrifying moments, silent. She thrashed, pulling her leg away, and nearly rolled off the bed.

"I thought you knew how to use it!" Jax shouted, catching Macy by her shoulders.

"I do! But…I've only seen it used on unconscious individuals." Arkon grasped her ankle to hold her leg still. "It's working. Hold her down, and I will seal her wounds as quickly as I can."

Jax met Macy's glistening, desperate eyes.

"I need something to bite down on," she said.

Jax tore a piece off the sheet and twisted it into a tight bundle. She opened her mouth, and he placed it between her teeth. She bit down.

He leaned over her, repositioning his tentacles to take hold of her thighs, and pressed some of his weight atop her. "Focus on me, Macy."

Her eyes widened for an instant before she squeezed them shut again. She writhed beneath him, and Jax increased the pressure on her limbs so she wouldn't jar Arkon as he worked.

"On me, Macy," he repeated, more firmly. "Listen to me. Hear me. What you did was foolish. You are luckier than you may ever know to be alive right now."

The cloth in her mouth muffled her scream. When she was able to open her eyes, she kept them on Jax. Her gaze was filled with pain, but there was something else beneath it. Determination.

"I told you to stay here, for your own safety, and you disobeyed me," Jax continued. "Somewhere beneath my worry is anger…but the youngling is alive because of you. You saved her life, and though you risked death, this is not your final day. You have proven yourself a hunter today, a warrior.

"My pride for you is beyond words."

Moisture flowed from her eyes. She grasped his arms tighter, digging her blunt nails into his skin.

Arkon turned her leg and squeezed the trigger again.

Macy arched her back. Jax shifted his weight to keep her pelvis on the bed and her thighs pinned. Her pupils expanded before rolling up, displaying only whites, and she sagged, limp, onto the bed.

"Macy!"

"What happened?" Arkon asked.

Jax pressed a shaky hand to her chest, trying to ignore his pounding hearts. He closed his eyes, clenched his jaw tight enough that he risked breaking his teeth, and stilled.

Faintly, he felt the beat of her heart under his palm; it was slow and weak, but it was there. Relief eased some of his panic.

"She lost consciousness," he replied. "Finish quickly."

As Arkon resumed his work, Jax cupped Macy's cheek. Her skin was cold and clammy; less than an hour before, she'd been warm, vibrant, full of life. "You *will* be fine, Macy," he said, voice rumbling from his chest.

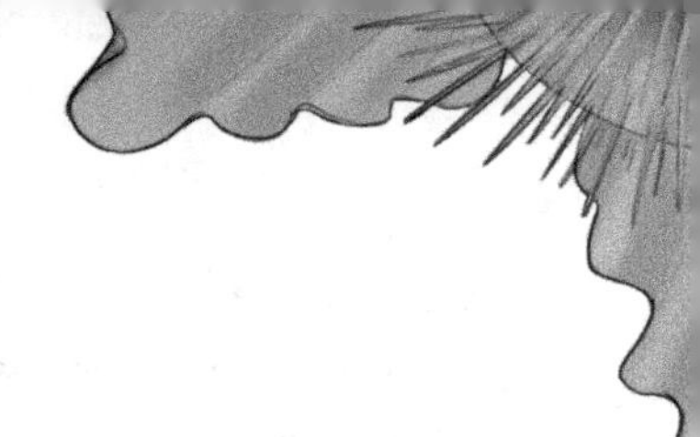

CHAPTER TWENTY-ONE

"She is resting, Rhea. Leave."

It hadn't been the voices that woke Macy, but the pain radiating from her leg, blazing along every nerve. Her throat was parched, and she was too warm. She was afraid to move, even to open her eyes, and longed for the oblivion that had claimed her before.

"I will not. I want to see the human," Rhea said again, voice hard with authority. "Let me pass."

"No." Jax's tone was equally firm. "I will send for you when she is awake, so she can turn you away by her own choice."

"I don't want to fight," Macy said. She opened her eyes and slowly turned her head toward the doorway, where Jax barred Rhea's entry.

Jax twisted to look at Macy. His features eased with relief, but he didn't move. "There is no fight. Rhea is leaving."

Rhea met Macy's eyes. "Will you let me speak, human?"

"Her name is Macy."

Macy stared at the female kraken and gave a small nod; it

was all the motion she could stand. Now that she'd regained consciousness, her leg throbbed, each beat a new wave of agony.

Frowning, Jax shifted aside. Rhea entered, with Melaina close behind. The girl hurried past her mother and grasped the low rail on the edge of the bed, bringing her face close to Macy's.

"Hi." Macy forced a smile.

Melaina smiled, too, but it quickly faded. "Why are you still in bed?"

Jax took up a position beside Rhea, folded his arms over his chest, and watched silently.

"My leg doesn't want to work right now."

"When it does, can we dance again? I like your music. I like dancing with you, too. I am sorry this is my fault."

"Melaina," Rhea intoned.

"I would love to dance with you again." Macy glanced at Rhea. "It was the best fun I've ever had."

"Me, too," Melaina grinned and lifted a tentacle, brushing it over Macy's arm.

"If you wanted your youngling to see Macy, you should have said so," Jax grumbled. "I would have let *her* through."

Rhea glared at Jax. "It is not Melaina alone who wishes to speak to her. I…have a few words." The female turned her attention back to Macy, and the heat went out of her gaze. "I was wrong. At least about you. If you hadn't found my Melaina, she…"

"It's okay," Macy said, and despite her discomfort, slipped a hand through the railing and brushed the backs of her fingers against Rhea's forearm.

The female kraken flinched, but her expression was more confused than alarmed.

"Thank you," Rhea said. She settled a hand on her daughter's shoulder. "Come, Melaina. We must allow her to rest."

Melaina opened her mouth to protest, but she snapped it

shut when she met her mother's stern gaze. "You promise we can dance again, Macy?" she asked as she was led away.

"I promise. As soon as I'm better."

After Rhea and Melaina exited, Jax moved to the bedside, sank down, and took Macy's hand. "How do you feel?"

"It hurts so much, Jax." There was no reason to pretend, with Melaina gone.

He frowned deeply, brow falling low, and touched her cheek. "You are warmer than normal, Macy, and you have not regained your color."

She closed her eyes. His palm was cool against her heated skin. "Do you remember what I said about infections?"

"That infections prevent wounds from healing."

"And could get worse." She opened her eyes. "I have a fever. My wound is likely infected, and there's a good chance this *will* get worse before it gets better."

Somehow, his expression grew even more distressed. "And if it does?"

Macy searched his face. She hated to worry him, hated that her recklessness was doing this to him…but if she hadn't gone out, who could say if the kraken would've found Melaina in time?

"It… The infection could get into my bloodstream…and I could die if it's not treated properly."

The look on his face hurt worse than her leg, if only briefly. She couldn't imagine what he was feeling — he'd likely thought her as good as dead when he found her with the razorback, and after the frantic return to the Facility and his desperate attempts to care for her injuries, she was still in danger of death.

"How do we treat it?" His voice was surprisingly steady.

"Antibiotics. Medicine. That's the only way to be sure."

"Medicine," he repeated, glancing past her. "There are countless bottles in the cabinets. Some of that *must* be medicine."

"But I don't know which to use, or how much to take, or if

any of it is still good." She covered his hands with hers, drawing his attention back. "If I get worse…I need to go back to The Watch."

His jaw muscles bulged, and he nodded. "Anything it takes to keep you safe."

"I love you."

"And I, you." He leaned down and kissed her forehead. "What do you need? What can I do, now?"

"Water."

His touch lingered, and their eyes held. So much passed between them in that moment — love, fear, desperation, and determination. Macy watched silently as he went to retrieve her water.

All those times she'd asked to be taken back to The Watch, all those times he'd denied her, and only now — when she didn't *want* to return — would he bring her without hesitation. Because her life was on the line, and that was more important to him than anything else.

Jax woke to Macy's moaning. He pushed himself upright — he'd fallen asleep leaning on the side of the bed — and shook away his grogginess. He hadn't intended to sleep. Hadn't wanted to take his eyes off her, for even a moment.

Her face glistened with a sheen of sweat, and the sheet Arkon had laid atop her was damp and bunched around her legs. Though her eyes were shut, and she appeared to be sleeping, she shifted from side to side, her expression drawn.

He pressed his palm to her forehead and frowned. She was hotter than before.

By the dimness of the overhead lights, it was night — many rooms in the Facility darkened automatically after sunset — and morning could be hours away. Her words lingered at the forefront of his mind.

If I get worse...I need to go back to The Watch.

Jax turned his attention to her leg; she'd kicked it from beneath the sheet, leaving her calf exposed. The faint, pale scars where Arkon had sealed her wounds were barely visible in the low light, but the thin, red veins snaking outward from them were unmistakable. Though he knew little about the way humans healed, this was clearly not normal.

This was *worse*.

He spread the sheet out over her and pressed a kiss to her cheek. "I will return as quickly as I can," he whispered.

If Macy heard, she made no indication.

He hurried out of the infirmary and down the corridor. He checked the computer room first; Arkon was not there. Gritting his teeth, he swallowed his rising panic. It would do him no good. He went to the pool next, where he gathered a diving suit and a mask. There was still no sign of his friend.

That left only two other likely places — Arkon's den, or the Mess. Jax moved toward the latter.

The voices from inside the Mess carried to him from down the corridor. He'd had little contact with his people since returning with Macy; he'd not sought them out, and no one had spoken to him about what had happened. There was no doubt word had already spread.

But he couldn't know how any of them would take the story.

He ignored the quickening of his hearts and entered the Mess without hesitation.

"We can't let this happen again. We need to keep a closer eye on our younglings, especially the females," one of the kraken said.

The group was smaller than when Jax had brought Macy to the Facility, but a similar tension thickened the air. They were clustered together near the far wall; Arkon, Dracchus, Kronus, and Ector were visible in the crowd.

"This does not often happen. Melaina is restless. She isn't the first, and she won't be the last," Ector said. His eyes shifted at that moment, falling on Jax.

The others responded to Ector's change in attention. Their conversation ended, and all eyes turned to Jax; he couldn't read their expressions, couldn't gauge their moods, save for Arkon's. There was an expectancy in the set of his brow, in the tight line of his lips, in his flattened pupils.

"I need your assistance, Arkon. We need to bring Macy back to her people," Jax said.

Without hesitation, Arkon moved to Jax's side.

"What?" Kronus moved forward, scowling. "She's already broken our terms once, Wanderer. We cannot allow it again."

"Whether with our people's approval or not, Kronus, I am taking her from this place."

"She stays," Kronus growled. "We cannot allow you to expose us for a *human*!"

Dracchus pushed through the others and loomed before Kronus; the two locked gazes and their skin flickered crimson.

"That human has earned her right to be considered one of us," Dracchus said. "She slew a razorback on her own, saving the life of a youngling and providing us ample meat in the process, at great risk to herself. She is one of us. If we can come and go at will, so can she."

"But he means to bring her back to her kind!"

"She will die if I do not," Jax said.

"So let her die," Kronus spat.

Jax advanced on Kronus; the group backed away. "If you are standing between me and the life of my mate, Kronus, I will kill you here."

"She is no proper mate. She is an unnatural, dis—"

Leaping the remaining distance between them, Jax hammered his fist into Kronus's jaw.

Kronus twisted aside with the force. Before the kraken fell, Jax wrapped his tentacles around Kronus's neck and took his face between both hands, holding his claws over Kronus's eyes.

"Speak of her again, and I will end you," Jax growled through bared teeth. "I will take you apart one piece at a time and spread you across the sea as I return her to her people."

Kronus stared, wide-eyed, at the claws hovering above him, body twitching as he fought to breathe.

"She is one of us," Jax said. When Kronus did not reply, Jax roared. "She is one of us!"

Frantically, Kronus nodded, though his range of motion was limited by the tentacles coiled around his neck.

"I am taking her away from here." Relinquishing his hold, Jax shoved Kronus away.

Kronus tumbled into the group behind him; most of them were the same kraken who'd followed him out after Ector had spared Macy's life in this very room.

Jax ran his gaze over the others slowly. "Do I have any other challenges to my intent?"

"I will accompany you," Dracchus said. He met Jax's eyes and held them.

"I do not know how the humans will react if they see us."

Dracchus shrugged his broad shoulders. "She did not know how we would react when she first came here. I would honor her courage."

"Thank you," Jax said.

"Her condition is poor?" Ector asked.

Jax nodded, pressing his lips into a tight line.

"Then go. Quickly."

CHAPTER TWENTY-TWO

The sea was relatively calm as the kraken sped along the surface. The coming sunrise had stained the water and clouds purple, and the patches of sky visible on the horizon were a blend of soft orange and pink.

Jax had seen the humans' home from afar, and, as they neared, Macy's name for it — The Watch — seemed increasingly fitting. He felt exposed beneath the light-crowned structure atop the cliffs. Boats bobbed beside the dock, and the dark shapes of humans walked along its length. Jax had seen many of the boats from below during his travels, but had never been close to one…not until the day of the storm, when he found Macy.

Uncertainty crept up his spine. Would they be able to help Macy in this place? Was she going to survive, would her wounds fully heal? What would the humans do if they saw a kraken?

One question, stronger and more troubling, rose above the others — would they ever be together again? If she survived, would her people let her leave?

Despite any misgivings, his path was clear; he knew what to do, knew there was only one way to be sure she was safe. He had to go with her. Had to place himself at the mercy of her people. He had to ensure her survival, even at the risk of his own.

When she agreed to go to the Facility for the first time, had Macy felt the same fear blossoming in her stomach?

He tightened his hold on her and stopped, turning to Arkon and Dracchus.

"I will go on with her from here. You two stay back," he said.

"Nonsense," Arkon protested. "I will go with you, Jax."

"I am not afraid of these humans." Dracchus's nostrils flared as he shifted his gaze to The Watch.

"No. It is too dangerous. I will take her, and whatever happens, both of you will return to our people. They cannot stand to lose three of us at once."

"And what of you?" Arkon's brow was low, his eyes hard.

"For her, anything," Jax said. The words washed over him, easing the tension in his muscles. Macy had sacrificed much — her comfort, her friends and family, her home, her freedom — since they'd met. He would do the same, and more, if it meant saving her.

Arkon clenched his jaw and forced air through his siphons. "We will not leave you. We'll keep watch from the sea."

"Good luck, Wanderer," Dracchus said.

Jax nodded. "Thank you both."

He turned away from them, ducked beneath the surface, and swam toward the dock.

The humans will help her. She will recover.

He angled himself upward as he neared the end of the dock.

They will *help her.*

Adjusting his hold on Macy, he pulled himself onto the end of the dock with one arm and his front tentacles. The structure floated on the surface of the water, and its swaying, combined with the sense of *heaviness* he always felt in the air, set him off-balance.

"What the hell is that?" someone shouted from nearby.

"Oh, shit!" A second human stumbled back, calves hitting the side of his boat. He tumbled into it with a crash.

Jax cradled Macy in his arm. He shifted her wrist and brushed his fingertip over the control there, summoning the projection. She'd shown him how to perform some of the basic functions just to pass the time one day. He knew the symbols by their shapes, rather than their meanings, and touched them in the order she'd demonstrated.

He took the mask in hand and set it aside gently as humans approached, their footsteps heavy. Their hushed voices held a mixture of fear and awe. Carefully, Jax drew back Macy's hood, uncovering her sweat-dampened hair and looked up at the humans. "Help her. Please."

"That's Macy!" One of the humans turned his head and yelled over his shoulder. "Get Breckett!"

"What is that?" another human asked.

"I don't know… A monster."

"*Help her*," Jax repeated. Even with the suit on, even after hours in the water, the unnatural heat of Macy's body flowed into his skin.

"And it fucking speaks!"

"Get her." They shoved one of their number forward.

"Hell no! You see that things claws? Its *teeth*?"

Jax growled. "She doesn't have time for this!" He moved forward; all the humans scurried back, stumbling over one another.

"What the hell is this?" someone shouted from the far end of the dock. Heavy footfalls plodded nearer.

The crowd of humans parted and glanced back at the two newcomers. One was tall and broad-shouldered, his face covered in hair. The other was familiar to Jax.

Camrin.

"Macy!" the larger male called. He shoved through the

cluster of frightened humans without hesitation and barely looked at Jax as he snatched Macy from the kraken's arms. He smoothed her hair back. "Macy girl?"

Jax backed away slightly, spreading his hands to the side and sinking down. They were unsettled by his appearance, fearful because they did not know what he was, and he didn't want to push them to violence.

Camrin grasped Macy's hand and pulled it to his chest. "Macy…"

"She is sick. Infected," Jax said.

"Infected?" one of the men asked and looked at the others. Several of the humans retreated farther.

"The wounds on her leg are infected. She was attacked by a razorback."

"What *are* you?" Camrin asked, staring at Jax with wide eyes.

"She needs help, needs medicine," Jax said, keeping his gaze on the larger male.

The big human looked up from Macy, and for the first time, he looked directly at Jax. His eyes widened, and his mouth moved beneath his thick face-hair. "Did you do this?"

"No. I would never hurt her." Jax gestured toward the water. "She was attacked by a razorback, and it bit her leg before she killed it."

The emotion on the man's face didn't diminish, and he didn't look away.

"What…what are we going to do with this thing?" someone asked.

A different human leaned forward. "You really think it's not the one that hurt her?"

The large man shook his head. "If he did, why would he bring her here?"

"I will not leave her," Jax said. "I only want her to be healed."

"We can take it to one of those old tanks. Enough of them are empty that it won't hurt to use one." Camrin said.

"I'm taking my daughter to Doc Rhodes. Will you go with these men if they take you to place to hold you until we figure all this out?" the large man asked. His eyes were hard, but there was an undeniable honesty in them.

This man was Macy's father, who she'd spoken of so fondly.

"Yes. I wish none of you harm. Just...save her."

Macy's father nodded and turned to the others. "It brought my Macy back, so it deserves fair treatment until we get some questions answered. Understood?"

The other humans made stammering replies, shifting their attention back to Jax. Macy stirred, moaning, and opened her eyes. They were glassy with fever. "Dad?"

"Yes, Macy girl. I'm here."

"Jax?" she asked. "Where's Jax?"

"Who is Jax?" Camrin asked.

"I want Jax." She shook her head back and forth, slowly.

"Shhh," the large man soothed. "You're sick. We're getting you to the Doc."

"Jax!"

Macy's father hurried down the dock as her cries continued, her voice weak and desperate. Camrin followed immediately behind. Jax watched with his jaw clenched, his chest tight, and his stomach churning. It took all his willpower to prevent himself from calling for her, from chasing after her. She needed medicine; he wouldn't delay that any longer.

The remaining humans stood, staring at Jax, for several moments before they finally acted. Several stepped into boats — teetering to maintain their balance, seemingly unwilling to take their eyes off the kraken — and gathered weapons. Some hefted poles with pointed, barbed tips, others knives of varying size.

"A-Alright," one of the men said. "Just listen to what we say, and we won't have to use these. Follow me. Everyone else is going to be behind you, just in case you try anything."

Jax nodded, and when they made room for him, he slowly

rose and moved forward. The man who'd instructed him turned reluctantly and started walking.

Their gazes were heavy on his back as the humans fell in behind him. Jax focused on keeping his movements smooth and steady, on giving them no reason to make use of their weapons. He breathed deeply and evenly and did his best to match the pace of the male in front of him, who kept glancing over his shoulder.

They moved up a stone path cut between the cliffs. Jax tilted his head back to look up at the structures built atop the stone to either side; to his left, a device jutted past the edge of the cliff. It was a large metal arm, and a thick rope hung from its tip, the hook at the end swaying in the breeze.

Behind him, the humans muttered to one another nervously. Any one of them could lunge at any moment and bury their weapon in Jax's back. Any one of them could be his end. And he'd brought Macy into the Facility, knowing the same had been true for his people; any one of them might have killed her at any time.

As they crested the path, Jax's nervousness was temporarily forgotten. It had always been difficult to determine the size of The Watch from the sea. The sight of it now, from within, was stunning. The structures were so varied; a few bore a vague resemblance to the Facility, but many more were constructed of some sort of stone or wood, sometimes mixing materials.

There were more humans in the pathways between the buildings. All of them stared at Jax as the male in front of him led him onto a path that doubled back toward the water — toward the large building overlooking the dock.

Two of the humans hurried forward and slid open the big doors. They escorted Jax into a huge, dimly lit room. Rows of cylindrical glass tanks, all filled with water, ran from one wall to the other. The foremost were full of various fish; was this how the humans kept their food fresh?

Raised metal platforms ran between the tanks, set at the same level as the lids. The lead human climbed a ladder to get atop the platform. Two more humans followed him before they told Jax to follow. They directed him to one of the empty tanks.

One of the men bent down and manipulated a control on the lid. It slid open, and a light came on at the base of the tank, illuminating the water.

"Go on in," the man said. "Please."

Jax clenched his jaw. It was a cage; he'd have room enough to turn about, and no little more than that. He moved forward — slowly — and lowered himself into the water.

Surprisingly, its temperature matched that of the sea, and it was familiarly salty. A series of narrow slits ringed the bottom; water seemed to cycle through them.

"Does it need air?" one of the men asked.

"I don't know," someone replied. "Ask it. It talks, doesn't it?"

"If it is no trouble to you," Jax said. The men hushed and stared at him.

"How'd you learn to speak like us?" the closest human — the one working the lid — asked.

"We learned from humans, long ago."

The men exchanged glances, and then the one at the controls swallowed. "O-Okay. Going to close it up. Keep your head down."

Jax sank to the bottom and watched as the lid slid shut. The gentle sound of water flowing around him would have been soothing at another time, in another situation. Only Macy's recovery would ease him now.

For an instant, the entire tank vibrated. Then several slits — not unlike the ones on the bottom — opened on the lid. Jax poked his head into the small space between the lid and the water.

"Alright, um…a couple of us will, uh, stay here. If you need anything, we'll try to help," said the human crouched there.

Most of the others had already descended the ladder and were walking toward the door, glancing back as they moved. Their forms were distorted through the curved glass of the tank.

"I need to know if Macy is okay," Jax replied.

It did not comfort him when he received no answer.

MACY FLOATED in a haze of pain, darkness, and noise. There were voices, so many voices; raised voices, quiet voices, voices calling her name over and over.

Then silence. Blissful silence.

She slept, unaware of who she was, where she was. Her pain became distant. And she dreamt. She dreamt of waves, of strange, emerald eyes, and the secure embrace of strong limbs, cocooning her, protecting her from the world.

Her rock.

Her love.

Jax.

Jax!

"Jax," Macy rasped, her broken voice thunderous in the silence.

She opened her eyes. Her vision was a blur of bright light; it cleared slowly, until she realized she was staring at a white ceiling.

"You're awake!" cried a lovingly familiar voice.

Aymee's arms slipped around Macy in a tight embrace.

Macy raised her hand and brushed her fingers over Aymee's soft curls. When she turned her head, she saw her parents approaching.

"Oh, we were so worried!" Macy's mother, Madeline, said, brushing tears from her face. "We all thought you were gone. We thought you were...d-d..."

"Dead," Macy said. That had been the idea. She'd never

meant to come back here, but now that she had, her own eyes misted. She'd missed them so damned much.

Breckett stepped closer and swept the hair from her forehead. "It was a close one, Macy. If it weren't for that…" He looked away, brow furrowed.

"Jax." Dread flooded Macy as she searched her father's face.

Where was Jax? He'd brought her here, had promised to if she got worse. She remembered…remembered…the dock. Jax with his head bowed, arms spread; a stance of surrender. He'd revealed himself. For her.

"Where is he, dad?"

"That monster?" Madeline asked. "He won't hurt you anymore."

"He's not a monster, mom. Jax would never hurt me!" Macy fixed her gaze on Breckett. "Dad, *where* is he? Is he here? Is he safe?"

"Shh," Aymee soothed, pressing a hand to Macy's chest and guiding her back down.

Macy hadn't realized she'd been struggling to sit up.

Aymee glanced at Macy's parents. "I think you should both go, for now." She shook her head before they could argue. "She's my patient, and she doesn't need to get any more worked up right now. She needs rest."

Breckett frowned, staring at Macy. Finally, he sighed and leaned forward, pecking a kiss on her brow. "We'll see you soon, Macy girl."

Once they'd said their goodbyes, Breckett led Madeline from the room.

"Where is he, Aymee?" Macy asked as soon as the door closed.

Aymee settled down on the bedside and searched her face. "This…Jax… He really is good?"

"Yes. He'd never hurt me." Macy caught one of Aymee's

hands and clutched it between her own. "Please, tell me he's okay."

"He's here. The people are wary of him, and there has been talk that he was the one who hurt you."

"That's not true!" Macy exclaimed, struggling to rise.

Aymee carefully guided her back down. "I know, I know. I believe you. People are just scared right now. He's…different."

Macy recalled the first time she'd seen Jax — his claws, his teeth, his inhuman lower half… She'd feared him then, too. She understood, and yet she hated to hear him called a monster.

"Is he safe?" she asked.

"Yeah. They have him in one of the storage tanks in the warehouse. Your dad and some people from the town council have tried questioning him for a couple days now, but he refuses to answer them. He just keeps asking if you're okay."

Relief eased some of Macy's tension; they could ask as many questions as they wanted, so long as they didn't harm him. "How long have I been here?"

"Three days. It was bad, Macy. If he hadn't brought you here…you would have died. We pumped antibiotics into your bloodstream to kill the infection, but your fever only broke last night." Aymee grinned. "Your leg is a mess. Whoever patched you up had no idea what they were doing, but it probably saved your life. Whatever sea creature did that to you, you're lucky you didn't lose your leg outright."

"Jax and Arkon saved me."

"Arkon? Do you mean…there are more like him?"

Macy hesitated. This was Aymee, who she'd trusted more than anyone in the world. Still did. But she understood, now, Jax's early hesitance to share anything about his people. "Yes. There are more."

"Are they good?" Aymee asked.

"They distrust humans. They had a…bad past. But yes, I

believe they are. They're more like us than you can imagine, Aymee. Humans *made* them."

After having Aymee help her sit up, Macy told her friend everything, from the disastrous boat ride to her battle with the razorback. She apologized several times for the hurt she'd caused by allowing everyone to believe her dead. Macy left nothing out, not even her relationship with Jax.

Aymee listened raptly.

"So...you had sex with him?" There was no disgust in Aymee's voice, only curiosity.

Macy's cheeks heated, but she nodded and smiled. "I know it sounds strange, maybe unnatural to some, but...yes. And I love him, Aymee. He's mine, and I'm...I'm his. We joined."

Aymee bit her lip, brow creasing.

"Please," Macy begged, clutching Aymee's hand to her chest, "don't judge me. Don't—"

"I'm not, Mace. Never. It's just..." She inhaled deeply and met Macy's eyes. "There's something I need to tell you."

Macy frowned. "What is it?"

"My dad had me scan you when you were brought in, and I found... At first, I thought..." Aymee closed her eyes for a moment, inhaled deeply, and opened them again. "Did you and Camrin go through with your joining?"

"What? No! No, we never even made it to land before the storm hit."

"You're pregnant, Macy."

Macy recoiled as though she'd been slapped, hands falling to rest on her stomach — her slightly rounded stomach. She stared at Aymee with a mixture of shock and fear.

She and Jax were too different, practically alien to one another. The possibility of a child had never crossed her mind. How could it even be possible?

And yet, Aymee wouldn't lie about this. The kraken were part human...human enough that she and Jax had created a life.

Macy hugged her abdomen. What would it look like? What would it *be*? Would…would it be okay?

No, not *it*. Her *baby*.

"What?"

Macy and Aymee started, snapping their heads toward Camrin. He stood in the doorway, his expression shocked as he stared at Macy.

"Y-You and…that *thing*?"

"Camrin!" Macy called, but he was gone, the door slamming behind him. She turned to Aymee, her heart pounding. "What will he do?"

"I don't know. Stay here. My orders. Your *doctor's* orders. I'll make sure he doesn't do anything stupid."

"Thank you," Macy breathed. "Don't let him hurt Jax."

"I won't."

THE FISH in the other tanks swam in endless circles, clustering in schools that moved with uncanny coordination. Jax had seen it in the sea; here, it looked strange, and reminded him of the funnel of water he'd once watched rise out of the water during an intense storm.

Sudden light caught his attention — the doors slid open, and a human entered the building, its form little more than a distorted silhouette from Jax's view.

He pulled himself up, raising his head out of the water.

"I need to talk to that *thing*. Get out." The voice was familiar, but only slightly.

"We're not supposed to leave it unattended," one of the guards said.

"It won't be. I'll be here."

"Are you okay, Camrin?"

"Just get out!"

Shuffling footsteps clanged on the walkway. Jax watched the humans descend the ladder and head for the exit, just as another figure entered.

"Camrin!" the female called as the doors closed. "What are you doing?"

Camrin ignored her and marched toward Jax's tank. As he neared, the grim set of his features became apparent.

"What did you do to her?" Camrin demanded and banged a fist against the side of the tank.

Jax's hearts skipped. "What happened to her?"

"Nothing," the female said as she drew up next to Camrin. "You need to stop."

"Stop? *Stop?* That fucking *thing*—" Camrin glared at Jax, "—that creature *touched* her!"

"Is she alive? Is she healed?" Jax growled. Camrin's problem didn't matter; only Macy mattered.

"You weren't supposed to be in there, listening to what I was telling my patient," the female said.

"I had a right to know! She was supposed to be *mine*, and you're my friend!"

"That doesn't mean you're entitled to her private information! If she wanted you to know, she would have told you in her own time."

Jax slammed his fist into the glass. The tank rattled, and a thin crack appeared in the side. Camrin and the woman turned their attention toward him.

"Is she safe?" he demanded through bared teeth.

"Macy is fine," the woman said calmly.

"She's not fine! She has a fucking monster growing inside her!"

"What is he speaking of?" Jax kept his gaze on the woman.

"That's enough, Camrin," she warned, eyes narrowed. "This needs to stop, right now. Regardless of what happened, Macy is still your friend, and how would she feel to hear you talking like this?"

Camrin clenched his jaw, gaze flickering between Jax and the woman.

"Think. You don't want to do anything that will hurt her. And hurting him," the woman waved toward Jax, "will hurt her."

"It's wrong. It's…foul."

"All that matters right now is that she's alive and safe."

Camrin growled, hands fisted at his sides.

"Go home. Please. I know you're hurting, but this won't help."

He was silent for a time, glaring at Jax. Without another word, he turned and left, sliding one of the doors open only wide enough to shove through.

The female looked at Jax.

"Let me out," he said. "Take me to her."

Regret filled her eyes. "I can't do that."

"I will break out if I must."

"That'll make things worse. A lot of people think you're dangerous, and that'll just prove to them their fears are justified." She stepped closer, her gaze moving over him, pausing first at his claws, then his tentacles.

A few more blows and the tank would shatter. He'd be free to find Macy.

And how would that help? He didn't know The Watch, didn't know where she was, and the place was full of humans. Though they'd escorted him here with simple weaponry in hand, he'd seen the long guns the guards carried now. They'd kill him, and he'd never know for sure if she was safe.

"I *need* to see her," he rasped. It brought her eyes back to his.

"Macy just woke up. She…told me everything."

"So you know I did not harm her. You know I am only here to ensure she is safe."

"Yes. And I believe her. Believe you. But there are a lot of folks here who won't. Camrin and I are her friends, but others… They're not going to see past what you are very easily. Being here could be dangerous for you, and now, for her."

The concern in the female's voice broke through Jax's desperation for a moment; she cared for Macy, deeply. "You are Aymee."

She smiled. "She talked about me?"

He nodded. "Yes. With…love."

"And I love her, which is why we need to get both of you out of here. Not now, but soon. Can you trust me enough to give me some time?"

Aymee held his gaze as he searched her eyes.

"Macy trusts you. So do I."

She nodded. "Thank you."

"What did he mean, Aymee? What monster is growing inside of her?"

"Not a monster. A baby. Yours."

Jax froze; his muscles refused to move, his breathing ceased, and his hearts were still. It seemed like many moments passed in that state. The entire world was motionless. When he could finally move, it was a struggle to speak. "She…how? How can you know?"

"She told me how your kind were made. That you have human DNA. When her father brought her in, I was the one to check her, and I…saw it. It doesn't look like a normal human fetus. And she's… It's far more developed than it should be by now. She's only been gone for a month and a half, but the fetus looks like it's in its second trimester. How long do your kind carry babies?"

"Four months." He barely heard his own response. Offspring were so rare for the kraken, so precious… The thought of procreating with Macy had never crossed his mind. How could it even be possible?

What would their youngling be? Human, kraken, or something else entirely? What would his people think of the child? Would they rejoice, knowing that there was a chance to grow again, to thrive, or would they think such offspring abominations to both kinds?

The doors opened wider, and light from outside streamed into the building. Aymee glanced behind her.

"I have to go. Please, be patient. I'll talk to her, and we'll make a plan. Just know that she is okay."

He nodded numbly and watched as she turned and hurried out, gesturing to the guards on her way. Jax closed his eyes and dropped to the bottom of the tank. His mind swirled like the churning sea beneath a fierce storm, but he took some solace in the knowledge that Macy had woken up and was well.

Aymee had given her word.

Jax would see Macy soon.

CHAPTER TWENTY-THREE

AYMEE PRESSED THE BOOSTER GUN TO MACY'S CALF AND PULLED the trigger.

It pierced Macy's skin with a *pop*, and she flinched, hissing through her teeth. The shots had become a daily occurrence over the last few days, and they seemed to be working — her pain had diminished to tolerable levels. It still hurt every time she was forced to roll out of bed and walk, but Macy didn't complain. Every step was one closer to seeing Jax again.

Tonight.

Macy would have already gone to see him, if not for her leg; she couldn't manage more than twenty or so steps before it was too much for her damaged muscles. These days apart from him had been the longest of her life. Only the knowledge that Jax wasn't being harmed had afforded her any patience.

"I'll pack a few of these with your other supplies," Aymee said, removing the cartridge from the dispenser and tossing it in a bin.

"Thank you, Aymee." Macy said massaged her calf. "More than you'll ever know."

Aymee smiled and pecked a kiss on Macy's cheek. "As crazy as all of this is, I'm happy for you, and fascinated by him."

Macy arched a brow.

"Oh, stop! You know what I mean. We thought we were *it* on this planet. I mean, even if they weren't here before us, they're still alien beings who can think and talk like us." Aymee sat beside Macy on the bed. "And there's something…alluring about him. I mean, he's frightening and all, too, but…he's beautiful."

"He is." Macy chuckled; the sparkle in Aymee's eyes meant she was already envisioning how she'd paint Jax's picture.

Aymee's features grew suddenly somber. "I'm going to miss you, Mace."

Macy's eyes stung. "I'm going to miss you, too."

"At least I'll know you're alive this time." She looked down at Macy's stomach. "And you're not going to get out of letting me meet your baby."

Macy embraced Aymee, holding her close. "We're supposed to grow old together, right? Even if I live somewhere else, we'll still see each other."

"I know. And we can leave letters for each other in the supply case. Do you remember the place?"

"Near the rock that looks like a krull drinking from the water." Macy smiled to herself. "Where we used to build little houses in the sand, and you'd paint the stones pretty colors."

Aymee pulled back and grinned. "The very place."

There was a knock on the door; it opened before either of them could respond. Doctor Kent Rhodes, Amy's father, peered in.

"How are you feeling, Macy?" he asked.

"Anxious, but good." Macy had been fearful when Aymee said she'd told Doctor Rhodes everything, but her fears were unfounded. His warm demeanor — which she'd known since she was a little girl — hadn't changed, and he'd shown nothing but concern for her wellbeing.

It had been his decision to erase Macy's scans. While no one else was likely to see them, he didn't want to take the chance of them getting into the wrong hands and stirring up trouble for Macy and Jax.

"Good, good. You need to exercise that leg, but don't push it too hard, okay?" He cleared his throat and glanced behind him. "You have another visitor."

Doctor Rhodes opened the door wider to reveal Camrin.

"Can I talk to you, Macy?" Camrin asked.

Macy nodded when Aymee gave her a questioning glance.

"Okay," Aymee said. "I'll go find your dad, and I want you up and walking when we get back."

"I will. Thank you, Aymee."

With a nod, Aymee moved toward the door. "Be nice, Cam. If you upset her—"

He held up his hands. "I won't. I promise."

Camrin entered, and Aymee and her father left. Once the door closed, he turned to face Macy. He was silent as she scooted to the edge of the bed and lowered her feet to the floor.

"I tried to find you after the storm," he finally said, stepping closer. "You have no idea how panicked I was when I woke up on the beach and you weren't there. The boat barely made it back here, but the first thing I did was try to form a search party. Only my father and Breckett were willing to go. Everyone else figured you were already dead...but I had to try. We searched for days, up and down the coastline, all along the cliffs, but...we couldn't find you."

Guilt assailed Macy; she knew the pain her decision would cause. Though Jax hadn't left her much of a choice, she'd been the one to embrace her situation, to enjoy her newfound freedom and let everyone she knew believe she'd perished.

"And all this time, you've been with him," Camrin said, stopping in front of her.

"Camrin—"

"No. I'm not here to attack you, Macy. I'm here to say…I'm sorry." He knelt and took her hands in his. "You're my friend. Always have been. When I saw you in his arms, saw you *alive*, I was overjoyed. I wasn't thinking about our future together, or what I'd say to you when you woke. I was just so damn thankful you were alive."

Teardrops flowed over her cheeks, and she dropped her gaze, squeezing his hands. "I've wronged you, Camrin. So much…"

"I can't lie and tell you it doesn't hurt, Macy."

"I know." She met his eyes. "I should have told you years ago how I really felt. I've wasted so many…so many years, so many years of your life. You could've found someone worthy of your love."

"Macy, you are—"

"No, I'm not. I never felt for you what I do for Jax. I loved you, but it was never the kind of love you wanted or needed from me. You were familiar. You were safe, and I used…used you horribly. I thought that maybe, after we joined, it would change — that *I* would change — but I know now it would've been a mistake."

Camrin stared at their hands, silent.

"I'm so, so sorry, Camrin."

He was silent for a long while before his tongue slipped out to wet his lips. "I think I've always known, deep down. I…I didn't want it to be true, and I fought against it so damned hard because all I wanted…I wanted you, Macy, but more than that, I wanted to make you *happy*."

"You did, Camrin. You were there for me through it all. You made my days a little brighter." She cupped his face, forcing him to look at her. "You did nothing wrong. *Nothing*. It was me. What I needed, what I wanted…"

"Is locked in a tank in the warehouse."

Macy frowned and looked away. This time, Camrin guided

her to face him, curling a finger beneath her chin. "I'm jealous as hell of him, Macy, and I wish you felt that way about me…but I really do want you to be happy. Which is why I want to help you."

Her eyes widened. "What?"

He smirked. "Do you think I don't know you and Aymee have something planned? She's not exactly the most subtle person around here, and I've known you both since we were little kids."

"You'll help us?"

"Whatever you need from me, Macy."

Macy threw her arms around him. "Thank you!"

With Camrin's support, she made several slow laps around the room, detailing the plan as she walked. Before long, the door opened, and Aymee entered with Breckett close behind.

"You're walking," Breckett said, grinning through his thick beard.

Macy smiled. "Barely, but it's getting better."

"How much longer do you think it'll be before she can come home?" he asked.

"Well…" Aymee looked at Macy and raised her brows.

"I'm not coming home."

Breckett frowned, his gaze moving from Macy to Aymee, then Camrin, and back again. "What are you talking about?"

"I need your help, dad."

His frown deepened. "You two, out."

Without a word, Aymee and Camrin departed.

Breckett stared at Macy for a long while after the door was closed, nostrils flaring with his heavy exhalations. "Just when I get you back, you're going to leave again?" His eyes glistened.

Unable to hold back her tears, Macy stumbled forward and threw her arms around her father. He stepped forward and caught her, drawing her into the shelter of his embrace.

"Tell me you know what you're doing, Macy girl," he rasped. "Tell me you're going to be okay."

"I will be. Jax loves me, dad, and I love him. I know he's different, that he's not...not human, but if you could only spend time with him..."

"Damn it, I have. And all he did was ask after you. Wouldn't tell me anything else...he just wanted to know if you were okay, if he could see you." He sniffed and tilted his head down, kissing her atop her head and tickling her face with his beard. "I just want you to be safe and happy. I'll still break his neck if he hurts you, doesn't matter where you go."

Macy laughed and squeezed him tighter; her laughter quickly faded. "What about mom?"

He pulled back and took hold of her upper arms with his big, rough hands. "She'll...she'll come to terms with it, in time. I need you to know, Macy girl, that she never really blamed you for your sister. Your mom...she broke that day, and she's never been quite right since. But I'll take care of her while you're gone."

Macy nodded. "You'll tell her I love her?"

"Course I will. Now, what do you need my help with?"

"We're leaving tonight, but there's no way I can get down to the water on my own. Even if I use crutches...I don't need anyone asking why I'm out there on my own in the middle of the night. If you're with me, though..."

"I'll take you, Macy."

"You will?"

"I will. But how're you going to get him out of the tank? The town council put a lock on it until they decide what to do about all this, and we don't have the key."

"We'll...figure it out. Aymee is going to speak with him soon. But afterward... We need to make sure everyone understands this is *my* choice. That I left with him willingly. I don't want anyone to hunt him — to hunt *us*. He's not a danger to anyone."

"I'll tell them, but there're fools in this town who'll run their mouths regardless. What about the guards?"

"Camrin is going to lure them away. We don't want anyone to get hurt."

"If those men aren't far enough away when that tank is broken, they're going to hear it, Macy. They'll come."

Macy frowned. "Jax will just have to be faster than them. He doesn't want to hurt anyone. He never hurt me, either, even when I gave him cause to, but all of this… It's put his people at risk, and now he's exposed."

"And you can't much blame a man — or whatever he is — for fighting for his life when his back's in the corner." He lifted a hand and tugged his fingers through his beard. "All right. When do I need to be here?"

"Come at sunset. It'll…it'll give us a little more time to talk."

He wrapped her in a strong, secure embrace. "Love you, Macy girl."

"I love you too, dad."

JAX WATCHED the guard leaning against the next tank over; the man's head bobbed as he drifted toward sleep. The other guard sat on the floor near the entrance, back against the wall, and was using the tip of a knife to pick at a chunk of wood. Their conversation had died off long before, and idleness was taking a toll on them.

For five days, Jax had been trapped inside this damned tank, with no idea of where Macy was, or what she was doing. The guards changed twice each day and once every night. Most of them couldn't help but walk up to the tank and ogle Jax with wonder at some point during their vigil; their faces were becoming familiar to him. A few had even attempted to talk with him; Jax wasn't interested.

He trusted Aymee, but he wasn't happy about the situation.

His muscles bristled with tension, with the need to move, to stretch, to *swim*. They gave him fresh fish several times a day, and though they tasted fine, there was no satisfaction in eating them. Not without the preceding hunt. He missed the open water. Missed exploring. Missed *freedom*.

More than all that, he missed Macy — the smile on her face, the sound of her laughter, sharing meals with her and lying beside her in the open air, admiring the stars.

Just as the sleepy guard began to tip forward, the door opened. The light was bright enough that Jax was momentarily blinded. After his eyes had adjusted, he watched as a newcomer — clearly Aymee, once she drew nearer — spoke with the guards, who had both moved to meet her.

Jax didn't bother surfacing yet. After a brief conversation, the guards picked up their long guns and left, one of them raising his arms overhead and stretching as he moved. Only when the door was closed and Aymee stood in front of the tank did Jax rise.

"We don't have much time," she said. "We're going to make our move tonight. Macy will be ready to leave, and we need to figure out how to get you out of this tank."

His hearts quickened, and excitement swept through him, heightened by his need for action. "How?"

"We're not really sure how it'll play out. Macy's father is going to take her to the docks to wait for you, and Camrin is going to lure the guards away." Her eyes strayed to the crack in the glass. "The main thing is we want to keep anyone from getting hurt, so we need to be quick and quiet."

"You need to try to call Arkon and Dracchus."

Her eyes widened. "They're here?"

"Arkon said he would wait and watch. He is in the water, not far offshore. He and Dracchus will help, if you can contact them and lead them to this place."

"How do I contact them?"

"A sign." Jax ducked under the surface and showed her the quick series of arm and hand movements. She repeated them with him several times until she got them right.

"What does that mean?" she asked when he came back up.

"*Swim with me.*"

"Swim with you? Not *help*? Or *danger*?"

"It is the only sign I can think of that doesn't require tentacles or a color change, but still holds enough meaning to catch their attention."

"What do you want me to tell—"

The door opened.

Aymee glanced over her shoulder. "I need to go. Tonight."

She turned and went to meet the guards. Their voices were too muffled by distance for Jax to make out, so he sank down and closed his eyes. His tentacles twitched with anticipation, but all he could do was wait.

Tonight.

CHAPTER TWENTY-FOUR

"IT HAS BEEN FIVE DAYS," DRACCHUS GROWLED.

Arkon exhaled through his siphons and dropped his forehead to the rock he was leaning against. "I am aware."

"How long do you intend to wait?"

"I will *not* leave them behind, Dracchus."

Grunting, Dracchus moved forward along the stone, shifting his gaze to the human settlement. "That is not what I was implying. It is past time for us to go and get them."

The idea was appealing; the two kraken had waited in the water since Jax returned Macy to her people, lurking along the cliffs as the tide rose and fell. Dracchus had very nearly charged in when the humans took up weapons and led Jax away, but Arkon had managed to stop him. Jax had been calm, and that was a good sign.

Or a very, very bad one.

"What do you propose?" Arkon asked. "Do you know where either of them are? Do you know what structures they have up on the cliffs, their layouts, their defenses? We don't even know how many humans are up there."

"Perhaps if you spent as much time thinking about what we

can do, rather than why we shouldn't do anything, you would have come up with a plan of your own." Dracchus's scowl was deep; even after everything that had transpired, Arkon couldn't deny his satisfaction at seeing it.

"I would love nothing more than to go in there and see my friends again." Arkon lifted his head and looked at the dock.

Most of the ships that had departed with the dawn had already returned, just ahead of the sunset. Humans moved in and out of the vessels, hauling barrels and netfuls of fish. Arkon couldn't help his fascination as he watched them.

The kraken hunted together, survived together, but their society — if it could be called that — was comprised of staunch individuals. They congregated and worked together when necessary, but rarely displayed the warmth and familiarity the humans showed to one another.

The humans touched frequently — slapping each other on the back, clasping hands, even embracing. When they were near each other, they seemed to speak incessantly. They worked hard, males and females *together*, utilizing many devices — deceptively simple devices — as aids. They weren't without their clashes, but those seemed few and far between.

"There is a female on the dock I have not seen before," Dracchus said.

"Hmm?" Arkon shifted his gaze toward the land.

The female looked over her shoulder before stepping off the side of the dock; with the tide low, the narrow stretch of beach wrapping around the inside curve of the cliffs was exposed, ending near the rocks where Arkon and Dracchus waited. She moved along the sand, toward the kraken. As she walked, she did something that gave Arkon pause.

"Do you see that?" he asked.

"Perhaps it is a mistake. There is no way she would know that sign."

But the female, after glancing behind her once more,

repeated the arm motions exactly. She swept her gaze across the water.

"She would know it if Jax showed her. I will move closer. Speak to her," Arkon said.

"If the men on the dock are alerted to our presence, they will be more watchful from now on. We will lose any opportunity we might have had to rescue Jax."

"She's repeating the sign deliberately. Jax must have taught her and sent her to look for us."

Dracchus looked back at the woman, his frown, somehow, deepening. "Fine. Keep low and keep hidden."

Arkon pushed off the rock and dipped below the surface, swimming toward the woman. As the water grew shallower, he altered his skin to match the bottom and slowed, digging his claws and the tips of his tentacles into the soft sand to anchor himself from the tide. He lifted his head above the surface, and his breath caught in his throat.

The wind had swept the female's long, brown hair — its spiraling strands so unlike Macy's — into her face. She slipped her fingers into her hair and tugged it back, revealing a delicate face with dark eyes and pink lips. Her features were similar to Macy's only in that she was also human. Her skin was darker, and she was taller, with long, graceful limbs.

She was *beautiful*.

The female made the sign again.

"Where are they?" she asked.

"Here."

The female leapt backward. When her feet hit the sand, she fell, landing on her rear. She searched the nearby water with rounded eyes, moving them directly over Arkon twice.

"Where are you?"

"I am here." Arkon allowed a flash of his normal color to pass across his face.

Her lips parted as she met his gaze. "Macy said you changed

color, but I guess I just didn't expect *this*." She moved onto her hands and knees and crawled toward him.

"You know Macy? Is she all right?"

She stopped as the surf rolled in, running over her wrists and dampening her clothes. "She's got a long recovery ahead, but she's doing well. My name is Aymee. Are you...Arkon?"

His eyes widened. This was Aymee, the friend Macy had spoken of? His wildest imaginings hadn't done her justice.

"I...yes. Yes, I am. Arkon."

"Do you not speak English as well as Jax does?"

Surprise skittered over Aymee's face as Arkon's camouflage faltered; he was suddenly quite nervous, more than ever in his life, and his tongue felt somehow dry. Less than a body's length of distance lay between them, just a bit of sand and water. "I, uh...yes. I mean...no. I speak well enough, thank you. I'm just a bit weary?"

Arkon squeezed his eyes shut and gave himself a mental shake. She'd sought him for a reason; Jax and Macy had sent her, and that was more important right now.

"If you've been waiting out here all this time, I'm sure you are." Her eyes moved over him slowly. "You are fascinating."

He smiled as warmth spread over his skin. "Why have you come to find us, Aymee? What is happening?"

"Is Dracchus here, too?"

Arkon's gaze flicked toward the rocks for a moment. "He is close by...but he's not very good company." He was suddenly glad Dracchus had stayed behind; he didn't want anyone else to see this female, for fear they'd desire her. Arkon wanted Aymee to be his alone.

She grinned. "So Macy told me." A wave crashed over Arkon, forcing Aymee to turn her face away as she was sprayed. "They're leaving tonight, but Jax needs your help."

His smile faded. "They are okay, are they not?"

"They're fine." Aymee turned toward the dock, watching

silently, then looked back to Arkon. "That building up there with the crane, do you see it?" she asked, pointing over her shoulder.

He followed her gesture with his eyes; he felt it safe to assume that the large device hanging over the edge of the cliff was the *crane*. One end of a large building was visible nearby it. "I do."

"He's in there, but he's locked in a tank. No one has hurt him, though. It's just a precaution."

"How do we get inside to get him out?"

"The warehouse doors themselves aren't locked. It's just a place where the fishermen store catches and their supplies. Someone's going to lead the guards away for a little while, so you have a chance to slip inside to get him out." She frowned. "We don't want *anyone* hurt, including you."

Arkon glanced toward the rocks again; Dracchus's body was mostly hidden by his camouflage, but Arkon could just make out orange, staring eyes. "That should not be an issue."

"Macy's father is going to carry her to the docks to wait, so you and Dracchus need to be ready and waiting tonight for our friend to lead the guards away." Her gaze moved over him again. "With that camouflage, you should be able to get up there once it's dark and wait nearby. Right?"

"We will manage, Aymee. Are your people armed?"

"The guards are, which is why we're going to get them as far from the warehouse as we can."

"We'll be especially careful, then."

She turned her head toward the dock for a moment before looking back at Arkon. "Can you show me your normal color, one more time?"

Almost without thinking, he shifted his face to its natural coloring; he was unable to look away from her.

Aymee smiled. "You really are beautiful."

Her words were unexpected, but they were not what left him

speechless for a moment; that was the result of her smile and the light dancing in her eyes.

"I need to go. I'm glad to have met you, Arkon."

"And I will never forget you, Aymee."

He remained in place as she pushed to her feet — not because he didn't try to move, but because his body didn't respond to the command. She attempted to brush the sand off her clothing; it clung to the wet patches on her arms and legs stubbornly. Her torso was wet, also, and the fabric clung to her, accentuating the shapely form hidden beneath. His knowledge of human anatomy didn't stop him from wondering exactly how she looked under her coverings.

Finally, he regained his senses enough to pry his attention from Aymee. He turned and swam back to his companion.

"And?" Dracchus grumbled.

"Jax and Macy are leaving this place. They will need us to go in and help."

"Good," he replied. "I am tired of waiting."

"That's unfortunate. None of this is happening until after nightfall."

Dracchus bared his teeth in a sneer, and the two settled in to await the cover of darkness.

CHAPTER TWENTY-FIVE

With the overhead lights dimmed, the primary illumination in the warehouse was cast by the occupied tanks. Jax's vision was warped beyond the glass, but the guards were in sight; they stood several body-lengths apart, in the clear space near the door, bouncing a ball back and forth to each other. Their guns leaned against the wall.

Jax remained at the bottom of the tank, watching, *waiting*. His tentacles were folded under him, slowly coiling and relaxing. It was the only relief — however minor — for his tension. Anticipation had thrummed through his veins since Aymee's visit. He assumed it had been hours, but it felt like days had passed in that time, and his eyes had continually drifted to the tiny crack on the inside of the glass.

Not while the humans are here.

Fast as Jax was, the humans would reach their guns before he could stop them.

He had to trust in the plan; had to trust that Macy, Aymee, and Camrin knew what they were doing.

Macy was awake and well. Aymee hadn't been lying, but it was still difficult to accept. Until he could see his mate with

347

his own eyes, touch her with his own limbs, he would be consumed with worry. Of all the things he'd done in his life — after all the dangers he'd willingly faced — letting the humans take Macy away from him had been the most difficult.

The doors slid open slightly, granting Jax a distorted view of the dark purple sky beyond. A figure entered and walked into the light. Camrin.

Jax remained in place as one of the guards bounced the ball; the other missed it, stumbling forward to catch it.

The three humans spoke. The pounding of Jax's hearts gradually strengthened, soon drowning out the sound of flowing water inside the tank.

Camrin gestured toward Jax, and one of the guards glanced at the tank over his shoulder, frowning.

Was this a betrayal? Was Camrin telling them of the escape plan?

Clenching his fists, Jax drew back against the glass. He bunched his tentacles beneath him, ready to spring forward. He'd be out of this tank one way or another. *Tonight.* His eyes rose to the crack for an instant.

Camrin smiled and took a step toward the doors, waving for the guards to follow. The two humans hesitated, exchanging a glance with one another.

It would take a massive amount of force to break through the tank in a single blow, but there wouldn't be time for anything more. The guards' distraction wouldn't count for much beyond it.

One of the guards slapped the other on the shoulder, and the men hurried to catch up to Camrin, picking up their long guns at the door. The three humans exited one at a time. The doors slid shut, returning the front of the warehouse to relative darkness.

Jax's anxiety eased, but only slightly. He forced himself to count his heartbeats. The humans needed to be far enough away that they wouldn't hear the glass breaking.

One hundred.

Two hundred.

He imagined the humans walking side-by-side, laughing and talking, as they moved away from the warehouse. How many heartbeats before they were far enough?

Four hundred.

How long would they be gone?

Macy would be waiting at the docks; Jax would get to her by any means necessary. He flattened himself against the backside of the tank, focused on the crack, and surged forward.

Something moved at the edge of his attention.

He faltered, flaring his tentacles to stop his momentum. His shoulder struck the glass — not with enough force to break it, but enough to hurt.

The doors had opened again. He watched as two dark figures slithered through the gap and slid the doors shut. Their familiar gaits filled him with a joy he hadn't expected, and he quickly forgot the throbbing ache in his shoulder.

Arkon hurried to the tank as Jax broke the surface. Dracchus, sweeping his gaze from side-to-side suspiciously, took position nearby.

"Why do they need to keep fish in these tanks, when the sea is so close by?" Dracchus asked.

"This allows them a ready food supply they can store indefinitely," Arkon replied. He ran his hands over the outside of the tank, studying its construction. "It means that, though they are reliant upon hunts to catch the food initially, they are never a single failed hunt away from starvation."

"They grow plants to eat, too," Jax said, speaking through the slits in the lid, "which matters just as little as what they use the tanks for. Open the top."

"Good to see you, too, Jax." Arkon stretched up and grabbed

the edge of the metal platform, pulling himself up in a single, fluid motion.

"You know I am overjoyed to see you. Both of you." Jax turned to glance at Arkon's shadowed form through the narrow slits.

"I am glad you yet live, Wanderer." Dracchus moved forward and stopped immediately in front of the tank, tilting his head back to examine the thing. His eyes shifted to the crack.

"This device should be simple enough to operate..." Arkon blew air through his siphons.

Jax clenched his jaw. "But?"

"It appears as though they've put some sort of locking mechanism on it. The manual release for the lid is immobile, and I believe it must be free to move, even for the electronic controls to function."

"Can you open it, Arkon?"

"I just need a few moments to puzzle it out."

Every moment was precious, but the chance of escaping this cage without raising any sort of alarm couldn't be easily dismissed. Jax counted his heartbeats as he waited.

"How long will the humans be away?" Dracchus asked.

"I do not know," Jax replied.

The large kraken grunted and turned away, looking between the other tanks.

Angling his head to glimpse Arkon, Jax frowned. "Arkon?"

"It is...somewhat more complicated than I anticipated." Something rattled on the lid.

"We don't have time for this, Arkon."

"It will not be much longer."

"Wanderer," Dracchus growled, "we must go. They will put all three of us in these cages if they return."

Jax spread his fingers and raked his claws impatiently along the glass. "I know."

Dracchus ducked beneath the walkway and disappeared from Jax's view.

Arkon rattled something on the lid again, and then banged on it; the sound vibrated through the glass and made ripples on the surface of the water.

"Arkon."

"I'm doing what I can, Jax!"

Jax's gaze flickered to the door; it was still closed, but he expected, the guards to walk in at any moment. Their eyes would go wide, and they'd raise their guns. Water and kraken blood would spill on the floor.

"Can you open it, or not?"

"Yes. I think so. I just need time."

"We don't have any time." Dracchus emerged from under the platform. "Macy awaits at the docks. The humans will return at any moment." As he advanced toward the tank, he hefted something in his hands — a long metal tool with a bulky end.

Dracchus met Jax's gaze.

Jax nodded and shifted to the rear of the tank, pressing himself against the glass.

Gripping the tool in both hands, Dracchus drew himself up on his tentacles and twisted. Muscles rippled beneath his dark skin as he swung. The head of the tool crashed into the glass, and cracks shot in all directions, radiating from the point of impact.

"What was that?" Arkon demanded. "What is he doing?"

Dracchus drew back once more. When the tool hit the glass a second time, the damaged portion collapsed inward, only to be swept out by the rush of escaping water. Dracchus hit the glass repeatedly as water pooled around his tentacles, opening the hole wider.

"That was not necessary!" Arkon moved onto the walkway and lowered himself to the floor behind Dracchus.

Turning to direct a heavy, lingering glance at Arkon, Dracchus tossed the tool aside. It clanged on the stone floor.

Jax pulled himself out of the tank, latching onto the edge of the walkway to swing clear of the broken glass on the floor. He landed in the last of the draining water and stretched his arms and tentacles. His muscles ached sweetly with their restored range of motion.

The kraken stared at one another; the only sounds were those of the water running into an unseen drain and the waves breaking on the cliffs outside.

"We need to leave." Jax shifted his eyes from Arkon to Dracchus and back again.

"I would have opened it soon enough," Arkon said.

Dracchus grunted.

"Come. Now." Jax didn't look behind him as he moved toward the doors, darkening his skin on the way. The shadows would be their only cover until they reached the dock. He grasped one of the handles, paused to listen for anything out of the ordinary, and slid the door open.

Leaning out, he glanced inland. A pair of lights set over the warehouse doors illuminated the area directly ahead, but the path leading down into the town was dark. He could see the glow of more lights beyond, where the main cluster of buildings stood; they'd have to cross that area if they followed the stone path down to the dock.

Jax pushed the door wider and slipped out into the relatively cool air, adjusting his skin to match his surroundings as he moved. He felt exposed in the light, even with his camouflage, and longed to reach the water as quickly as possible now that he'd been freed from the confines of the tank.

He longed to reach Macy.

He crept to the cliff edge and peered over, running his gaze along the dock, past the bobbing ships, and to its end. Three dark figures stood there, features indistinct in the soft glow of the rising moon. Their shadows stretched out over the shimmering water.

The door slid closed. From the corner of his eye, Jax saw Arkon approach.

"Almost there, Jax."

"Yes. Almost. Let us remain alert as we descend, just—"

A voice drew Jax's attention toward the town. Dracchus paused nearby, and each of them stared down the darkened path.

"—be nothing. The crane rattling in the wind, maybe," said a human voice, drawing nearer with each moment. "I don't know. We need to get back up there before someone notices we're gone."

"You sure you heard something?" asked a second voice.

"Yeah," replied the first.

Jax looked to Arkon and Dracchus; both wore expressions of indecision for a fleeting moment, and he imagined they felt the same paralyzing flash of fear he did.

The humans were not yet on the path, but would be soon. With their guns.

Below, the waves crashed into the cliffs, drowning out any further conversation from the approaching humans. The tide was not low enough, now, to reveal the narrow strand of beach that hugged the cliffs, but it was difficult for Jax to determine the water's depth from his vantage.

If they didn't break themselves on the ground below, they could get caught in the waves, which would smash them against the cliff face. Not typically life-threatening for kraken, but it would significantly slow their escape.

He had no desire to harm any humans...but he would not be caged again.

His companions had moved forward; they stood to either side of Jax, staring down into the sea. Jax met Dracchus's gaze first. The amber eyes were steady, betraying no fear. Dracchus nodded.

Jax shifted his attention to Arkon. His violet eyes were lively beneath a brow set firm in determination. Arkon nodded.

Inhaling deeply, Jax glanced at the dark figures on the end of the dock once more.

Tonight.

He bunched his tentacles beneath himself and jumped.

Wind whistled past Jax's earholes. His stomach leapt into his throat. Then the surface — so far away, a moment before — rushed up to meet him. He threw his hands forward to break through just before he hit with a startling impact that sent a jolt throughout his body.

The current caught him immediately, sweeping him back toward land. Drawing in water through his siphons, he propelled himself away, pushing with his tentacles and pulling with his arms. His muscles burned with strain. The waves lifted him up, as though the sea meant to toss him atop the cliff, back into one of the tanks.

Jax couldn't tolerate any more obstacles between himself and Macy. Couldn't accept any further delay. He drove forward with everything he had, and more. His body screamed in protest.

Finally, he broke away from the strongest current and directed himself toward the end of the dock. He glanced behind; Arkon and Dracchus signaled with glowing skin. They were unharmed.

He surfaced where the dock ended, rising into the silvery light of the rising moon, and lifted his gaze. His eyes found Macy, and he saw nothing more.

The black diving suit covered her from neck to toe. Her blonde hair — paler in the moonlight — fell around her shoulders, ends flowing in the breeze. Her expression was drawn, but the moment her eyes fell upon him, her lips tilted up into a wide smile.

"Jax!" She stepped forward, and her leg gave out beneath her. Her father's big arms encircled her to keep her from falling. Her smile didn't diminish as she extended her arms toward Jax.

"Careful, Macy girl," her father rumbled. He was staring at Jax, mouth lost in his face-hair.

Moving closer to the dock, Jax grabbed the edge with his tentacles and pulled himself high enough to take Macy's hips between his hands. Her father reluctantly released his hold. She wrapped her arms around Jax's neck as he lowered her into the water.

"You're here." Her voice brimmed with emotion as she pecked kisses over his face. "I missed you so much."

"As I missed you." He pressed his lips to her cheek, thrilling in the feel of her body, reveling in her scent.

Her mouth found his, and they locked in a lingering kiss, neither wanting to pull away.

"It got away!" The shout was distant, nearly drowned out by the wind and sea, but everyone heard it; Jax and Macy broke their kiss and looked toward the clifftop warehouse.

"You need to go," Aymee said. She knelt and held out Macy's mask.

Macy yanked up her hood and took the mask, raising it into place.

"I'll leave supplies in the place we discussed." Aymee held out a sealed canister. "These meds should see you through for now, though."

Macy's father took the canister. "I have something for you before you go," he said, opening the lid. He reached into his pocket and produced a small wooden box, which he slid into the container before resealing it. "Your heart's always been with sea...you just forgot it for a while. Sarina's was, too...keep this with you, where it belongs."

"Thank you," Macy said, voice trembling, as Jax accepted the canister. "I love you both."

"Love you too, Macy girl," her father replied gruffly. He shifted his gaze to Jax. "You take care of her, or I'll break you. Don't care how big you are, or how many arms you have."

Jax nodded; this was the bond of family she'd talked about. The protectiveness, the caring, the *love*. "She is the most precious thing on land or sea, and will always be treated as such."

Macy's father nodded. "Go. Get away from here."

Wrapping her legs around Jax's waist, Macy said her final farewells.

Jax turned; Dracchus was studying the humans with a mild look of confusion on his face, as though he couldn't quite understand what they were. Arkon stared, unabashed, at Aymee. "Come. Let us return to our people."

CHAPTER TWENTY-SIX

THE DAYS MACY HAD SPENT WAITING TO BE BACK IN JAX'S ARMS were the longest she'd ever experienced; now that she was in his embrace again, she never wanted to let go.

Arkon and Dracchus crowded around Jax in the entry chamber, waiting for the water to drain. Macy caught Arkon's gaze and smiled at him. She doubted she'd be able to adequately express her gratitude — he and Dracchus had gone to The Watch with Jax and waited for days to ensure she was safe.

"Pressurization normalized," the computer said, and the interior door slid open. "Welcome back, diver one-two-seven."

Macy removed the mask and tugged off the hood as Jax carried her through the doorway.

He placed her gently on her feet and shifted a hand to her stomach. Her breath caught; there was barely contained emotion on his face. "Is it true, Macy?"

She placed a shaky hand over his, hating that the suit was between them, and nodded. "Aymee showed me the scans before she erased them. I…I never thought it was possible. Even when I noticed the changes in myself, and displayed the symptoms, it never crossed my mind."

"Never thought what was a possibility?" Dracchus asked.

Jax held her gaze, brow creased in question. Macy nodded.

"She is carrying a youngling," Jax said. "Our youngling." A slow smile spread across his lips.

"That...how...I don't understand," Arkon stammered.

"*How* doesn't matter, only that it *is*," Jax said. He tipped his head forward, pressed his forehead to Macy's, and closed his eyes. His hand moved slowly over her belly.

"A youngling?" Dracchus stared at Macy.

She placed her hand on the back of Jax's neck. She was excited and terrified at once; there was no going back to The Watch, now, and she didn't know anything about childbirth. What if something went wrong? What if something was wrong with the baby?

Aymee's scans had put some of Macy's worries to rest. She'd nearly cried when she saw the baby's tiny hands and short, thin tentacles and heard the beating of its three hearts. By all appearances, their baby was a kraken. It was everything else that concerned her — would it heal like Jax? Would it grow claws to protect itself?

Would the baby be able to breathe underwater?

"This...this could be a blessing to our people," Arkon said. "If we can reproduce with humans, perhaps we can overcome the way we were designed, and return from the brink of extinction."

Macy pulled back from Jax and stared at Arkon; now that she knew the truth, she couldn't forget about the past conflict between their peoples.

"Why are you looking at me that way?" he asked, tilting his head.

"If the others found out, what would they do, Arkon?" Macy asked. "The kraken have hated humans for so long, and if they discover this... What will this mean for human women? What would the kraken *do*?"

"Nothing."

All eyes fell on Dracchus; Macy guessed the others were as surprised by his response as she was.

"The kraken have struggled," he continued, "but that does not mean we will provoke another war against the humans. If our people can come together, you are the start of it, and you will need to be the example we follow."

His words were a relief, but a kernel of doubt remained. What she'd seen of most of the other kraken hadn't been reassuring, thus far, and she couldn't guess how they'd react to this news. She hoped Dracchus was right...

But desperation could drive people to do terrible things.

"We do not need to discuss this now," Jax said, running a hand down Macy's back. "Are you ready to return to our den?"

"I'm ready."

They thanked Arkon and Dracchus again and said their goodbyes. Jax bent down and carefully lifted Macy to his chest; her leg throbbed, but the pain was nothing compared to what it had been. He carried her through soothingly familiar corridors, past several rooms that held surprisingly fond memories, and, finally, into the cabin she'd chosen to share with him.

"Is my imprisonment reinstated?"

"No. They'll not keep you here like that again. You are kraken, now, but more, you are *mine*. No one will treat you that way again, so long as I live."

He set her down on the edge of the bed and sank to eye-level before her, raising his palms to her face. The pads of his thumbs brushed over her cheekbones. "I almost lost you, Macy. I have never been so afraid."

"I know, and I'm sorry." She placed her hands over his and searched his eyes; the echoes of his fear lingered in their emerald depths, but his love shone brighter. "I just couldn't stand by and do nothing, Jax. I can't... I hate feeling useless. When I heard Melaina was missing, I thought of Sarina, and how devastated Rhea would be if she lost her daughter. I needed to help. I know you and the hunters would've done everything you could to find her, but I…I had Sam."

"I do not want apologies, Macy. It was dangerous and foolish, but you saved a life. And now…" Jax dropped his gaze. "You are safe, and that is all that matters."

He drew her into an embrace, and she wrapped her arms around him, pressing her cheek to his warm, solid chest. She took comfort in his presence, in his strength.

"I'm so glad they didn't hurt you, Jax."

"I would do it again, even at risk of death…because they saved you when I could not. You gave up everything for me, Macy, and I would do the same and more for you."

Macy lifted her head and kissed him, taking in his breath, tasting his essence. "Thank you for saving me that day."

His tentacles slipped around her, drawing her even closer. "You are by far the greatest treasure I have ever taken from the sea."

EPILOGUE

MACY BIT DOWN ON HER SCREAM, DIGGING HER FINGERS INTO THE backs of her thighs. Pain and exhaustion saturated every cell in her body. Rhea and Helen were on either side of the bed, keeping Macy's legs parted and bent, and Thana was hunkered at the foot of the bed. As much as it hurt, Macy *had* to push when instinct demanded.

"Almost there!" Thana exclaimed.

"You are doing so well," Rhea soothed, brushing her hand over Macy's damp hair.

Macy concentrated on her breathing; any second, she'd need to push again. Hours of labor had steadily sapped her strength. She didn't feel human anymore; she was a mindless, baying animal.

The urge came again. She pushed, and couldn't contain her scream this time. "Jax!"

There was a bang.

Rhea lifted her gaze toward the door. "What are you doing?"

"I will not wait out there any longer," Jax said, moving to Macy's side.

She looked up at him; his eyes were wide beneath a creased brow, his pupils narrow slits across their green backdrop.

"This is a female's place, Wanderer," Rhea said firmly.

"And this is my female," he replied, not looking away from Macy. He placed his hand on her shoulder. "My place is at her side."

Macy had argued that she wanted him there to begin with, but the females had been insistent.

Rhea opened her mouth to say more when another contraction hit. Macy sucked in a deep breath, reared up, and pushed.

"The youngling is coming!" Thana said.

Immense pressure filled Macy, crushing her insides. She released one more cry. Relief flooded her abruptly. She fell back against the bed, limp, and closed her eyes.

A loud, high wail filled the room. Jax tightened his grip on Macy's shoulder.

"She is a female," Thana declared happily.

Macy opened her eyes as Thana tied and cut the umbilical cord. Rhea wiped the baby's face with a towel, and then the newborn was in Macy's arms.

She stared down at her daughter's tiny features; though the baby favored its kraken blood, she possessed some distinctly human features. Macy brushed her finger over the little nose, along the soft brows, and through the fine hairs atop her head. She moved her eyes down to the small, webbed fingers with their dainty claws. The baby's skin was nearly the same shade as Jax's, darkening near her waist, where her eight tentacles were drawn up in a tight bundle.

Jax sank down beside the bed, leaning over the low side rail, and gently ran the back of one finger over the baby's cheek. "We have a child," he said, voice filled with awe. "A daughter. She is so small…"

Macy turned her smile toward Jax. "You're a father."

Though the bewilderment in his expression didn't fade, the corners of his mouth lifted.

"It is the mother's place to name the youngling," Rhea said. "She needs a strong name, so she will thrive."

Macy knew the kraken took inspiration for their names from stories they'd heard through the holograms — stories from ancient Earth mythology, barely remembered in The Watch. She'd listened to a few of them with Jax and Arkon, but none of the names stood out to her.

"Jax?" she asked.

He finally pulled his gaze away from their daughter. "What is it, Macy?"

"Would you name her?"

"But it's the female's place," Rhea argued.

"You thought Jax was strange *before* he took a human as a mate," Macy said gently, "so why start conforming now? We do things differently."

Rhea blew air from her siphons, though a smile tugged at her lips. "So be it."

Jax's eyes were back on the baby; he lightly traced her cheeks and chin with his bent knuckle. Macy lifted her up, and he carefully pressed his palm to the baby's chest, covering it completely. He was silent for a long while, not looking away from their child. One small tentacle wrapped around his wrist.

"Sarina," he said finally.

Macy's breath caught, and her eyes stung. "Really?"

He nodded, and with his free hand, cupped Macy's cheek, brushing away the first of her falling tears with the pad of his thumb. "She is birthed of land and sea, and will know the love of two peoples. She is...a new beginning. We cannot forget the past, but we can shape the future."

Her heart expanded with love for Jax and their daughter, and she drew the baby close. Sarina began rooting, and Rhea helped Macy position the baby at her breast to feed.

Macy wrapped her arm around Jax's head when he leaned in, turning her face to kiss him.

"*You* are the greatest treasure in the sea, Jax. You've given me more than I could ever have hoped for."

"Anything and everything for you." Jax looked down at Sarina and caressed her head. "Both of you."

ALSO BY TIFFANY ROBERTS

THE INFINITE CITY

Entwined Fates

Silent Lucidity

Shielded Heart

Vengeful Heart

Untamed Hunger

Savage Desire

Tethered Souls

THE KRAKEN

Treasure of the Abyss

Jewel of the Sea

Hunter of the Tide

Heart of the Deep

Rising from the Depths

Fallen from the Stars

Lover from the Waves

THE SPIDER'S MATE TRILOGY

Ensnared

Enthralled

Bound

THE VRIX

The Weaver

The Delver

The Hunter

<u>THE CURSED ONES</u>

His Darkest Craving

His Darkest Desire

<u>ALIENS AMONG US</u>

Taken by the Alien Next Door

Stalked by the Alien Assassin

Claimed by the Alien Bodyguard

Saved by the Alien Crime Boss

<u>STANDALONE TITLES</u>

Claimed by an Alien Warrior

Dustwalker

Escaping Wonderland

Yearning For Her

The Warlock's Kiss

Ice Bound: Short Story

<u>ISLE OF THE FORGOTTEN</u>

Make Me Burn

Make Me Hunger

Make Me Whole

Make Me Yours

<u>VALOS OF SONHADRA COLLABORATION</u>

Tiffany Roberts - Undying

Tiffany Roberts - Unleashed

VENYS NEEDS MEN COLLABORATION

Tiffany Roberts - To Tame a Dragon

Tiffany Roberts – To Love a Dragon

ABOUT THE AUTHOR

Tiffany Roberts is the pseudonym for Tiffany and Robert Freund, a husband and wife writing duo. The two have always shared a passion for reading and writing, and it was their dream to combine their mighty powers to create the sorts of books they want to read. They write character driven sci-fi and fantasy romance, creating happily-ever-afters for the alien and unknown.

Sign up for our Newsletter!
Check out our social media sites and more!
http://www.authortiffanyroberts.com

www.ingramcontent.com/pod-product-compliance
Lightning Source LLC
Chambersburg PA
CBHW061057210726
48294CB00001B/192